VAMPIRES
Classic Tales

Edited and with an Introduction by
Mike Ashley

DOVER PUBLICATIONS, INC.
Mineola, New York

Acknowledgments
See page ix.

Copyright

Bibliographical Note

Vampires: Classic Tales, first published by Dover Publications, Inc., in 2011, is a new anthology of twelve stories reprinted from standard texts. A new Introduction, written by Mike Ashley, has been specially prepared for the present edition.

Library of Congress Cataloging-in-Publication Data

Vampires: classic tales / edited and with an introduction by Mike Ashley.
    p. cm.
  Includes bibliographical references.
  ISBN-13: 978-0-486-48113-5
  ISBN-10: 0-486-48113-1
  1. Vampires—Fiction. 2. Horror tales, American. I. Ashley, Mike.
PS648.V35V295 2011
813'.54080375—dc22

2010052827

Manufactured in the United States by Courier Corporation
48113101
www.doverpublications.com

Contents

Introduction   v

Blood Gothic   1
Nancy Holder

Let the Dead Rest   7
Ernst Raupach

The Mysterious Stranger   33
Karl von Wachsmann

The Pale Lady   70
Alexandre Dumas

Blood Chess   106
Tanith Lee

The Fate of Madame Cabanel   117
Eliza Lynn Linton

A Kiss of Judas   132
Julian Osgood Field

The Crimson Weaver   174
R. Murray Gilchrist

The Woman With the "Oily Eyes"   182
Dick Donovan

Emptiness   215
Brian Stableford

With the Vampires   231
  Sidney Bertram

Appendix: A Fragment   241
  Lord Byron

INTRODUCTION
The Romance of Vampires

THIS BOOK CONTAINS a selection of vampire stories both old and new. Generally I've reprinted lesser-known stories with an intent to show both the origins of the vampire in fiction and some of the diversity that has emerged over the years.

Vampire fiction has been with us for at least two hundred years and our fascination with it remains undiminished. If anything, it is at the height of its popularity. It is not difficult to see why, with the vampire so often portrayed as a tragic hero or, in the case of women, a voluptuous temptress or *femme fatale*.

The success of the topic in books in recent years can be traced to Anne Rice's *Interview with the Vampire* (1976) and its sequels, and the theme was further popularized with the TV series *Buffy the Vampire Slayer* (1997–2003) and Stephenie Meyers's series that began with *Twilight* (2005). Between them, Rice and Meyers's books have sold over 200 million copies, which probably makes vampires the most widely read of all genre fiction.

And it owes all its success to Lord Byron.

Well, not quite—but he has a lot to answer for.

It barely needs repeating, but one of the most influential literary gatherings happened at the Villa Diodati on the shores of Lake Geneva in June 1816. Present were Byron and his personal physician, Dr. John Polidori, the young Mary Godwin and her future husband, the poet Percy Shelley, and Mary's half-sister Claire Clairmont. During a storm they read from a collection of Gothic horror stories, *Tales from the Dead*, and Byron challenged each of them to write a ghost story. The most famous work to emerge from this was Mary Shelley's novel, *Franken-stein*. Byron and Percy Shelley soon gave up their efforts, but Byron's unfinished "fragment" was used by Polidori as the basis for his own story, "The Vampyre," which was published in the *New Monthly Magazine* in April 1819. The publisher of the magazine, Henry Colburn, attributed the story to Byron, which vexed the poet, who refuted it in a letter published in *The Times* of London on June 5, 1819. "I am not the author and never heard of the work in question until now," he wrote, adding, "I have, besides, a personal dislike to 'vampires' and the little acquaintance I have with them would by no means induce me to divulge their secrets."

By then Polidori had already proclaimed his authorship but for years the suspicion remained that it was by Byron. This was compounded by the fact that the name Polidori chose for the vampire, Lord Ruthven, had already been used by Lady Caroline Lamb in her novel *Glenarvon* (1816) and Ruthven was clearly based on Byron. Polidori likewise modeled his Ruthven on Byron, and it is from this story that the romantic yet tragic image of the vampire has grown.

Polidori's story is frequently reprinted in anthologies, so I have not included it here, but Byron's original is less readily available, so I have included that in an appendix because of its historical significance. Although Byron did not get as far as resurrecting his vampire, he was nevertheless seeking to write what is now regarded as the first modern fusion of the vampire myth and gothic tale in English fiction. And by completing the story, Polidori gave rise to the whole iconic vampire imagery of doomed nobility.

★

The idea of vampires, or at least demonic figures who devour flesh and blood, has been around for thousands of years. They appear in the legends and fables of ancient Egypt, Babylon, Greece, and Rome, where they are invariably female and called lamia. The Greek writer Phlegon, who lived at the time of the Emperor Hadrian in the second century, collected together a miscellany of stories and accounts of strange and inexplicable events known as *On Marvels,* and among them was the story of "The Bride of Corinth" about a young Athenian man who discovers his wife-to-be has risen from the dead. This story was the basis of the poem, "The Bride of Corinth" by Johann von Goethe, which appeared in 1797 at the height of the boom in Gothic literature.

But truth to tell, the idea of vampires was already so well entrenched in everyday parlance that it was possible to lampoon the idea as early as 1785. On October 18 that year the *Universal Register* (the forerunner of the London *Times*) ran an anonymous short story called "Opulence," wherein the first person narrator assists an alchemist in creating the philosopher's stone. The alchemist is killed, but the narrator takes the stone and with it becomes wealthy. However, his fortune attracts the interest of others who descend upon his estate and rob him of everything. He calls these thieves "vampires," because they bled him dry of everything, a metaphor still used today. A footnote to the story explains:

> In Poland and some other countries, a notion is entertained that some persons after they are dead and buried, have the power of sucking others till they die and to them they give the name vampire.

The Oxford English Dictionary notes that the word "vampire" had first appeared in print in England in 1734, so it was firmly in circulation by the time Polidori's story was published.

Soon after Polidori's story was published, another appeared in English, "Wake Not the Dead," in the anthology *Popular Tales and Romances of the Northern Nations*, published in 1823. It appeared anonymously but for years was attributed to Johann Ludwig Tieck, despite there not being any original German text amongst Tieck's accredited work. In fact, it is now firmly established that the story was by Ernst Raupach and it appears here correctly attributed, and correctly titled as "Let the Dead Rest" for the first time. This was the first story to develop what has become the traditional vampire imagery of a beautiful, seductive creature that shuns daylight, weakens its victims, and can only be despatched with a dagger through the heart.

Also of historical importance is "The Mysterious Stranger." Though first published in English in 1854, it had appeared in Germany at least ten years earlier and, as such, was the first vampire story to be set in the Carpathian mountains, the location of Dracula's castle in Bram Stoker's famous novel, which was published in May 1897. Although there is no evidence that Bram Stoker had read the story, there are sufficient similarities between it and *Dracula* for the antiquarian and ghost-story writer M. R. James to suggest that it must have served as the basis for the novel. For years the authorship of this story was treated as anonymous, but recent research has revealed that it was by the little-known German writer Karl von Wachsmann.

One other early story completes the fabric of the legend: "The Pale Lady" by Alexandre Dumas which, though written in 1848, was not translated into English until 1910, and has rarely been reprinted since. Like "The Mysterious Stranger," it is also set in the Carpathian mountains.

These early examples suffice to show how the vampire legend established itself in fiction, mostly in Germany and France, but drawing upon beliefs from central and eastern Europe. I have avoided the more familiar stories of this period such as Théophile Gautier's "Le Morte Amoreuse" (1839) and Sheridan Le Fanu's "Carmilla" (1871) in order to concentrate on stories that exemplify some major themes in vampire fiction. In "The Fate of Madame Cabanel" (1872), for instance, by Eliza Lynn Linton, we see how the belief in and fear of vampires has become so entrenched in remote communities that prejudices can soon erupt with tragic consequences. In "A Kiss of Judas" (1893), Julian Osgood Field considers a totally different origin of the vampire, linking the dead-alive to the children of Christ's betrayer, Judas. Donovan's little-known "The Woman With the 'Oily Eyes'" (1899) explores the idea of the *femme fatale* while Gilchrist's "The Crimson Weaver" (1895) weaves the vampire temptress into the imagery of the fantastic. Finally, "With the Vampires" (1903), which has never previously been reprinted, looks at the peril of those who enter the realm of the vampire bats.

There are three stories of more recent vintage. In "Blood Gothic," Nancy Holder shows the corrupting influence of the romantic vampire image. In "Blood Chess," Tanith Lee returns to the traditional vampire story but from a wholly new perspective. In "Emptiness," Brian Stableford considers the idea of vampire babies.

You will see from the dates that, aside from the more recent stories, only two of the older stories appeared after *Dracula*, and so none of the earlier stories could have been influenced by it. It's entirely likely that Donovan's "The Woman With the 'Oily Eyes'" had an earlier magazine publication, so it, too, could have been written prior to *Dracula's* appearance in May 1897. And there is no doubt that "With the Vampires" bears no relationship to *Dracula* at all. As a consequence all these stories draw their inspiration from older traditions and prevailing legends, and therefore develop their own treatment.

Between them, these stories demonstrate the versatility of the vampire story as well as the continuing strength of the legend.

August 2010   —MIKE ASHLEY

Copyright Acknowledgments
and Sources

The following stories are in copyright and have been reprinted by permission of the authors.

"Blood Gothic" by Nancy Holder, first published in *Shadows 8*, edited by Charles L. Grant (New York: Doubleday, 1985).

"Blood Chess" by Tanith Lee, first published in *Weird Tales* #331, Spring 2003.

"Emptiness" by Brian Stableford, first published in *Dreams of Decadence* #13, Winter 2000/Spring 2001.

The following stories are out of copyright and first appeared in the following sources.

"Let the Dead Rest" by Ernst Raupach first appeared in German as "Lasst die Todten Ruhen" in *Minerva* (Leipzig, 1822). Its first English translation was as "Wake Not the Dead" in *Popular Tales and Romances of the Northern Nations* (London: Simpkin, Marshall, 1823).

"The Mysterious Stranger" by Karl von Wachsmann first appeared in German in *Erzählungen und Novellen*, third series (Leipzig, 1844). Its first English translation was in *Chambers's Repository*, February 1854.

"The Pale Lady" by Alexandre Dumas first appeared in French, untitled, in *Les Mille et un Fantômes* (Brussels, 1848-1851). Its first English translation was in *Tales of the Supernatural* (Methuen, 1910).

"The Fate of Madame Cabanel" by Eliza Lynn Linton was first published in *All the Year Round*, 16 December 1872, and collected in *With a Silken Thread and Other Stories* (London: Chatto & Windus, 1880).

"A Kiss of Judas" by Julian Osgood Field was first published in *Pall Mall Magazine*, July 1893, and collected in *Aut Diabolus Aut Nihil and Other Tales* (London: Methuen, 1894), in both cases under the alias "X. L."

Blood Gothic

Nancy Holder

The name of Nancy Holder (b. 1953) will be well known to devotees of vampire fiction and particularly to followers of the Buffy the Vampire Slayer *series. She has written sixteen spin-off novels based on the series, starting with* Hallowe'en Rain *(1997, with Christopher Golden) as well as the best-selling* The Watchers Guide to Buffy the Vampire Slayer *(1998, also with Christopher Golden). Her short stories and novels have won her four Bram Stoker Awards presented by the Horror Writers of America for superior achievement, among them her first solo novel,* Dead in the Water *(1994). The following is one of her earliest short stories, which sets the tone for the anthology.*

Blood Gothic

Nancy Holder

SHE WANTED to have a vampire lover. She wanted it so badly that she kept waiting for it to happen. One night, soon, she would awaken to wings flapping against the window and then take to wearing velvet ribbons and cameo lockets around her delicate, pale neck. She knew it.

She immersed herself in the world of her vampire lover: she devoured Gothic romances, consumed late-night horror movies. Visions of satin capes and eyes of fire shielded her from the harshness of the daylight, from mortality and the vain and meaningless struggles of the world of the sun. Days as a kindergarten teacher and evenings with some overly eager, casual acquaintance could not pull her from her secret existence: always a ticking portion of her brain planned, proceeded, waited.

She spent her meager earnings on dark antiques and intricate clothes. Her wardrobe was crammed with white negligees and ruffled underthings. No crosses and no mirrors, particularly not in her bedroom. White tapered candles stood in pewter sconces, and she would read late into the night by their smoky flickerings, she scented and ruffled, hair combed loosely about her shoulders. She glanced at the window often.

She resented lovers—though she took them, thrilling to the fullness of life in them, the blood and the life—who insisted upon staying all night, burning their breakfast toast and making bitter coffee. Her kitchen, of course, held nothing but fresh ingredients and copper and ironware; to her chagrin, she could not do without ovens or stoves or refrigerators. Alone, she carried candles and bathed in cool water.

She waited, prepared. And at long last, her vampire lover began to come to her in dreams. They floated across the moors, glided through the fields of heather. He carried her to his crumbling castle, undressing her, pulling off her diaphanous gown, caressing her lovely body until, in the height of passion, he bit into her arched neck, drawing

2

the life out of her and replacing it with eternal damnation and eternal love.

She awoke from these dreams drenched in sweat and feeling exhausted. The kindergarten children would find her unusually quiet and self-absorbed, and it frightened them when she rubbed her spotless neck and smiled wistfully. *Soon and soon and soon,* her veins chanted, in prayer and anticipation. *Soon.*

The children were her only regret. She would not miss her inquisitive relatives and friends, the ones who frowned and studied her as if she were a portrait of someone they knew they were supposed to recognize. Those, who urged her to drop by for an hour, to come with them to films, to accompany them to the seashore. Those, who were connected to her—or thought they were—by the mere gesturing of the long and milky hands of Fate. Who sought to distract her from her one true passion; who sought to discover the secret of that passion. For, true to the sacredness of her vigil for her vampire lover, she had never spoken of him to a single earthly, earthbound soul. It would be beyond them, she knew. They would not comprehend a bond of such intentioned sacrifice.

But she would regret the children. Never would a child of their love coo and murmur in the darkness; never would his proud and noble features soften at the sight of the mother and her child of his loins. It was her single sorrow.

Her vacation was coming. June hovered like the mist and the children squirmed in anticipation. Their own true lives would begin in June. She empathized with the shining eyes and smiling faces, knowing their wait was as agonizing as her own. Silently, as the days closed in, she bade each of them a tender farewell, holding them as they threw their little arms around her neck and pressed fervent summertime kisses on her cheeks.

She booked her passage to London on a ship. Then to Romania, Bulgaria, Transylvania. The hereditary seat of her beloved, the fierce, violent backdrop of her dreams. Her suitcases opened themselves to her long, full skirts and her brooches and lockets. She peered into her hand mirror as she packed it. "I am getting pale," she thought, and the idea both terrified and delighted her.

She became paler, thinner, more exhausted as her trip wore on. After recovering from the disappointment of the raucous, modern cruise ship, she raced across the Continent to find refuge in the creaky trains and taverns she had so yearned for. Her heart thrilled as she meandered past the black silhouettes of ruined fortresses and ancient manor houses. She sat for hours in the mists, praying for the howling wolf to find her, for the bat to come and join her.

She took to drinking wine in bed, deep, rich, blood-red burgundy that glowed in the candlelight. She melted into the landscape within days, and cringed as if from the crucifix itself when flickers of her past life, her American, false existence, invaded her serenity. She did not keep a diary; she did not count the days as her summer slipped away from her. She only rejoiced that she grew weaker.

It was when she was counting out the coins for a Gypsy shawl that she realized she had no time left. Tomorrow she must make for Frankfurt and from there fly back to New York. The shopkeeper nudged her, inquiring if she were ill, and she left with her treasure, trembling.

She flung herself on her own rented bed. "This will not do. This will not do." She pleaded with the darkness. "You must come for me tonight. I have done everything for you, my beloved, loved you above all else. You must save me." She sobbed until she ached.

She skipped her last meal of veal and paprika and sat quietly in her room. The innkeeper brought her yet another bottle of burgundy and after she assured him that she was quite all right, just a little tired, he wished his guest a pleasant trip home.

The night wore on; though her book was open before her, her eyes were riveted to the windows, her hands clenched around the wineglass as she sipped steadily, like a creature feeding. Oh, to feel him against her veins, emptying her and filling her!

Soon and soon and soon...

Then, all at once, it happened. The windows rattled, flapped inward. A great shadow, a curtain of ebony, fell across the bed, and the room began to whirl, faster, faster still; and she was consumed with a bitter, deathly chill. She heard, rather than saw, the wineglass crash to the floor, and struggled to keep her eyes open as she was overwhelmed, engulfed, taken.

"Is it you?" she managed to whisper through teeth that rattled with delight and cold and terror. "Is it finally to be?"

Freezing hands touched her everywhere: her face, her breasts, the desperate offering of her arched neck. Frozen and strong and never-dying. Sinking, she smiled in a rictus of mortal dread and exultation. Eternal damnation, eternal love. Her vampire lover had come for her at last.

When her eyes opened again, she let out a howl and shrank against the searing brilliance of the sun. Hastily, they closed the curtains and quickly told her where she was: home again, where everything was warm and pleasant and she was safe from the disease that had nearly killed her.

She had been ill before she had left the States. By the time she had reached Transylvania, her anemia had been acute. Had she never noticed her own pallor, her lassitude?

Anemia. Her smile was a secret on her white lips. So they thought, but he *had* come for her, again and again. In her dreams. And on that night, he had meant to take her finally to his castle forever, to crown her the best-beloved one, his love of the moors and the mists.

She had but to wait, and he would finish the deed.

Soon and soon and soon.

She let them fret over her, wrapping her in blankets in the last days of summer. She endured the forced cheer of her relatives, allowed them to feed her rich food and drink in hopes of restoring her.

But her stomach could no longer hold the nourishment of their kind; they wrung their hands and talked of stronger measures when it became clear that she was wasting away.

At the urging of the doctor, she took walks. Small ones at first, on painfully thin feet. Swathed in wool, cowering behind sunglasses, she took tiny steps like an old woman. As she moved through the summer hours, her neck burned with an ungovernable pain that would not cease until she rested in the shadows. Her stomach lurched at the sight of grocery-store windows. But at the butcher's, she paused, and licked her lips at the sight of the raw, bloody meat.

But she did not go to him. She grew neither worse nor better.

"I am trapped," she whispered to the night as she stared into the flames of a candle by her bed. "I am disappearing between your world and mine, my beloved. Help me. Come for me." She rubbed her neck, which ached and throbbed but showed no outward signs of his devotion. Her throat was parched, bone-dry, but water did not quench her thirst.

At long last, she dreamed again. Her vampire lover came for her as before, joyous in their reunion. They soared above the crooked trees at the foothills, streamed like black banners above the mountain crags to his castle. He could not touch her enough, worship her enough, and they were wild in their abandon as he carried her in her diaphanous grown to the gates of his fortress.

But at the entrance, he shook his head with sorrow and could not let her pass into the black realm with him. His fiery tears seared her neck, and she thrilled to the touch of the mark even as she cried out for him as he left her, fading into the vapors with a look of entreaty in his dark, flashing eyes.

Something was missing; he required a boon of her before he could bind her against his heart. A thing that she must give to him...

She walked in the sunlight, enfeebled, cowering, She thirsted, hungered, yearned. Still she dreamed of him, and still he could not take the last of her unto himself.

Days and nights and days. Her steps took her finally to the schoolyard, where once, only months before, she had embraced and kissed the children, thinking never to see them again. They were all there, who had kissed her cheeks so eagerly. Their silvery laughter was like the tinkling of bells as dust motes from their games and antics whirled around their feet. How free they seemed to her who was so troubled, how content and at peace.

The children.

She shambled forward, eyes widening behind the shields of smoky glass.

He required something of her first.

Her one regret. Her only sorrow.

She thirsted. The burns on her neck pulsated with pain.

Tears of gratitude welled in her eyes for the revelation that had not come too late. Weeping, she pushed open the gate of the schoolyard and reached out a skeleton-limb to a child standing apart from the rest, engrossed in a solitary game of cat's cradle. Tawny-headed, ruddy-cheeked, filled with the blood and the life.

For him, as a token of their love.

"My little one, do you remember me?" she said softly.

The boy turned. And smiled back uncertainly in innocence and trust.

Then she came for him, swooped down on him like a great, winged thing, with eyes that burned through the glasses, teeth that flashed, once, twice. . . .

soon and soon and soon.

Let the Dead Rest
Ernst Raupach

This story was long attributed to Johann Ludwig Tieck, but thanks to the research of Rob Brautigam and Douglas Anderson, the proper credit can at last go to Ernst Raupach (1784–1852). Raupach was a German tutor and teacher who became a dramatist in the 1820s and produced, by one count, 117 plays. He was popular in his day but his reputation has since faded. Perhaps it will be restored a little with the recognition of his authorship of this story, which has long been held in high regard as one of the foundation texts of vampire fiction.

Let the Dead Rest

Ernst Raupach

Wake not the Dead:—they bring but gloomy night
And cheerless desolation into day;
For in the grave who mouldering lay,
No more can feel the influence of light,
Or yield them to the sun's prolific might;
Let them repose within their house of clay—
Corruption, vainly wilt thou e'er essay
To quicken:—it sends forth a pest'lent blight;
And neither fiery sun, nor bathing dew,
Nor breath of spring the dead can e'er renew.
That which from life is pluck'd, becomes the foe
Of life, and whoso wakes it waketh woe.
Seek not the dead to waken from that sleep
In which from mortal eye they lie enshrouded deep.

"Wilt thou for ever sleep? Wilt thou never more awake, my beloved, but henceforth repose for ever from thy short pilgrimage on earth? O yet once again return! and bring back with thee the vivifying dawn of hope to one whose existence hath, since thy departure, been obscured by the dunnest shades. What! dumb? forever dumb? Thy friend lamenteth, and thou heedest him not? He sheds bitter, scalding tears, and thou reposest unregarding his affliction? He is in despair, and thou no longer openest thy arms to him as an asylum from his grief? Say then, doth the paly shroud become thee better than the bridal veil? Is the chamber of the grave a warmer bed than the couch of love? Is the spectre death more welcome to thy arms than thy enamoured consort? Oh! return, my beloved, return once again to this anxious disconsolate bosom."

Such were the lamentations which Walter poured forth for his Brunhilda, the partner of his youthful passionate love; thus did he bewail over her grave at the midnight hour, what time the spirit that presides in the troublous atmosphere, sends his legions of monsters through mid-air; so that their shadows, as they flit beneath the moon and across the earth, dart as wild, agitating thoughts that chase each other o'er the sinner's bosom:—thus did he lament under the tall linden trees by her grave, while his head reclined on the cold stone.

Walter was a powerful lord in Burgundy, who, in his earliest youth, had been smitten with the charms of the fair Brunhilda, a beauty far surpassing in loveliness all her rivals; for her tresses, dark as the raven face of night, streaming over her shoulders, set off to the utmost advantage the beaming lustre of her slender form, and the rich dye of a cheek whose tint was deep and brilliant as that of the western heaven; her eyes did not resemble those burning orbs whose pale glow gems the vault of night, and whose immeasurable distance fills the soul with deep thoughts of eternity, but rather as the sober beams which cheer this nether world, and which, while they enlighten, kindle the sons of earth to joy and love. Brunhilda became the wife of Walter, and both being equally enamoured and devoted, they abandoned themselves to the enjoyment of a passion that rendered them reckless of aught besides, while it lulled them in a fascinating dream. Their sole apprehension was lest aught should awaken them from a delirium which they prayed might continue for ever. Yet how vain is the wish that would arrest the decrees of destiny! as well might it seek to divert the circling planets from their eternal course. Short was the duration of this phrenzied passion; not that it gradually decayed and subsided into apathy, but death snatched away his blooming victim, and left Walter to a widowed couch. Impetuous, however, as was his first burst of grief, he was not inconsolable, for ere long another bride became the partner of the youthful nobleman.

Swanhilda also was beautiful; although nature had formed her charms on a very different model from those of Brunhilda. Her golden locks waved bright as the beams of morn: only when excited by some emotion of her soul did a rosy hue tinge the lily paleness of her cheek: her limbs were proportioned in the nicest symmetry, yet did they not possess that luxuriant fullness of animal life: her eye beamed eloquently, but it was with the milder radiance of a star, tranquillizing to tenderness rather than exciting to warmth. Thus formed, it was not possible that she should steep him in his former delirium, although she rendered happy his waking hours—tranquil and serious, yet cheerful, studying in all things her husband's pleasure, she restored order and comfort in his family, where her presence shed a general influence all around. Her mild benevolence tended to restrain the fiery, impetuous disposition of Walter: while at the same time her prudence recalled him in some degree from his vain, turbulent wishes, and his aspirings after unattainable enjoyments, to the duties and pleasures of actual life. Swanhilda bore her husband two children, a son and a daughter; the latter was mild and patient as her mother, well contented with her solitary sports, and even in these recreations displayed the serious turn of her character. The boy possessed his father's fiery, restless disposition, tempered, however, with the solidity of his mother. Attached by his offspring more tenderly towards their mother, Walter now lived for several years very happily: his thoughts would frequently, indeed, recur to Brunhilda, but without their former violence, merely as we dwell upon the memory of a friend of our earlier days, borne from us on the rapid current of time to a region where we know that he is happy.

But clouds dissolve into air, flowers fade, the sands of the hourglass run imperceptibly away, and even so, do human feelings dissolve, fade, and pass away, and with them too, human happiness. Walter's inconstant breast again sighed for the ecstatic dreams of those days which he had spent with his equally romantic, enamoured Brunhilda—again did she present herself to his ardent fancy in all the glow of her bridal charms, and he began to draw a parallel between the past and the present; nor did imagination, as it is wont, fail to array the former in her brightest hues, while it proportionately obscured the latter; so that he pictured to himself, the one much more rich in enjoyment, and the other, much less so than they really were. This change in her husband did not escape Swanhilda; whereupon, redoubling her attentions towards him, and her cares towards their children, she expected, by this means, to reunite the knot that was slackened; yet the more she endeavoured to regain his affections, the colder did he grow,— the more intolerable did her caresses seem, and the more continually did the image of Brunhilda haunt his thoughts. The children, whose endearments were now become indispensable to him, alone stood between the parents as genii eager to affect a reconciliation; and, beloved by them both, formed a uniting link between them. Yet, as evil can be plucked from the heart of man, only ere its root has yet struck deep, its fangs being afterwards too firm to be eradicated; so was Walter's diseased fancy too far affected to have its disorder stopped, for, in a short time, it completely tyrannized over him. Frequently of a night, instead of retiring to his consort's chamber, he repaired to Brunhilda's grave, where he murmured forth his discontent, saying: "Wilt thou sleep for ever?"

One night as he was reclining on the turf, indulging in his wonted sorrow, a sorcerer from the neighbouring mountains, entered into this field of death for the purpose of gathering, for his mystic spells, such herbs as grow only from the earth wherein the dead repose, and which, as if the last production of mortality, are gifted with a powerful and supernatural influence. The sorcerer perceived the mourner, and approached the spot where he was lying.

"Wherefore, fond wretch, dost thou grieve thus, for what is now a hideous mass of mortality—mere bones, and nerves, and veins? Nations have fallen unlamented; even worlds themselves, long ere this globe of ours was created, have mouldered into nothing; nor hath any one wept over them; why then should'st thou indulge this vain affliction for a child of the dust—a being as frail as thyself, and like thee the creature but of a moment?"

Walter raised himself up:—"Let yon worlds that shine in the firmament" replied he, "lament for each other as they perish. It is true, that I who am myself clay, lament for my fellow-clay: yet is this clay impregnated with a fire,—with an essence, that none of the elements of creation possess—with love: and this divine passion, I felt for her who now sleepeth beneath this sod."

"Will thy complaints awaken her: or could they do so, would she not soon upbraid thee for having disturbed that repose in which she is now hushed?"

"Avaunt, cold-hearted being: thou knowest not what is love. Oh! that my tears could wash away the earthy covering that conceals her from these eyes;—that my groan of anguish could rouse her from her slumber of death!—No, she would not again seek her earthy couch."

"Insensate that thou art, and couldst thou endure to gaze without shuddering on one disgorged from the jaws of the grave? Art thou too thyself the same from whom she parted; or hath time passed o'er thy brow and left no traces there? Would not thy love rather be converted into hate and disgust?"

"Say rather that the stars would leave yon firmament, that the sun will henceforth refuse to shed his beams through the heavens. Oh! that she stood once more before me;—that once again she reposed on this bosom!—how quickly should we then forget that death or time had ever stepped between us."

"Delusion! mere delusion of the brain, from heated blood, like to that which arises from the fumes of wine. It is not my wish to tempt thee;—to restore to thee thy dead; else wouldst thou soon feel that I have spoken truth."

"How! restore her to me," exclaimed Walter casting himself at the sorcerer's feet. "Oh! if thou art indeed able to effect that, grant it to my earnest supplication; if one throb of human feeling vibrates in thy bosom, let my tears prevail with thee; restore to me my beloved; so shalt thou hereafter bless the deed, and see that it was a good work."

"A good work! a blessed deed!"—returned the sorcerer with a smile of scorn; "for me there exists nor good nor evil; since my will is always the same. Ye alone know evil, who will that which ye would not. It is indeed in my power to restore her to thee: yet, bethink thee well, whether it will prove thy weal. Consider too, how deep the abyss between life and death; across this, my power can build a bridge, but it can never fill up the frightful chasm."

Walter would have spoken, and have sought to prevail on this powerful being by fresh entreaties, but the latter prevented him, saying: "Peace! bethink thee well! and return hither to me tomorrow at midnight. Yet once more do I warn thee, 'Wake not the dead.' "

Having uttered these words, the mysterious being disappeared. Intoxicated with fresh hope, Walter found no sleep on his couch; for fancy, prodigal of her richest stores, expanded before him the glittering web of futurity; and his eye, moistened with the dew of rapture, glanced from one vision of happiness to another. During the next day he wandered through the woods, lest wonted objects by recalling the memory of later and less happier times, might disturb the blissful idea. that he should again behold her—again fold her in his arms, gaze on her beaming brow by day, repose on her bosom at night: and, as this sole idea filled his imagination, how was it possible that the least doubt should arise; or that the warning of the mysterious old man should recur to his thoughts?

No sooner did the midnight hour approach, than he hastened before the grave-field where the sorcerer was already standing by that of Brunhilda. "Hast thou maturely considered?" inquired he.

"Oh! restore to me the object of my ardent passion," exclaimed Walter with impetuous eagerness. "Delay not thy generous action, lest I die even this night, consumed with disappointed desire; and behold her face no more."

"Well then," answered the old man, "return hither again tomorrow at the same hour. But once more do I give thee this friendly warning, 'Wake not the dead.' "

All in the despair of impatience, Walter would have prostrated himself at his feet, and supplicated him to fulfil at once a desire now increased to agony; but the sorcerer had already disappeared. Pouring forth his lamentations more wildly and impetuously than ever, he lay upon the grave of his adored one, until the grey dawn streaked the east. During the day, which seemed to him longer than any he had ever experienced, he wandered to and fro, restless and impatient, seemingly without any object, and deeply buried in his own reflections, inquest as the murderer who meditates his first deed of blood: and the stars of evening found him once more at the appointed spot. At midnight the sorcerer was there also.

"Hast thou yet maturely deliberated?" inquired he, "as on the preceding night?"

"Oh what should I deliberate?" returned Walter impatiently. "I need not to deliberate; what I demand of thee, is that which thou hast promised me—that which will prove my bliss. Or dost thou but mock me? if so, hence from my sight, lest I be tempted to lay my hand on thee."

"Once more do I warn thee," answered the old man with undisturbed composure, " 'Wake not the dead'—let her rest."

"Aye, but not in the cold grave: she shall rather rest on this bosom which burns with eagerness to clasp her."

"Reflect, thou mayst not quit her until death, even though aversion and horror should seize thy heart. There would then remain only one horrible means."

"Dotard!" cried Walter, interrupting him, 'how may I hate that which I love with such intensity of passion? How should I abhor that for which my every drop of blood is boiling?"

"Then be it even as thou wishest," answered the sorcerer; "step back."

The old man now drew a circle round the grave, all the while muttering words of enchantment. Immediately the storm began to howl among the tops of the trees; owls flapped their wings, and uttered their low voice of omen; the stars hid their mild, beaming aspect, that they might not behold so unholy and impious a spectacle; the stone then rolled from the grave with a hollow sound, leaving a free passage for the inhabitant of that dreadful tenement. The sorcerer scattered into the yawning earth, roots and herbs of most magic power, and of most penetrating odour, so that the worms crawling forth from the earth congregated together, and raised themselves in a fiery column over the grave: while rushing wind burst from the earth, scattering the mould before it, until at length the coffin lay uncovered. The moonbeams fell on it, and the lid burst open with a tremendous sound. Upon this the sorcerer poured upon it some blood from out of a human skull, exclaiming at the same time, "Drink, sleeper, of this warm stream, that thy heart may again beat within thy bosom." And, after a short pause, shedding on her some other mystic liquid, he cried aloud with the voice of one inspired: "Yes, thy heart beats once more with the flood of life: thine eye is again opened to sight. Arise, therefore, from the tomb."

As an island suddenly springs forth from the dark waves of the ocean, raised upwards from the deep by the force of subterraneous fires, so did Brunhilda start from her earthy couch, borne forward by some invisible power. Taking her by the hand, the sorcerer led her towards Walter, who stood at some little distance, rooted to the ground with amazement.

"Receive again," said he, "the object of thy passionate sighs: mayest thou never more require my aid; should that, however, happen, so wilt thou find me, during the full of the moon, upon the mountains in that spot and where the three roads meet."

Instantly did Walter recognize in the form that stood before him, her whom he so ardently loved; and a sudden glow shot through his frame at finding her thus restored to him: yet the night-frost had chilled his limbs and palsied his tongue. For a while he gazed upon her without either motion or speech, and during this pause, all was again become hushed and serene; and the stars shone brightly in the clear heavens.

"Walter!" exclaimed the figure; and at once the well-known sound, thrilling to his heart, broke the spell by which he was bound.

"Is it reality? Is it truth?" cried he, "or a cheating delusion?"

"No, it is no imposture; I am really living:—conduct me quickly to thy castle in the mountains."

Walter looked around: the old man had disappeared, but he perceived close by his side, a coal-black steed of fiery eye, ready equipped to conduct him thence; and on his back lay all proper attire for Brunhilda, who lost no time in arraying herself. This being done, she cried; "Haste, let us away ere the dawn breaks, for my eye is yet too weak to endure the light of day." Fully recovered from his stupor, Walter leaped into his saddle, and catching up, with a mingled feeling of delight and awe, the beloved being thus mysteriously restored from the power of the grave, he spurred on across the wild, towards the mountains, as furiously as if pursued by the shadows of the dead, hastening to recover from him their sister.

The castle to which Walter conducted his Brunhilda, was situated on a rock between other rocks rising up above it. Here they arrived, unseen by any save one aged domestic, on whom Walter imposed secrecy by the severest threats.

"Here will we tarry," said Brunhilda, "until I can endure the light, and until thou canst look upon me without trembling as if struck with a cold chill." They accordingly continued to make that place their abode: yet no one knew that Brunhilda existed, save only that aged attendant, who provided their meals. During seven entire days they had no light except that of tapers: during the next seven, the light was admitted through the lofty casements only while the rising or setting-sun faintly illumined the mountain-tops, the valley being still enveloped in shade.

Seldom did Walter quit Brunhilda's side: a nameless spell seemed to attach him to her; even the shudder which he felt in her presence, and which would not permit him to touch her, was not unmixed with pleasure, like that thrilling awful emotion felt when strains of sacred music float under the vault of some temple; he rather sought, therefore, than avoided this feeling. Often too as he had indulged in calling to mind the beauties of Brunhilda, she had never appeared so fair, so fascinating, so admirable when depicted by his imagination, as when now beheld in reality. Never till now had her voice sounded with such tones of sweetness; never before did her language possess such eloquence as it now did, when she conversed with him on the subject of the past. And this was the magic fairy-land towards which her words constantly conducted him. Ever did she dwell upon the days of their first love, those hours of delight which they had participated together when the one derived all enjoyment from the other: and so rapturous, so enchanting, so full of life did she recall to his imagination that blissful season, that he even doubted whether he had ever experienced with her so much felicity, or had been so truly happy. And, while she thus vividly portrayed their hours of past delight, she delineated in still more glowing, more enchanting colours, those hours of approaching bliss which now awaited them, richer in enjoyment than any preceding ones. In this manner did she charm her attentive auditor with enrapturing hopes for the future, and lull him into dreams of more than mortal ecstasy; so that while he listened to her siren strain, he entirely forgot how little blissful was the latter period of their union, when he had often sighed at her imperiousness, and at her harshness both to himself and all his household. Yet even had he recalled this to mind would it have disturbed him in his present delirious trance? Had she not now left behind in the grave all the frailty of mortality? Was not her whole being refined and purified by that long sleep in which neither passion nor sin had approached her even in dreams? How different now was the subject of her discourse! Only when speaking of her affection for him, did she betray anything of earthly feeling: at other times, she uniformly dwelt upon themes relating to the invisible and future world; when in descanting and declaring the mysteries of eternity, a stream of prophetic eloquence would burst from her lips.

In this manner had twice seven days elapsed, and, for the first time, Walter beheld the being now dearer to him than ever, in the full light of day. Every trace of the grave had disappeared from her countenance; a roseate tinge like the ruddy streaks of dawn again beamed on her pallid cheek; the faint, mouldering taint of the grave was changed into a delightful violet scent; the only sign of earth that never disappeared. He no longer felt either apprehension or awe, as he gazed upon her in the sunny light of day: it was not until now, that he seemed to have recovered her completely; and, glowing with all his former passion towards her, he would have pressed her to his bosom, but she gently repulsed him, saying:—"Not yet—spare your caresses until the moon has again filled her horn."

Spite of his impatience, Walter was obliged to await the lapse of another period of seven days: but, on the night when the moon was arrived at the full, he hastened to Brunhilda, whom he found more lovely than she had ever appeared before. Fearing no obstacles to his transports, he embraced with all the fervour of a deeply enamoured and successful lover. Brunhilda, however, still refused to yield to his passion. "What!" exclaimed she, "is it fitting that I who have been purified by death from the frailty of mortality, should become thy concubine, while a mere daughter of the earth bears the title of thy wife: never shall it be. No, it must be within the walls of thy palace, within that chamber where I once reigned as queen, that thou obtainest the end of thy wishes,—and of mine also," added she, imprinting a glowing kiss on the lips, and immediately disappeared.

Heated with passion, and determined to sacrifice everything to the accomplishment of his desires, Walter hastily quitted the apartment, and shortly after the castle itself. He travelled over mountain and across heath, with the rapidity of a storm, so that the turf was flung up by his horse's hoofs; nor once stopped until he arrived home.

Here, however, neither the affectionate caresses of Swanhilda, nor those of his children could touch his heart, or induce him to restrain his furious desires. Alas! is the impetuous torrent to be checked in its devastating course by the beauteous flowers over which it rushes, when they exclaim:—"Destroyer, commiserate our helpless innocence and beauty, nor lay us waste?"—the stream sweeps over them unregarding, and a single moment annihilates the pride of a whole summer.

Shortly afterwards did Walter begin to hint to Swanhilda that they were ill-suited to each other; that he was anxious to taste that wild, tumultuous life, so well according with the spirit of his sex, while she, on the contrary, was satisfied with the monotonous circle of household enjoyments:—that he was eager for whatever promised novelty, while she felt most attached to what was familiarized to her by habit: and lastly, that her cold disposition, bordering upon indifference, but ill assorted with his ardent temperament: it was therefore more prudent that they should seek apart from each other that happiness which they could not find together. A sigh, and a brief acquiescence in his wishes was all the reply that Swanhilda made: and, on the following morning, upon his presenting her with a paper of separation, informing her that she was at liberty to return home to her father, she received it most submissively: yet, ere she departed, she gave him the following warning: "Too well do I conjecture to whom I am indebted for this our separation. Often have I seen thee at Brunhilda's grave, and beheld thee there even on that night when the face of the heavens was suddenly enveloped in a veil of clouds. Hast thou rashly dared to tear aside the awful veil that separates the mortality that dreams, from that which dreameth not? Oh, then woe to thee, thou wretched man, for thou hast attached to thyself that which will prove thy destruction."

She ceased: nor did Walter attempt any reply, for the similar admonition uttered by the sorcerer flashed upon his mind, all obscured as it was by passion, just as the lightning glares momentarily through the gloom of night without dispersing the obscurity.

Swanhilda then departed, in order to pronounce to her children, a bitter farewell, for they, according to national custom, belonged to the father; and, having bathed them in her tears, and consecrated them with the holy water of maternal love, she quitted her husband's residence, and departed to the home of her father's.

Thus was the kind and benevolent Swanhilda driven an exile from those halls where she had presided with grace;—from halls which were now newly decorated to receive another mistress. The day at length arrived on which Walter, for the second time, conducted Brunhilda home as a newly made bride. And he caused it to be reported among his domestics that his new consort had gained his affections by her extraordinary likeness to Brunhilda, their former mistress. How ineffably happy did he deem himself as he conducted his beloved once more into the chamber which had often witnessed their former joys, and which was now newly gilded and adorned in a most costly style: among the other decorations were figures of angels scattering roses, which served to support the purple draperies whose ample folds o'ershadowed the nuptial couch. With what impatience did he await the hour that was to put him in possession of those beauties for which he had already paid so high a price, but, whose enjoyment was to cost him most dearly yet! Unfortunate Walter! revelling in bliss, thou beholdest not the abyss that yawns beneath thy feet, intoxicated with the luscious perfume of the flower thou hast plucked, thou little deemest how deadly is the venom with which it is fraught, although, for a short season, its potent fragrance bestows new energy on all thy feelings.

Happy, however, as Walter was now, his household were far from being equally so. The strange resemblance between their new lady and the deceased Brunhilda filled them with a secret dismay—an undefinable horror; for there was not a single difference of feature, of tone of voice, or of gesture. To add too to these mysterious circumstances, her female attendants discovered a particular mark on her back, exactly like one which Brunhilda had. A report was now soon circulated, that their lady was no other than Brunhilda herself, who had been recalled to life by the power of necromancy. How truly horrible was the idea of living under the same roof with one who had been an inhabitant of the tomb, and of being obliged to attend upon her, and acknowledge her as mistress! There was also in

Brunhilda much to increase this aversion, and favour their superstition: no ornaments of gold ever decked her person; all that others were wont to wear of this metal, she had formed of silver: no richly coloured and sparkling jewels glittered upon her; pearls alone, lent their pale lustre to adorn her bosom. Most carefully did she always avoid the cheerful light of the sun, and was wont to spend the brightest days in the most retired and gloomy apartments: only during the twilight of the commencing or declining day did she ever walk abroad, but her favourite hour was when the phantom light of the moon bestowed on all objects a shadowy appearance and a sombre hue; always too at the crowing of the cock an involuntary shudder was observed to seize her limbs. Imperious as before her death, she quickly imposed her iron yoke on everyone around her, while she seemed even far more terrible than ever, since a dread of some supernatural power attached to her, appalled all who approached her. A malignant withering glance seemed to shoot from her eye on the unhappy object of her wrath, as if it would annihilate its victim. In short, those halls which, in the time of Swanhilda were the residence of cheerfulness and mirth, now resembled an extensive desert tomb. With fear imprinted on their pale countenances, the domestics glided through the apartments of the castle; and in this abode of terror, the crowing of the cock caused the living to tremble, as if they were the spirits of the departed; for the sound always reminded them of their mysterious mistress. There was no one but who shuddered at meeting her in a lonely place, in the dusk of evening, or by the light of the moon, a circumstance that was deemed to be ominous of some evil: so great was the apprehension of her female attendants, they pined in continual disquietude, and, by degrees, all quitted her. In the course of time even others of the domestics fled, for an insupportable horror had seized them.

The art of the sorcerer had indeed bestowed upon Brunhilda an artificial life, and due nourishment had continued to support the restored body: yet this body was not able of itself to keep up the genial glow of vitality, and to nourish the flame whence springs all the affections and passions, whether of love or hate; for death had for ever destroyed and withered it: all that Brunhilda now possessed was a chilled existence, colder than that of the snake. It was nevertheless necessary that she should love, and return with equal ardour the warm caresses of her spell-enthralled husband, to whose passion alone she was indebted for her renewed existence. It was necessary that a magic draught should animate the dull current in her veins and awaken her to the glow of life and the flame of love—a potion of abomination—one not even to be named without a curse—human blood, imbibed whilst yet warm, from the veins of youth. This was the hellish drink for which she thirsted: possessing no sympathy with the purer feelings of humanity; deriving no enjoyment from aught that interests in life and occupies its varied hours; her existence was a mere blank, unless when in the arms of her paramour husband, and therefore was it that she craved incessantly after the horrible draught. It was even with the utmost effort that she could forbear sucking even the blood of Walter himself, reclined beside her. Whenever she beheld some innocent child whose lovely face denoted the exuberance of infantine health and vigour, she would entice it by soothing words and fond caresses into her most secret apartment, where, lulling it to sleep in her arms, she would suck from its bosom the warm, purple tide of life. Nor were youths of either sex safe from her horrid attack: having first breathed upon her unhappy victim, who never failed immediately to sink into a lengthened sleep, she would then in a similar manner drain his veins of the vital juice. Thus children, youths, and maidens quickly faded away, as flowers gnawed by the cankering worm: the fullness of their limbs disappeared; a sallow line succeeded to the rosy freshness of their cheeks, the liquid lustre of the eye was deadened, even as the sparkling stream when arrested by the touch of frost; and their locks became thin and grey, as if already ravaged by the storm of life. Parents beheld with horror this desolating pestilence devouring their offspring; nor could simple charm, potion or amulet avail aught against it. The grave swallowed up one after the other; or did the miserable victim survive, he became cadaverous and wrinkled even in the very morn of existence. Parents observed with horror this devastating pestilence snatch away their offspring—a pestilence which, nor herb however potent, nor charm, nor holy taper, nor exorcism could avert. They either beheld their children sink one after the other into the grave, or their youthful forms, withered by the unholy, vampire embrace of Brunhilda, assume the decrepitude of sudden age.

At length strange surmises and reports began to prevail; it was whispered that Brunhilda herself was the cause of all these horrors; although no one could pretend to tell in what manner she destroyed her victims, since no marks of violence were discernible. Yet when young children confessed that she had frequently lulled them asleep in her arms, and elder ones said that a sudden slumber had come upon them whenever she began to converse with them, suspicion became converted into certainty, and those whose offspring had hitherto escaped unharmed, quitted their hearths and home—all their little possessions—the dwellings of their fathers and the inheritance of their children, in order to rescue from so horrible a fate those who were dearer to their simple affections than aught else the world could give.

Thus daily did the castle assume a more desolate appearance; daily did its environs become more deserted; none but a few aged decrepit old women and grey-headed menials were to be seen remaining of the once numerous retinue. Such will in the latter days of the earth be the last generation of mortals, when childbearing shall have ceased, when youth shall no more be seen, nor any arise to replace those who shall await their fate in silence.

Walter alone noticed not, or heeded not, the desolation around him; he apprehended not death, lapped as he was in a glowing elysium of love. Far more happy than formerly did he now seem in the possession of Brunhilda. All those caprices and frowns which had been wont to over cloud their former union had now entirely disappeared. She even seemed to doat on him with a warmth of passion that she had never exhibited even during the happy season of bridal love; for the flame of that youthful blood, of which she drained the veins of others, rioted in her own. At night, as soon as he closed his eyes, she would breathe on him till he sank into delicious dreams, from which he awoke only to experience more rapturous enjoyments. By day she would continually discourse with him on the bliss experienced by happy spirits beyond the grave, assuring him that, as his affection had recalled her from the tomb, they were now irrevocably united. Thus fascinated by a continual spell, it was not possible that he should perceive what was taking place around him. Brunhilda, however, foresaw with savage grief that the source of her youthful ardour was daily decreasing, for, in a short time, there remained nothing gifted with youth, save Walter and his children, and these latter she resolved should be her next victims.

On her first return to the castle, she had felt an aversion towards the offspring of another, and therefore abandoned them entirely to the attendants appointed by Swanhilda. Now, however, she began to pay considerable attention to them, and caused them to be frequently admitted into her presence. The aged nurses were filled with dread at perceiving these marks of regard from her towards their young charges, yet dared they not to oppose the will of their terrible and imperious mistress. Soon did Brunhilda gain the affection of the children, who were too unsuspecting of guile to apprehend any danger from her; on the contrary, her caresses won them completely to her. Instead of ever checking their mirthful gambols, she would rather instruct them in new sports: often too did she recite to them tales of such strange and wild interest as to exceed all the stories of their nurses. Were they wearied either with play or with listening to her narratives, she would take them on her knees and lull them to slumber. Then did visions of the most surpassing magnificence attend their dreams: they would fancy themselves in some garden where flowers of every hue rose in rows one above the other, from the humble violet to the tall sunflower, forming a parti-coloured broidery of every hue, sloping upwards towards the golden clouds where little angels whose wings sparkled with azure and gold descended to bring them delicious cakes or splendid jewels; or sung to them soothing melodious hymns. So delightful did these dream in short time become to the children that they longed for nothing so eagerly as to slumber on Brunhilda's lap, for never did they else enjoy such visions of heavenly forms. They were the most anxious for that which was to prove their destruction:—yet do we not all aspire after that which conducts us to the grave—after the enjoyment of life? These innocents stretched out their arms to approaching death because it assumed the mask of pleasure; for, which they were lapped in these ecstatic slumbers, Brunhilda sucked the life-stream from their bosoms. On waking, indeed, they felt themselves faint and exhausted, yet did no pain nor any mark betray the cause. Shortly, however, did their strength entirely fail, even as the summer brook is gradually dried up: their sports became less and less noisy; their loud, frolicsome laughter was converted into a faint smile; the full tones of their voices died away into a mere whisper. Their attendants were filled with horror and despair; too well did they conjecture the horrible truth, yet dared not to impart their suspicions to Walter, who was so devotedly attached to his horrible partner. Death had already smote his prey: the children were but the mere shadows of their former selves, and even this shadow quickly disappeared.

The anguished father deeply bemoaned their loss, for, notwithstanding his apparent neglect, he was strongly attached to them, nor until he had experienced their loss was he aware that his love was so great. His affliction could not fail to excite the displeasure of

Brunhilda: "Why dost thou lament so fondly," said she, "for these little ones? What satisfaction could such unformed beings yield to thee unless thou wert still attached to their mother? Thy heart then is still hers? Or dost thou now regret her and them because thou art satiated with my fondness and weary of my endearments? Had these young ones grown up, would they not have attached thee, thy spirit and thy affections more closely to this earth of clay—to this dust and have alienated thee from that sphere to which I, who have already passed the grave, endeavour to raise thee? Say is thy spirit so heavy, or thy love so weak, or thy faith so hollow, that the hope of being mine for ever is unable to touch thee?" Thus did Brunhilda express her indignation at her consort's grief, and forbade him her presence. The fear of offending her beyond forgiveness and his anxiety to appease her soon dried up his tears; and he again abandoned himself to his fatal passion, until approaching destruction at length awakened him from his delusion.

Neither maiden, nor youth, was any longer to be seen, either within the dreary walls of the castle, or the adjoining territory:—all had disappeared; for those whom the grave had not swallowed up had fled from the region of death. Who, therefore, now remained to quench the horrible thirst of the female vampire save Walter himself? and his death she dared to contemplate unmoved; for that divine sentiment that unites two beings in one joy and one sorrow was unknown to her bosom. Was he in his tomb, so was she free to search out other victims and glut herself with destruction, until she herself should, at the last day, be consumed with the earth itself, such is the fatal law to which the dead are subject when awoke by the arts of necromancy from the sleep of the grave.

She now began to fix her bloodthirsty lips on Walter's breast, when cast into a profound sleep by the odour of her violet breath he reclined beside her quite unconscious of his impending fate: yet soon did his vital powers begin to decay; and many a grey hair peeped through his raven locks. With his strength, his passion also declined; and he now frequently left her in order to pass the whole day in the sports of the chase, hoping thereby to regain his wonted vigour. As he was repos-ing one day in a wood beneath the shade of an oak, he perceived, on the summit of a tree, a bird of strange appearance, and quite unknown to him; but, before he could take aim at it with his bow, it flew away into the clouds; at the same time letting fall a rose-coloured root which dropped at Walter's feet, who immediately took it up and, although he was well acquainted with almost every plant, he could not remember to have seen any at all resembling this. Its delightfully odoriferous scent induced him to try its flavour, but ten times more bitter than wormwood it was even as gall in his mouth; upon which, impatient of the disappointment, he flung it away with violence. Had he, however, been aware of its miraculous quality and that it acted as a counter charm against the opiate perfume of Brunhilda's breath, he would have blessed it in spite of its bitterness: thus do mortals often blindly cast away in displeasure the unsavoury remedy that would otherwise work their weal.

When Walter returned home in the evening and laid him down to repose as usual by Brunhilda's side, the magic power of her breath produced no effect upon him; and for the first time during many months did he close his eyes in a natural slumber. Yet hardly had he fallen asleep, ere a pungent smarting pain disturbed him from his dreams; and, opening his eyes, he discerned, by the gloomy rays of a lamp that glimmered in the apartment, what for some moments transfixed him quite aghast, for it was Brunhilda, drawing with her lips, the warm blood from his bosom. The wild cry of horror which at length escaped him terrified Brunhilda, whose mouth was besmeared with the warm blood. "Monster!" exclaimed he, springing from the couch, "is it thus that you love me?"

"Aye, even as the dead love," replied she, with a malignant coldness.

"Creature of blood!" continued Walter, "the delusion which has so long blinded me is at an end: thou are the fiend who hast destroyed my children—who hast murdered the offspring of my vassals." Raising herself upwards and, at the same time, casting on him a glance that froze him to the spot with dread, she replied. "It is not I who have murdered them;—I was obliged to pamper myself with warm youthful blood, in order that I might satisfy thy furious desires— thou art the murderer!"—These dreadful words summoned, before Walter's terrified conscience, the threatening shades of all those who had thus perished; while despair choked his voice.

"Why," continued she, in a tone that increased his horror, "why dost thou make mouths at me like a puppet? Thou who hadst the courage to love the dead—to take into thy bed, one who had been sleeping in the grave, the bed-fellow of the worm—who hast clasped in thy lustful arms, the corruption of the tomb—dost thou, unhallowed as thou art, now raise this hideous cry for the sacrifice of a few

lives?—They are but leaves swept from their branches by a storm.—
Come, chase these idiot fancies, and taste the bliss thou hast so dearly
purchased." So saying, she extended her arms towards him; but this
motion served only to increase his terror, and exclaiming: "Accursed
Being,"—he rushed out of the apartment.

All the horrors of a guilty, upbraiding conscience became his companions, now that he was awakened from the delirium of his unholy
pleasures. Frequently did he curse his own obstinate blindness, for
having given no heed to the hints and admonitions of his children's
nurses, but treating them as vile calumnies. But his sorrow was now
too late, for, although repentance may gain pardon for the sinner, it
cannot alter the immutable decrees of fate—it cannot recall the murdered from the tomb. No sooner did the first break of dawn appear,
than he set out for his lonely castle in the mountains, determined no
longer to abide under the same roof with so terrific a being; yet vain
was his flight, for, on waking the following morning, he perceived
himself in Brunhilda's arms, and quite entangled in her long raven
tresses, which seemed to involve him, and bind him in the fetters of
his fate; the powerful fascination of her breath held him still more
captivated, so that, forgetting all that had passed, he returned her
caresses, until awakening as if from a dream he recoiled in unmixed
horror from her embrace. During the day he wandered through the
solitary wilds of the mountains, as a culprit seeking an asylum from
his pursuers; and, at night, retired to the shelter of a cave; fearing less
to couch himself within such a dreary place, than to expose himself
to the horror of again meeting Brunhilda; but alas! it was in vain that
he endeavoured to flee her. Again, when he awoke, he found her
the partner of his miserable bed. Nay, had he sought the centre of
the earth as his hiding place; had he even imbedded himself beneath
rocks, or formed his chamber in the recesses of the ocean, still had
he found her his constant companion; for, by calling her again into
existence, he had rendered himself inseparably hers; so fatal were the
links that united them.

Struggling with the madness that was beginning to seize him, and
brooding incessantly on the ghastly visions that presented themselves
to his horror-stricken mind, he lay motionless in the gloomiest recesses
of the woods, even from the rise of sun till the shades of eve. But, no
sooner was the light of day extinguished in the west, and the woods
buried in impenetrable darkness, than the apprehension of resigning
himself to sleep drove him forth among the mountains. The storm

played wildly with the fantastic clouds, and with the rattling leaves, as they were caught up into the air, as if some dread spirit was sporting with these images of transitoriness and decay: it roared among the summits of the oaks as if uttering a voice of fury, while its hollow sound rebounding among the distant hills, seemed as the moans of a departing sinner, or as the faint cry of some wretch expiring under the murderer's hand: the owl too, uttered its ghastly cry as if foreboding the wreck of nature. Walter's hair flew disorderly in the wind, like black snakes wreathing around his temples and shoulders; while each sense was awake to catch fresh horror. In the clouds he seemed to behold the forms of the murdered; in the howling wind to hear their laments and groans; in the chilling blast itself he felt the dire kiss of Brunhilda; in the cry of the screeching bird he heard her voice; in the mouldering leaves he scented the charnel-bed out of which he had awakened her. "Murderer of thy own offspring," exclaimed he in a voice making night, and the conflict of the element still more hideous, "paramour of a blood-thirsty vampire, reveller with the corruption of the tomb!" while in his despair he rent the wild locks from his head. Just then the full moon darted from beneath the bursting clouds; and the sight recalled to his remembrance the advice of the sorcerer, when he trembled at the first apparition of Brunhilda rising from her sleep of death;—namely, to seek him at the season of the full moon in the mountains, where three roads met. Scarcely had this gleam of hope broke in on his bewildered mind than he flew to the appointed spot.

On his arrival, Walter found the old man seated there upon a stone as calmly as though it had been a bright sunny day and completely regardless of the uproar around. "Art thou come then?" exclaimed he to the breathless wretch, who, flinging himself at his feet, cried in a tone of anguish:—"Oh save me—succour me—rescue me from the monster that scattereth death and desolation around her.

"I am acquainted with all," returned the sorcerer. "Thou now perceivest how wholesome was the advice—'Wake not the dead.'"

"And wherefore a mere mysterious warning? Why didst thou not rather disclose to me at once all the horrors that awaited my sacrilegious profanation of the grave?"

"Wert thou able to listen to any other voice than that of thy impetuous passions? Did not thy eager impatience shut my mouth at the very moment I would have cautioned thee?"

"True, true:—thy reproof is just: but what does it avail now;—I need the promptest aid."

"Well," replied the old man, "there remains even yet a means of rescuing thyself, but it is fraught with horror and demands all thy resolution."

"Utter it then, utter it; for what can be more appalling, more hideous than the misery I now endure?"

"Know then," continued the sorcerer, "that only on the night of the new moon does she sleep the sleep of mortals; and then all the supernatural power which she inherits from the grave totally fails her. 'Tis then that thou must murder her."

"How! murder her!" echoed Walter.

"Aye," returned the old man calmly, "pierce her bosom with a sharpened dagger, which I will furnish thee with; at the same time renounce her memory for ever, swearing never to think of her intentionally, and that, if thou dost involuntarily, thou wilt repeat the curse."

"Most horrible! yet what can be more horrible than she herself is?—I'll do it."

"Keep then this resolution until the next new moon."

"What, must I wait until then?" cried Walter, "alas ere then either her savage thirst for blood will have forced me into the night of the tomb, or horror will have driven me into the night of madness."

"Nay," replied the sorcerer, "that I can prevent;" and, so saying, he conducted him to a cavern further among the mountains. "Abide here twice seven days," said he; "so long can I protect thee against her deadly caresses. Here wilt thou find all due provision for thy wants; but take heed that nothing tempt thee to quit this place. Farewell, when the moon renews itself, then do I repair hither again." So saying, the sorcerer drew a magic circle around the cave, and then immediately disappeared.

Twice seven days did Walter continue in this solitude, where his companions were his own terrifying thoughts, and his bitter repentance. The present was all desolation and dread; the future presented the image of a horrible deed which he must perforce commit; while the past was empoisoned by the memory of his guilt. Did he think on his former happy union with Brunhilda, her horrible image presented itself to his imagination with her lips defiled with dropping blood: or, did he call to mind the peaceful days he had passed with Swanhilda, he beheld her sorrowful spirit with the shadows of her murdered children. Such were the horrors that attended him by day: those of night were still more dreadful, for then he beheld Brunhilda herself, who, wandering round the magic circle which she could not pass, called upon his name till the cavern re-echoed the horrible sound. "Walter, my beloved," cried she, "wherefore dost thou avoid me? Art thou not mine, forever mine—mine here, and mine hereafter? And dost thou seek to murder me?—ah! commit not a deed which hurls us both to perdition—thyself as well as me." In this manner did the horrible visitant torment him each night, and, even when she departed, robbed him of all repose.

The night of the new moon at length arrived, dark as the deed it was doomed to bring forth. The sorcerer entered the cavern; "Come," said he to Walter, "let us depart hence, the hour is now arrived:" and he forthwith conducted him in silence from the cave to a coal-black steed, the sight of which recalled to Walter's remembrance the fatal night. He then related to the old man Brunhilda's nocturnal visits and anxiously inquired whether her apprehensions of eternal perdition would be fulfilled or not. "Mortal eye," exclaimed the sorcerer, "may not pierce the dark secrets of another world, or penetrate the deep abyss that separates earth from heaven." Walter hesitated to mount the steed. "Be resolute," exclaimed his companion, "but this once is it granted to thee to make the trial, and, should thou fail now, nought can rescue thee from her power."

"What can be more horrible than she herself?—I am determined:" and he leaped on the horse, the sorcerer mounting also behind him.

Carried with a rapidity equal to that of the storm that sweeps across the plain they in brief space arrived at Walter's castle. All the doors flew open at the bidding of his companion, and they speedily reached Brunhilda's chamber, and stood beside her couch. Reclining in a tranquil slumber; she reposed in all her native loveliness, every trace of horror had disappeared from her countenance; she looked so pure, meek and innocent that all the sweet hours of their endearments rushed to Walter's memory, like interceding angels pleading in her behalf. His unnerved hand could not take the dagger which the sorcerer presented to him. "The blow must be struck even now:" said the latter, "shouldst thou delay but an hour, she will lie at daybreak on thy bosom, sucking the warm life drops from thy heart."

"Horrible! most horrible!" faltered the trembling Walter, and turning away his face, he thrust the dagger into her bosom, exclaiming—"I curse thee for ever!—and the cold blood gushed upon his hand. Opening her eyes once more, she cast a look of ghastly horror on her husband, and, in a hollow dying accent said—"Thou too art doomed to perdition."

"Lay now thy hand upon her corpse," said the sorcerer, "and swear the oath."—Walter did as commanded, saying, "Never will I think of her with love, never recall her to mind intentionally, and, should her image recur to my mind involuntarily, so will I exclaim to it: be thou accursed."

"Thou hast now done everything," returned the sorcerer;—"restore her therefore to the earth, from which thou didst so foolishly recall her; and be sure to recollect thy oath: for, shouldst thou forget it but once, she would return, and thou wouldst be inevitably lost. Adieu— we see each other no more." Having uttered these words he quitted the apartment, and Walter also fled from this abode of horror, having first given direction that the corpse should be speedily interred.

Again did the terrific Brunhilda repose within her grave; but her image continually haunted Walter's imagination, so that his existence was one continued martyrdom, in which he continually struggled, to dismiss from his recollection the hideous phantoms of the past; yet, the stronger his effort to banish them, so much the more frequently and the more vividly did they return; as the night-wanderer, who is enticed by a fire-wisp into quagmire or bog, sinks the deeper into his damp grave the more he struggles to escape. His imagination seemed incapable of admitting any other image than that of Brunhilda: now he fancied he beheld her expiring, the blood streaming from her beautiful bosom: at others he saw the lovely bride of his youth, who reproached him with having disturbed the slumbers of the tomb; and to both he was compelled to utter the dreadful words, "I curse thee for ever." The terrible imprecation was constantly passing his lips; yet was he in incessant terror lest he should forget it, or dream of her without being able to repeat it, and then, on awaking, find himself in her arms. Else would he recall her expiring words, and, appalled at their terrific import, imagine that the doom of his perdition was irrecoverably passed. Whence should he fly from himself? or how erase from his brain these images and forms of horror? In the din of combat, in the tumult of war and its incessant pour of victory to defeat; from the cry of anguish to the exultation of victory—in these he hoped to find at least the relief of distraction: but here too he was disappointed. The giant fang of apprehension now seized him who had never before known fear; each drop of blood that sprayed upon him seemed the cold blood that had gushed from Brunhilda's wound; each dying wretch that fell beside him looked like her, when expiring, she exclaimed,—"Thou too art doomed to perdition"; so that the aspect of death seemed more full of dread to him than aught beside, and this unconquerable terror compelled him to abandon the battle-field. At length, after many a weary and fruitless wandering, he returned to his castle. Here all was deserted and silent, as if the sword, or a still more deadly pestilence had laid everything waste: for the few inhabitants that still remained, and even those servants who had once shewn themselves the most attached, now fled from him, as though he had been branded with the mark of Cain. With horror he perceived that, by uniting himself as he had done with the dead, he had cut himself off from the living, who refused to hold any intercourse with him. Often, when he stood on the battlements of his castle, and looked down upon desolate fields, he compared their present solitude with the lively activity they were wont to exhibit, under the strict but benevolent discipline of Swanhilda. He now felt that she alone could reconcile him to life, but durst he hope that one, whom he so deeply aggrieved, could pardon him, and receive him again? Impatience at length got the better of fear; he sought Swanhilda, and, with the deepest contrition, acknowledged his complicated guilt; embracing her knees as he beseeched her to pardon him, and to return to his desolate castle, in order that it might again become the abode of contentment and peace. The pale form which she beheld at her feet, the shadow of the lately blooming youth, touched Swanhilda. "The folly," said she gently, "though it has caused me much sorrow, has never excited my resentment or my anger. But say, where are my children?" To this dreadful interrogation the agonized father could for a while frame no reply: at length he was obliged to confess the dreadful truth. "Then we are sundered for ever," returned Swanhilda; nor could all his tears or supplications prevail upon her to revoke the sentence she had given.

Stripped of his last earthly hope, bereft of his last consolation, and thereby rendered as poor as mortal can possibly be on this side of the grave. Walter returned homewards; when, as he was riding through the forest in the neighbourhood of his castle, absorbed in his gloomy meditations, the sudden sound of a horn roused him from his reverie. Shortly after he saw appear a female figure clad in black, and mounted on a steed of the same colour: her attire was like that of a huntress, but, instead of a falcon, she bore a raven in her hand; and she was attended by a gay troop of cavaliers and dames. The first salutations bring passed, he found that she was proceeding the same road as himself; and, when she found that Walter's castle was close at hand, she requested that he would lodge her for that night, the evening being far advanced. Most willingly did he comply with this request, since the appearance of the beautiful stranger had struck him greatly; so wonderfully did she resemble Swanhilda, except that her locks were brown, and her eye dark and full of fire. With a sumptuous banquet did he entertain his guests, whose mirth and songs enlivened the lately silent halls. Three days did this revelry continue, and so exhilarating did it prove to Walter that he seemed to have forgotten his sorrows and his fears; nor could he prevail upon himself to dismiss his visitors, dreading lest, on their departure, the castle would seem a hundred times more desolate than before hand his grief be proportionally increased. At his earnest request, the stranger consented to stay seven, and again another seven days. Without being requested, she took upon herself the superintendence of the household, which she regulated as discreetly and cheerfully as Swanhilda had been wont to do, so that the castle, which had so lately been the abode of melancholy and horror, became the residence of pleasure and festivity, and Walter's grief disappeared altogether in the midst of so much gaiety. Daily did his attachment to the fair unknown increase; he even made her his confidant; and, one evening as they were walking together apart from any of her train, he related to her his melancholy and frightful history. "My dear friend," returned she, as soon as he had finished his tale, "it ill beseems a man of thy discretion to afflict thyself on account of all this. Thou hast awakened the dead from the sleep of the grave and afterwards found,—what might have been anticipated, that the dead possess no sympathy with life. What then? thou wilt not commit this error a second time.

Thou hast however murdered the being whom thou hadst thus recalled again to existence—but it was only in appearance, for thou couldst not deprive that of life which properly had none. Thou hast, too, lost a wife and two children: but at thy years such a loss is most easily repaired. There are beauties who will gladly share thy couch, and make thee again a father. But thou dreadst the reckoning of hereafter:—go, open the graves and ask the sleepers there whether that hereafter disturbs them." In such manner would she frequently exhort and cheer him, so that, in a short time, his melancholy entirely disappeared. He now ventured to declare to the unknown the passion

with which she had inspired him, nor did she refuse him her hand.
Within seven days afterwards the nuptials were celebrated, and the
very foundations of the castle seemed to rock from the wild tumultuous uproar of unrestrained riot. The wine streamed in abundance; the
goblets circled incessantly; intemperance reached its utmost bounds,
while shouts of laughter almost resembling madness burst from the
numerous train belonging to the unknown. At length Walter, heated
with wine and love, conducted his bride into the nuptial chamber:
but, oh! horror! scarcely had he clasped her in his arms ere she trans-
formed herself into a monstrous serpent, which entwining him in its
horrid folds, crushed him to death. Flames crackled on every side of
the apartment; in a few minutes after, the whole castle was enveloped
in a blaze that consumed it entirely: while, as the walls fell in with a
tremendous crash, a voice exclaimed aloud—"Wake not the dead!"

The Mysterious Stranger
Karl von Wachsmann

Here is another author who has not received due recognition. When this story first appeared in translation in England, in Chambers's Repository *for February 1854, it bore no author credit and has remained anonymous until now.[1] Its original source was unknown and when Montague Summers included it in his anthology* Victorian Ghost Stories *in 1934, he wrongly dated it 1860. As a consequence, the story has been robbed of its true importance. It first appeared in Germany in 1844 and is therefore the earliest known vampire story to be set in the Carpathian mountains, the setting for Dracula's castle.*

Karl von Wachsmann (1787–1862) was born in what is now Zielona Gora in western Poland, but what was then called Grünberg in Silesia, an area well steeped in vampire lore and legend. He wrote many stories collected in over thirty volumes of Erzählungen und Novellen, *but precious few of them have been translated or credited, and there may be more discoveries to be made.*

[1] I am indebted to Douglas A. Anderson and Thomas Honegger for tracing the identity of the author of this story and for providing background details.

33

The Mysterious Stranger
Karl von Wachsmann

"To die? to sleep!
Perchance to dream? Ay, there's the rub."—*Hamlet*.

BOREAS, THAT fearful north-west wind, which in the spring and autumn stirs up the lowest depths of the wild Adriatic, and is then so dangerous to vessels, was howling through the woods, and tossing the branches of the old knotty oaks in the Carpathian Mountains, when a party of five riders, who surrounded a litter drawn by a pair of mules, turned into a forest-path, which offered some protection from the April weather, and allowed the travellers in some degree to recover their breath. It was already evening, and bitterly cold; the snow fell every now and then in large flakes. A tall old gentleman, of aristocratic appearance, rode at the head of the troop. This was the Knight of Fahnenberg, in Austria. He had inherited from a childless brother a considerable property, situated in the Carpathian Mountains; and he had set out to take possession of it, accompanied by his daughter Franziska, and a niece about twenty years of age, who had been brought up with her.

Next to the knight rode a fine young man some twenty and odd years—the Baron Franz von Kronstein; he wore, like the former, the broad-brimmed hat with hanging feathers, the leather collar, the wide riding-boots—in short, the travelling-dress which was in fashion at the commencement of the seventeenth century. The features of the young man had much about them that was open and friendly, as well as some mind; but the expression was more that of dreamy and sensitive softness than of youthful daring, although no one could deny that he possessed much of youthful beauty. As the cavalcade turned into the oak wood the young man rode up to the litter, and chatted with the ladies who were seated therein. One of these—and to her

34

his conversation was principally addressed—was of dazzling beauty. Her hair flowed in natural curls round the fine oval of her face, out of which beamed a pair of star-like eyes, full of genius, lively, fancy, and a certain degree of archness. Franziska von Fahnenberg seemed to attend but carelessly to the speeches of her admirer, who made many kind inquiries as to how she felt herself during the journey, which had been attended with many difficulties: she always answered him very shortly; almost contemptuously; and at length remarked, that if it had not been for her father's objections, she would long ago have requested the baron to take her place in their horrid cage of a litter, for, to judge by his remarks, he seemed incommoded by the weather; and she would so much rather be mounted on the spirited horse, and face wind and storm, than be mewed up there, dragged up the hills by those long-eared animals, and mope herself to death with ennui. The young lady's words, and, still more, the half-contemptuous tone in which they were uttered, appeared to make the most painful impression on the young man: he made her no reply at the moment, but the absent air with which he attended to the kindly-intended remarks of the other young lady, showed how much he was disconcerted.

"It appears, dear Franziska," said he at length in a kindly tone, "that the hardships of the road have affected you more than you will acknowledge. Generally so kind to others, you have been very often out of humour during the journey, and particularly with regard to your humble servant and cousin, who would gladly bear a double or treble share of the discomforts, if he could thereby save you from the smallest of them."

Franziska showed by her look that she was about to reply with some bitter jibe, when the voice of the knight was heard calling for his nephew, who galloped off at the sound.

"I should like to scold you well, Franziska," said her companion somewhat sharply, "for always plaguing your poor Cousin Franz in this shameful way; he who loves you so truly, and who, whatever you may say, will one day be your husband."

"My husband!" replied the other angrily. "I must either completely alter my ideas, or he his whole self, before that takes place. No, Bertha! I know that this is my father's darling wish, and I do not deny the good qualities Cousin Franz may have, or really has, since I see you are making a face; but to marry an effeminate man—never!"

"Effeminate! you do him great injustice," replied her friend quickly. "Just because instead of going off to the Turkish war, where little honour was to be gained, he attended to your father's advice, and stayed at home, to bring his neglected estate into order, which he accomplished with care and prudence; and because he does not represent this howling wind as a mild zephyr—for reasons such as these you are pleased to call him effeminate."

"Say what you will, it is so," cried Franziska obstinately. "Bold, aspiring, even despotic, must be the man who is to gain my heart; these soft, patient, and thoughtful natures are utterly distasteful to me. Is Franz capable of deep sympathy, either in joy or sorrow? He is always the same—always quiet, soft and tiresome."

"He has a warm heart, and is not without genius," said Bertha.

"A warm heart! that may be," replied the other; "but I would rather be tyrannized over, and kept under a little by my future husband, than be loved in such a wearisome manner. You say he has genius, too. I will not exactly contradict you, since that would be unpolite, but it is not easily discovered. But even allowing you are right in both statements, still the man who does not bring these qualities into action is a despicable creature. A man may do many foolish things, he may even be a little wicked now and then, provided it is in nothing dishonourable; and one can forgive him, if he is only acting on some fixed theory for some special object. There is, for instance, your own faithful admirer, the Castellan of Glogau, Knight of Woislaw; he loves you most truly, and is now quite in a position to enable you to marry comfortably. The brave man has lost his right hand—reason enough for remaining seated behind the stove, or near the spinning-wheel of his Bertha; but what does he do?—He goes off to the war in Turkey; he fights for a noble thought—"

"And runs the chance of getting his other hand chopped off, and another great scar across his face," put in her friend.

"Leaves his lady-love to weep and pine a little," pursued Franziska, "but returns with fame, marries, and is all the more honoured and admired! This is done by a man of forty, a rough warrior, not bred at court, a soldier who has nothing but his cloak and sword. And Franz—rich, noble—but I will not go on. Not a word more on this detested point, if you love me, Bertha."

Franziska leaned back in the corner of the litter with a dissatisfied air, and shut her eyes as though, overcome by fatigue, she wished to sleep.

"This awful wind is so powerful, you say, that we must make a detour to avoid its full force," said the knight to an old man, dressed in a fur-cap and a cloak of rough skin, who seemed to be the guide of the party.

"Those who have never personally felt the Boreas storming over the country between Sessano and Triest, can have no conception of the reality," replied the other. "As soon as it commences, the snow is blown in thick long columns along the ground. That is nothing to what follows. These columns become higher and higher, as the wind rises, and continue to do so until you see nothing but snow above, below, and on every side—unless, indeed, sometimes, when sand and gravel are mixed with the snow, and at length it is impossible to open your eyes at all. Your only plan for safety is to wrap your cloak around you, and lie down flat on the ground. If your home were but a few hundred yards off, you might lose your life in the attempt to reach it."

"Well, then, we owe you thanks, old Kumpan," said the knight, though it was with difficulty he made his words heard above the roaring of the storm; "we owe you thanks for taking us this round, as we shall thus be enabled to reach our destination without danger."

"You may feel sure of that, noble sir," said the old man. "By midnight we shall have arrived, and that without any danger by the way, if —" Suddenly the old man stopped, he drew his horse sharply up, and remained in an attitude of attentive listening.

"It appears to me we must be in the neighbourhood of some village," said Franz von Kronstein; "for between the gusts of the storm I hear a dog howling."

"It is no dog, it is no dog!" said the old man uneasily, and urging his horse to a rapid pace. "For miles around there is no human dwelling; and except in the castle of Klatka, which indeed lies in the neighbourhood, but has been deserted for more than a century, probably no one has lived here since the creation.—But there again," he continued; "well, if I wasn't sure of it from the first."

"That howling seems to fidget you, old Kumpan," said the knight, listening to a long-drawn fierce sound, which appeared nearer than before, and seemed to be answered from a distance.

"That howling comes from no dogs," replied the old guide uneasily. "Those are reed-wolves; they may be on our track; and it would be as well if the gentlemen looked to their firearms."

"Reed-wolves? What do you mean?" inquired Franz in surprise.

"At the edge of this wood," said Kumpan, "there lies a lake about a mile long, whose banks are covered with reeds. In these a number of wolves have taken up their quarters, and feed on wild birds, fish and such like. They are shy in the summer-time, and a boy of twelve might scare them; but when the birds migrate, and the fish are frozen up, they prowl about at night, and then they are dangerous. They are worst, however, when Boreas rages, for then it is just as if the fiend himself possessed them: they are so mad and fierce that man and beast become alike their victims; and a party of them have been known even to attack the ferocious bears of these mountains, and, what is more, to come off victorious." The howl was now again repeated more distinctly, and from two opposite directions. The riders in alarm felt for their pistols, and the old man grasped the spear which hung at his saddle.

"We must keep close to the litter; the wolves are very near us," whispered the guide. The riders turned their horses, surrounded the litter, and the knight informed the ladies, in a few quieting words, of the cause of this movement.

"Then we shall have an adventure—some little variety!" cried Franziska with sparkling eyes.

"How can you talk so foolishly?" said Bertha in alarm.

"Are we not under manly protection? Is not Cousin Franz on our side?" said the other mockingly.

"See, there is a light gleaming among the twigs; and there is another," cried Bertha. "there must be people close to us."

"No, no," cried the guide quickly. "Shut up the door, ladies. Keep close together, gentlemen. It is the eyes of wolves you see sparkling there." The gentlemen looked towards the thick underwood, in which every now and then little bright spots appeared, such as in summer would have been taken for glow-worms; it was just the same greenish-yellow light, but less unsteady, and there were always two flames together. The horses began to be restive, they kicked and dragged at the rein; but the mules behaved tolerably well.

"I will fire on the beasts, and teach them to keep their distance," said Franz, pointing to the spot where the lights were thickest.

"Hold, hold, Sir Baron!" cried Kumpan quickly, and seizing the young man's arm. "You would bring such a host together by the report, that, encouraged by numbers, they would be sure to make the first assault. However, keep your arms in readiness, and if an old she-wolf springs out—for these always lead the attack—take good aim and kill her, for then there must be no further hesitation." By this time the horses were almost unmanageable, and terror had also infected the mules. Just as Franz was turning towards the litter to say a word to his cousin, an animal, about the size of a large hound, sprang from the thicket and seized the foremost mule.

"Fire, baron! A wolf!" shouted the guide.

The young man fired, and the wolf fell to the ground. A fearful howl rang through the wood. "Now, forward! Forward without a moment's delay!" cried Kumpan. "We have not above five minutes' time. The beasts will tear their wounded comrade to pieces, and, if they are very hungry, partially devour her. We shall, in the meantime, gain a little start, and it is not more than an hour's ride to the end of the forest. There—do you see—these are the towers of Klatka between the trees—out there where the moon is rising, and from that point the wood becomes less dense."

The travellers endeavoured to increase their pace to the utmost, but the litter retarded their progress. Bertha was weeping with fear, and even Franziska's courage had diminished, for she sat very still. Franz endeavoured to reassure them. They had not proceeded many moments when the howling recommenced, and approached nearer and nearer.

"There they are again and fiercer and more numerous than before," cried the guide in alarm.

The lights were soon visible again, and certainly in greater numbers. The wood had already become less thick, and the snowstorm having ceased, the moonbeams discovered many a dusky form amongst the trees, keeping together like a pack of hounds, and advancing nearer and nearer till they were within twenty paces, and on the very path of the travellers. From time to time a fierce howl arose from their centre, which was answered by the whole pack, and was at length taken up by single voices in the distance.

The party now found themselves some few hundred yards from the ruined castle of which Kumpan had spoken. It was, or seemed by moonlight to be, of some magnitude. Near the tolerably preserved principal building lay the ruins of a church, which must have once been beautiful, placed on a little hillock, dotted with single oak-trees and bramble-bushes. Both castle and church were still partially roofed in; and a path led from the castle gate to an old oak-tree, where it joined at right angles the one along which the travellers were advancing. The old guide seemed in much perplexity.

"We are in great danger, noble sir," said he. "The wolves will very soon make a general attack. There will then be only one way of escape: leaving the mules to their fate, and taking the young ladies on your horses."

"That would be all very well, if I had not thought of a better plan," replied the knight. "Here is the ruined castle; we can surely reach that, and then, blocking up the gates, we must just await the morning."

"Here? In the ruins of Klatka?—Not for all the wolves in the world!" cried the old man. "Even by daylight no one likes to approach the place, and, now, by night!—The castle, Sir Knight, has a bad name."

"On account of robbers?" asked Franz.

"No; it is haunted," replied the other.

"Stuff and nonsense!" said the baron. "Forward to the ruins; there is not a moment to be lost."

And this was indeed the case. The ferocious beasts were but a few steps behind the travellers. Every now and then they retired, and set up a ferocious howl. The party had just arrived at the old oak before mentioned, and were about to turn into the path to the ruins, when the animals, as though perceiving the risk they ran of losing their prey, came so near that a lance could easily have struck them. The knight and Franz faced sharply about, spurring their horses amidst the advancing crowds, when suddenly, from the shadow of the oak stepped forth a man, who in a few strides placed himself between the travellers and their pursuers. As far as one could see in the dusky light, the stranger was a man of a tall and well-built frame; he wore a sword by his side, and a broad-brimmed hat was on his head. If the party were astonished at his sudden appearance, they were still more so at what followed. As soon as the stranger appeared, the wolves gave over their pursuit, rumbled over each other, and set up a fearful howl. The stranger now raised his hand, appeared to wave it, and the wild animals crawled back into the thickets like a pack of beaten hounds.

Without casting a glance at the travellers, who were too much overcome by astonishment to speak, the stranger went up the path which led to the castle, and soon disappeared beneath the gateway.

"Heaven have mercy on us!" murmured old Kumpan in his beard, as he made the sign of the cross.

"Who was that strange man?" asked the knight with surprise, when he had watched the stranger as long as he was visible, and the party had resumed their way.

The old guide pretended not to understand, and, riding up to the mules, busied himself with arranging the harness, which had become disordered in their haste: more than a quarter of an hour elapsed before he rejoined them.

"Did you know the man who met us near the ruins, and who freed us from our four-footed pursuers in such a miraculous way?" asked Franz of the guide.

"Do I know him? No, noble sir; I never saw him before," replied the guide hesitatingly. "He looked like a soldier, and was armed," said the baron. "Is the castle, then, inhabited?"

"Not for the last hundred years," replied the other. "It was dismantled because the possessor in those days had iniquitous dealings with some Turkish-Sclavonian hordes, who had advanced as far as this; or rather"—he corrected himself hastily—"he is said to have had such, for he might have been as upright and good a man as ever ate cheese fried in butter."

"And who is now the possessor of the ruins and of these woods?" inquired the knight.

"Who but yourself, noble sir?" replied Kumpan. "For more than two hours we have been on your estate, and we shall soon reach the end of the wood."

"We hear and see nothing more of the wolves," said the baron after a pause. "Even their howling has ceased. The adventure with the stranger still remains to me inexplicable, even if one were to suppose him a huntsman—"

"Yes, yes; that is most likely what he is," interrupted the guide hastily, whilst he looked uneasily round him. "The brave good man, who came so opportunely to our assistance, must have been a huntsman. Oh, there are many powerful woodsmen in this neighbourhood! Heaven be praised!" he continued, taking a deep breath, "there is the end of the wood, and in a short hour we shall be safely housed."

And so it happened. Before an hour had elapsed, the party passed through a well-built village, the principal spot on the estate, towards the venerable castle, the windows of which were brightly illuminated, and at the door stood the steward and other dependents, who, having received their new lord with every expression of respect, conducted the party to the splendidly furnished apartments.

Nearly four weeks passed before the travelling adventures again came on the *tapis*. The knight and Franz found such constant employment in looking over all the particulars of the large estate, and endeavouring to introduce various German improvements, that they were very little at home. At first, Franziska was charmed with everything in a neighbourhood so entirely new and unknown. It appeared to her so romantic, so very different from her German Fatherland, that she took the greatest interest in everything, and often drew comparisons between the countries, which generally ended unfavourably for Germany. Bertha was of exactly the contrary opinion: she laughed at her cousin, and said that her liking for novelty and strange sights must indeed have come to a pass, when she preferred hovels in which the smoke went out of the doors and windows instead of the chimney, walls covered with soot, and inhabitants not much cleaner, and of unmannerly habits, to the comfortable dwellings and polite people of Germany. However, Franziska persisted in her notions, and replied that everything in Austria was flat, *ennuyant*, and common; and that a wild peasant here, with his rough coat of skin, had ten times more interest for her than a quiet Austrian in his holiday suit, the mere sight of whom was enough to make one yawn.

As soon as the knight had got the first arrangements into some degree of order, the party found themselves more together again. Franz continued to show great attention to his cousin, which, however, she received with little gratitude, for she made him the butt of all her fanciful humours, that soon returned when after a longer sojourn she had become more accustomed to her new life. Many excursions into the neighbourhood were undertaken, but there was little variety in the scenery, and these soon ceased to amuse.

The party were one day assembled in the old-fashioned hall, dinner had just been removed, and they were arranging in which direction they should ride. "I have it," cried Franziska suddenly, "I wonder we never thought before of going to view by day the spot where we fell in with our night-adventure with wolves and the Mysterious Stranger."

"You mean a visit to the ruins—what were they called?" said the knight.

"Castle Klatka," cried Franziska gaily. "Oh, we really must ride there! It will be so charming to go over again by daylight, and in safety, the ground where we had such a dreadful fright."

"Bring round the horses," said the knight to a servant "and tell the steward to come to me immediately." The latter, an old man, soon after entered the room.

"We intend taking a ride to Klatka," said the knight: "we had an adventure there on our road."

"So old Kumpan told me," interrupted the steward.

"And what do you say about it?" asked the knight.

"I really don't know what to say," replied the old man, shaking his head. "I was a youth of twenty when I first came to this castle, and now my hair is grey; half a century has elapsed during that time. Hundreds of times my duty has called me into the neighbourhood of those ruins, but never have I seen the Fiend of Klatka."

"What do you say? Whom do you call by that name?" inquired Franziska, whose love of adventure and romance was strongly awakened.

"Why, people call by that name the ghost or spirit who is supposed to haunt the ruins," replied the steward. "They say he only shows himself on moonlight nights ——"

"That is quite natural," interrupted Franz smiling. "Ghosts can never bear the light of day; and if the moon did not shine, how could the ghost be seen? For it is not supposed that any one for a mere freak would visit the ruins by torch-light."

"There are some credulous people who pretend to have seen this ghost," continued the steward. "Huntsmen and wood-cutters say they have met him by the large oak on the cross-path. That, noble sir, is supposed to be the spot he inclines most to haunt, for the tree was planted in remembrance of the man who fell there."

"And who was he?" asked Franziska with increasing curiosity.

"The last owner of the castle, which at that time was a sort of robber's den, and the headquarters of all depredators in the neighbourhood," answered the old man. "They say this man was of superhuman strength, and was feared not only on account of his passionate temper, but of his treaties with the Turkish hordes. Any young woman, too, in the neighbourhood to whom he took a fancy, was carried off to his tower and never heard of more. When the measure of his iniquity was full, the whole neighbourhood rose in a mass, besieged his stronghold, and at length he was slain on the spot where the huge oak-tree now stands."

"I wonder they did not burn the whole castle, so as to erase the very memory of it," said the knight.

"It was a dependency of the church, and that saved it," replied the other. "Your great-grandfather afterwards took possession of it, for it had fine lands attached. As the Knight of Klatka was of good family, a monument was erected to him in the church, which now lies as much in ruin as the castle itself."

"Oh, let us set off at once! Nothing shall prevent my visiting so interesting a spot," said Franziska eagerly. "The imprisoned damsels who never reappeared, the storming of the tower, the death of the knight, the nightly wanderings of his spirit round the old oak, and, lastly, our own adventure, all draw me thither with an indescribable curiosity."

When a servant announced that the horses were at the door, the young girls tripped laughingly down the steps which led to the coach-yard. Franz, the knight, and a servant well acquainted with the country, followed; and in a few minutes the party were on their road to the forest.

The sun was still high in the heavens when they saw the towers of Klatka rising above the trees. Everything in the wood was still, except the cheerful twitterings of the birds as they hopped about amongst the bursting buds and leaves, and announced that spring had arrived.

The party soon found themselves near the old oak at the bottom of the hill on which stood the towers, still imposing in their ruin. Ivy and bramble bushes had wound themselves over the walls, and forced deep roots so firmly between the stones that they in a great measure held these together. On the top of the highest spot, a small bush in its young fresh verdure swayed lightly in the breeze.

The gentlemen assisted their companions to alight, and leaving the horses to the care of the servant, ascended the hill to the castle. After having explored this in every nook and cranny, and spent much time in a vain search for some trace of the extraordinary stranger, whom Franziska declared she was determined to discover, they proceeded to an inspection of the adjoining church. This they found to have better withstood the ravages of time and weather; the nave, indeed, was in complete dilapidation, but the chancel and altar were still under roof, as well as a sort of chapel which appeared to have been a place of honour for the families of the old knights of the castle. Few traces remained, however, of the magnificent painted glass which must once have adorned the windows, and the wind entered at pleasure through the open spaces.

The party were occupied for some time in deciphering the inscriptions on a number of tombstones, and on the walls, principally within the chancel. They were generally memorials of the ancient lords, with figures of men in armour, and women and children of all ages. A flying raven and various other devices were placed at the corners. One gravestone, which stood close to the entrance of the chancel, differed widely from the others: there was no figure sculptured on it, and the inscription, which, on all besides, was a mere mass of flattering eulogies, was here simple and unadorned; it contained only these words: "Ezzelin von Klatka fell like a knight at the storming of the castle"—on such a day and year.

"That must be the monument of the knight whose ghost is said to haunt these ruins," cried Franziska eagerly.

"What a pity he is not represented in the same way as the others—I should so like to have known what he was like!"

"Oh, there is the family vault, with steps leading down to it, and the sun is lighting it up through a crevice, said Franz, stepping from the adjoining vestry.

The whole party followed him down the eight or nine steps which led to a tolerably airy chamber, where were placed a number of coffins of all sizes, some of them crumbling into dust. Here, again, one close to the door was distinguished from the others by the simplicity of its design, the freshness of its appearance, and the brief inscription: "Ezzelinus de Klatka, Eques."

As not the slightest effluvium was perceptible, they lingered some time in the vault; and when they reascended to the church, they had a long talk over the old possessors, of whom the knight now remembered he had heard his parents speak. The sun had disappeared, and the moon was just rising as the explorers turned to leave the ruins. Bertha had made a step into the nave, when she uttered a slight exclamation of fear and surprise. Her eyes fell on a man who wore a hat with drooping feathers, a sword at his side, and a short cloak of somewhat old-fashioned cut over his shoulders. The stranger leaned carelessly on a broken column at the entrance; he did not appear to take any notice of the party; and the moon shone full on his pale face.

The party advanced towards the stranger.

"If I am not mistaken," commenced the knight; "we have met before."

Not a word from the unknown.

"You released us in an almost miraculous manner," said Franziska, "from the power of those dreadful wolves. Am I wrong in supposing it is to you we are indebted for that great service?"

"The beasts are afraid of me," replied the stranger in a deep fierce tone, while he fastened his sunken eyes on the girl, without taking any notice of the others.

"Then you are probably a huntsman," said Franz, "and wage war against the fierce brutes."

"Who is not either the pursuer or the pursued? All persecute or are persecuted, and Fate persecutes all," replied the stranger without looking at him.

"Do you live in these ruins?" asked the knight hesitatingly.

"Yes; but not to the destruction of your game, as you may fear, Knight of Fahnenberg," said the unknown contemptuously. "Be quite assured your property shall remain untouched—"

"Oh! my father did not mean that," interrupted Franziska, who appeared to take the liveliest interest in the stranger. "Unfortunate events and sad experiences have, no doubt, induced you to take up your abode in these ruins, of which my father would by no means dispossess you."

"Your father is very good, if that is what he meant," said the stranger in his former tone; and it seemed as though his dark features were drawn into a slight smile; "but people of my sort are rather difficult to turn out."

"You must live very uncomfortably here," said Franziska, half vexed, for she thought her polite speech had deserved a better reply.

"My dwelling is not exactly uncomfortable, only somewhat small, still quite suitable for quiet people," said the unknown with a kind of sneer. "I am not, however, always quiet; I sometimes pine to quit the narrow space, and then I dash away through forest and field, over hill and dale; and the time when I must return to my little dwelling always comes too soon for me."

"As you now and then leave your dwelling," said the knight, "I would invite you to visit us, if I knew—"

"That I was in a station to admit of your doing so," interrupted the other; and the knight started slightly, for the stranger had exactly expressed the half-formed thought. "I lament," he continued coldly, "that I am not able to give you particulars on this point—some difficulties stand in the way: be assured, however, that I am a knight, and of at least as ancient a family as yourself."

"Then you must not refuse our request," cried Franziska, highly interested in the strange manners of the unknown. "You must come and visit us."

"I am no boon-companion, and on that account few have invited me of late," replied the other with his peculiar smile; "besides, I generally remain at home during the day; that is my time for rest. I belong, you must know, to that class of persons who turn day into night, and night into day, and who love everything uncommon and peculiar."

"Really? So do I! And for that reason, you must visit us," cried Franziska. "Now," she continued smiling, "I suppose you have just risen, and you are taking your morning airing. Well, since the moon is your sun, pray pay a frequent visit to our castle by the light of its rays. I think we shall agree very well, and that it will be very nice for us to be acquainted."

"You wish it? You press the invitation?" asked the stranger earnestly and decidedly.

"To be sure, for otherwise you will not come," replied the young lady shortly.

"Well, then, come I will," said the other, again fixing his gaze on her. "If my company does not please you at any time, you will have yourself to blame for an acquaintance with one who seldom forces himself, but is difficult to shake off."

When the unknown had concluded these words, he made a slight motion with his hand, as though to take leave of them, and passing under the doorway, disappeared among the ruins. The party soon after mounted their horses, and took the road home.

It was the evening of the following day, and all were again seated in the hall of the castle. Bertha had that day received good news. The knight Woislaw had written from Hungary, that the war with the Turks would be brought to a conclusion during the year, and that although he had intended returning to Silesia, hearing of the knight of Fahnenberg having gone to take possession of his new estates, he should follow the family there, not doubting that Bertha had accompanied her friend. He hinted that he stood so high in the opinion of his duke on account of his valuable services, that in future his duties would be even more important and extensive; but before settling down to them, he should come and claim Bertha's promise to become his wife. He had been much enriched by his master, as well as by booty taken from the Turks. Having formerly lost his right hand in the duke's service, he had essayed to fight with his left; but this did not succeed very admirably, and so he had an iron one made by a very clever artist. This hand performed many of the functions of a natural one, but there had been still much wanting; now, however, his master had presented him with one of gold, an extraordinary work of art, produced by a celebrated Italian mechanic. The knight described it as something marvellous, especially as to the superhuman strength with which it enabled him to use the sword and lance. Franziska naturally rejoiced in the happiness of her friend, who had had no news of her betrothed for a long time before. She launched out every now and then, partly to plague Franz, and partly to express her own feelings, in the highest praise and admiration of the bravery and enterprise of the knight, whose adventurous qualities she lauded to the skies. Even the scar on his face, and his want of a right hand, were reckoned as virtues; and Franziska at last saucily declared that a rather ugly man was infinitely more attractive to her than a handsome one, for as a general rule handsome men were conceited and effeminate. Thus, she added, no one could term their acquaintance of the night before handsome, but attractive and interesting he certainly was. Franz and Bertha simultaneously denied this. His gloomy appearance: the deadly hue of his complexion, the tone of his voice, were each in turn depreciated by Bertha, while Franz found fault with the contempt and arrogance obvious in his speech. The knight stood between the two parties. He thought there was something in his bearing that spoke of good family, though much could not be said for his politeness; however, the man might have had trials enough in his life to make him misanthropical. Whilst they were conversing in this way, the door suddenly opened, and the subject of their remarks himself walked in.

"Pardon me, Sir Knight," he said coldly, "that I come, if not uninvited, at least unannounced; there was no one in the ante-chamber to do me that service."

The brilliantly lighted chamber gave a full view of the stranger. He was a man about forty, tall, and extremely thin. His features could not be termed uninteresting—there lay in them something bold and daring; but the expression was on the whole anything but benevolent. There was contempt and sarcasm in the cold grey eyes, whose glance, however, was at times so piercing, that no one could endure it long. His complexion was even more peculiar than the features: it could neither be called pale nor yellow; it was a sort of grey, or, so to speak, dirty white, like that of an Indian who has been suffering long from fever; and was rendered still more remarkable by the intense blackness of his beard and short cropped hair. The dress of the unknown was knightly, but old-fashioned and neglected; there were great spots of rust on the collar and breastplate of his armour; and his dagger and the hilt of his finely-worked sword were marked in some places with mildew. As the party were just going to supper, it was only natural to invite the stranger to partake of it; he complied, however, only in so far that he seated himself at the table, for he ate no morsel. The knight, with surprise, inquired the reason.

"For a long time past, I have accustomed myself never to eat at night," he replied with a strange smile. "My digestion is quite unused to solids, and indeed would scarcely confront them. I live entirely on liquids."

"Oh, then, we can empty a bumper of Rhine-wine together," cried the host.

"Thanks; but I neither drink wine nor any cold beverage," replied the other; and his tone was full of mockery. It appeared as if there was some amusing association connected with the idea.

"Then I will order you a cup of hippocras"—a warm drink composed of herbs—"it shall be ready immediately," said Franziska.

"Many thanks, fair lady; not at present," replied the other. "But if I refuse the beverage you offer me now, you may be assured that as soon as I require it—perhaps very soon—I will request that, or some other of you."

Bertha and Franz thought the man had something inexpressibly repulsive in his whole manner, and they had no inclination to engage him in conversation; but the baron, thinking that perhaps politeness required him to say something, turned towards the guest, and commenced in a friendly tone: "It is now many weeks since we first became acquainted with you; we then had to thank you for a signal service—"

"And I have not yet told you my name, although you would gladly know it," interrupted the other dryly. "I am called Azzo; and as"—this he said again with his ironical smile—"with the permission of the Knight of Fahnenberg, I live at the castle of Klatka, you can in future call me Azzo von Klatka."

"I only wonder you do not feel lonely and uncomfortable amongst those old walls," began Bertha. "I cannot understand—"

"What my business is there? Oh, about that I will willingly give you some information, since you and the young gentleman there takes such a kindly interest in my person," replied the unknown in his tone of sarcasm.

Franz and Bertha both started, for he had revealed their thoughts as though he could read their souls. "You see, lady," he continued, "there are a variety of strange whims in the world. As I have already said, I love what is peculiar and uncommon, at least what would appear so to you. It is wrong in the main to be astonished at anything, for, viewed in one light, all things are alike; even life and death, this side of the grave and the other, have more resemblance than you would imagine. You perhaps consider me rather touched a little in my mind, for taking up my abode with the bat and the owl; but if so, why not consider every hermit and recluse insane? You will tell me that those are holy men. I certainly have no pretension that way; but as they find pleasure in praying and singing psalms, so I amuse myself with hunting. Oh, you can have no idea of the intense pleasure of dashing away in the pale moonlight, on a horse that never tires, over hill and dale, through forest and woodland! I rush among the wolves, which fly at my approach, as you yourself perceived, as though they were puppies fearful of the lash."

"But still it must be lonely, very lonely for you," remarked Bertha.

"So it would by day; but I am then asleep," replied the stranger dryly; "at night I am merry enough."

"You hunt in an extraordinary way," remarked Franz hesitatingly.

"Yes; but, nevertheless, I have no communication with robbers, as you seem to imagine," replied Azzo coldly.

Franz again started—that very thought had just crossed his mind. "Oh, I beg your pardon; I do not know—" he stammered.

"What to make of me," interrupted the other. "You would, therefore, do well to believe just what I tell you, or at least to avoid making conjectures of your own, which will lead to nothing."

"I understand you: I know how to value your ideas, if no one else does," cried Franziska eagerly. "The humdrum, everyday life of the generality of men is repulsive to you; you have tasted the joys and pleasures of life, at least what are so called, and you have found them tame and hollow. How soon one tires of the things one sees all around! Life consists in change. Only in what is new, uncommon, and peculiar, do the flowers of the spirit bloom and give forth scent. Even pain may become a pleasure if it saves one from the shallow monotony of everyday life—a thing I shall hate till the hour of my death."

"Right, fair lady—quite right! Remain in this mind: this was always my opinion, and the one from which I have derived the highest reward," cried Azzo; and his fierce eyes sparkled more intensely than ever. "I am doubly pleased to have found in you a person who shares my ideas. Oh, if you were a man, you would make me a splendid companion; but even a woman may have fine experiences when once these opinions take root in her, and bring forth action!"

As Azzo spoke these words in a cold tone of politeness, he turned from the subject, and for the rest of his visit only gave the knight monosyllabic replies to his inquiries, taking leave before the table was cleared. To an invitation from the knight, backed by a still more pressing one from Franziska to repeat his visit, he replied that he would take advantage of their kindness, and come sometimes.

When the stranger had departed, many were the remarks made on his appearance and general deportment. Franz declared his most decided dislike to him. Whether it was as usual to vex her cousin, or whether Azzo had really made an impression on her, Franziska took his part vehemently. As Franz contradicted her more eagerly than usual, the young lady launched out into still stronger expressions; and there is no knowing what hard words her cousin might have received had not a servant entered the room.

The following morning Franziska lay longer than usual in bed. When her friend went to her room, fearful lest she should be ill, she found her pale and exhausted. Franziska complained she had passed a very bad night; she thought the dispute with Franz about the stranger must have excited her greatly, for she felt quite feverish and exhausted, and a strange dream, too, had worried her, which was evidently a consequence of the evening's conversation. Bertha, as usual, took the young man's part, and added, that a common dispute about a man whom no one knew, and about whom any one might form his own opinion, could not possibly have thrown her into her present state. "At least," she continued, "you can let me hear this wonderful dream."

To her surprise; Franziska for a length of time refused to do so.

"Come, tell me," inquired Bertha, "what can possibly prevent you from relating a dream—a mere dream? I might almost think it credible, if the idea were not too horrid, that poor Franz is not very far wrong when he says that the thin, corpse-like, dried-up, old-fashioned stranger has made a greater impression on you than you will allow."

"Did Franz say so?" asked Franziska. "Then you can tell him he is not mistaken. Yes, the thin, corpse-like, dried-up, whimsical stranger is far more interesting to me than the rosy-cheeked, well-dressed, polite, and prosy cousin."

"Strange," cried Bertha. "I cannot at all comprehend the almost magic influence which this man, so repulsive, exercises over you."

"Perhaps the very reason I take his part, may be that you are all so prejudiced against him," remarked Franziska pettishly. "Yes, it must be so; for that his appearance should please my eyes, is what no one in his senses could imagine. But," she continued, smiling and holding out her hand to Bertha, "is it not laughable that I should get out of temper even with you about this stranger?—I can more easily understand it with Franz—and that this unknown should spoil my morning, as he has already spoiled my evening and my night's rest?"

"By that dream, you mean?" said Bertha, easily appeased, as she put her arm round her cousin's neck and kissed her. "Now, do tell it to me. You know how I delight in hearing anything of the kind."

"Well, I will, as a sort of compensation for my peevishness towards you," said the other, clasping her friend's hands. "Now, listen! I had walked up and down my room for a long time; I was excited—out of spirits—I do not know exactly what. It was almost midnight ere I lay down, but I could not sleep. I tossed about, and at length it was only from sheer exhaustion that I dropped off. But what a sleep it was! An inward fear ran through me perpetually. I saw a number of pictures before me, as I used to do in childish sicknesses. I do not know whether I was asleep or half awake. Then I dreamed, but as dearly as if I had been wide awake, that a sort of mist filled the room, and out of it stepped the knight Azzo. He gazed at me for a time, and then letting himself slowly down on one knee, imprinted a kiss on my throat. Long did his lips rest there; and I felt a slight pain, which always went on increasing, until I could bear it no more. With all my strength I tried to force the vision from me, but succeeded only after a long struggle. No doubt I uttered a scream, for that awoke me from my trance. When I came a little to my senses, I felt a sort of superstitious fear creeping over me—how great you may imagine when I tell you that, with my eyes open and awake, it appeared to me as if Azzo's figure were still by my bed, and then disappearing gradually into the mist, vanished at the door!"

"You must have dreamed very heavily, my poor friend," began Bertha, but suddenly paused. She gazed with surprise at Franziska's throat. "Why, what is that?" she cried. "Just look: how extraordinary— a red streak on your throat!"

Franziska raised herself, and went to a little glass that stood in the window. She really saw a small red line about an inch long on her neck, which began to smart when she touched it with her finger.

"I must have hurt myself by some means in my sleep," she said after a pause; "and that in some measure will account for my dream."

The friends continued chatting for some time about this singular coincidence—the dream and the stranger; and at length it was all turned into a joke by Bertha. Several weeks passed. The knight had found the estate and affairs in greater disorder than he at first imagined; and instead of remaining three or four weeks, as was originally intended, their departure was deferred to an indefinite period. This postponement was likewise in some measure occasioned by Franziska's continued indisposition. She who had formerly bloomed like a rose in its young fresh beauty, was becoming daily thinner, more sickly and exhausted, and at the same time so pale, that in the space of a month not a tinge of red was perceptible on the once glowing cheek. The knight's anxiety about her was extreme, and the best advice was procured which the age and country afforded; but all to no purpose. Franziska complained from time to time that the horrible dream with which her illness commenced was repeated, and that always on the day following she felt an increased and indescribable weakness. Bertha naturally set this down to the effect of fever, but the ravages of that fever on the usually dear reason of her friend filled her with alarm.

The knight Azzo repeated his visits every now and then. He always came in the evening, and when the moon shone brightly. His manner was always the same. He spoke in monosyllables, and was coldly polite to the knight; to Franz and Bertha, particularly to the former, contemptuous and haughty; but to Franziska, friendliness itself. Often when, after a short visit, he again left the house, his peculiarities became the subject of conversation. Besides his old way of speaking, in which Bertha said there lay a deep hatred, a cold detestation of all mankind with the exception of Franziska, two other singularities were observable. During none of his visits, which often took place at supper-time, had he been prevailed upon to eat or drink anything, and that without giving any good reason for his abstinence. A remarkable alteration, too, had taken place in his appearance; he seemed an entirely different creature. The skin, before so shrivelled and stretched, seemed smooth and soft, while a slight tinge of red appeared in his cheeks, which began to look round and plump. Bertha, who could not at all conceal her ill-will towards him, said often, that much as she hated his face before, when it was more like a death's-head than a human being's, it was now more than ever repulsive; she always felt

a shudder run through her veins whenever his sharp piercing eyes
rested on her. Perhaps it was owing to Franziska's partiality, or to the
knight Azzo's own contemptuous way of replying to Franz, or to his
haughty way of treating him in general, that made the young man
dislike him more and more. It was quite observable, that whenever
Franz made a remark to his cousin in the presence of Azzo, the latter
would immediately throw some ill-natured light on it, or distort it
to a totally different meaning. This increased from day to day, and at
last Franz declared to Bertha, that he would stand such conduct no
longer, and that it was only out of consideration for Franziska that he
had not already called him to account.

At this time the party at the castle was increased by the arrival of
Bertha's long-expected guest. He came just as they were sitting down
to supper one evening, and all jumped up to greet their old friend.
The knight Woislaw was a true model of the soldier, hardened and
strengthened by war with men and elements. His face would not have
been termed ugly, if a Turkish sabre had not left a mark running from
the right eye to the left cheek, and standing out bright red from the
sunburned skin. The frame of the Castellan of Glogau might almost
be termed colossal. Few would have been able to carry his armour,
and still fewer move with his lightness and ease under its weight. He
did not think little of this same armour, for it had been a present from
the palatine of Hungary on his leaving the camp. The blue wrought-
steel was ornamented all over with patterns in gold; and he had put it
on to do honour to his bride-elect, together with the wonderful gold
hand, the gift of the duke. Woislaw was questioned by the knight and
Franz on all the concerns of the campaign; and he entered into the
most minute particulars relating to the battles, which, with regard to
plunder, had been more successful than ever. He spoke much of the
strength of the Turks in a hand-to-hand fight, and remarked that he
owed the duke many thanks for his splendid gift, for in consequence
of its strength many of the enemy regarded him as something superhuman. The sickliness and deathlike paleness of Franziska was too
perceptible not to be immediately noticed by Woislaw; accustomed
to see her so fresh and cheerful, he hastened to inquire into the cause
of the change. Bertha related all that had happened, and Woislaw
listened with the greatest interest. This increased to the utmost at
the account of the often-repeated dream, and Franziska had to give
him the most minute particulars of it; it appeared as though he had

met with a similar case before, or at least had heard of one. When the
young lady added, that it was very remarkable that the wound on her
throat which she had at first felt had never healed, and still pained
her, the knight Woislaw looked at Bertha as much as to say, that this
last fact had greatly strengthened his idea as to the cause of Franziska's
illness.

It was only natural that the discourse should next turn to the
knight Azzo, about whom every one began to talk eagerly. Woislaw
inquired as minutely as he had done with regard to Franziska's illness, about what concerned this stranger, from the first evening of
their acquaintance down to his last visit, without, however, giving any
opinion on the subject. The party were still in earnest conversation,
when the door opened, and Azzo entered. Woislaw's eyes remained
fixed on him, as he, without taking any particular notice of the new
arrival, walked up to the table, and seating himself, directed most
of the conversation to Franziska and her father, and now and then
made some sarcastic remark when Franz began to speak. The Turkish
war again came on the *tapis*, and though Azzo only put in an occasional remark, Woislaw had much to say on the subject. Thus they
had advanced late into the night, and Franz said smiling to Woislaw:
"I should not wonder if day had surprised us, whilst listening to your
entertaining adventures."

"I admire the young gentleman's taste," said Azzo, with an ironical
curl of the lip. "Stories of storm and shipwreck are, indeed, best heard
on *terra firma*, and those of battle and death at a hospitable table or in
the chimney-corner. One had then the comfortable feeling of keeping a whole skin, and being in no danger, not even of taking cold."
With the last words, he gave a hoarse laugh, and turning his back on
Franz, rose, bowed to the rest of the company, and left the room. The
knight, who always accompanied Azzo to the door, now expressed
himself fatigued, and bade his friends good night.

"That Azzo's impertinence is unbearable," cried Bertha when he
was gone. "He becomes daily more rough, unpolite, and presuming.
If only on account of Franziska's dream, though of course he cannot help that, I detest him. Now, tonight, not one civil word has he
spoken to any one but Franziska, except, perhaps, some casual remark
to my uncle."

"I cannot deny that you are right, Bertha," said her cousin. "One
may forgive much to a man whom fate had probably made somewhat

misanthropical; but he should not overstep the bounds of common politeness. But where on earth is Franz?" added Franziska, as she looked uneasily round.—The young man had quietly left the room whilst Bertha was speaking.

"He cannot have followed the knight Azzo to challenge him?" cried Bertha in alarm.

"It were better he entered a lion's den to pull his mane!" said Woislaw vehemently. "I must follow him instantly," he added, as he rushed from the room. He hastened over the threshold, out of the castle, and through the court, before he came up to them. Here a narrow bridge with a slight balustrade passed over the moat by which the castle was surrounded. It appeared that Franz had only just addressed Azzo in a few hot words, for as Woislaw, unperceived by either, advanced under the shadow of the wall, Azzo said gloomily: "Leave me, foolish boy—leave me; for by that sun"—and he pointed to the full moon above them—"you will see those rays no more if you linger another moment on my path."

"And I tell you, wretch, that you either give me satisfaction for your repeated insolence, or you die," cried Franz, drawing his sword.

Azzo stretched forth his hand, and grasping the sword in the middle, it snapped like a broken reed. "I warn you for the last time," he said in a voice of thunder, as he threw the pieces into the moat. "Now, away—away, boy, from my path, or, by those below us, you are lost!"

"You or I! you or I!" cried Franz madly, as he made a rush at the sword of his antagonist, and strove to draw it from his side. Azzo replied not; only a bitter laugh half escaped from his lips; then seizing Franz by the chest, he lifted him up like an infant, and was in the act of throwing him over the bridge, when Woislaw stepped to his side. With a grasp of his wonderful hand, into the springs of which he threw all his strength, he seized Azzo's arm, pulled it down, and obliged him to drop his victim. Azzo seemed in the highest degree astonished. Without concerning himself further about Franz, he gazed in amazement on Woislaw.

"Who are thou who darest to rob me of my prey?" he asked hesitatingly. "Is it possible? Can you be —?"

"Ask not, thou bloody one! Go, seek thy nourishment! Soon comes thy hour!" replied Woislaw in a calm but firm tone.

"Ha, now I know!" cried Azzo eagerly. "Welcome, blood-brother! I give up to you this worm, and for your sake will not crush him. Farewell; our paths will soon meet again."

"Soon, very soon; farewell!" cried Woislaw, drawing Franz towards him. Azzo rushed away, and disappeared.

Franz had remained for some moments in a state of stupefaction, but suddenly started as from a dream. "I am dishonoured, dishonoured for ever!" he cried, as he pressed his clenched hands to his forehead.

"Calm yourself; you could not have conquered," said Woislaw.

"But I will conquer, or perish!" cried Franz incensed. "I will seek this adventurer in his den, and he or I must fall."

"You could not hurt him," said Woislaw. "You would infallibly be the victim."

"Then show me a way to bring the wretch to judgment," cried Franz, seizing Woislaw's hands, while tears of anger sprang to his eyes. "Disgraced as I am, I cannot live."

"You shall be revenged, and that within twenty-four hours, I hope; but only on two conditions—"

"I agree to them! I will do anything—" began the young man eagerly.

"The first is, that you do nothing, but leave everything in my hands," interrupted Woislaw. "The second, that you will assist me in persuading Franziska to do what I shall represent to her as absolutely necessary. That young lady's life is in more danger from Azzo than your own!"

"How? What?" cried Franz fiercely. "Franziska's life in danger, and from that man? Tell me, Woislaw, who is this fiend?"

"Not a word will I tell either the young lady or you, until the danger is passed," said Woislaw firmly. "The smallest indiscretion would ruin everything. No one can act here but Franziska herself, and if she refuses to do so she is irretrievably lost."

"Speak, and I will help you. I will do all you wish, but I must know—"

"Nothing, absolutely nothing," replied Woislaw. "I must have both you and Franziska yield to me unconditionally. Come now, come to her. You are to be mute on what has passed, and use every effort to induce her to accede to my proposal."

Woislaw spoke firmly, and it was impossible for Franz to make any further objection; in a few moments they both entered the hall, where they found the young girls still anxiously awaiting them.

"Oh, I have been so frightened," said Franziska, even paler than usual, as she held out her hand to Franz. "I trust all has ended peaceably."

"Everything is arranged; a couple of words were sufficient to settle the whole affair," said Woislaw cheerfully.

"But Master Franz was less concerned in it than yourself, fair lady."

"I! How do you mean?" said Franziska in surprise.

"I allude to your illness," replied the other.

"And you spoke of that to Azzo? Does he, then, know a remedy which he could not tell me himself?" she inquired, smiling painfully.

"The knight Azzo must take part in your cure; but speak to you about it he cannot, unless the remedy is to lose all its efficacy," replied Woislaw quietly.

"So it is some secret elixir, as the learned doctors say, who have so long attended me, and through whose means I only grow worse," said Franziska mournfully.

"It is certainly a secret, but is as certainly a cure," replied Woislaw.

"So said all, but none has succeeded," said the young lady peevishly.

"You might at least try it," began Bertha.

"Because your friend proposes it," said the other smiling. "I have no doubt that you, with nothing ailing you, would take all manner of drugs to please your knight; but with me the inducement is wanting, and therefore also the faith."

"I did not speak of any medicine," said Woislaw.

"Oh! a magical remedy! I am to be cured—what was it the quack who was here the other day called it—'by sympathy'? Yes, that was it."

"I do not object to your calling it so, if you like," said Woislaw smiling; "but you must know, dear lady, that the measures I shall propose must be attended to literally, and according to the strictest directions."

"And you trust this to me?" asked Franziska.

"Certainly," said Woislaw hesitating; "but—"

"Well, why do you not proceed? Can you think that I shall fail in courage?" she asked.

"Courage is certainly necessary for the success of my plan," said Woislaw gravely; "and it is because I give you credit for a large share of that virtue, I venture to propose it at all, although for the real harmlessness of the remedy I will answer with my life, provided you follow my directions exactly."

"Well, tell me the plan, and then I can decide," said the young lady.

"I can only tell you that when we commence our operations," replied Woislaw.

"Do you think I am a child to be sent here, there, and everywhere, without a reason?" asked Franziska, with something of her old pettishness.

"You did me great injustice, dear lady, if you thought for a moment I would propose anything disagreeable to you, unless demanded by the sternest necessity," said Woislaw; "and yet I can only repeat my former words."

"Then I will not do it," cried Franziska. "I have already tried so much, and all ineffectually."

"I give you my honour as a knight, that your cure is certain, but—you must pledge yourself solemnly and unconditionally to do implicitly what I shall direct," said Woislaw earnestly.

"Oh, I implore you to consent, Franziska. Our friend would not propose anything unnecessary," said Bertha, taking both her cousin's hands.

"And let me join my entreaties to Bertha's," said Franz.

"How strange you all are!" exclaimed Franziska, shaking her head; "you make such a secret of that which I must know if I am to accomplish it, and then you declare so positively that I shall recover, when my own feelings tell me it is quite hopeless."

"I repeat, that I will answer for the result," said Woislaw, "on the condition I mentioned before, and that you have courage to carry out what you commence."

"Ha! now I understand; this, after all, is the only thing which appears doubtful to you," cried Franziska. "Well, to show you that our sex are neither wanting in the will nor in the power to accomplish deeds of daring, I give my consent."

With the last words, she offered Woislaw her hand.

"Our compact is thus sealed," she pursued smiling. "Now say, Sir Knight, how am I to commence this mysterious cure?"

"It commenced when you gave your consent," said Woislaw gravely. "Now, I have only to request that you will ask no more questions, but hold yourself in readiness to take a ride with me tomorrow an hour before sunset. I also request that you will not mention to your father a word of what has passed."

"Strange!" said Franziska.

"You have made the compact; you are not wanting in resolution; and I will answer for everything else," said Woislaw encouragingly.

"Well, so let it be. I will follow your directions," said the lady, although she still looked incredulous.

"On our return you shall know everything; before that, it is quite impossible," said Woislaw in conclusion. "Now go, dear lady, and take some rest; you will need strength for to-morrow."

It was on the morning of the following day, the sun had not risen above an hour, and the dew still lay like a veil of pearls on the grass, or dripped from the petals of the flowers, swaying in the early breeze, when the knight Woislaw hastened over the fields towards the forest, and turned into a gloomy path, which by the direction, one could perceive, led towards the towers of Klatka. When he arrived at the old oak-tree we have before had occasion to mention, he sought carefully along the road for traces of human footsteps, but only a deer had passed that way; and seemingly satisfied with his search, he proceeded on his way, though not before he had half drawn his dagger from its sheath, as though to assure himself that it was ready for service in time of need.

Slowly he ascended the path; it was evident he carried something beneath his cloak. Arrived in the court, he left the ruins of the castle to the left, and entered the old chapel. In the chancel, he looked eagerly and earnestly around. A deathlike stillness reigned in the deserted sanctuary, only broken by the whispering of the wind in an old thorn-tree which grew outside. Woislaw had looked round him ere he perceived the door leading down to the vault; he hurried towards it, and descended. The sun's position enabled its rays to penetrate the crevices, and made the subterranean chamber so light, that one could read easily the inscriptions at the head and feet of the coffins. The knight first laid on the ground the packet he had hitherto carried under his cloak, and then going from coffin to coffin, at last remained stationary before the oldest of them. He read the inscription carefully, drew his dagger thoughtfully from its case, and endeavoured to raise the lid with its point. This was no difficult matter, for the rusty iron nails kept but a slight hold of the rotten wood. On looking in, only a heap of ashes, some remnants of dress, and a skull were the contents. He quickly closed it again, and went on to the next, passing over those of a woman and two children. Here things had much the same appearance, except that the corpse held together till the lid was raised, and then fell into dust, a few linen rags and bones being alone perceptible In the third, fourth, and nearly the next half-dozen, the bodies were in better preservation: in some, they looked a sort of yellow brown mummy; whilst in others, a skinless skull covered with hair grinned from the coverings of velvet, silk, or mildewed embroideries; all, however, were touched with the loathsome marks of decay. Only one more coffin now remained to be inspected; Woislaw approached it, and read the inscription. It was the same that had before attracted the Knight of Fahnenberg: Ezzelin von Klatka, the last possessor of the tower, was described as lying therein. Woislaw found it more difficult to raise the lid here; and it was only by the exertion of much strength he at length succeeded in extracting the nails. He did all, however, as quietly as if afraid of rousing some sleeper within; he then raised the cover, and cast a glance on the corpse. An involuntary "Ha!" burst from his lips as he stepped back a pace. If he had less expected the sight that met his eyes, he would have been far more overcome. In the coffin lay Azzo as he lived and breathed, and as Woislaw had seen him at the supper-table only the evening before. His appearance, dress and all were the same; besides, he had more the semblance of sleep than of death—no trace of decay was visible—there was even a rosy tint on his cheeks. Only the circumstance that the breast did not heave, distinguished him from one who slept. For a few moments Woislaw did not move; he could only stare into the coffin. With a hastiness in his movements not usual with him, he suddenly seized the lid, which had fallen from his hands, and laying it on the coffin, knocked the nails into their places. As soon as he had completed this work, he fetched the packet he had left at the entrance, and laying it on the top of the coffin, hastily ascended the steps, and quitted the church and the ruins.

The day passed. Before evening, Franziska requested her father to allow her to take a ride with Woislaw, under pretence of showing him the country. He, only too happy to think this a sign of amendment in his daughter, readily gave his consent; so followed by a single servant, they mounted and left the castle. Woislaw was unusually silent and serious. When Franziska began to rally him about his gravity, and the approaching sympathetic care, he replied that what was before her was no laughing matter; and that although the result would be certainly a cure, still it would leave an impression on her whole future life. In such discourse they reached the wood, and at length the oak, where they left their horses. Woislaw gave Franziska his arm, and they ascended the hill slowly and silently. They had just reached one of the half-dilapidated outworks where they could catch a glimpse of the open country, when Woislaw, speaking more to himself than to his companion, said: "In a quarter of an hour, the sun will set, and in another hour the moon will have risen; then all must be accomplished. It will soon be time to commence the work."

"Then, I should think it was time to entrust me with some idea of what it is," said Franziska, looking at him.

"Well, lady," he replied, turning towards her, and his voice was very solemn, "I entreat you, Franziska von Fahnenberg, for your own good, and as you love the father who clings to you with his whole soul, that you will weigh well my words, and that you will not interrupt me with questions which I cannot answer until the work is completed. Your life is in the greatest danger from the illness under which you are labouring; indeed, you are irrecoverably lost if you do not fully carry out what I shall now impart to you. Now, promise me to do implicitly as I shall tell you; I pledge you my knightly word it is nothing against Heaven, or the honour of your house; and, besides, it is the sole means for saving you." With these words, he held out his right hand to his companion, while he raised the other to heaven in confirmation of his oath.

"I promise you," said Franziska, visibly moved by Woislaw's solemn tone, as she laid her little white and wasted hand in his.

"Then, come; it is time," was his reply, as he led her towards the church. The last rays of the sun were just pouring through the broken windows. They entered the chancel, the best preserved part of the whole building; here there were still some old kneeling-stools, placed before the high-altar, although nothing remained of that but the stonework and a few steps; the pictures and decorations had all vanished.

"Say an Ave; you will have need of it," said Woislaw, as he himself fell on his knees.

Franziska knelt beside him, and repeated a short prayer. After a few moments, both rose. "The moment has arrived! The sun sinks, and before the moon rises, all must be over," said Woislaw quickly.

"What am I to do?" asked Franziska cheerfully.

"You see there that open vault!" replied the knight Woislaw, pointing to the door and flight of steps: "You must descend. You must go alone; I may not accompany you. When you have reached the vault you will find, close to the entrance, a coffin, on which is placed a

small packet. Open this packet, and you will find three long iron nails
and a hammer. Then pause for a moment; but when I begin to repeat
the Credo in a loud voice, knock with all your might, first one nail,
then a second, and then a third, into the lid of the coffin, right up to
their heads."

Franziska stood thunderstruck; her whole body trembled, and she
could not utter a word. Woislaw perceived it.

"Take courage, dear lady!" said he. "Think that you are in the hands
of Heaven, and that without the will of your Creator, not a hair can
fall from your head. Besides, I repeat, there is no danger."

"Well, then, I will do it," cried Franziska, in some measure regain-
ing courage.

"Whatever you may hear, whatever takes place inside the coffin,"
continued Woislaw, "must have no effect upon you. Drive the nails
well in, without flinching: your work must be finished before my
prayer comes to an end."

Franziska shuddered, but again recovered herself. "I will do it;
Heaven will send me strength," she murmured softly.

"There is one thing more," said Woislaw hesitatingly; "perhaps it is
the hardest of all I have proposed, but without it your cure will not
be complete. When you have done as I have told you, a sort of"—he
hesitated—"a sort of liquid will flow from the coffin; in this dip your
finger, and besmear the scratch on your throat."

"Horrible!" cried Franziska. "This liquid is blood. A human being
lies in the coffin."

"An *unearthly* one lies therein! That blood is your own, but it flows
in other veins," said Woislaw gloomily. "Ask no more; the sand is
running out."

Franziska summoned up all her powers of mind and body, went
towards the steps which led to the vault, and Woislaw sank on his
knees before the altar in quiet prayer. When the lady had descended,
she found herself before the coffin on which lay the packet before
mentioned. A sort of twilight reigned in the vault, and everything
around was so still and peaceful, that she felt more calm, and going
up to the coffin, opened the packet. She had hardly seen that a hammer and three long nails were its contents when suddenly Woislaw's
voice rang through the church, and broke the stillness of the aisles.
Franziska started, but recognized the appointed prayer. She seized one
of the nails, and with one stroke of the hammer drove it at least an
inch into the cover. All was still; nothing was heard but the echo of

the stroke. Taking heart, the maiden grasped the hammer with both hands, and struck the nail twice with all her might, right up to the head into the wood. At this moment commenced a rustling noise; it seemed as though something in the interior began to move and to struggle. Franziska drew back in alarm. She was already on the point of throwing away the hammer, and flying up the steps, when Woislaw raised his voice so powerfully, and it sounded so entreatingly, that in a sort of excitement, such as would induce one to rush into a lion's den, she returned to the coffin, determined to bring things to a conclusion. Hardly knowing what she did, she placed a second nail in the centre of the lid, and after some strokes, this was likewise buried to its head. The struggle now increased fearfully, as if some living creature were striving to burst the coffin. This was so shaken by it, that it cracked and split on all sides. Half distracted, Franziska seized the third nail; she thought no more of her ailments, she only knew herself to be in terrible danger, of what kind she could not guess: in an agony that threatened to rob her of her senses, and in the midst of the turning and cracking of the coffin, in which low groans were flow heard, she struck the third nail in equally tight. At this moment, she began to lose consciousness. She wished to hasten away, but staggered; and mechanically grasping at something to save herself by, she seized the corner of the coffin, and sank fainting beside it on the ground.

A quarter of an hour might have elapsed, when she again opened her eyes. She looked around her. Above was the starry sky, and the moon, which shed her cold light on the ruins and on the tops of the old oak-trees. Franziska was lying outside the church walls, Woislaw on his knees beside her, holding her hand in his.

"Heaven be praised that you live!" he cried, with a sigh of relief. "I was beginning to doubt whether the remedy had not been too severe, and yet it was the only thing to save you."

Franziska recovered her full consciousness very gradually. The past seemed to her like a dreadful dream. Only a few moments before, that fearful scene; and now this quiet all around her. She hardly dared at first to raise her eyes, and shuddered when she found herself only a few paces removed from the spot where she had undergone such terrible agony. She listened half unconsciously, now to the pacifying words Woislaw addressed to her, now to the whistling of the servant, who stood by the horses, and who, to wile away his time, was imitating the evening-song of a belated cow-herd.

"Let us go," whispered Franziska, as she strove to raise herself. "But what is this? My shoulder is wet, my throat, my hand—"

"It is probably the evening dew on the grass," said Woislaw gently.

"No; it is blood!" she cried, springing up with horror in her tone. "See, my hand is full of blood!"

"Oh, you are mistaken—surely mistaken," said Woislaw stammering. "Or perhaps the wound on your neck may have opened! Pray, feel whether this is the case." He seized her hand, and directed it to the spot.

"I do not perceive anything; I feel no pain," she said at length, somewhat angrily.

"Then, perhaps, when you fainted, you may have struck a corner of the coffin, or have torn yourself with the point of one of the nails," suggested Woislaw.

"Oh, of what do you remind me!" cried Franziska shuddering. "Let us away—away! I entreat you, come! I will not remain a moment longer near this dreadful, dreadful place."

They descended the path much quicker than they came. Woislaw placed his companion on her horse, and they were soon on their way home.

When they approached the castle, Franziska began to inundate her protector with questions about the preceding adventure; but he declared that her present state of excitement must make him defer all explanations till the morning, when her curiosity should be satisfied. On their arrival, he conducted her at once to her room, and told the knight his daughter was too much fatigued with her ride to appear at the supper-table.

On the following morning, Franziska rose earlier than she had done for a long time. She assured her friend it was the first time since her illness commenced that she had been really refreshed by her sleep, and, what was still more remarkable, she had not been troubled by her old terrible dream. Her improved looks were not only remarked by Bertha, but by Franz and the knight; and with Woislaw's permission, she related the adventures of the previous evening. No sooner had she concluded, than Woislaw was completely stormed with questions about such a strange occurrence.

"Have you" said the latter, turning towards his host, "ever heard of Vampires?"

"Often," replied he; "but I have never believed in them."

"Nor did I," said Woislaw; "but I have been assured of their existence by experience."

"Oh, tell us what occurred," cried Bertha eagerly, as a light seemed
to dawn on her.

"It was during my first campaign in Hungary," began Woislaw,
"when I was rendered helpless for some time by this sword-cut of a
janizary across my face, and another on my shoulder. I had been taken
into the house of a respectable family in a small town. It consisted of
the father and mother, and a daughter about twenty years of age. They
obtained their living by selling the very good wine of the country,
and the taproom was always full of visitors. Although the family were
well to do in the world, there seemed to brood over them a continual
melancholy, caused by the constant illness of the only daughter, a
very pretty and excellent girl. She had always bloomed like a rose,
but for some months she had been getting so thin and wasted, and
that without any satisfactory reason: they tried every means to restore
her, but in vain. As the army had encamped quite in the neighbourhood, of course a number of people of all countries assembled in the
tavern. Amongst these there was one man who came every evening,
when the moon shone, who struck everybody by the peculiarity of
his manners and appearance; he looked dried up and deathlike, and
hardly spoke at all; but what he did say was bitter and sarcastic. Most
attention was excited towards him by the circumstance, that although
he always ordered a cup of the best wine, and now and then raised it
to his lips, the cup was always as full after his departure as at first."

"This all agrees wonderfully with the appearance of Azzo," said
Bertha, deeply interested.

"The daughter of the house," continued Woislaw, "became daily
worse, despite the aid not only of Christian doctors, but of many
amongst the heathen prisoners, who were consulted in the hope that
they might have some magical remedy to propose. It was singular that
the girl always complained of a dream, in which the unknown guest
worried and plagued her."

"Just the same as your dream, Franziska," cried Bertha.

"One evening," resumed Woislaw, "an old Sclavonian—who had
made many voyages to Turkey and Greece, and had even seen the
New World—and I were sitting over our wine, and sat down at the
table. The bottle passed quickly between my friend and me, whilst we
talked of all manner of things, of our adventures, and of passages in our
lives, both horrible and amusing. We went on chatting thus for about

an hour, and drank a tolerable quantity of wine. The unknown had remained perfectly silent the whole time, only smiling contemptuously every now and then. He now paid his money, and was going away. All this had quietly worried me—perhaps the wine had got a little into my head—so I said to the stranger: 'Hold, you stony stranger; you have hitherto done nothing but listen, and have not even emptied your cup. Now you shall take your turn in telling us something amusing, and if you do not drink up your wine, it shall produce a quarrel between us.' 'Yes,' said the Sclavonian, 'you must remain; you shall chat and drink, too;' and he grasped—for although no longer young, he was big and very strong—the stranger by the shoulder, to pull him down to his seat again: the latter, however, although as thin as a skeleton, with one movement of his hand flung the Sclavonian to the middle of the room, and half stunned him for a moment. I now approached to hold the stranger back. I caught him by the arm; and although the springs of my iron hand were less powerful than those I have at present, I must have gripped him rather hard in my anger, for after looking grimly at me for a moment, he bent towards me and whispered in my ear: 'Let me go from the gripe of your fist, I see you are my brother, therefore do not hinder me from seeking my bloody nourishment. I am hungry!' Surprised by such words, I let him loose, and almost before I was aware he had left the room. As soon as I had in some degree recovered from my astonishment, I told the Sclavonian what I had heard. He started, evidently alarmed. I asked him to tell me the cause of his fears, and pressed him for an explanation of those extraordinary words. On our way to his lodging, he complied with my request. 'The stranger,' said he, 'is a Vampire!'

"How?" cried the knight, Franziska, and Bertha simultaneously, in a voice of horror. "So this Azzo was—"

"Nothing less. He also was a Vampire!" replied Woislaw. "But at all events his hellish thirst is quenched for ever; he will never return.— But I have not finished. As in my country vampires had never been heard of, I questioned the Sclavonian minutely. He said that in Hungary, Croatia, Dalmatia, and Bosnia, these hellish guests were not uncommon. They were deceased persons, who had either once served as nourishment to vampires, or who had died in deadly sin, or under excommunication; and that whenever the moon shone, they rose from their graves, and sucked the blood of the living."

"Horrible!" cried Franziska. "If you had told me all this before-hand, I should never have accomplished the work."

"So I thought; and yet it must be executed by the sufferers themselves, while some one else performs the devotions," replied Woislaw. "The Sclavonian," he continued after a short pause, "added many other facts with regard to these unearthly visitants. He said that whilst their victim wasted, they themselves improved in appearance, and that a vampire possessed enormous strength—"

"Now I can understand the change your false hand produced on Azzo," interrupted Franz.

"Yes, that was it," replied Woislaw. "Azzo, as well as the other vampire, mistook its great power for that of a natural one, and concluded I was one of his own species.—You may now imagine, dear lady," he continued, turning to Franziska, "how alarmed I was at your appearance when I arrived: all you and Bertha told me increased my anxiety; and when I saw Azzo, I could doubt no longer that he was a vampire. As I learned from your account that a grave with the name Ezzelin von Klatka lay in the neighbourhood, I had no doubt that you might be saved if I could only induce you to assist me. It did not appear to me advisable to impart the whole facts of the case, for your bodily powers were so impaired, that an idea of the horrors before you might have quite unfitted you for the exertion; for this reason, I arranged everything in the manner in which it has taken place."

"You did wisely," replied Franziska shuddering. "I can never be grateful enough to you. Had I known what was required of me, I never could have undertaken the deed."

"That was what I feared," said Woislaw; "but fortune has favoured us all through."

"And what became of the unfortunate girl in Hungary? " inquired Bertha.

"I know not," replied Woislaw. "That very evening there was an alarm of Turks, and we were ordered off. I never heard anything more of her."

The conversation upon these strange occurrences continued for some time longer. The knight determined to have the vault at Klatka walled up for ever. This took place on the following day; the knight alleging as a reason that he did not wish the dead to be disturbed by irreverent hands.

Franziska recovered gradually. Her health had been so severely shaken, that it was long ere her strength was so much restored as to allow of her being considered out of danger. The young lady's character underwent a great change in the interval. Its former strength was, perhaps, in some degree diminished, but in place of that, she had acquired a benevolent softness, which brought out all her best qualities. Franz continued his attentions to his cousin; but, perhaps, owing to a hint from Bertha, he was less assiduous in his exhibition of them. His inclinations did not lead him to the battle, the camp, or the attainment of honours; his great aim was to increase the good condition and happiness of his tenants, and to this he contributed the whole energy of his mind. Franziska could not withstand the unobtrusive signs of the young man's continued attachment; and it was not long ere the credit she was obliged to yield to his noble efforts for the welfare of his fellow-creatures, changed into a liking, which went on increasing, until at length it assumed the character of love. As Woislaw insisted on making Bertha his wife before he returned to Silesia, it was arranged that the marriage should take place at their present abode. How joyful was the surprise of the knight of Fahnenberg, when his daughter and Franz likewise entreated his blessing, and expressed their desire of being united on the same day! That day soon came round, and it saw the bright looks of two happy couples.

The Pale Lady

Alexandre Dumas

Unlike the previous two authors, Alexandre Dumas (1802–1870) is world-renowned as the author of The Three Musketeers *(1844) and* The Count of Monte Cristo *(1846), and plenty more besides. He is less often associated with supernatural fiction, although he did write* The Wolf-Leader *(1857), an early werewolf tale. His shorter weird tales were collected in* Les Mille et un Fantômes *(1849), which included the following story. When Dumas first arrived in Paris in 1823, determined to make his fortune as a playwright, he went to the theatre to see* Le Vampire, *a play by Charles Nodier based on Polidori's "The Vampyre." Through the play, Dumas became acquainted with Nodier, and after Nodier's death in 1844 Dumas revised the play and it saw a new run in 1851. The following story would have been completed shortly before Dumas began work on the play, which shows his continued fascination with the subject.*

The Pale Lady

Alexandre Dumas

1. Among the Carpathians

I AM A Pole by birth, a native of Sandomir, a land where legends become articles of faith, and where we believe in our family traditions as firmly as in the Gospel—perhaps more firmly. Not one of our castles but has its spectre, not one of our cottages but owns its familiar spirit. Among rich and poor alike, in castle and cot equally, the two principles of good and ill are acknowledged.

Sometimes the two are at variance and fight one against the other. Then are heard mysterious noises in passages, howls in old, half-ruined towers, shakings of walls—so terrible and appalling that cot and castle are both left desolate, while the inhabitants, whether peasants or nobles, fly to the nearest church to seek protection from holy cross or blessed relics, the only preservatives effectual against the demons that harass our homes.

Moreover in the same land two still more terrible principles, principles still more fierce and implacable, are face to face—to wit, tyranny and freedom.

In the year 1825 broke out between Russia and Poland one of those death struggles that seem bound to drain the life-blood of a people to its last drop, as the blood of a particular family is often exhausted.

My father and two brothers had risen in revolt against the new Czar, and had gone forth to range themselves beneath the flag of Polish independence, so often torn down, so often raised again.

One day I learnt that my younger brother had been killed; another day I was told that my elder brother was mortally wounded; lastly, after a long 24 hours during which I listened with terror to the booming of the cannon coming constantly nearer and nearer, I beheld my

71

father ride in with a hundred horsemen—all that was left of three thousand men under his command. He came to shut himself up in our castle, resolved, if need be, to perish buried beneath its ruins.

Fearless for himself, my father trembled at the fate that threatened me. For him death was the only penalty, for he was firmly resolved never to fall alive into the hands of his enemies: but for me slavery, dishonour, shame might be in store.

From among the hundred men left him my father chose ten, summoned the Intendant of the Estate, handed him all the gold and jewels we possessed, and remembering how, at the date of the second partition of Poland, my mother, then scarcely a child, had found unassailable refuge in the Monastery of Sahastru, situated in the heart of the Carpathian Mountains, bade him conduct me thither. The cloister which had sheltered the mother would doubtless be no less hospitable to the daughter.

Our farewells were brief, notwithstanding the fond love my father bore me. By tomorrow in all likelihood the Russians would be within sight of the castle, so that there was not a moment to lose. Hurriedly I donned a riding-habit which I was in the habit of wearing when following the hounds with my brothers. The most trusty mount in the stables was saddled for me, my father slipped his own pistols, masterpieces of the Toula gunsmiths' art, into my holsters, kissed me and gave the order to start.

That night and next day we covered a score of leagues, riding up the banks of one of the nameless rivers that flow from the hills to join the Vistula. This forced march to begin with had carried us completely out of the reach of our Russian foes.

The last rays of the setting sun showed us the snowy summits of the Carpathians gleaming through the dusk. Towards the close of next day we arrived at their base, and eventually during the forenoon of the third day we found ourselves winding along a mountain gorge.

Our Carpathian hills differ widely from Western ranges, which are civilised in comparison. All that nature has to show of strange and wild and grand is seen in its completest majesty. Their storm-beaten peaks are lost in the clouds and shrouded in eternal snow; their boundless fir-woods bend over the burnished mirror of lakes that are more like seas, crystal clear waters which no keel has ever furrowed, no fisherman's net ever disturbed.

The human voice is seldom heard in these regions, and then only to raise some rude Moldavian folksong to which the cries of wild animals reply, song and cries blending together to wake the lonely echoes that seem astounded to be roused at all.

Mile after mile you travel beneath the gloomy vaults of the forest interrupted only by the unexpected marvels which the waste reveals to the wayfarer at almost every step, moving his astonishment and admiration.

Danger lurks everywhere, danger compounded of a thousand varying perils; but there is no time to be afraid, the perils are too sublime to admit of common terror. Now it is the sudden formation of cataracts owing to the melting of the ice, which, dashing down from rock to rock, unexpectedly overwhelm the narrow path the traveller is following, a path traced by the sportsman and the game he pursues; now it is the fall of trees undermined by the lapse of time, which tear up their roots from the soil and come crashing down with a sound like that of an earthquake; now it is the onrush of a hurricane which enfolds the climber in storm-clouds riven by the darting zig-zags of the lightning, writhing and coiling like a serpent.

Then, after these Alpine peaks, after these primeval forests, as you have had giant mountains and boundless woods, you next have illimitable steppes, a veritable sea with its waves and tempests, barren, rugged wastes, where the eyes wander and lose themselves on the far-distant horizon. It is not terror now that seizes the spectator, it is irresistible melancholy, a profound sadness. The look of all the country-side, far as the eye can range, is everlastingly the same. You mount only to descend again slopes that are all alike; this you do twenty times over, searching in vain for a beaten track, till finding yourself thus lost in solitude, amid pathless deserts, you deem yourself alone with nature, and your melancholy turns into despair.

Movement seems a vain thing that will advance to whit; you will meet with neither village, nor castle, nor cottage, no smallest trace of human occupation. Only now and again, adding yet another note of sadness to the dreary landscape, a little lake, bare and treeless, without reeds or rushes or brushwood, lying asleep in the bottom of a ravine like another Dead Sea, bars your way with its greenish waters, from which rise at your approach a cloud of aquatic birds uttering long discordant screams. You make a detour; you climb the hill before you, you go down into another valley, you climb another hill, and this does on and on till finally you come to the end of the range of foothills, which grow gradually lower and lower.

But now, if you make a bend to the south, the landscape recovers all its grandeur again and you catch sight of a new range, higher and more picturesque-looking and more inviting. It is all plumed with woods, and refreshed by countless watercourses. Shade and moisture give back life to the countryside; the tinkle of the hermit's bell is heard, a caravan is seen winding along the hillside. Finally, under the dying rays of the sinking sun, you sight, looking like a covey of white birds crouched side by side, the houses of a village grouped close together to guard against nocturnal attack.

For with life, danger is there again, and it is not now, as in the first range crossed, packs of wolves and bears that are to be feared, but hordes of Moldavian robbers.

However, we drew near our destination in spite of every difficulty. Ten days' constant travelling had sped without accident, and already we could make out the summit of Mount Pion, a giant a whole head taller than his fellow giants, on whose southern slopes lies the Monastery of Sahastru, to which I was bound. Another three days and we stood before the gates.

It was the end of August and the day had been one of blazing heat; the relief was intense when, towards four o'clock, we first began to inhale the fresh evening breeze. We had passed by the ruined towers of Niantzo, and were descending upon a plain just opening to view through a gap in the mountains. We could already, from the point we had reached, trace the course of the Bistriza, and note its banks besprinkled with red water-poppies and great white campanulas. We were making our way along the brink of a precipice at the foot of which rolled the river, as yet no more than a mountain torrent, our path being barely wide enough to allow our beasts to go two abreast.

The guide went first, perched sideways on his horse, singing a native stave to a monotonous air, the words of which I followed with no small interest and pleasure.

The winger was composer too. As for the tune, one must be a born mountaineer to appreciate to the full its wild melancholy and unsophisticated gloom. The words ran thus:

> "In the marsh-lands of Stavila,
> Where the fight has oft been sore,
>   See yonder dead man lying!
> 'Tis no son of Illyria,
> 'Tis a brigand, fell and fierce,

Who beguiled a gentle maid,
    And robbed and burned and slew.

"A bullet sped like a hurricane
And struck the robber low,
    In his throat's a yatagan!
But for three long days, oh mystery,
Beneath the grim and lonely pine,
His warm blood wets the ground
    And stains red the Ovigan.

"His blue eyes shine no more;
Let us away, let none come nigh
    The swamp where the dead thief lies.
'Tis a vampire! The wild wolf
Runs howling from the horrid thing!
In terror o'er the bare hillside
    The vulture wings away."

Suddenly a gun-shot rang out and a musket ball whistled through the air. The song stopped, and our guide rolled mortally wounded down the precipice, while his horse stood shivering on the brink, peering wonderingly into the depths of the abyss into which his master had disappeared.

Simultaneously a great shouting was raised, and we saw ourselves surrounded by a band of brigands, some thirty strong; we were entirely surrounded. All seized their weapons, and though caught unawares, my companions, being old soldiers inured to action, never lost their heads, but returned the fire vigorously. To give an example myself, I grasped a pistol, and seeing how disadvantageous our present position was, cried: "Forward!" and spurred my horse in the direction of the level country.

But we had to do with mountaineers, who sprang lightly from rock to rock like very demons of the abyss, firing as they leapt, and never losing the menacing position they had taken up on our flank. Moreover, our attempt at escape had been foreseen. At a spot where the road widened and the mountain formed a small plain, a young chief awaited us at the head of ten or a dozen horsemen. On seeing us, they put their horses to a gallop, and dashed forward to charge us in front, while the rest who were pursuing us slipped down the mountain-sides and surrounded us on every side, so as to cut off our retreat completely.

The situation was very serious; yet, inured as I was from childhood to scenes of strife and bloodshed, I could examine my surroundings without a detail escaping me.

Our adversaries were one and all clad in sheepskins and wore enormous round hats garlanded with wild flowers, after the Hungarian fashion. Each carried a long Turkish firepiece; these they brandished in the air after discharging, uttering barbarous shouts the while. In their belts they had besides a curved sabre and a brace of pistols.

Their leader was a young man of barely twenty-two, with a pale face, long dark eyes and hair falling in ringlets about his shoulder. His costume consisted of the flowing Moldavian gown edged with fur and confined at the waist by a scarf of alternate gold and silken stripes. A curved sabre flashed in his hand, and four pistols glittered in his belt.

During the fight he kept up a string of hoarse, inarticulate cries, which scarcely seemed to belong to human speech; yet they sufficiently expressed his orders, for his men obeyed them implicitly, throwing themselves flat on the ground to avoid our fire, springing up anon to deliver their own, bringing down such as were still capable of defence, finishing off the wounded, and presently turning the fight into a mere butchery. Soon I had seen two-thirds of my defenders fall one after the other. Four only were left, who closed about me, never thinking of asking quarter, which they were certain not to receive, hoping one thing only, to sell their lives as dearly as possible.

Then the young chief gave a cry more expressive than ever, pointing his sabre at us. Doubtless the order was to envelop this final handful in a circle of fire, and shoot us down all together, for the long-barrelled Moldavian muskets covered us simultaneously. I felt our last hour was come; I raised my eyes and hands to heaven in a last supplication, and waited for death.

At this supreme moment I saw another young warrior descend— no, *descend* is not the word; I should say dash down, leaping from rock to rock. Then he halted, standing on a boulder, dominating the whole scene like a statue on its pedestal, and pointing to the field of carnage, pronounced the simple word:

"Enough!"

All eyes looked up at the voice. Each man appeared ready to obey this new leader. One bandit only raised his gun to his shoulder again, and fired.

One of our men gave a cry; the ball had broken his left arm. He turned instantly to rush at the man who had wounded him; but before his horse had taken four paces forward, a flash shone out above our heads, and the mutinous brigand rolled over, his skull shattered by a bullet.

Such a press of strong and varying emotions had brought me to the end of my strength, and I fell fainting to the ground.

When I recovered consciousness I was lying on the grass, my head supported against the knees of a man whose hand, very white and covered with rings, I could see about my waist. Standing in front of me, with arms crossed and his sabre under his arm, was the young Moldavian chieftain who had directed the attack against us.

"Kostaki," my protector was saying in French and with a tone of authority, "you must go this instant and draw off your men, and leave me to look after the girl."

"Brother, brother," replied the individual to whom these words were addressed, and who appeared to find extreme difficulty in containing himself; "brother, beware of exhausting my patience. I leave you the Castle, leave the Forest to me. Within the Castle you are master, but here I am all-powerful. Here it would need but one word to compel you to obey me."

"Kostaki, I am the elder—that is to say, I am master everywhere, in the Castle no less than in the Forest, there as well as here. Oh yes! I am of the blood of the Brankovans as much as you. 'Tis Royal blood and is wont to be obeyed. I order, and I must be obeyed."

"You order, you, Gregoriska; your lackeys, yes, but not my soldiers."

"Your soldiers are brigands, Kostaki—brigands I will have hanged from the battlements of our towers, if they do not give me instant obedience."

"Well, then, order them, and see if they obey!"

Then I felt my supporter draw away his knees and lay my head down softly against a stone. I followed him anxiously with my eyes, and I saw the same young chief who had tumbled, so to speak, from the skies into the middle of the fight, and whom hitherto I had only been able to catch a glimpse of, having swooned at the very instant he had first spoken.

He was a young man of twenty-four, of tall stature, with great blue eyes in which was legible a remarkable endowment of resolution and determination. His long flaxen hair, characteristic of the Slav race, fell about his shoulders like the Archangel Michael's, framing his young, fresh cheeks; his lips parted in a disdainful smile, showing a double row of pearls; his gaze was the eagle's confronting the lightning.

He was dressed in a kind of tunic of black velvet; a little cap, like that which the painter Raphael wears in his portraits, adorned with an eagle's feather, was on his head; he wore tight breeches and embroidered high boots. Round his waist was a sash containing a hunting-knife, while a shoulder-belt carried a short, double-barrelled carbine, the accuracy of which one of the bandits had just been given an opportunity of appreciating.

He extended his arm, and the gesture seemed to command the obedience even of his brother; he pronounced a few words in Moldavian, and these words appeared to produce a profound impression on the brigands.

Then, using the same language, the young chief spoke in his turn, and I could guess that his words were a mixture of threats and imprecations.

But to all his long and fierce harangue the elder of the two brothers vouchsafed not one word of reply.

The brigands bowed before his imperious glance, and, at a gesture from him, ranged themselves behind us.

"Well, so be it, Gregoriska," said Kostaki, returning to the French tongue. "The woman shall not be taken to the cavern, then; but she shall be mine none the less. She is to my taste, I have won her in fight, and I will have her." And with the words, he darted towards me and lifted me in his arms.

"The woman shall be taken to the Castle, I repeat, and given into my mother's care; and I mean to see it is done," replied my protector.

"My horse, bring me my horse!" cried Kostaki in Moldavian.

A dozen bandits sprang forward to obey, and led up the horse to their chief.

Gregoriska glanced around him, seized a masterless horse by the bridle, and leapt on its back without touching the stirrups.

Kostaki flung himself into the saddle almost as lightly as his brother, although he still held me in his arms, and dashed off at a gallop.

Gregoriska's steed seemed fired with the same spirit, and kept head and flank steadily on a level with the head and flank of Kostaki's mount.

It was a strange sight, the two horsemen speeding side by side, in gloomy silence, never losing one another for a single instant from view, though without seeming to look, giving the rein to their horses, which pursued a wild and desperate course through woods and amid rocks and precipices.

My head was thrown back so as to let me see Gregoriska's fine eyes fixed upon my own. Kostaki, observing this, raised my head, and I could henceforth see only his dark, sombre gaze, devouring my face. I dropped my lids, but in vain; through their shade I could still feel the same piercing glance penetrating to my inmost bosom and lacerating my heart. Then a strange hallucination took possession of me; I thought I was the lost Lenore of Bürger's famous ballad, in the act of being carried off by the spectral horse and horseman, and presently when I felt we were slackening speed, it was with a feeling of sheer terror I opened my eyes, firmly convinced I should see surrounding me only shattered graveyard crosses and open tombs.

What I did behold was hardly less gloomy, to wit, the inner courtyard of a Moldavian castle built in the fourteenth century.

2. The Castle of Brankovan

Then Kostaki let me slip out of his arms on to the ground, and in another moment got down beside me; but, quick as he had been, he had not been quick enough to anticipate Gregoriska. As the latter had said, within the Castle he was undisputed master.

Seeing the arrival of the two young chiefs and the strange woman they had brought along with them, the servants ran eagerly forward, but though their attentions were divided between Kostaki and Gregoriska, it was plain the greatest obsequiousness, the deepest respect, were reserved for the last named.

Two women approached; Gregoriska gave them an order in Moldavian, and signed me to follow them. The gesture was accompanied by a look expressive of so much respect that I did not hesitate to obey. Five minutes afterwards I was in a bedchamber, which, bare and uncomfortable as it must have appeared to the least exacting of mortals, was manifestly the best the Castle contained.

It was a vast, square apartment, provided with a sort of divan covered with green serge, serving as a seat by day and a bed by night. Five or six great oak settles, an enormous cupboard or wardrobe, and in one corner of the room a canopied chair resembling a great, richly carved church stall, completed the furniture. As to window curtains or bed hangings, such things were out of the question. The way thither was by a staircase adorned with three statues, more than life-size, of dead and gone Brankovans, standing in niches.

In another few minutes the baggage was brought up, my trunks among the rest. The women offered to help me; but while repairing the disorder produced in my costume by the events of the day, I retained my long riding-habit, as better matching my hosts' personal appointments than any other costume I could have adopted.

Scarcely had I completed these little changes of dress when I heard someone knocking softly at the door.

"Come in," I said, speaking naturally enough in French, French being, as you are aware, a second mother tongue to us Poles.

Gregorista appeared, saying, "Ah, madame, I am happy to know that you speak French!"

"And I too, sir," I replied, "I am happy to know that language, since, thanks to my doing so, I have been able to appreciate your generous conduct towards me. It was in that tongue you championed me against the evil designs of your brother, and in the same language I now offer you the expression of my heartfelt gratitude."

"Thank you, madame. It was no more than natural I should take the side of a woman situated as you were. I was hunting in the mountain when I heard irregular but long-continued firing. I knew it must be a question of some attack by armed violence, and made for the scene of action. I arrived in the nick of time, thanks be to God. But may I ask you now, madame, by what strange chance a lady of distinction like yourself came to expose herself to the risks of our wild mountains?"

"I am a Pole, sir," I replied. "My two brothers have just been killed in the war against Russia; my father, whom I left prepared to defend our Castle against the enemy, has doubtless rejoined them by this time. For myself, I was flying to escape from those scenes of massacre, and seeking, by my father's orders, an asylum in the cloister of Sahastru, where my mother in her youth and under similar circumstances, had found a secure refuge."

"You are the foe of the Russians; so much the better!" cried the young man, "this will be a strong point in your favour in our Castle here, and we shall require all our strength to sustain the struggle that is brewing. And now, I know who you are, learn, madame, who we are; the name Brankovan is not unknown to you, is it, madame?"

I bowed assent.

"My mother is the last Princess of the name, the last descendant of that illustrious chief who was done to death the Cantimirs, the caitiff courtiers of Peter I. My mother married as her first husband my father, Serban Waivady, a Prince as she was a Princess, but of less illustrious race.

"My father had been brought up at Vienna, where he had learnt to appreciate the advantages of civilisation. He resolved to make a European of me, and we started on travels embracing France, Italy, Spain and Germany.

"My mother—it is not a son's part, I know, to tell you that I am going to, but inasmuch as, for your own safety, it behoves you to know us intimately, you will understand the necessity for the revelation— my mother, who, during the earlier years of my father's absence, when I was still quite a child, had had guilty relations with a party chieftain (this," added Gregoriska with a laugh, "is what men who have wantonly attacked you are entitled in our country)—my mother, I saw, who had had guilty relations with a certain Count Giordaki Koproli, half Greek, half Moldavian, wrote to my father, confessing all and asking for divorce, declaring in support of her demand that she could not bear, Brankovan as she was, to continue the wife of a man who deliberately day by day was making himself more and more of a stranger to his native land. Alas! my father was never called upon to agree to the request—one that may seem extraordinary to you, but which with us is looked upon as the simplest and most natural thing in the world; he had just died of an aneurism, from which he had long suffered, and it was I who received the letter.

"There was nothing for me to do, beyond expressing my heartfelt wishes for my mother's happiness. This I did in a letter, in which I announced to her the news of her widowhood. In the same letter I begged her permission to continue my travels, and this was readily granted.

"My fixed resolution had been to settle in France or Germany, so as to avoid meeting a man who hated me and for whom I could not possibly feel affection for, that is to say, my mother's second husband. But suddenly one day I received news that Count Giordaki Koproli had been assassinated, by all accounts at the hands of the old Cossack troopers of my father's.

"I hurried home; I loved my mother and understood her present isolation and her natural craving to have beside her at such a moment such persons as were bound to her by close ties of kinship. True she had never shown any very tender affection for me, but still she was my mother. One morning, without a word to announce my arrival, I entered the Castle of my ancestors.

"There I found a young man whom I took at first for a stranger, but whom I learnt later was my brother. This was Kostaki, the child of adultery, now legitimized by my mother's second marriage—Kostaki, the untamable being you have yourself seen, whose passions are his only law, who holds nothing sacred in all the world but his mother, who only obeys me as the tiger does the man that has mastered him by sheer force—and this with a never-ceasing growl of protest in vain hope of one day devouring me.

"Inside the Castle, within the home of the Brankovans and Waivadys, I am still master; but once outside its walls, once in the open country, he is again the savage child of the woods and mountains, resolved to make everything bend to his own iron will. How came he to yield today, what made his men obey another? I cannot say; perhaps force of habit, some relic of traditional respect. I should not care to put my authority to a second proof. Stay here, do not quit this room, this court, in a word the circuit of these walls—and I can guarantee your safety; take one step outside the Castle—and I can promise nothing, except to sacrifice my life in your defence."

"Then cannot I continue my journey to the Monastery of Sahastru, as my father wished?"

"Try if you will; command, and I shall obey; but the end will be —I shall be left a dead man by the wayside, and you will never reach your destination."

"What is to be done, then?"

"Best stay here and await events; have patience and profit by circumstances. Recognise that you are fallen into a bandit's den, and that your courage alone can save you, your presence of mind alone release you. My mother, despite her preference for Kostaki, the son of her love, is kind and generous. Moreover, she is a Brankovan, in other words a true princess. You shall be presented to her; she will defend you against the brute passions of Kostaki. Place yourself under her protection; you are fair to look upon and she will love you. Indeed," he went on, looking at me with an indescribable expression on his face, "who could see you and not love you? Come now to the hall where supper is prepared and where my mother waits you. Show neither embarrassment nor distrust, and speak Polish—no one understands that tongue here; I will translate your words to my mother, and rest assured I will only say what should be said. Above all, not a word of what I have just told you; not a breath of our mutual understanding. You do not know yet all the wiles and subterfuges of the most straightforward of my countrymen. Now come."

I followed him down the staircase I have described, now lighted by pinewood torches burning in iron hands protruding from the walls. Evidently so unusual an illumination had been made in my honour.

Arrived at the great hall, Gregoriska threw open the door and pronounced a Moldavian word, which I learnt subsequently means 'the stranger.' Hereupon a tall, imposing woman came forward to meet us—the Princess Brankovan.

Her white hair was coiled in plaits about her head, on which rested a little cap of sable, surmounted by an aigrette, sign of her princely origin. She wore a sort of tunic of cloth of gold covered with pearls, falling over a long skirt of Turkish material, trimmed with the same fur as her headdress. In her hand she carried a rosary with amber beads, which she was turning rapidly between her fingers.

Beside her stood Kostaki, wearing the magnificent and imposing Magyar costume which lent him a still stranger and more exotic look than ever. It consisted of a gown of green velvet with ample sleeves, falling below the knee, breeches of red cashmere, and Turkish slippers of morocco leather embroidered in gold; his head was uncovered, and his long locks, so black as to be almost blue, tumbled about his bare neck, confined merely by the slender white line of the edging of a silken shirt.

He gave me an awkward bow, and said a few words in Moldavian which I could not understand.

"You can speak French, brother," Gregoriska said to him. "Madame is Polish, and understands the language." Upon this, Kostaki made some remarks in French, which were all but as unintelligible to me as those he had uttered in Moldavian; but the Princess now extended her hand imperiously, and imposed silence on them both. I could plainly see she was telling her sons it was her place to receive me.

Then she began in Moldavian a speech of welcome, which the expression of her face made it easy to gather the drift of. She signed me to the table, offered me a seat by her side, embraced the whole house in a sweeping gesture, as if to tell me it was all at my disposal; then sitting down first with kindly dignity, she made the sign of the cross and began a prayer.

This ended, all took their places—places determined by etiquette, Gregoriska's being next below mine. I was a stranger, and consequently occupied a place of honour next to Kostaki, who sat beside his mother Smerande.

Gregoriska had likewise changed his dress. He now wore the Magyar tunic like his brother; only his was of garnet-red and his breeches of blue cashmere. A magnificent decoration hung at his neck—the Nisham of the Sultan Mahmoud.

The rest of the household supped at the same table, each in the due subordination given him by his position among the friends or dependents of the family.

The meal was a gloomy one; not once did Kostaki address me, though his brother took pains to converse with me and always in French. As for their mother, she offered me some of every dish herself, with the air of grave solemnity which never left her. Gregoriska had said truly, she was a veritable Princess.

After supper, Gregoriska came forward, and approaching his mother, explained to her in Moldavian the desire I must be feeling to be alone, and how needful rest was for me after the emotions of a day such as I had passed. Smerande bowed her head in assent, reached me her hand, kissed me on the brow, as she might have done to a daughter, and wished me a good night and sound repose in her Castle.

Gregoriska was right; I longed eagerly for a moment's solitude. So I thanked the Princess, who led me to the door of the hall, where I found waiting for me the two women who had previously attended me.

I made my bow to the mistress of the house, saluted her two sons, and retired to the same apartment, the room I had quitted an hour before to come down to supper. Meantime the divan had been converted into a bed, the only change that had been effected.

I thanked my tire-women, and informed them by signs that I would undress myself. On this they left the room at once, with marks of respect that showed they had received orders to obey me implicitly.

I was left alone in the vaste apartment, which my light was insufficient even to illuminate from end to end; I could only make out bits at a time, as I moved my candle from place to place, never the whole room at once. The light was strangely blended, the moonbeams entering through the curtainless window, and struggling to diminish the glimmer of my taper.

Besides the door by which I had entered, and which opened on to the staircase, my room possessed two others, but massive bolts attached to these and fastening from inside, sufficed to reassure me on this score.

Next I examined the entrance door. Like the others, it was well provided with means of defence. Then I threw open my window, and found a sheer precipice beneath it.

I saw plainly enough that Gregoriska had made a deliberate choice of this particular chamber to ensure me against danger. Presently, coming back to my divan, I discerned a little note lying on a table by my bedside. I opened it and read in Polish:

"Sleep at ease; you will have nothing to fear, so long as you remain within the Castle walls.—*Gregoriska.*"

I followed the advice given me, and, weariness prevailing over all other feelings, I lay down and fell fast asleep.

3. The Two Brothers

Henceforward I was established at the Castle of Brankovan, and from that moment began the drama I am about to relate.

The two brothers both fell in love with me, each in his own peculiar way.

Kostaki did not wait a day before he told me he loved me, declared I should be his or no one's, swore he would kill me sooner than suffer me to belong to another, no matter who.

Gregoriska said nothing; but he lavished infinite care and solicitude upon me. All the resources of a brilliant education, all the recollections of a youth passed at the most famous Courts of Europe, were laid under contribution to please me. Alas! the task was only too easy; at the first sound of his voice, I had felt that he was the chosen one of my soul; at the first look of his eyes, I had felt my heart was his.

At the end of three months, Kostaki had repeated a hundred times over that he loved me. I detested him. At the end of the same period, Gregoriska had never spoken one word of love, and I knew that, ask me when he might, I should be his, heart and soul.

Kostaki had given up his out-of-door life altogether. He never left the Castle now, having for the time being abdicated his authority in favour of a sort of lieutenant, who came to him from time to time for orders, and disappeared to execute them.

Smerande likewise manifested a passionate affection for me, the intensity of which terrified me. She openly championed Kostaki, and seemed to be more jealous of me than he was himself. Only, as she understood neither Polish nor French, while I knew no Moldavian, she could not well make any pressing appeals to me in her boy's favour. Still she had learnt to say three words in French, which she would repeat to me every time her lips were laid upon my forehead:

"Kostaki aime Hedwig"—Kostaki loves Hedwig.

One day I learnt a terrible piece of news, which seemed to crown my misfortunes. The four men who had survived the fight with the brigands had been released, and had returned to Poland, under pledge that one of them should come back within three months to bring me news of my father's fate. One of the four did so come back, only to tell me our Castle had been taken, set fire to, and utterly destroyed, while my father had been killed in trying to defend it.

I was left all alone in the world. Kostaki redoubled his eager appeals and Smerande her tenderness; but I could now urge my mourning for my father as an obstacle. Kostaki only insisted the more, saying that the more lonely and forlorn I was, the more I needed a protector, while his mother was as importunate or perhaps more importunate than himself.

Gregoriska had spoken to me of the power the Moldavians possess over themselves in cases where they desire to keep their true feelings hid; and he was in himself a living example of this faculty. It was impossible to be more certain of the love of a man than I was of his; yet if I had been asked what proof I had to allege for my certainty, I could have given none. No one, in the Castle, had ever seen his hand touch mine, or his eyes seek mine. Jealousy alone could enlighten Kostaki as to his brother's rivalry, as my love alone could inform me of his love.

Nevertheless, I must admit, this excessive self-control of Gregoriska's troubled me. I believed, I felt he loved me, but how could I be sure? I wanted some tangible proof. I was still in this uncertainty, when one evening, just after I had retired to my room for the night, I heard a soft tapping at one of the two doors I have mentioned before as fastening on the inside. From the way the knocks were given, I guessed it was a friend. I went to the door and asked who was there.

"Gregoriska," replied a voice whose accents there was little fear of my mistaking.

"What do you want with me?" I asked, trembling all over.

"If you trust me," cried Gregoriska, "if you believe me to be a man of honour, grant me what I ask."

"And what is that?"

"Put out your light, as if you had gone to bed, and in half an hour's time open your door to let me in."

"Come back in half an hour," was my only and unhesitating answer. Then I put out my light and waited.

My heart beat violently, for I felt sure it was a question of some all-important eventuality. The half hour slipped by, and I heard the taps repeated more softly even than the first time.

Meanwhile I had withdrawn the bolts, so that I had merely to pull the door open.

Gregoriska came in, and, without his saying a word to that effect, I closed the door behind him and shot the bolts. He stood still a moment, mute and motionless, gesturing me to be silent. Then, assured that no immediate danger threatened us, he led me to the middle of the vast apartment, and, seeing from the way I trembled that I could hardly stand, brought me a chair. I sat down, or rather let myself sink helplessly into it.

"God in Heaven!" I explained, "what is the matter, and why these excessive precautions?"

"Because my life—though that is nothing—because your life, perhaps, depends upon the conversation we are going to have together."

In great alarm, I seized his hand in mine, which he lifted to his lips, looking into my eyes the while to ask my pardon for such an act of presumption. I dropped my eyes before his—a confession of self-surrender.

"I love you," he said in a voice as sweet and melodious as a song; "do you love me?"

"Yes," I told him.

"Are you ready to be my wife?"

"Yes."

He drew his hand across his forehead with a deep-drawn sigh of happiness.

"Then you will not refuse to follow me?"

"I will follow you anywhere and everywhere!"

"You understand, of course," he went on, "that we can only win happiness by flight."

"Oh, yes!" I cried, "let us fly, let us fly!"

"Hush," he said, shuddering, "hush."

"You are right," and I went up to him trembling.

"This is what I have done," he said; "this is why I have been so long without confessing my love to you. It was because I desired, once secure of your affection, that nothing might have power to hinder our union. I am rich, Hedwig, enormously rich, but after the fashion of the Moldavian nobles—rich in lands, in flocks and herds, in serfs. Well, I have sold to the Monastery of Hango a million francs worth of land, cattle and villages. They have given me three hundred thousand francs of the purchase money in previous stones, a hundred thousand francs in gold, the rest in letters of credit upon Vienna. Will a million be enough for you?"

I pressed his hand. "Your love would have been enough alone, Gregoriska, be sure of that."

"Well, now, listen; tomorrow I am going to the Monastery of Hango to make my final arrangements with the Superior. He has horses ready for me; these horses will await us at nine o'clock, in hiding, a hundred paces from the Castle. After supper you are to go up to your room the same as today; the same as today you are to put out your light; the same as today you are to open the door and I will come in. But tomorrow, instead of my going out alone, you are to follow me; we will gain the gate opening on the country, we will find our horses, we will spring on their backs, and by next day's dawn we shall be thirty leagues away."

"Ah! why is it not next day's dawn already!"

"Hedwig, my darling!"—and Gregoriska pressed me to his heart; our lips met in a long kiss.

He had well said when I opened my chamber door to him that he was a man of honour; was well aware that without possessing my body, he possessed my heart.

The night passed without my having closed an eye. I pictured myself borne away in his arms as I had been by Kostaki. Only now, the ride which had been so fearful, so appalling, so grim, was a sweet, soft, entrancing motion, the very rapidity of which added a voluptuous charm, for speed has a charm and pleasure of its own. Daylight came at last, and I left my room. I seemed to detect something even more morose than usual in the greeting Kostaki vouchsafed me on my appearance. His smile was more than ironical, it was threatening, sinister. As for Smerande, her attitude seemed much as usual.

In the course of breakfast Gregoriska ordered his horses, without Kostaki paying any attention apparently to the circumstance. About eleven, he took leave of us, announcing that he would not be back before evening, and begged his mother not to delay dinner for him. Then, turning to me, he made his excuses for quitting me so suddenly.

He left the great hall, his brother staring after him until he crossed the threshold. As he did so, a lightning flash of hate and malignity shot from Kostaki's eyes that made me shudder.

The day passed amid such fears and anxieties as may be imagined. I had confided our projects to no living soul, hardly in my prayers had I dared to tell God of them; yet I felt as though these plans were known to all the world, that every look cast my way had power to penetrate my heart and read my inmost thoughts.

Dinner was a veritable torture; sombre and silent. Kostaki scarcely opened his mouth. When he did, it was only to address a curt phrase or two to his mother in Moldavian, and every time the tones of his voice made me shudder in spite of myself.

When I rose to go back to my room, Smerande kissed me as usual, and as she kissed me she spoke the sentence which for quite a week now I had not heard her utter:

"Kostaki loves Hedwig."

The words pursued me like a threat; arrived in my chamber I seemed to hear a voice of fate still murmuring in my ear, "Kostaki loves Hedwig,"—but Kostaki's love, Gregoriska had told me so, meant death.

About seven in the evening, as twilight was falling, I saw Kostaki cross the castle court; he wheeled round to look in my direction, but I started back to avoid his seeing me. I felt anxious, for as long as the situation of my window allowed me to follow his movements, I had observed that he was making his way towards the stables. I made bold to unbolt my door, and slipped into the next room, from the window of which I could see perfectly what he was about.

Yes, he was going to the stables. Presently he brought out his favourite horse, saddled the animal with his own hands, and this with a minute care that showed he attached the greatest importance to the smallest details. He wore the same costume as on the day I had first seen him, but on this occasion his only weapon was his sabre. His mount saddled, he cast his eyes once more to my window. Then, not seeing me, he leapt into the saddle, rode out by the same gate by which his brother had left the castle and would return, and away at a hard gallop in the direction of the Monastery of Hango.

Then my heart contracted in a spasm of dread; a fatal presentiment told me that Kostaki was going to meet and confront his brother.

I lingered at the window as long as I could make out the track, which a quarter of a league from the Castle made a bend, and disappeared among the first trees of the forest; but darkness was rapidly descending, and every trace of the road soon became invisible.

I lingered on and on. At last the very excess of my disquietude restored my energy, and as it was evidently in the great hall below that I was likely to receive the first tidings of one or other of the two brothers, I went down thither. My first look was for Smerande; but the calmness of her face told me she was under no special apprehension. She was giving her orders for the customary supper, and places were laid as usual for the two brothers.

I dared not question anyone—indeed, who could I question? Nobody in the Castle, Kostaki and Gregoriska excepted, could speak either of the only two languages I knew myself.

The slightest sound set me trembling.

Nine o'clock was the ordinary hour for the meal. I had come down at half-past eight; I watched anxiously the minute hand, the movement of which was almost visible on the huge face of the Castle clock. Soon the quarter sounded, sad and solemn; then the hand went on its silent way again, and once more I watched the minutes marked off, slowly but surely.

A few minutes before nine I thought I heard a horse gallop into the courtyard. Smerande heard it too, and turned her head towards the window; but the night was too dark for her to see anything.

If she had but cast one glance at me, how easily she might have guessed what was passing in my heart. We heard but one horse only; indeed what else was to be expected? My heart told me only one horseman would return, but which?

Steps sounded in the ante-chamber—slow, heavy steps that seemed to oppress my soul. The door opened. I saw a shadow outlined in the gloom.

The shadow halted on the threshold. My heart trembled in suspense. The shadow came forward, and as it entered further and further into the lighted rooms I breathed again. Another second of such tension and my heart would have stopped beating.

Gregoriska stood before me, but pale as a dead man. To look at him was to see that something dreadful had happened.

"Is it you, my Kostaki?" asked Smerande.

"No, mother," answered Gregoriska in a hoarse, toneless voice.

"Ah, it is you, is it?" she now said; "and how long do you expect your mother to wait for you?"

"Why, mother," protested Gregoriska, glancing at the time-piece, "it is only nine o'clock."

And indeed that moment the hour struck.

"Very true," said Smerande. "Where is your brother?"

In spite of myself, I could not help thinking it was the same question God had asked of Cain.

Gregoriska said nothing.

"Has no one seen Kostaki?" questioned Smerande.

The Vatar (major-domo), after making inquiries of those around him, answered, "about seven the Count went to the stable, saddled his horse himself, and set out on the road to Hango."

At that moment my eyes met Gregoriska's. I cannot tell if it was reality or hallucination, but I seemed to see a drop of blood in the middle of his forehead.

I put my finger slowly to my own brow, indicating the spot where I thought I saw the stain. Gregoriska understood me; he took out his handkerchief and wiped his face.

"Yes, yes," muttered Smerande.

"He must have fallen in with a bear or a wolf, and gone after it for his diversion."

"Is that a reason for a son to keep his mother waiting? Where did you leave him, Gregoriska? tell me that."

"Mother," replied Gregoriska in a startled but firm voice, "my brother and I did not set out together."

"Well and good," ended Smerande. "Bring in supper, take your places at table, and shut the gates; those who are still outside must sleep outside."

The first two orders were executed to the letter. Smerande took her place, while Gregoriska seated himself at her right, and myself at her left. Then the serving-men left the hall to carry out the third, that is, to shut the Castle gates.

At that moment a great noise rose from the courtyard and a terrified domestic dashed into the hall crying:

"Princess, Count Kostaki's horse has just galloped into the bailey riderless and dripping with blood."

"Alas!" faltered Smerande, rising from her seat, pale and menacing, "it was in like plight his father's horse came back one night."

I looked at Gregoriska; he was not pale now, he was livid.

The fact is, Count Koproli's horse had dashed one evening into the Castle yard, dripping with blood, and an hour later the retainers had found his body covered with wounds, and brought it home.

Smerande now took a torch from the hands of one of the serving-men, walked to the door, threw it open, and went down the steps into the courtyard.

The horse, in a state of extreme terror, was being held in by main force by three or four grooms, who were doing all they could to soothe the animal. Smerande drew near, looked at the bloodstained saddle, and presently discovered the horse had received a wound in the face.

"Kostaki has been killed by a blow in front," she said, "in a duel, and by a single adversary. Search for the body, my lads; afterwards we will search till we find his murderer."

As the horse had come back by the Hango gate of the Castle, all the men hurried out the same way, and soon we could see their torches flitting about the fields and diving into the forest, just as the fire-flies flash and gleam on a fine summer's evening in the plains about Nice or Pisa.

Smerande, as though convinced the search would soon be success-ful, stood waiting under the archway. Not a tear flowed from the eyes of the bereaved mother; yet it was plain that despair was tearing her entrails.

Gregoriska was behind her and I was next Gregoriska. On leaving the great hall he had made as if to offer me his arm, but had hesitated, and finally given up the intention, apparently afraid.

In about a quarter of an hour we saw a single torch reappear at the turning of the road, then two more, and finally the whole number. Only now, instead of being dispersed about the country, they were massed round a common centre—which it soon became manifest consisted of a litter and a man stretched upon it.

The funereal band advanced slowly but surely, and in another ten minutes was at the gateway. On observing the unhappy mother wait-ing for her dead son, the bearers uncovered instinctively, and marched sad and silent into the Castle yard.

Smerande joined the procession, and we came after her. In this order we all reached the great hall, where they laid down the body.

Then, with a gesture of supreme dignity, Smerande beckoned all to draw back, and, going up to the dead man, knelt down before him, parted the long hair which fell like a veil before his face, gazed long at his features, with dry eyes still, then, opening the Moldavian gown he wore, lifted the blood-stained shirt.

The wound was in the right side of the breast, and must have been made by a straight blade and a double-edged one. I remembered I had noticed that very day in Gregoriska's belt the long hunting-knife that served as a bayonet for his carbine.

I looked for the weapon now; but it had disappeared.

Smerande called for water, dipped her handkerchief in it and washed the wound. A gush of bright, fresh, scarlet blood welled up and reddened the lips of the gash.

The whole scene was at once odious and sublime. The vast gloomy hall, thick with the smoke of pine torches, the wild faces, the fiercely gleaming eyes, the strange dresses, the mother gazing at the still warm blood, and reckoning how long her son had been dead, the deep silence, only broken by the sobs of the bandits whose chief Kostaki had been, all was impressive and awe-inspiring to the last degree.

Lastly, Smerande put her lips to her son's brow; then, rising to her full height and tossing back the long coils of her white hair which had become unfastened, she cried, "Gregoriska, Gregoriska!"

Gregoriska shuddered, shook his head, and coming out of his lethargy, answered, "Yes, mother?"

"Come here, son, and hear me."

Gregoriska obeyed with a shudder, but obey he did. The nearer he approached the corpse, the more abundantly did the red blood gush from the wound. Happily Smerande was not looking that way, for at sight of this accusing flood, she would have had no need to look further for the murderer.

"Gregoriska," she went on, "I know very well that you and Kostaki were enemies. I know quite well that you are a Waivady by your father, and he a Koproli by his; but through your mother you are both of you Brankovans. I know that you are a man of the Western cities, he a child of the Eastern hills; but still, by virtue of the womb that bore you both, you are brothers. Well! Gregoriska, I would know this, if you mean to lay your brother to rest beside his father without the oath of vengeance having been pronounced; if I may weep my dead in peace and confidence as a woman should, putting my trust in you to punish as a man's part is?"

"Tell me the name of my brother's murderer, madame, and command me; I swear that ere an hour is past, if you so order, he shall have ceased to live."

"Nay! swear, Gregoriska, swear, under penalty of my curse, do you hear, my son? swear the murderer shall die, that you will not leave one stone upon another of his house, that his mother, children, brothers, his wife or his betrothed, shall perish by your hand. Swear, invoking the anger of Heaven upon your head, if you fail to keep the sacred obligation. If you break the oath, be prepared for wretchedness, the execration of your friends, your mother's malediction."

Gregoriska laid his hand upon the corpse. "I swear the murderer shall die," he said.

On this strange oath, of which I and the dead man alone perhaps could grasp the true sense, I saw, or I thought I saw, an appalling prodigy follow.

The dead man's eyes opened and fixed themselves on mine with a keener look than I had ever seen in them, and as though the double ray they shot had been a material thing, I felt a red-hot iron pierce to my very heart.

It was more than my strength could bear, and I swooned away.

4. The Cloister of Hango

When I came to myself, I was in my chamber, lying upon my bed, while one of my two tire-women was watching beside me.

I asked where Smerande was, and was told she was praying beside her son's body. Then I asked where Gregoriska was, and learned that he was at the Monastery of Hango.

Flight was needless, for was not Kostaki dead? Marriage was impossible; I could never wed a fratricide.

Three days and three nights dragged by, filled with strange and fantastic dreams. Awake or asleep, I could never lose sight of those two eyes glaring alive and eager in the dead face—a horrid vision!

On the third day Kostaki was to be buried, and early on that day they brought me a full suit of widow's weeds, saying Smerande sent them me. I dressed myself and came downstairs.

The rooms seemed utterly empty; every soul was in the Castle chapel. I made my way thither; and as I crossed the threshold, Smerande, whom I had not seen for three days, came forward to meet me in the doorway.

She looked like a carven image of Grief. Slow as a statue she laid her icy lips on my forehead, and in a voice that seemed to come from the tomb, she pronounced her customary phrase: "Kostaki loves you."

You can form no conception of the effect these words produced on me. This declaration of love, made in the present instead of in the past tense, this *loves you* instead of *loved you*, this passion from the world of the dead singling me out among the living, made a profound and terrible impression on my mind.

At the same time a strange, uncanny feeling crept over me that in very deed I was the wife of the dead man, and not the betrothed of the living brother. The coffin yonder drew me to him in spite of myself; I was attracted reluctantly and painfully, as they say a bird is fascinated by a serpent. I looked for Gregoriska, and saw him standing, pale and sad, beside a pillar. His eyes were raised to Heaven; I cannot say if he saw me.

The monks from Hango surrounded the bier, singing the funeral psalms of the Greek rite, sometimes melodious enough, more often harsh and monotonous. I longed to pray too, but the words died upon my lips; my mind was so confounded I seemed to be present at a consistory of demons rather than among a company of priests of God.

When they lifted the body to carry it to the grave, I tried to follow; but my strength failed me. I felt my limbs bend under me, and I leant against the doorway for support. Then Smerande approached me, signing to Gregoriska, who also came up in obedience to the gestures. Smerande addressed me in Moldavian.

"My mother bids me repeat to you word for word what she is going to say," put in Gregoriska.

Smerande resumed, and when she had ended, he said:

"These are my mother's words," and, translating into French:

"You weep my son, Hedwig; you loved him, did you not? I thank you for your tears and for your love; henceforward you are my daughter as truly as if Kostaki had been your husband—henceforth you have a country, a mother, a home. We will shed the guerdon of tears we owe the dead, then we will both remember our dignity and show ourselves worthy of him who is no more. . . . I, his mother, you his wife! Farewell! return to your chamber; for myself, I will follow my son to his last resting-place. When I come back, I shall shut myself up with my grief, and when you see me again, I shall have conquered it. Rest assured I shall kill it, for I will not have it kill me."

I could only reply by a groan to those affecting words. I returned to my room, and the funeral procession started and presently disappeared at the bend of the road. The Cloister of Hango was only half a league from the Castle as the crow flies; but irregularities of the ground forced the road to make wide detours, and to anyone following the highway, it was pretty nearly a two hours' journey.

We were in the month of November, and the days were short and chilly. At five in the afternoon it was quite dark. About seven I saw the torches reappear and the mourners returning. All was over; the dead man lay in the tomb of his fathers.

I have already described the strange fancy which had persistently possessed my mind ever since the fatal event which had put us all in mourning, and more particularly since I had seen those eyes, which death had closed, re-open and fix themselves on mine. Tonight, worn out by the emotions of the day, I felt more depressed than ever. I listened to the hours one after the other sounding on the Castle clock, and grew sadder and sadder the nearer the flight of time brought me to the minute when Kostaki must have died.

I heard a quarter to nine strike. Then an extraordinary sensation came over me, a sort of shuddering horror that run over my whole body and froze it; then along with this an invincible drowsiness obscured my senses, weighed down my bosom and darkened my eyes. I stretched out my arms and stepped backwards to my bed, on which I fell in a half swoon.

Still my senses were not so completely deadened as to prevent my hearing a footstep approaching the door of my chamber. I seemed to notice the door opening, after which I neither saw nor heard anything more.

But I felt a sharp throb of pain at my neck, before I finally relapsed into complete unconsciousness.

At midnight I awoke, to find my lamp still burning. I tried to rise, but I was so weak I had to repeat the effort before I succeeded. However, I fought down this feebleness, and still feeling the same pricking sensation in my neck now that I was awake as I had felt in my sleep, I dragged myself along the walls as far as the mirror and looked at myself.

A pin-prick, or something like it, marked the carotid artery. I thought some insect had bitten me in my sleep, and as I was worn out with fatigue, I lay down and went to sleep again.

Next morning I awoke as usual; and as usual I made to spring out of bed the moment my eyes were open; but I experienced a feeling of extreme exhaustion such as I had felt only once before in my life, on the morning after I had been bled. I looked at my face in the glass, and I was struck with my own pallor.

The hours dragged by sad and sombre, and all day long I had an unaccustomed and unaccountable craving to stay where I was, every change of place or position being a weariness of the flesh.

Night came, and they brought me my lamp. My women, or so I understood from their signs, offered to stay with me; but I refused with thanks, and they left me to myself.

At the same time as before I began to feel the same sensations. I endeavoured this time to rise and summon help; but I could not get as far as the door. I heard vaguely the sound of the clock chiming a quarter to nine; then came foot-steps, and the door opened. But I could neither hear nor see anything more; as on the first evening, I had fallen back fainting on my bed.

As before, I felt a sharp pain at the side of my neck; as before, I roused at midnight, only now I awoke weaker and paler than ever.

Next day the same horrid fancy held undisputed possession of my mind. I had made up my mind to go down to Smerande, weak and feeble as I was, when one of my women came into my room, uttering the name of Gregoriska, who followed her across the threshold.

I tried to get up from my chair to receive him, but fell back again exhausted by the effort. He gave a cry at the sight, and dashed forward to my assistance; but I had still strength enough left to wave him off.

"What are you come here for?" I asked him.

"Alas!" he said, "I was coming to bid you farewell! I was coming to tell you that I am leaving a world that is intolerable to me without your love and your presence; I was coming to tell you I am retiring to a cell in the Monastery of Hango!"

"You must forego my presence, but my love is yours still, Gregoriska," I returned. "Alas! I love you still, and my great grief is, that henceforth such love is next door to a crime."

"Then I may hope you will pray for me, Hedwig?"

"Yes; only I shall not have long to pray," I added,

"What is wrong with you, tell me, and why are you so pale?"

"Wrong—wrong! Nay! doubtless God is taking pity on me, calling me to him."

Gregoriska came near and took my hand, which I had not the strength to withdraw, and, looking me hard in the face, said:

"This pallor is not natural, Hedwig; what does it mean?"

"If I were to tell you what I think, Gregoriska, you would deem me mad."

"No, no! tell me, Hedwig. I beseech you, tell me. We are here in a country that is like no other country, in a family that is like no other family. Tell me, tell me all, I beseech you."

So I told him all—the strange hallucination which came over me at the hour when Kostaki must have died, the horror, the drowsiness, the icy chill, the prostration that laid me fainting on my bed, the sound of footsteps I seemed to hear, the opening door I seemed to see, and then the sharp pang of pain followed by a pallor and exhaustion growing greater day by day.

I had supposed my narrative would strike Gregoriska as merely the first stage of mania, and I concluded it with some natural timidity; but I saw, on the contrary, that he was profoundly impressed by what I had said.

He reflected a moment.

"So you fell asleep," he asked, "every evening at a quarter to nine?"

"Yes—in spite of all the efforts I make to resist the drowsiness."

"Then, you seem to see the door open?"

"Yes—although I always bolt it."

"Then, you feel a sharp pain in the neck?"

"Yes—though my neck shows scarcely any trace of a wound."

"Will you let me see this trace?" he asked next.

In reply, I bent my head sideways so as to show the place, which he examined carefully.

"Hedwig," he said, after a moment's silence, "Hedwig, do you trust me?"

"Can you ask!" I cried indignantly.

"Do you believe my word?"

"As I believe in the Holy Gospels."

"Very well, then, Hedwig; on my word, I swear you have not a week to live, unless you agree to do this very day what I am going to tell you. . . ."

"And if I agree?"

"If you agree, you will be saved, perhaps."

"Perhaps?"

But he would say no more.

"Come what may, Gregoriska," I resumed, "I will do whatever you bid me to do."

"Then listen," he said, "and above all do not be too much alarmed. In your country, as in Hungary, there is a tradition."

I shuddered, for I remembered the tradition in question.

"Ah!" he went on, "then you know what I mean?"

"Yes!" I told him, "yes, in Poland I have seen persons subject to this horrible fate."

"You allude to vampires, do you not?"

"Yes, in my childhood I saw a dreadful sight in the cemetery of a village belonging to my father—the exhumation of forty peasants who had died one after the other, all in a fortnight, without an explanation of the cause of death. Seventeen exhibited all the marks of vampirism, that is to say, their bodies were found fresh, rosy, and looking as if still alive; the remainder were their victims."

"And what was done to deliver the countryside from the scourge?"

"A stake was driven through their hearts, and this done, the bodies burned."

"Yes, that is what is ordinarily done, but in your case it is not enough. To deliver you from the phantom, I must first know who it is, and, by God! I will know. Yes, if need be, I will fight hand to hand with him, be he who he may."

"Oh, Gregoriska, you terrify me!" I cried in alarm.

"I said, 'be he who he may,' and I repeat it. But to bring this awful enterprise to a good end, you must agree to everything I am going to ask you to do."

"Say on."

"Be ready at seven this evening; come down to the chapel—and come alone. You must conquer your weakness, Hedwig, you *must*. There we will receive the nuptial benediction. Agree to this, beloved; to defend you efficiently, I must have the right, before God and men, to watch over your safety. We will return here when the rite is complete, and then—and then. . . ."

"Oh! Gregoriska," I ejaculated. "If it is he, if it is Kostaki, he will kill you!"

"Have no fear, my beloved, my Hedwig; only agree."

"You may rest assured I shall do whatever you ask."

"Till tonight, then."

"Yes, do you whatever is needful; I will second you to the best of my powers. Now go."

He left me; and a quarter of an hour later, I saw a horseman bounding along the road to the Monastery, and knew it was Gregoriska.

No sooner had he vanished from my sight than I knelt down and prayed such prayers as are never uttered in your lukewarm irreligious Western land; thus occupied, I awaited seven o'clock, offering up to God and the Saints the holocaust of my meditations. I only rose from my knees as the clock struck the hour.

I was weak as a dying woman, pale as the sheeted dead. I threw a long, black veil over my head, and descended the stairs, supporting myself by the walls. I reached the chapel without having encountered a living soul.

Gregoriska was waiting for me there, along with Father Basil, Superior of the Cloister of Hango. My betrothed wore by his side a holy sword, heirloom of an old Crusader who had been at the taking of Constantinople with Villehardouin and Baldwin of Flanders.

"Hedwig," he said, striking his hand upon his sword, "with God's good help, here is a weapon will break the spell that threatens your life. Come boldly hither; this holy man is ready, after hearing my confession, to receive and sanctify our marriage vows."

The ceremony began; never perhaps before had it been performed in simpler and at the same time more solemn guise. The Priest, or *Pope* according to the phraseology of the Greek Church, had neither acolyte nor assistant; with his own hands he placed the wedding crowns upon our heads. Both clad in mourning raiment, we marched about the altar, taper in hand; then Father Basil pronounced the ceremonial words, adding further:

"And now go, my children, and God give you force and courage to wrestle with the Enemy of Mankind. You are armed in your innocence and the justice of your cause; you will overcome the Demon. Go, and Heaven's blessing go with you."

We kissed the holy books and left the chapel; then for the first time I rested on Gregoriska's arm, and at the touch of his valiant arm, at the contact of his noble heart, life seemed to flow back again into my veins. I felt confident of victory, now that Gregoriska was with me.

Half past eight struck. At the sound, Gregoriska spoke.

"Hedwig," he said, "we have no time to lose. Will you go to sleep as usual and slumber through it all? or will you remain up and dressed and see everything?"

"By your side I fear nothing; I will stay awake, I prefer to see it all."

Gregoriska drew from his bosom a twig of box consecrated by the priest and still wet with holy water, and gave it me.

"Take this branch," said he, "lie down on your bed, repeat the prayers to the Virgin and wait. Fear nothing, God is with us. Above all, never quit hold of your talisman; with it you can command even the powers of hell. Do not cry nor call for help; pray, wait and hope."

I lay down on the bed and crossed my hands over my bosom, on which I placed the branch the priest had blessed.

Meantime Gregoriska concealed himself behind the great canopied chair I have described before, which cut off a corner of the room.

I counted the minutes, one by one, and no doubt Gregoriska did the same. The clock struck the three quarters.

Instantly I felt the old drowsiness, the same sensations of horror and icy cold, creeping over me; but I put the Holy branch to my lips, and found relief.

Then I heard distinctly the noise of slow and measured footsteps sounding on the stairs and coming nearer and nearer to the door. It opened slowly and noiselessly as if moved by a supernatural force, and then . . .

And then I beheld Kostaki, pale as I had seen him lying on the litter; his long dark hair falling about his shoulders dripped with blood; he wore his usual dress, only it was open at the breast, showing the bleeding wound.

He was dead, a corpse. Flesh, clothes, bearing, were those of a dead man; only the eyes, those awful eyes, were alive.

At the sight, strange to say, instead of an increase of terror, I felt fresh courage. Doubtless God gave me His courage that I might judge my position calmly, and defy the Powers of Evil. At the first step the spectre took towards my bed, I fixed my eyes boldly on his leaden orbs and held out the holy branch at him.

The phantom strove to advance, but a power stronger than his own held him rooted to the spot; he hesitated, muttering:

"Oh, she is not asleep, she knows all."

He spoke in Moldavian, and yet I understood the sense of his words, as if they had been uttered in a tongue I was familiar with.

We stood face to face, and I could not withdraw my eyes from his. Presently, without needing to turn my head in his direction, I saw Gregoriska come out from behind the canopied stall, looking like the Angel of Destruction, and holding his sword in his right hand. With the left he made the sign of the cross and stepped slowly forwards, his sword's point threatening the spectre. On seeing his brother, Kostaki too drew his sabre with a screech of eldritch laughter; but scarcely had his sabre touched the consecrated steel ere the phantom arm fell back powerless and inert.

Kostaki heaved a sigh full of hatred and despair.

"What would you of me?" he asked his brother.

"In the name of the living God, I adjure you," said Gregoriska, "to answer my questions."

"Speak," replied the phantom, gnashing his teeth.

"Did I lay wait for you?"

"No."

"Did I attack you?"

"No."

"Did I strike you?"

"No."

"You threw yourself upon my sword point and nothing else. Therefore in the eyes of God and men I am innocent of the crime of fratricide; therefore you have not received a divine mission, but an infernal behest; therefore you have left the tomb, not as a holy shade, but an accursed spectre. I command you, return to your tomb."

"With her, yes!" cried Kostaki, making a supreme effort to reach and seize me.

"No! alone!" thundered Gregoriska in reply, "this woman is mine."

And as he pronounced the words, he touched with the point of his consecrated sword the raw wound in his brother's breast. Kostaki uttered a scream as if a falchion of fire had seared him, and, putting his left hand to his bosom, he took a step back.

Simultaneously, and keeping step for step with his ghostly adversary, Gregoriska advanced upon him; then, his eyes upon the dead man's eyes, his sword at his brother's breast, he began to drive the spectre before him slowly, sternly, solemnly. It was something like the passage of Don Juan and the Commendatore—the spectre recoiling before the consecrated blade and the irresistible will of God's Champion, the latter following him up pace for pace without a word. Both were breathless, both ghastly pale, the living man pushing the dead before him, forcing him to forsake the Castle that was his home in the past, for the tomb, his abiding place henceforth.

Oh, it was a horrid sight, a dreadful, dreadful sight!

And yet, urged by a superior force, a force mysterious, unknown, invisible, not knowing myself what I did, I rose from the bed and followed them. We descended the staircase, our only light Kostaki's blazing eye-balls. We traversed the gallery and the Castle yard; we passed the gate at the same measured pace—the phantom stepping backwards, Gregoriska with outstretched arm, myself behind them both.

The fantastic procession continued for a full hour. The dead man had to be led back to his tomb; only, instead of the beaten road, Kostaki and Gregoriska went straight to their end, paying scant heed to hindrances and obstacles. Indeed these had ceased to exist; beneath their feet rough places grew smooth, torrents dried up, trees fell back, rocks flew open. The same miracle worked for me as for them; but the heavens seemed to my eyes shrouded in a veil of darkness; moon and stars had disappeared and all I could see in the gloom was the flashing of the vampire's eyes of fire.

In this fashion we reached Hango, in this fashion we passed through the hedge of arbutus which fenced in the cemetery. The moment we were inside, I made out through the obscurity the tomb of Kostaki, side by side with his father's. Nothing was hid from me that night. At the edge of the open grave Gregoriska halted, saying,

"Kostaki, all is not yet over for you; a voice from Heaven tells me you will be pardoned if you repent. Promise to go back into your tomb, promise to leave it no more, promise to give God the devotion you have vowed to Hell."

"Never," replied Kostaki.

"Repent," reiterated Gregoriska.

"Never."

"For the last time, Kostaki, I appeal to you."

"Never."

"Well, then, call Satan to your help, as I call God to mine, and we shall see yet once again who will be victorious."

Two cries range out simultaneously and the swords crossed amid a myriad sparks; the fight lasted a minute, which seemed a century to me.

Kostaki fell; I saw the terrible sword whirl in the air, I saw it plunged into his body, nailing it to the freshly upturned earth. A last blood-curdling scream, which had nothing human about it, rent the air.

Gregoriska stood still over his adversary, but faintly and staggering. I ran up and caught him in my arms.

"Are you wounded?" I asked him anxiously.

"No," he answered me, "but in such a contest, dear Hedwig, 'tis not the wound that kills but the stress and struggle. I have striven with Death, and to Death I belong."

"Beloved, beloved," I cried, "begone from here, and life will come back, perhaps."

"No," he said solemnly, "here is my tomb, Hedwig. But waste no time, take a handful of this earth saturated with his blood and lay it on the bite he gave you; it is the only means to guard you in the future against his odious love."

I shuddered, but obeyed. Stopping to gather up the bloodstained mould, I saw Kostaki's corpse pinned to the earth; the holy sword was through his heart, and an abundant jet of rich black blood gushed from the wound, as if he had died but an instant before. I kneaded a little mould with the blood, and applied the horrid talisman to my neck.

"Now, Hedwig, my adored Hedwig," faltered Gregoriska in a thin, weak voice, "listen heedfully to my last behests. Leave the country at the earliest opportunity; in distance lies your only safety. Father Basil had received my last instructions today, and he will carry them out. Hedwig, a kiss, the last, the only kiss, my Hedwig, before I die"—and with these words on his lips, Gregoriska fell dead beside his brother.

Under any other circumstances, in a graveyard, beside an open tomb, with two corpses lying side by side, I should have gone mad; but, I have already said so, God had given me a strength to match the terrible occurences which He made me not only witness but play a part in.

I looked about me in search of help, and at that moment I saw the cloister door open, and the monks, Father Basil at their head, advancing towards me, two by two, carrying lighted torches and chanting the prayers of the dead.

Father Basil had just returned to the Monastery, and, foreseeing what had befallen, he had come straight to the cemetery, all his monks with him.

He found me, a living woman, standing over two dead men.

Kostaki's face was disfigured by a last hideous convulsion; but Gregoriska wore a calm and almost smiling aspect. As he had directed, the latter was buried by his sinful brother's side—God's servant keeping watch and ward over the Devil's.

Smerande, when she heard of this fresh calamity and the part I had played in it, desired to see me. She came to visit me at the Cloister of Hango, and learnt from my lips all that had happened that dreadful night.

I told her the fantastic history in all its dreadful details, but she heard me, as Gregoriska had, without a great surprise or horror.

"Hedwig," she said to me, when I had finished, after a moment's silence, "strange as the story is you have just told me, yet you have spoken only the plain truth. The race of the Brankovans is accursed to the third and fourth generation because a Brankovan once killed a priest. But the curse is now run out; for though a wife, you are a virgin, and I am the last of my race. If my son has bequeathed you a million take it. When I am gone, except for the few pious legacies I propose to leave, you shall have the remainder of my fortune. Now follow your bridegroom's advice, and return with all haste to the countries where God does not suffer the accomplishment of these appalling prodigies. I need no one to help me mourn my sons. Farewell. Take no more heed of me; my lot to come concerns only myself and my God."

And, kissing me on the brow as of old, she left me, to shut herself up in her bedchamber in the Castle of Brankovan.

A week later I started to France. As Gregoriska had hoped, my nights presently ceased to be haunted by the dreadful phantom. Health returned, and the only penalty remaining from my hideous adventure is this deathly pallor, which accompanies to the tomb every living creature that has once felt the embrace of a Vampire.

Blood Chess

Tanith Lee

Tanith Lee (b. 1947) is one of the leading British writers of supernatural and fantasy fiction. She has won two World Fantasy Awards for her short fiction and the British Fantasy Award for her novel, Death's Master *(1979). She has long been fascinated by the vampire legend, and vampires appear in many of her short stories, the best of which will be found in* Dreams of Dark and Light *(1986) and* Women as Demons *(1989), as well as in the novel* Sabella *(1980). The following is one of Lee's more recent vampire tales and may seem traditional at first, but it soon takes on a life of its own.*

Blood Chess
Tanith Lee

Winter and the Sorian Approach

A CRUMBLING stone staircase leads down the mountain-hill from the castle. About a mile above the valley, there is a walled terrace, and here the gigantic chessboard is laid out. It is old and faded, the black squares grey, the blood-red squares a life-less pink. As she crosses the chessboard, each square taking a full three steps, Ismira glances down at it, at the cracks in its paving where wild flowers push up in spring, and where, now winter is approaching, they die.

She is not a vampire, but the people in the valley are afraid of her, thinking she must be. Her brother is the vampire. In the valley they call him the Sorian. He comes from the land of Soriath, over the mountains, so the name is not inappropriate—but really they are trying to distance him in the only way they can. They are aware of his true name, which is Yane, and never use it.

Ismira knows her brother will return during the night, By going down to the village, she is also warning them.

There is an afternoon frost. When she reaches the village street, the tall trees by the well are clouded with cold. Icicles thin as needles spike the roofs. Already the ball of the sun is rolling off the sky.

Before she would often come here in full daylight, striving to convince them she was only herself, had no fear of sunlight, and did not require blood. But when she saw this did no good, she did not do it any more.

All the doors are shut and the street and alleys empty. Somewhere a dog howls and is struck—she hears the blow—to silence it.

Ismira stops in the centre of the street, by the well. In her long black garments, her long black hair curling down like a fleece to her shoulder-blades, she is only what they must expect.

As she stands waiting, the sun too runs away, afraid she will see its redness and desire its blood.

Yane, the Sorian, once said to her, in one of his intermittent fevers: "The sun—give me the sun to drink—it's *full* as a wineskin—"

After a time of merely standing there, Ismira sees a door is being eased open in the side of the big house, the one with the carvings that pretend to the decoration of the castle on the mountain-hill. Something is thrust out. It drops and lies motionless on the street.

Ismira goes over to this object, which turns out to be a young woman of about sixteen, clothed in white, and with her fair hair washed and braided. She is not unconscious, as sometimes they are. She stares up at Ismira from the dirt.

"Don't make me, lady—let me go—"

"I can't. Get up and come with me."

Shaking and temporarily past tears, the girl does so. She will probably walk meekly behind Ismira all the way back up the mountain. Now and then, one of them will dash off, and never be seen by Ismira again. She suspects the village pursues and murders them.

Ismira herself has done what she must. She has procured the sacrifice for her brother's needs, and also warned the village by her presence that he is imminent.

The sky burns crimson.

Ismira and the sacrifice plod doggedly up the terrible, ruinous stair.

"Look," says Ismira, encouragingly, as the epic bulk of the castle looms over them, touched with ruby by the falling sun they have, through climbing, managed to keep sight of. Now the girl starts to cry.

Ismira hardens her heart, at which act she has, over the fifteen years since her tenth birthday, become adept.

Why attempt reassurance? These ones the village select by unlucky lot. Each of them knows what will happen.

They pass the chessboard. The weeping girl takes no notice of it. All the flowers have been abruptly frost bitten to death, and above, in the castle garden, scarcely any leaves remain on the tangled trees, and those that do are like silver daggers.

The Return of Yane

The girl's name is Thental. She sits crying on and on.

Once it begins to be very dark, Ismira walks about the castle, the rooms, passages and annexes, lighting a few lamps and enormous candles. She wonders if the girl would be more comfortable in the great hall. But the kitchen, with its huge fire, will be much warmer.

Coming back into the kitchen, there is Thental, still crying.

Ismira has given her white bread and an apple, and wine for courage, none of which has Thental tried.

How dismal it all is, Ismira thinks, lighting another candle on the branch above the hearth. She hopes Yane will soon arrive.

As if reading her mind, Thental checks her sobs.

"Does he fly here, on his bat wings?" she asks.

Ismira senses an unpleasant pettiness in the question. Thental knows she is being given to a monster, the monster must therefore live up to his legends.

"No, in fact, he'll ride across the pass."

"Some demon will have told you he's near."

"Also no. Common sense, and memory. Snow will soon fall and close all the passes. It's always on this night Yane comes back. Have none of you realized?"

The girl shudders. Her head darts up and her shining hair, loosened by now, flutters candlelit round her head like a bridal veil.

"Is that a clatter of wings?"

Ismira says nothing. She can hear it too, and quite obviously the noise is that of hoofs clattering into the yard outside.

Yane will stable his horse in the stall Ismira has prepared, before he enters the kitchen; they have no servants, of course. But the girl springs up and falls now on her knees, tightly shutting her eyes, and praying.

Ismira feels sorry for her, but also it is all so tiresome, this. "*Shush!*" she exclaims sharply, and Thental becomes quiet as the grave.

It will be useless to try to reason with her. Ismira, long since, additionally gave that up with the sacrifices who accompany her to the castle, their names written helpfully on little scraps of book paper and wrapped round their wrists.

They pose there then, in stasis, Ismira seated on the wooden chair, Thental kneeling abject on the stone-flagged floor.

Outside now a sound of boots, then the door is pushed wide. Yane strides in out of the night, bringing the night in with him, cold and mysterious, across cloak and hair.

Ismira sees, as so often, Thental stare, then avert her gaze.

Yane is very handsome. His blue-black hair falls to his waist; he is tall and straight, his body hard and fined from constant journeys, his large dark eyes full of a luminous introspection fatal to most women.

Ismira gets up. She takes him a cup of wine.

Yane thanks her. He drinks the wine. Then he glances at the girl kneeling on the floor, staring at him between fingers she has clamped over her eyes.

"Is she for me?"

"Who else?"

"Dear God," says Yane. He sighs, perhaps an affectation. He walks across and sits in the wooden chair, and looks at Thental. Thental does not look back, but nor does she cry any more. "Well," says Yane, "good evening. Isn't the floor rather hard on your knees?"

Thental blinks. She puts down her hands.

"Don't kill me," she says quietly, "don't damn my soul."

"I'm not interested in your soul. Keep it." Thental grunts. She lowers her head, desolate now. Yane stands up, frowning with irritation and tiredness. Ismira has drawn a bath for him, across the passage, with extra water heating on the fire there. He goes out to this, and Ismira moves around the kitchen, seeing to the supper, constantly detouring past Themtal kneeling on the floor.

An Evening At Home

When Yane enters again he is more relaxed, wrapped in a dressing-robe of scarlet, black, and gold. He goes to Thental at once and lifts her off the floor, and sits her at the table in a chair adjacent to his own.

She is evidently exhausted by her fright, far worse than Yane from his travels. He takes advantage of that, feeding her scraps of meat and cheese, and making her sip the wine.

Her head droops on to his shoulder. He kisses her hair absently. Ismira watches all this from the other end of the table.

It has ceased to offend, puzzle, or upset her.

She thinks back to the day the horsemen came to her father's house in another country, not this one, and not Soriath either. That was the day of her tenth birthday. While her proud father sat in talk with the riders, Ismira's chilly mother took her aside. "Listen to me, Ismira. Today you're to go away to another place. We've never treated you as we do our other children, and this is because, you must now understand, you're no child of ours at all. You are the cuckoo's egg left to hatch in this house. We bore it because we must, and we've done you no harm. You've been raised nobly, as our true children have, although without our love. Under the circumstances, you'll agree, you could hardly expect any." Astounded, shocked beyond reason, Ismira stood listening. Her mother—who was not—told her she was the child of an ancient and corrupt family who exerted much power in this region and elsewhere. The Scaratha, they were called. Due to their way of living, which was that of vampires, blood-drinkers, and creatures of darkness and horror, they kept no children of their own in their domiciles before the age of ten. At that age they would send for and claim them, whether the vampire strain was prevalent or not. "You have been closely observed, more for our sakes than yours," said Ismira's unmother, with great distaste. "You show no symptoms of any of that. Even so you are a fiend, the child of fiends. It's made me sick to have you in this house. I have seldom touched you and won't now. Get out and go to your own, you foul abomination."

"What are you brooding on, Ismi?" asks Yane from along the table. The girl from the village has fallen asleep against him, soothed by his glamorous kindness and the Eastern incense he has rubbed into his hair.

"The past," says Ismira.

"Oh, that. Don't think of that. Let me tell you what I saw on my way here—something better than the Eastern markets, for all their glitter and show. Better even than the moon-and-star night over the City of Rome."

"What?" inquires Ismira. She knows what he will say.

"I saw the sun."

"Which will make you ill. It always does."

"Yes, it always does, but this was three days ago. And you see, I'm cool and well. Perhaps I'm growing used to the sun, or it to me."

"The wineskin full of blood," says Ismira. She becomes angry with him, because, in his fevers she must nurse him, and she hates the chore, and also is infuriated to see him suffer so stupidly by his own lack of control. *He is addicted to the sun,* she sometimes thinks, *worse than blood.*

But Yane boasts, "I crept out of my deep hiding cave, and I beheld a sunrise in the mountains. The sky was redder than any blood. I'm cool and hale, Ismi. Can't you see? Perhaps, in a day or so, I can try again."

"The sun isn't for you."

But you can see it every day! Don't you know how jealous I am of you, Ismi?"

She too frowns. She considers how Yane rides about the world, journeying to lands she has never, will never, see. How she remains at home, tending the castle, alone, save for the winter months when Yane comes back, often flaming with sun-fever, crazy and devilish, and girls must be collected from the village, one every thirty days, for Yane's pleasure.

I'm his skivvy, Ismira thinks. *And he is jealous?*

This is why they value those of their kind who are not vampiric. They take them in and load them with codes of honour and high dreams of loyalty, and make them into useful servants of the house.

Ismira can hear Yane talking endlessly, in raptures about the sun. She pretends—she is quite clever at pretence—that she attends to him. She loves him, admires him, but resents him. They may have two hundred years more like this, for, left to themselves, the Scaratha are all long-lived. The rest of the castle inhabitants perished in a war with other Scaratha ten years ago. But other castles and fortresses exist still well-stocked with their kind. Sometimes Yane promises to take her visiting. He never does, and doubtless never will.

She considers leaving him and going off on her own. Wherever she went—on foot, alone, unsafe ways for a women, even—*especially*—a Scaratha woman to travel—she would in the end fetch up with the Scaratha. She would have no other place to go. And then her life would be the same as it is here, save with more to do, more persons to love, admire and tend—the higher echelons of the practising vampires.

Now Yane is speaking to Thental, the flower-like sacrifice. "Time for bed, sweetheart."

He has put something in the wine. The girl stirs and smiles at him, sleepy and adoring, ready as a summer peach on the vine.

He half carries this now-willing and pliable companion—perhaps she thinks this is her wedding night?—away along the passage, and up the steps of a tower to the bedroom Yane has there. Ismira has put fresh embroidered sheets on the bed, sprinkled lavender and other herbs. Scented lamps burn, and the window is heavily shuttered against sunrise, and locked. Ismira keeps the key.

Up there Yane the Sorian will make love to the girl, exquisitely, and also he will drink her blood, with passionate discretion. It will do her no harm whatsoever. He is wholesome, his teeth clean and flawless. Even the marks on her throat will fade when, after seven or so nights, he turns her out of bed, with enough money and jewels to make her rich beyond her most avaricious dreams. He will also escort her—by night—along the valley. That is Yane's gallantry. He knows about women travelling on their own, particularly with wealth about them. He will make sure she reaches some sort of safety, for the Scaratha are careful with the goods they handle. After a certain point, however, once he has discharged his duty by her, or his payment for her services, Yane will leave the girl. If something happens to Thental then—or has happened in the past to any of the countless others— that will not be Yane's fault.

Ismira tidies the table. She hauls a pitcher of cold water and adds it to a wooden tub of hot, and rinses the platters and knives. The precious cups of emerald crystal, rimmed and stemmed with gold, she replaces on the stone top of the hearth, among the candles, vases of dead flowers, iron keys, onions, and other things.

Outside the wind is rising. It howls like the dog in the village they had struck to make it silent. Who will strike the wind?

The villages naturally believe that all who are brought here die, drained like bottles. Or else they are turned into undead devils, and subsequently roam the countryside, preying on the sheep, or small unguarded children, which in fact lammergeyers or starving wolves have picked off. One day perhaps, the village may rebel against the castle. But probably they will not, for Scaratha power, though so isolate and scattered, is yet omnipresent and much dreaded.

Ismira blows out the kitchen candles. She takes one with her, and goes about the castle again, replenishing the lights. Later, when her brother has had tonight's fill of the girl, he will ramble through the passages enter the great hall, take down old swords, and musical instruments to play. The castle is a rare treat for Yane—how not, when he is hardly ever here.

As she retires to her room beyond the kitchen, Ismira hopes the sun will not have made him ill, and that he has enjoyed Thental. But when she falls asleep, Ismira dreams of riding his horse away and away, her own black hair and cloak rippling in the race of their speed. Dimly in the distance she thinks she sees the acres of a sea, the domes of the East, the moonlit columns of Rome. *I am Ismira,* she sings in her sleep, *nor was I born in Soriath*—

The Chess-Game

It was how the Scaratha taught their young the rules of existence— that is, the *vampiric*, more-valued young, although the others, the lesser, but so-useful breed, were allowed to stand by and watch. In this way Ismira had been part of the audience at the chess-games, played out on the huge board half-way down the mountain-hill.

They commenced at dusk, often not concluding until midnight, all by torchlight—and in the village below, no doubt the people covered their heads in fear. This was before the war among the Scaratha had wiped away all but two of the castle's indigenous population.

Scaratha chess was not like humanly employed chess, of course.

There were no pawns, for humanity was all made up of pawns, as far as the Scaratha were concerned. Here, the Scaratha hunted each *other* over the squares, which then were kept vivid with paint. A knight might take a queen, a queen a priest, as they pleased. Physical figures performed these actions. Deliberately, always, the *wrong* moves were educated into the Scaratha young, so they should learn to break all the other rules of the world.

Only at the very end would the victors fasten on their conquered own. This was not like a war. None died. They milked their victims, in mutual delight, of blood. Tokens, *love* tokens, which still meant some-one had won. Blood to the Scaratha was not a food, but a covenant. From human things they took it as of right; from their own they took it as the sigil of conquest. And life was all a game, like chess. The spilled blood had dripped, during these playings, through the paint into the chessboard, then coloured red for blood and black for night. Because of the nourishment of those libations, when finally allowed by neglect, flowers came to break cracks in the squares. The flowers were very strong, tougher from being kept down, from fighting back. Only harsh frost could kill them now, and in the spring others would come, rising from death as gods and vampires allegedly did.

How Fair the Day

Waking early as always, Ismira gets up. She sets about the business of the morning, equably, quietly. She anticipates nothing of it, but it has a surprise for her after all.

She is in the great hall, clearing up the mess of spent candles and replacing them with fresh, when Thental steals in like a slim white ray around the door.

Sometimes these girls do venture down, while Yane lies sleeping in the dark. Then, by now besotted with the vampire from Soriath, they talk on and on of his virtues to Ismira. It is her task too, to give them food and drink, to keep them healthy, bathed and appealing, for her brother.

When she turns to Thental, however, Ismira is briefly bemused. It seems to her the girl has impudently put on Yane's dressing-robe of chessboard red and black, edged with gold.

But no. The gold is Thental's dishevelled hair, and the white her own skin, some of it. The red and black, which are thick on her naked body, are rich red blood and skeins of black hair, that seems to have been torn out at the roots.

Thental lifts her head and smiles at Ismira.

"How fair the day. I've done what I came for. Just as I swore I would, I did it. He had my sister a year back. I never forgot, never. I can cry always just thinking of her. I told them this time, let it be me, I'll go. And so they let me. See this? My little dagger, razor sharp. The hilt's silver, that helps with killing a demon-thing. I bartered for it off a pedlar. He bedded me for it. Sensible trade, worth every jolt." Thental raises the dagger high. If it was ever silver, now it is not. It is blood-red, like most of the rest of her. "What a lot he had in him," Thental remarks of this blood, conversational, moving nearer. "Some of it after all was mine. What he drank from me last night. I stabbed him through as he slept. Then I hacked off his head—quite a job I had of that, but I managed. It's how you must do it with that kind— your *kind*—I'll do it for you—" she runs headlong at Ismira. Ismira, Scaratha though not vampire, kills the girl instantly with one swift sidelong blow that breaks her neck.

Then Ismira stands there, staring at the wreckage, thinking about the other wreckage which will be all that is left of Yane in the tower.

Presently, Ismira sits down.

She considers graves, digging them, which is easy, she has dug a couple, if some years ago. She thinks of her glorious brother, she thinks of the human heritage she has never had, the vampire Scaratha heritage she has also, being second rate, never had.

Yane's horse is in the stable. The snows have not yet begun. The sun, for Ismira, provides no difficulty—though later, she can always make believe it does . . .

Ismira goes over to Thental, the fragile white flower which grew strong enough to crack the paving of the chessboard, but which the frost of Ismira's hand then finished. Human flowers do not recover from that, nor vampire flowers, so Ismira has discovered.

Ismira dips her finger in the still-wet blood Thental has thoughtfully brought with her, Yane's blood. Ismira licks the finger. It means nothing to her, nothing at all. But, as with the sun of this fair day, she can always pretend.

The Fate of Madame Cabanel
Eliza Lynn Linton

Eliza Lynn (1822–1898) was a popular and very forthright novelist during the mid- to late Victorian period but, more significantly, she styled herself an "independent woman" and was a strong advocate of women's rights. Doubtless the seeds for this were sown when the young Eliza lost her mother soon after she was born and was raised by a stern, religious father. It is significant that when she married William Linton in 1858 she retained her maiden name and styled herself E. Lynn Linton thereafter. It was not a marriage made in heaven, and the two lived separate lives after 1864. Eliza continued to support herself by her writing—she had, since 1848, been the first salaried woman journalist in Britain. Her most famous, indeed notorious, book was The True History of Joshua Davidson, Christian and Communist *(1872), which highlighted the inequalities and prejudices in Victorian England. That same attitude towards bigotry is behind the following short story written at the same time and published in* All the Year Round *in December 1872.*

The Fate of Madame Cabanel

Eliza Lynn Linton

Progress had not invaded, nor had science enlightened, the little hamlet of Pieuvrot, in Brittany. They were a simple, ignorant, superstitious set who lived there, and the luxuries of civilization were known to them as little as its learning. They toiled hard all the week on the ungrateful soil that yielded them but a bare subsistence in return; they went regularly to mass in the little rock-set chapel on Sundays and saints' days; believed implicitly all that monsieur le cure said to them, and many things which he did not say; and they took all the unknown, not as magnificent, but as diabolical.

The sole link between them and the outside world of mind and progress was Monsieur Jules Cabanel, the proprietor, par excellence, of the place; *maire, juge de paix*, and all the public functionaries rolled into one. And he sometimes went to Paris whence he returned with a cargo of novelties that excited envy, admiration, or fear, according to the degree of intelligence in those who beheld them.

Monsieur Jules Cabanel was not the most charming man of his class in appearance, but he was generally held to be a good fellow at bottom. A short, thickset, low-browed man, with blue-black hair cropped close like a mat, as was his blue-black beard, inclined to obesity and fond of good living, he had need have some virtues behind the bush to compensate for his want of personal charms. He was not bad, however; he was only common and unlovely. Up to fifty years of age he had remained the unmarried prize of the surrounding country; but hitherto he had resisted all the overtures made by maternal fowlers, and had kept his liberty and his bachelorhood intact. Perhaps his handsome housekeeper, Adèle, had something to do with his persistent celibacy. They said she had, under their breath as it were, down at *la Veuve Prieur's*; but no one dared to so much as hint the like to herself. She was a proud, reserved kind of woman; and had strange notions of her own dignity which no one cared to

118

disturb. So, whatever the underhand gossip of the place might be, neither she nor her master got wind of it.

Presently and quite suddenly, Jules Cabanel, who had been for a longer time than usual in Paris, came home with a wife. Adèle had only twenty-four hours' notice to prepare for this strange home-coming; and the task seemed heavy. But she got through it in her old way of silent determination; arranged the rooms as she knew her master would wish them to be arranged; and even supplemented the usual nice adornments by a voluntary bunch of flowers on the salon table.

"Strange flowers for a bride," said to herself little Jeannette, the goose-girl who was sometimes brought into the house to work, as she noticed heliotrope—called in France *la fleur des veuves*—scarlet poppies, a bunch of belladonna, another of aconite—scarcely, as even ignorant little Jeannette said, flowers of bridal welcome or bridal significance. Nevertheless, they stood where Adèle had placed them; and if Monsieur Cabanel meant anything by the passionate expression of disgust with which he ordered them out of his sight, madame seemed to understand nothing, as she smiled with that vague, half-deprecating look of a person who is assisting at a scene of which the true bearing is not understood. Madame Cabanel was a foreigner, and an Englishwoman; young, pretty and fair as an angel.

"*La beauté du diable*," said the Pieuvrotines, with something between a sneer and a shudder; for the words meant with them more than they mean in ordinary use. Swarthy, ill-nourished, low of stature and mea-gre in frame as they were themselves, they could not understand the plump form, tall figure and fresh complexion of the Englishwoman. Unlike their own experience, it was therefore more likely to be evil than good. The feeling which had sprung up against her at first sight deepened when it was observed that, although she went to mass with praiseworthy punctuality, she did not know her missal and signed herself *à travers*. La beauté du diable, in faith!

"*Pouf!*" said Martin Briolic, the old gravedigger of the little cem-etery; "with those red lips of hers, her rose cheeks and her plump shoulders, she looks like a vampire and as if she lived on blood."

He said this one evening down at *la Veuve Prieur's*; and he said it with an air of conviction that had its weight. For Martin Briolic was reputed the wisest man of the district; not even excepting Monsieur le curé who was wise in his own way, which was not Martin's—nor Monsieur Cabanel who was wise in his, which was neither Martin's

nor le curé's. He knew all about the weather and the stars, the wild
herbs that grew on the plains and the wild shy beasts that eat them;
and he had the power of divination and could find where the hidden
springs of water lay far down in the earth when he held the baguette
in his hand. He knew too, where treasures could be had on Christmas
Eve if only you were quick and brave enough to enter the cleft in the
rock at the right moment and come out again before too late; and he
had seen with his own eyes the White Ladies dancing in the moonlight; and the little imps, the Infins, playing their prankish gambols
by the pit at the edge of the wood. And he had a shrewd suspicion as
to who, among those black-hearted men of La Crèche-en-bois—the
rival hamlet—was a loup-garou, if ever there was one on the face
of the earth and no one had doubted that! He had other powers of
a yet more mystic kind; so that Martin Briolic's bad word went for
something, if, with the illogical injustice of ill-nature his good went
for nothing.

Fanny Campbell, or, as she was now Madame Cabanel, would have
excited no special attention in England, or indeed anywhere but at
such dead-alive, ignorant, and consequently gossiping place as Pieuvrot. She had no romantic secret as her background; and what history
she had was commonplace enough, if sorrowful too in its own way.
She was simply an orphan and a governess; very young and very poor;
whose employers had quarrelled with her and left her stranded in
Paris, alone and almost moneyless; and who had married Monsieur
Jules Cabanel as the best thing she could do for herself. Loving no
one else, she was not difficult to be won by the first man who showed
her kindness in her hour of trouble and destitution; and she accepted
her middle-aged suitor, who was fitter to be her father than her husband, with a clear conscience and a determination to do her duty
cheerfully and faithfully—all without considering herself as a martyr
or an interesting victim sacrificed to the cruelty of circumstances. She
did not know however, of the handsome housekeeper Adèle, nor of
the housekeeper's little nephew—to whom her master was so kind
that he allowed him to live at the Maison Cabanel and had him well
taught by the curé. Perhaps if she had, she would have thought twice
before she put herself under the same roof with a woman who for a
bridal bouquet offered her poppies, heliotrope and poison-flowers.

If one had to name the predominant characteristic of Madame
Cabanel it would be easiness of temper. You saw it in the round,
soft, indolent lines of her face and figure; in her mild blue eyes and

placid, unvarying smile; which irritated the more petulant French temperament and especially disgusted Adèle. It seemed impossible to make madame angry or even to make her understand when she was insulted, the housekeeper used to say with profound disdain; and, to do the woman justice, she did not spare her endeavours to enlighten her. But madame accepted all Adèle's haughty reticence and defiant continuance of mistress-hood with unwearied sweetness; indeed, she expressed herself gratified that so much trouble was taken off her hands, and that Adèle so kindly took her duties on herself.

The consequences of this placid lazy life, where all her faculties were in a manner asleep, and where she was enjoying the reaction from her late years of privation and anxiety, was, as might be expected, an increase in physical beauty that made her freshness and good condition still more remarkable. Her lips were redder, her cheeks rosier, her shoulders plumper than ever; but as she waxed, the health of the little hamlet waned, and not the oldest inhabitant remembered so sickly a season, or so many deaths. The master too, suffered slightly; the little Adolphe desperately. This failure of general health in undrained hamlets is not uncommon in France or in England; neither is the steady and pitiable decline of French children; but Adèle treated it as something out of all the lines of normal experience; and, breaking through her habits of reticence spoke to every one quite fiercely of the strange sickliness that had fallen on Pieuvrot and the Maison Cabanel; and how she believed it was something more than common; while as to her little nephew, she could give neither a name nor find a remedy for the mysterious disease that had attacked him. There were strange things among them, she used to say, and Pieuvrot had never done well since the old times were changed. Jeannette used to notice how she would sit gazing at the English lady, with such a deadly look on her handsome face when she turned from the foreigner's fresh complexion and grand physique to the pale face of the stunted, meagre, fading child. It was a look, she said afterwards, that used to make her flesh get like ice and creep like worms.

One night Adèle, as if she could bear it no longer, dashed down to where old Martin Briolic lived, to ask him to tell her how it had all come about—and the remedy.

"Hold, Ma'am Adèle," said Martin, as he shuffled his greasy tarot cards and laid them out in triplets on the table; 'there is more in this than one sees. One sees only a poor little child become suddenly sick; that may be, is it not so, and no harm done by man? God sends sickness to us all and makes my trade profitable to me. But the little Adolphe has not been touched by the Good God. I see the will of a wicked woman in this. Hem!' Here he shuffled the cards and laid them out with a kind of eager distraction of manner, his withered hands trembling and his mouth uttering words that Adèle could not catch.

"Saint Joseph and all the saints protect us!" he cried; "the foreigner—the Englishwoman—she whom they call Madame Cabanel—no rightful madame she!—Ah, misery!"

"Speak, Father Martin! What do you mean!" cried Adèle, grasping his arm. Her black eyes were wild; her arched nostrils dilated; her lips, thin, sinuous, flexible, were pressed tight over her small square teeth. "Tell me in plain words what you would say!"

"Broucolaque!" said Martin in a low voice.

"It is what I believed!" cried Adèle. "It is what I knew. Ah, my Adolphe! woe on the day when the master brought that fair-skinned devil home!"

"Those red lips don't come by nothing, Ma'am Adèle," cried Martin nodding his head. "Look at them—they glisten with blood! I said so from the beginning; and the cards, they said so too. I drew 'blood' and a 'bad fair woman' on the evening when the master brought her home, and I said to myself, 'Ha, ha, Martin; you are on the track, my boy—on the track. Martin!'—and, Ma'am Adèle, I have never left it! Broucolaque! that's what the cards say, Ma'am Adèle. Vampire. Watch and see; watch and see; and you'll find that the cards have spoken true."

"And when we have found, Martin?" said Adèle in a hoarse whisper.

The old man shuffled his cards again. "When we have found, Ma'am Adèle?" he said slowly.

"You know the old pit out there by the forest?—the old pit where the lutins run in and out, and where the White Ladies wring the necks of those who come upon them in the moonlight? Perhaps the White Ladies will do as much for the English wife of Monsieur Cabanel; who knows?"

"They may," said Adèle, gloomily.

"Courage, brave woman!" said Martin. "They will."

The only really pretty place about Pieuvrot was the cemetery. To be sure there was the dark gloomy forest which was grand in its own mysterious way; and there was the broad wide plain where you might wander for a long summer's day and not come to the end of it; but these were scarcely places where a young woman would care to go by herself; and for the rest, the miserable little patches of cultivated ground, which the peasants had snatched from the surrounding waste and where they had raised poor crops, were not very lovely. So Madame Cabanel, who, for all the soft indolence that had invaded her, had the Englishwoman's inborn love for walking and fresh air, haunted the pretty little graveyard a good deal. She had no sentiment connected with it. Of all the dead who laid there in their narrow coffins, she knew none and cared for none; but she liked to see the pretty little flower-beds and the wreaths of immortelles, and the like; the distance too, from her own home was just enough for her; and the view over the plain to the dark belt of forest and the mountains beyond, was fine.

The Pieuvrotines did not understand this. It was inexplicable to them that any one, not out of her mind, should go continually to the cemetery—not on the day of the dead and not to adorn the grave of one she loved—only to sit there and wander among the tombs, looking out on to the plain and the mountains beyond when she was tired.

"It was just like—"The speaker, one Lesouëf, had got so far as this, when he stopped for a word. He said this down at *la Veuve Prieur's* where the hamlet collected nightly to discuss the day's small doings, and where the main theme, ever since she had come among them, three months ago now, had been Madame Cabanel and her foreign ways and her wicked ignorance of her massbook and her wrong-doings of a mysterious kind generally, interspersed with jesting queries, banded from one to the other, of how Ma'am Adèle liked it?—and what would become of le petit Adolphe when the rightful heir appeared?—some adding that monsieur was a brave man to shut up two wild cats under the same roof together; and what would become of it in the end? Mischief of a surety.

"Wander about the tombs just like what, Jean Lesouëf?" said Martin Briolic. Rising, he added in a low but distinct voice, every word falling clear and clean: "I will tell you like what, Lesouëf—like a vampire! La femme Cabanel has red lips and red cheeks; and Ma'am Adèle's little nephew is perishing before your eyes. La femme Cabanel has red lips and red cheeks; and she sits for hours among the tombs. Can you read the riddle, my friends? For me it is as clear as the blessed sun."

"Ha, Father Martin, you have found the word—like a vampire!" said Lesouëf with a shudder.

"Like a vampire!" they all echoed with a groan.

"And I said vampire the first," said Martin Briolic. "Call to mind I said it from the first."

"Faith and you did!" they answered; "and you said true."

So now the unfriendly feeling that had met and accompanied the young Englishwoman ever since she came to Pieuvrot had drawn to a focus. The seed which Martin and Adèle had dropped so sedulously had at last taken root; and the Pieuvrotines would have been ready to accuse of atheism and immorality anyone who had doubted their decision, and had declared that pretty Madame Cabanel was only a young woman with nothing special to do, a naturally fair complexion, superb health—and no vampire at all, sucking the blood of a living child or living among the tombs to make the newly buried her prey.

The little Adolphe grew paler and paler, thinner and thinner; the fierce summer sun told on the half-starved dwellers within those foul mud-huts surrounded by undrained marshes; and Monsieur Jules Cabanel's former solid health followed the law of the rest. The doctor, who lived at Crèche-en-bois, shook his head at the look of things; and said it was grave. When Adèle pressed him to tell her what was the matter with the child and with monsieur, he evaded the question; or gave her a word which she neither understood nor could pronounce. The truth was, he was a credulous and intensely suspicious man; a viewy man who made theories and then gave himself to the task of finding them true. He had made the theory that Fanny was secretly poisoning both her husband and the child; and though he would not give Adèle a hint of this, he would not set her mind at rest by a definite answer that went on any other line.

As for Monsieur Cabanel, he was a man without imagination and without suspicion; a man to take life easily and not distress himself too much for the fear of wounding others; a selfish man but not a cruel one; a man whose own pleasure was his supreme law and who could not imagine, still less brook, opposition or the want of love and respect for himself. Still, he loved his wife as he had never loved a woman before. Coarsely moulded, common-natured as he was, he loved her with what strength and passion of poetry nature had given him; and if the quantity was small, the quality was sincere. But that quality was sorely tried when—now Adèle, now the doctor—hinted mysteriously, the one at diabolical influences, the other at underhand proceedings of which it behoved him to be careful, especially careful what he ate and drank and how it was prepared and by whom;

Adèle adding hints about the perfidiousness of English women and the share which the devil had in fair hair and brilliant complexions. Love his young wife as he might, this constant dropping of poison was not without some effect. It told much for his steadfastness and loyalty that it should have had only so small effect.

One evening however, when Adèle, in an agony, was kneeling at his feet—madame had gone out for her usual walk—crying: "Why did you leave me for such as she is?—I, who loved you, who was faithful to you, and she, who walks among the graves, who sucks your blood and our child's—she who has only the devil's beauty for her portion and who loves you not?"—something seemed suddenly to touch him with electric force.

"Miserable fool that I was!" he said, resting his head on Adèle's shoulders and weeping. Her heart leapt with joy. Was her reign to be renewed? Was her rival to be dispossessed?

From that evening Monsieur Cabanel's manner changed to his young wife but she was too easy-tempered and unsuspicious to notice anything, or if she did, there was too little depth in her own love for him—it was so much a matter of untroubled friendliness only—that she did not fret but accepted the coldness and brusqueness that had crept into his manner as good-naturedly as she accepted all things. It would have been wiser if she had cried and made a scene and come to an open fracas with Monsieur Cabanel. They would have understood each other better; and Frenchmen like the excitement of a quarrel and a reconciliation.

Naturally kind-hearted, Madame Cabanel went much about the village, offering help of various kinds to the sick. But no one among them all, not the very poorest—indeed, the very poorest the least—received her civilly or accepted her aid. If she attempted to touch one of the dying children, the mother, shuddering, withdrew it hastily to her own arms; if she spoke to the adult sick, the wan eyes would look at her with a strange horror and the feeble voice would mutter words in a patois she could not understand. But always came the same word, "*broucolaque*"!

"How these people hate the English!" she used to think as she turned away, perhaps just a little depressed, but too phlegmatic to let herself be uncomfortable or troubled deeply.

It was the same at home. If she wanted to do any little act of kindness to the child, Adèle passionately refused her. Once she snatched him rudely from her arms, saying as she did so: "infamous *broucolaque!*

before my very eyes?" And once, when Fanny was troubled about her husband and proposed to make him a cup of beef-tea à l'Anglaise, the doctor looked at her as if he would have looked through her; and Adèle upset the saucepan; saying insolently—but yet hot tears were in her eyes—"Is it not fast enough for you, madame? Not faster, unless you kill me first!"

To all of which Fanny replied nothing; thinking only that the doctor was very rude to stare so fixedly at her and that Adèle was horribly cross; and what an ill-tempered creature she was; and how unlike an English housekeeper!

But Monsieur Cabanel, when he was told of the little scene, called Fanny to him and said in a more caressing voice than he had used to her of late: 'Thou wouldst not hurt me, little wife? It was love and kindness, not wrong, that thou wouldst do?'

"Wrong? What wrong could I do?" answered Fanny, opening her blue eyes wide. "What wrong should I do to my best and only friend?"

"And I am thy friend? thy lover? thy husband? Thou lovest me dear?" said Monsieur Cabanel.

"Dear Jules, who is so dear; who so near?" she said kissing him, while he said fervently:

"God bless thee!"

The next day Monsieur Cabanel was called away on urgent business. He might be absent for two days, he said, but he would try to lessen the time; and the young wife was left alone in the midst of her enemies, without even such slight guard as his presence might prove.

Adèle was out. It was a dark, hot summer's night, and the little Adolphe had been more feverish and restless than usual all the day. Towards evening he grew worse; and though Jeannette, the goose-girl, had strict commands not to allow madame to touch him, she grew frightened at the condition of the boy; and when madame came into the small parlour to offer her assistance, Jeannette gladly abandoned a charge that was too heavy for her and let the lady take him from her arms.

Sitting there with the child in her lap, cooing to him, soothing him by a low, soft nursery song, the paroxysm of his pain seemed to her to pass and it was as if he slept. But in that paroxysm he had bitten both his lip and tongue; and the blood was now oozing from his mouth. He was a pretty boy; and his mortal sickness made him at this moment pathetically lovely. Fanny bent her head and kissed the pale still face;—and the blood that was on his lips was transferred to hers.

While she still bent over him—her woman's heart touched with a mysterious force and prevision of her own future motherhood—Adèle, followed by old Martin and some others of the village, rushed into the room.

"Behold her!" she cried, seizing Fanny by the arm and forcing her face upwards by the chin—"behold her in the act! Friends, look at my child—dead, dead in her arms; and she with his blood on her lips! Do you want more proofs? Vampire that she is, can you deny the evidence of your own senses?"

"No! no!" roared the crowd hoarsely. "She is a vampire—a creature cursed by God and the enemy of man; away with her to the pit. She must die as she has made others to die!"

"Die, as she has made my boy to die!" said Adèle; and more than one who had lost a relative or child during the epidemic echoed her words, "Die, as she has made mine to die!"

"What is the meaning of all this?" said Madame Cabanel, rising and facing the crowd with the true courage of an Englishwoman. "What harm have I done to any of you that you should come about me, in the absence of my husband, with these angry looks and insolent words?"

"What harm hast thou done?" cried old Martin, coming close to her. "Sorceress as thou art, thou hast bewitched our good master; and vampire as thou art, thou nourishest thyself on our blood! Have we not proof of that at this very moment? Look at thy mouth—cursed *broucolaque*; and here lies thy victim, who accuses thee in his death!"

Fanny laughed scornfully, "I cannot condescend to answer such folly," she said lifting her head. "Are you men or children?"

"We are men, madame," said Legros the miller; "and being men we must protect our weak ones. We have all had our doubts—and who more cause than I, with three little ones taken to heaven before their time?—and now we are convinced."

"Because I have nursed a dying child and done my best to soothe him!" said Madame Cabanel with unconscious pathos.

"No more words!" cried Adèle, dragging her by the arm from which she had never loosed her hold. "To the pit with her, my friends, if you would not see all your children die as mine has died—as our good Legros have died!"

A kind of shudder shook the crowd; and a groan that sounded in itself a curse burst from them.

"To the pit!" they cried. "Let the demons take their own!"

Quick as thought Adèle pinioned the strong white arms whose shape and beauty had so often maddened her with jealous pain; and before the poor girl could utter more than one cry Legros had placed his brawny hand over her mouth. Though this destruction of a monster was not the murder of a human being in his mind, or in the mind of any there, still they did not care to have their nerves disturbed by cries that sounded so human as Madame Cabanel's. Silent then, and gloomy, that dreadful cortege took its way to the forest, carrying its living load; gagged and helpless as if it had been a corpse among them. Save with Adèle and old Martin, it was not so much personal animosity as the instinctive self-defence of fear that animated them. They were executioners, not enemies; and the executioners of a more righteous law than that allowed by the national code. But one by one they all dropped off, till their numbers were reduced to six; of whom Legros was one, and Lesouëf, who had lost his only sister, was also one.

The pit was not more than an English mile from the Maison Cabanel. It was a dark and lonesome spot, where not the bravest man of all that assembly would have dared to go alone after nightfall, not even if the curé had been with him; but a multitude gives courage, said old Martin Briolic; and half a dozen stalwart men, led by such a woman as Adèle, were not afraid of even lutins or the White Ladies.

As swiftly as they could for the burden they bore, and all in utter silence, the cortege strode over the moor; one or two of them carrying rude torches; for the night was black and the way was not without its physical dangers. Nearer and nearer they came to the fatal bourn; and heavier grew the weight of their victim. She had long ceased to struggle; and now lay as if dead in the hands of her bearers. But no one spoke of this or of aught else. Not a word was exchanged between them; and more than one, even of those left, began to doubt whether they had done wisely, and whether they had not better have trusted to the law. Adèle and Martin alone remained firm to the task they had undertaken; and Legros too was sure; but he was weakly and humanly sorrowful for the thing he felt obliged to do. As for Adèle, the woman's jealousy, the mother's anguish and the terror of superstition, had all wrought in her so that she would not have raised a finger to have lightened her victim of one of her pains, or have found her a woman like herself and no vampire after all.

The way got darker; the distance between them and their place of execution shorter; and at last they reached the border of the pit where this fearful monster, this vampire—poor innocent Fanny Cabanel— was to be thrown. As they lowered her, the light of their torches fell on her face.

"Grand Dieu!" cried Legros, taking off his cap; "she is dead!"

"A vampire cannot die," said Adèle, "It is only an appearance. Ask Father Martin."

"A vampire cannot die unless the evil spirits take her, or she is buried with a stake thrust through her body," said Martin Briolic sententiously.

"I don't like the look of it," said Legros; and so said some others. They had taken the bandage from the mouth of the poor girl; and as she lay in the flickering light, her blue eyes half open; and her pale face white with the whiteness of death, a little return of human feeling among them shook them as if the wind had passed over them.

Suddenly they heard the sound of horses' hoofs thundering across the plain. They counted two, four, six; and they were now only four unarmed men, with Martin and Adèle to make up the number. Between the vengeance of man and the power and malice of the wood-demons, their courage faded and their presence of mind deserted them. Legros rushed frantically into the vague darkness of the forest; Lesouëf followed him; the other two fled over the plain while the horsemen came nearer and nearer. Only Adèle held the torch high above her head, to show more clearly both herself in her swarthy passion and revenge and the dead body of her victim. She wanted no concealment; she had done her work, and she gloried in it. Then the horsemen came plunging to them—Jules Cabanel the first, followed by the doctor and four gardes champêtres.

"Wretches! murderers!" was all he said, as he flung himself from his horse and raised the pale face to his lips.

"Master," said Adèle; "she deserved to die. She is a vampire and she has killed our child."

"Fool" cried Jules Cabanel, flinging off her hand. "Oh, my loved wife! thou who did no harm to man or beast, to be murdered now by men who are worse than beasts!"

"She was killing thee," said Adèle. "Ask monsieur le docteur. What ailed the master, monsieur?"

"Do not bring me into this infamy," said the doctor looking up from the dead. "Whatever ailed monsieur, she ought not to be here.

You have made yourself her judge and executioner, Adèle, and you must answer for it to the law."

"You say this too, master?" said Adèle.

"I say so too," returned Monsieur Cabanel. "To the law you must answer for the innocent life you have so cruelly taken—you and all the tools and murderers you have joined to you."

"And is there to be no vengeance for our child?"

"Would you revenge yourself on God, woman?" said Monsieur Cabanel sternly.

"And our past years of love, master?"

"Are memories of hate, Adèle," said Monsieur Cabanel, as he turned again to the pale face of his dead wife.

"Then my place is vacant," said Adèle, with a bitter cry. "Ah, my little Adolphe, it is well you went before!"

"Hold, Ma'am Adèle!" cried Martin.

But before a hand could be stretched out, with one bound, one shriek, she had flung herself into the pit where she had hoped to bury Madame Cabanel; and they heard her body strike the water at the bottom with a dull splash, as of something falling from a great distance.

"They can prove nothing against me, Jean," said old Martin to the garde who held him. "I neither bandaged her mouth nor carried her on my shoulders. I am the gravedigger of Pieuvrot, and, *ma foi*, you would all do badly, you poor creatures, when you die, without me! I shall have the honour of digging madame's grave, never doubt it; and, Jean," he whispered, "they may talk as they like, those rich aristos who know nothing. She is a vampire, and she shall have a stake through her body yet! Who knows better than I? If we do not tie her down like this, she will come out of her grave and suck our blood; it is a way these vampires have."

"Silence there!" said the garde, commanding the little escort. "To prison with the assassins; and keep their tongues from wagging."

"To prison with martyrs and the public benefactors," retorted old Martin. "So the world rewards its best!"

And in this faith he lived and died, as a forçat at Toulon, maintaining to the last that he had done the world a good service by ridding it of a monster who else would not have left one man in Pieuvrot to perpetuate his name and race. But Legros and also Lesouëf, his companion, doubted gravely of the righteousness of that act of theirs on that dark summer's night in the forest; and though they always maintained that they should not have been punished, because of their good motives, yet they grew in time to disbelieve old Martin Briolic and his wisdom, and to wish that they had let the law take its own course unhelped by them—reserving their strength for the grinding of the hamlet's flour and the mending of the hamlet's sabots—and the leading of a good life according to the teaching of monsieur le cure and the exhortations of their own wives.

A Kiss of Judas

Julian Osgood Field

Julian Osgood Field (1852–1925) was a wealthy American writer and socialite who spent most of his life in London and the great cities of Europe, just like the protagonist in the following story. Field was arrogant and self-centered and loved to be the center of attention. He had few scruples, which is apparent from the titles of his memoirs, Things I Shouldn't Tell *(1924)* and Uncensored Recollections *(1924). He was imprisoned for forgery in 1901 and was an undischarged bankrupt. In 1911 he involved Lady Ida Sitwell in a case of fraud that led to both of them being imprisoned in 1915, he for eighteen months hard labor. I do not know how much this affected him but, like Oscar Wilde, he died as he had lived—way beyond his means. Some critics have called the following story overlong, and there is no doubt that Field wrote like he talked, loving the sound of his own voice, but the end result is a mini-novel full of period atmosphere that must be savored on the journey to the inevitable climax.*

A Kiss of Judas
Julian Osgood Field

"Woman of outer darkness, fiend of death,
From what inhuman cave, what dire abyss,
Hast thou invisible that spell o'erheard?
What potent hand hath touched thy quickened corse,
What song dissolved thy cerements, who unclosed
Those faded eyes and filled them from the stars?"
Walter Savage Landor, Gebir.

Chapter I

Towards the end of September, about eight years ago, the steamship *Albrecht*, under the command of the popular Captain Pellegrini, had on its voyage down the Danube, as far as Rustchuck, the honour of counting among its passengers a gentleman to whom not inaptly might have been addressed the somewhat audacious remark made by Charles Buller to the late Lord Houghton: "I often think how puzzled your Maker must be to account for your conduct." And, indeed, a more curious jumble of lovable and detestable qualities then went to the making up of the personality labelled for formal purposes Lieutenant-Colonel Richard Ulick Verner Rowan, but familiarly known to society as "Hippy" Rowan, it would, we think, at least in the restricted kingdom of charming men, have been difficult to find. Selfish almost to cruelty, and yet capable of acts of generous self-sacrifice which many a better man could not perhaps have risen to; famous for his unnecessary harshness in the numerous wars in which he had distinguished himself, and yet enjoying the well-merited reputation of being the best-natured man in London; Hippy Rowan, thanks to the calm and healthy spirit of philosophy within him, had in the course of his fifty odd years of mundane experiences—which had been varied and of a character calculated to embitter a more delicate nature—never allowed a touch of cynicism to chill his heart, albeit perchance a warmer corner therein was reserved for his enemies than for his friends. It is not so easy or natural as many may imagine to be content with a great deal; but in the golden days when much had been his—at the meridian of his altogether pleasant life, in which even the afternoon shadows were in no wise indicative of the terrors of advancing night—Dick Rowan was possessed of the same serene spirit of content which distinguished him in the later and more troublous times when he found himself forced to look gout and debt in the face on an income barely double the wages he had formerly given to his *cordon bleu*.

Although, when we present him for the first time to our readers, Colonel Rowan is past fifty, and has been for the last twenty odd years what he himself termed "hopelessly and irretrievably ruined," which meant that he could count on but little over a thousand pounds per annum for his maintenance. In former days he had been far more well-to-do, and, indeed, for a very short time—a period of about twelve months—he had been the possessor of a very large sum of money, wealth suddenly inherited, which he had squandered in the most extravagant fashion.

Disraeli used to say, "When I meet a man whose name I cannot remember, I give myself two minutes then, if it be a hopeless task, I always say, 'And how is the old complaint?'" Now, if the great Tory leader could be imagined by any miracle forgetting the name of his highly-esteemed friend Hippy Rowan, and meeting him and asking him the above searching and comprehensive question, the reply doubtless would have been, "I only got back last week," or "I'm going next month," or something after that fashion; for very certainly Colonel Rowan would have interpreted "the old complaint" to signify his passionate love for Paris, the theatre of his splendid follies, the sepulchre of his fortune indeed, but the Mecca whither the faithful feet of the voluptuary were ever eager to speed—the shrine at which his knees, even when gouty, were glad to kneel. The sole surviving representative of one of the most patrician families of Ireland, a man of remarkable personal beauty—his good looks, by the way, in his youth would have been best described by the slang adjective "showy" – for, ever a man of gigantic stature and herculean build, his bright auburn hair and beard had given him during the

earlier part of his career a loud and flaming aspect which rendered
him a hopelessly compromising Clavaroche for any Jacqueline to
keep clandestine appointments with—as he was reckless and daring
to a degree but rarely attained even by his fellow-countrymen, to
whom temerity is often ascribed as a national failing. Dick Rowan
had certainly distinguished himself in his martial profession; and the
same may be said of that portion of his life passed in the House of
Commons, in which august assembly he had for many years helped
to represent an Irish county. But to the twelve months of riotous living in Paris already spoken of, Hippy, beyond all doubt, chiefly owed
his fame; and his laurels, both as a warrior and as legislator, paled
before the roses which crowned his wine cup filled with Yquem of
'37, and the myrtles sacred to Venus of which he wove garlands for
that goddess by Seine side. But his career as one of the acknowledged
leaders of *la haute noce* in the capital of pleasure had been brief though
brilliant. Persistently playing the "rubicon" at four louis a point at the
Petit Club, while at the same time constantly assuming the onerous
responsibilities of an open bank at the Jockey, possess, when unfailing
bad luck attends such gallant endeavours to win the smiles of fickle
fortune, at least the advantage not common to all evils, of providing
in themselves their own antidote and cure; and so, at the end of
twelve brief months devoted to such pastimes, and others no less
costly though less avowable, the gallant colonel had been forced to
acknowledge his defeat, and retire with his never-failing grace from
the French capital, exchanging indeed with regret *Dugléré* for the
Speaker, and leaving with a sigh the sparkle of the Grand Seize for
the comparative respectability of St. Stephen's.

    All this had taken place twenty years and more before the opening
of our story, and in the course of this score of years Hippy, by reason
of certain prolonged and dangerous rambles undertaken by him for
purposes of sport and amusement in all kinds of outlandish countries,
had acquired among his friends a not inconsiderable reputation as a
traveller, and he who, while his money lasted, had been quite content
to limit his wanderings to explorations in the *pays du tendre*, when
forced by unmerciful disaster to fold his pleasure tent and steal away,
had sought to solace his soul for the loss of his fortune by "going
to and fro in the earth" after the fashion of the prince in whose
service indeed that very fortune had been spent—one year suffering
himself to be entertained by the Emir of Bokhara, and in the course
of the next twelve months accepting the hospitality of the Imaum of

Muscat; becoming acquainted in his rambles, gun and notebook in hand, with all sorts and conditions of men, from overeign despots, nay, demi-gods, to slaves ranking far below quadrupeds; by no means altogether limiting his pastimes to sport pure and simple, but, for instance, leaving Pall Mall one day to see if Schliemann had forgotten nothing in the Trojan plain, and endeavouring to catch Beke tripping in Sinai the next; in all these expeditions being, of course, greatly aided by his rare and precious gift of easily and accurately acquiring all languages and dialects, the choice Arabic with which it amused him to surprise the Shereef of Wazan being no less fluent than the Polish in which he flirted with pretty patriots in the land of Kosciuszco.

But the expedition on which he was bent when we introduce him to our readers was one calling for the lead of neither pencil nor pellet, but a journey of purely social purport. The all too-brief days of Hippy's magnificence in Paris had been, so far as they went, concurrent with the reign of splendid folly which has made the name of Djavil Pacha famous in the annals of apolausticism; and some of the most happy hours of Rowan's Parisian existence having been passed in the celebrated apartment on the corner of the Rue Taitbout and the Boulevard des Italiens, inhabited by the Turkish millionaire, between his excellency and the gallant colonel a warm feeling of friendship had sprung up—not the mere passing liking born with the bisque and ceasing with the coffee, but a genuine sympathy which lasted when the banquet was all over and the lights put out, which expressed itself in various graceful and cordial fashions after both had retired from Paris, and which, just before our story opens, had taken the form of an invitation from Djavil to his friend to spend a few days with him at his palace on the Bosphorus, a summons which Dick Rowan was now steaming down the Danube to obey.

He had chosen this particularly monotonous and uncomfortable way of reaching his friend for reasons which do not concern us; but the thought of the unpleasant railway journey from Rustchuck to Varna which awaited him, and then the Black Sea to encounter, did not tend to assuage the twinges of gout and irritability which assailed him by fits and starts as, during the two dreary days he watched the shores on either side glide slowly by—seeing on the right Hungary at length give place to Servia, and then Servia to Turkey, while perpetual Wallachia, sad and desolate, stretched unceasingly and forever to the left—walking up and down the deck leaning on the arm of his trusty valet, or rather, Ancient or Lieutenant, Adams by name, a man almost as well known and fully as well informed as his master, a Cockney who, without any control over the aspirates in his native English, spoke eight other different languages, including Arabic, accurately and fluently, and whose knowledge of Oriental countries dated indeed from the days when he had been page-boy to the great Eltchi in Constantinople. There were but few passengers on board,—an abnormally small number in fact,—and to this circumstance, doubtless, was it due that Rowan, who as a rule paid but little attention to his fellow-travellers, happened to remark a mysterious-looking individual—a man, and apparently not an old one—who sat quite apart from the others and by himself, muffled up to the eyes in a very voluminous, albeit rather dirty, white silk handkerchief, and who was evidently an invalid, judging from the listless way in which he sat, the extreme pallor of the only part of his face which could be seen, and above all, the fever-fed light which glared from between sore and lashless eyelids. He was dressed entirely in black, and although his clothes were somewhat shabby, they betokened carelessness on the part of their wearer rather than poverty; and Adams had noticed and called his master's attention to the fact that on one finger of the man's thin, yellow, dirty hand, which every now and then he would lift to rearrange still higher up about his face the silken muffler, sparkled a diamond, which the omniscient valet recognised to be a stone of value.

"What an extremely disagreeable-looking man, Adams!" pettishly murmured the colonel in English, as he and his servant in their perambulations up and down the deck for the twentieth time on the first morning of the journey passed by where the mysterious stranger sat. "And how he stares at us! He has the eyes of a lunatic, and there is evidently something horrible the matter with his face. Perhaps he's a leper. Ask the captain about him."

But the ever-amiable Captain Pellegrini had not much information to impart, save indeed that the man was certainly neither a madman nor a leper, nor indeed, so far as he knew, an invalid. He was a Moldavian, Isaac Lebedenko by name, a young man, a medical student or doctor, the captain thought; but, at all events, a man in very well-to-do circumstances, for he always spent his money freely.

"I have known him off and on for two years, please your Excellency," said the skipper. "Though I must confess I have never seen his face properly, for he's always muffled up in that way. He takes his meals by himself, and of course pays extra for doing so, and in fact he always, so far as I know, keeps entirely to himself and never speaks to anyone. But the steward's boy, who has waited on him and seen his face, says there is nothing the matter with him, except indeed that he's the ugliest man he ever saw."

"Perhaps he's consumptive," suggested the colonel. But the all-wise Adams shook his head. That was quite inadmissible. He had seen the man walk, and had noticed his legs. Phthisis could not deceive him, he could recognise its presence at a glance. This man was as strong on his legs as a panther; no consumption there.

"Well," said the colonel impatiently, "there's evidently something wrong with him, no matter what, and I'm glad I'm not condemned to remain long in his society, for he certainly has the most unpleasant look in his eyes that I've seen since we left the lepers." And then he turned the current of the conversation, and the subject dropped.

That night very late, when the colonel was sitting quite alone on deck smoking a cigarette and thinking over his approaching visit to Djavil, wondering what persons his old friend would have invited to his palace to meet him, and a thousand souvenirs of the long-past pleasant Paris days thronging to his mind as he dreamily glanced up at the moon which smiled over slowly-receding Servia, a voice close by his ear, a slow, husky, sibilant, high-pitched whisper, broke the stillness, saying in lisping French, "May I ask, Monsieur, by what right you dare to question persons about me?" and, turning, he saw standing by his shoulder the horrible man in shabby black, his eyes glaring with exceptional ferocity from between the red bare lids, and the diamond-decorated claw-like hand grasping convulsively the soiled white muffler, presumably to prevent the vehemence of his speech from causing it to slip down.

Hippy rose to his feet at once, and as he did so his face passed close to the half-shrouded countenance of the man who had addressed him, and the familiar sickening smell of animal musk, full of disgusting significance to the experienced traveller, assailed his nostrils.

"What do you mean?" he exclaimed, shrinking back, his disgust quite overpowering for the moment every other sentiment. "Stand back! Don't come near me!"

The man said nothing, stood quite still, but Rowan saw plainly in the moonlight the red-encircled eyes gleam with renewed ferocity, the yellow claw-like hand wearing the diamond ring and grasping the dirty muffler agitated by a convulsive spasm, and heard beneath the silken covering the husky breathing caught as in a sob.

Hippy recovered himself at once. "Forgive me. Monsieur," he said coldly. "You startled me. Might I beg you to repeat your question?" The man said nothing. It was evident that he had perceived the disgust he had inspired, and that his anger, his indignation, mastered him, and that he dared not trust himself to speak. "You asked me, I think," continued the colonel in a more gentle tone—for his conscience smote him as he reflected that he might perhaps involuntarily have caused pain to one who, notwithstanding his unpleasant aspect and arrogant, not to say hostile, attitude, was doubtless merely an invalid and sufferer—"You asked me, I think, Monsieur, by what right I made inquiries concerning you? Pray pardon me for having done so. I have, indeed, no excuse to offer, but I am really sorry if I have offended you. I merely asked the captain"—But the man interrupted him, his voice, which was tremulous with passion, coming as a husky, wheezy hiss, which rendered the strong lisp with which he pronounced the French the more noticeable and grotesque.

"You asked him—you dared ask him, if I were not a leper. He told Hoffmann, the steward's boy, who told me. You can't deny it! Dog of an Englishman!" Here, gasping for want of breath, and apparently quite overpowered by his anger, the man took a step towards Rowan. This outburst of violent vituperation came as a great relief to the colonel. Like most persons of refined feeling, he could stand any wounds better than those inflicted by self-reproach, and the suspicion that perhaps by careless rudeness he had caused pain to one worthy only of pity had been as gall to him. The man's violent hostility and bad language entirely altered and brightened the aspect of affairs.

"I am sorry," said Hippy, with ironical politeness, "that my nationality should not meet with the honour of your approval. It is not, hélas! the proud privilege of all to be able to boast that they are natives of Moldavia, you know! *Pour le reste*, all I can do is to repeat my apology for—" But the man interrupted him again.

"Apology!" he echoed, if indeed any word indicative of resonance can be applied to the hoarse, damp, lisping whisper in which he spoke—"Apology! Ah, yes! You English curs are all cowards, and only think of apologies. You dare not fight, canaille, but you shall! I'll force you to!" And again he took a step forward, but this time in so menacing a fashion that the colonel, half amused and half disgusted, thought it prudent to step back.

"Take care!" he said, half raising his stick as if to push the man back as an unclean thing. "Keep your distance;" and then, speaking quickly,

for he feared an assault from the infuriated Moldavian, and was desirous of avoiding such an absurd complication, he continued, "If you
can prove to me that I ought to meet you, I shall be happy to do so.
You're right, of course, in thinking duels are no longer the fashion in
England. But I'm an exception to the rule. I've fought two already,
and shall be happy to add to the number by meeting you if it can be
arranged. But that's hardly a matter you and I can properly discuss
between ourselves, is it? Captain Pellegrini knows me. I'll leave my
address with him. I have friends in Turkey, and shall be staying in the
neighbourhood of Constantinople for a fortnight, so, if you care to
send me your seconds, I will appoint gentlemen to receive them.
Allow me to wish you good-night!" and Rowan raised his hat with
much formal politeness, and stepped aside as if to depart. But the man
sprang forward like a cat and stood in his way.

"Coward!" he exclaimed, extending both arms as if to bar Rowan's
passage. "Cur! like all your countrymen! You think to run away from
me, but you shall not! You shall go on your knees and beg my pardon,
you accursed Englishman—you dog—you—" But just as the enraged
Moldavian reached this point in his fury an awful thing happened.
The yellow, claw-like hand having been withdrawn from clutching at
the dirty muffler, the vehemence of the man's speech began gradually
to disarrange this covering, causing it little by little to sink lower and
lower and thus to disclose by degrees to Rowan a sight so strange,
so awful, that, impelled by a morbid curiosity, he involuntarily bent
his head forward as his horror-stricken eyes eagerly noted every step
in the infernal progress of this revelation. And thus, gazing at the
slowly slipping silk, he saw first, beardless, hollow cheeks, twitching
with emotion, but of a most hideous pallor, of indeed that awful hue
inseparably associated with the idea of post-mortem changes; then, in
the middle of this livid leanness, lighted only by those fever-fed, red-
lidded eyes, the beginning—the broad base springing from the very
cheekbones as it were—of a repulsive prominence which apparently
went narrowing on to some termination which as yet the scarf hid,
but which the horrified colonel felt every second surer and yet more
sure could not resemble the nasal organ of a man, but rather the—ah,
yes! the silk fell, and in the moonlight Rowan saw the end he had
foreseen, the pointed nose as of a large ferret, and beneath it, far in
under it, nervously working, the humid, viscous horror of a small
mouth almost round, but lipless, from which came in hurried, husky
sibilance the lisping words of hate and menace.

This awful revelation, although partly expected, was so inexpress-ibly horrible when it came, that, doubtless, the expression of disgust in Rowan's face deepened so suddenly in acuteness and intensity as to arrest the attention of the monster who inspired it, infuriated though he was; for he paused in the lisping tumult of his violence, and, as he paused, became suddenly aware that the muffler had slipped down. Then, as this knowledge came to him, and now rightly interpreting the horror he saw written in the colonel's countenance, and goaded thus to a fresh fit of fury, too despairing and violent even for words, he, with an inarticulate moan or whimper, rushed blindly forward with extended arms to attack his enemy. But the colonel, who had foreseen this onslaught, stepped quickly to one side, and, as he did so, quite overpowered by disgust, he could not resist the temptation of giving the hostile monster a violent push with his heavy walking-stick—a thrust of far greater force than he had indeed intended, for it caused the man to totter and fall forward just as two or three sailors, who from a distance had witnessed the last incidents of the dispute, ran up and stood between the adversaries.

"That man," exclaimed the colonel in German, pointing with his stick to where the Moldavian lay sprawling on his knees, hastily read-justing the muffler around his hideous face, "tried to assault me, and I defended myself. Look after him, but beware of him. He is a wild beast, not a man!"

The men looked at the colonel, whom they knew to be some important grandee held in great honour by their captain, and then at the shabby mass of black clothes sprawling on the deck, and then at each other, and marvelled greatly, open-mouthed, not knowing what to say or think or do.

"I shall see the captain about this to-morrow," continued Rowan. "But in the meantime, as I say, look after this—this—man, but beware of him!" And so speaking, he turned and strode away in the direction of his cabin.

Just before reaching the stairway he turned and looked back. There in the moonlight stood the man in black, gazing after him, the awful face hidden once more in the dirty muffler which was now stained on one side with the blood which came trickling down from a wound on the brow. As he saw the colonel turn, the man raised his clenched fist and shook it very slowly, solemnly, and deliberately, the gesture of a warning and of a curse, and the sailors, fearing further violence, closed around him. Then the colonel turned and went his way to bed.

The following morning Rowan of course made his faithful Adams (who by the way was never astonished at anything, having acquired through long residence in the East the stolidity of the Oriental) fully acquainted with the strange events of the preceding night, but charged him to say nothing to anybody.

"I have thought the matter over," said the colonel, "and have decided merely to tell the captain that I had a few words with the man, and in a heated moment struck him, and then give Pellegrini his Excellency's address where we shall be for the next fortnight, so that if this man wants to communicate with me in any way, he can. Of course, any question of a duel with such a brute is absurd. I'd as soon accept a challenge from a stoat or a ferret. But after all, the initial fault was mine. This wretched creature is not responsible either for his face or for his mariners, and I feel I owe him some reparation for my impertinent curiosity. So I'll just say a word to Pellegrini and give him our address at Djavil Pacha's, to give to this man if he requires it. I hope he won't attempt to assault me again today."

"I'll keep a sharp lookout he doesn't, sir," said Adams, but such precautions were unnecessary. Nothing more was seen of the Moldavian, who presumably was confined to his cabin by his wound, and the following morning at early dawn the colonel and his servant left the steamer at Rustchuck and took the train to Varna and the Black Sea, en route for the splendours of the Bosphorus.

Chapter II

From one end to the other of the Bosphorus, both on the coast of Europe and on the coast of Asia, are numerous little towns and villages—the *faubourgs*, as it were, of Constantinople—which, in the *belle saison*, are inhabited by members of the Turkish aristocracy and strangers of distinction; and in one of these, on the European side, within less than an hour's journey by steamboat from the Stamboul bridge, was situated the palace of Hippy Rowan's friend,—the whilom plunger of the Petit and Jockey Clubs,—the famous Djavil Pacha.

Of the building we need say but little. It was white—partly marble and partly wood, painted to resemble marble—low, rambling, and commodious, but of no special style of architecture, and certainly not Turkish, or even Oriental, but rather Italian in its outward aspect.

The principal beauty and advantage of the residence was the extensive garden which surrounded it, and which, rising in banks of flowers and verdure at the back, in front sloped down to a splendid marble terrace, washed by the waters of the Bosphorus, which led to the Pacha's private landing-place and quay, whereby was moored the private steam-launch of his excellency. Djavil Pacha was a bachelor, kept no harem, and lived in European style, his head cook and the chief assistants of that artist having been imported direct from Bignon's, and the palace throughout furnished by a *tapissier* from Paris, the only concession to Turkish prejudices which a careful observer might have remarked being the absence of statuary and paintings in the house—the Koran, as we know, forbidding the reproduction in painting of animate objects, and Djavil having, before leaving the French capital, disposed of his splendid canvases and marbles in the Rue Drouot—whether induced to make this sacrifice by religious motives or for more sordid reasons, who shall say?

In Constantinople—which, by the way, is the most backbiting, tittle-tattling, scandal-mongering little village in the world—the ex-ambassador and old Parisian *viveur* was greatly blamed for living in so thoroughly European a fashion, keeping open house, constantly entertaining the most distinguished members, male and female, of the European colony, and, in fact, conducting his life by the Bosphorus very much on the same lines as any man of wealth and refinement might conduct his by the Seine, the Danube, the Neva, or the Thames. The clever and ambitious Djavil, however, cared nothing for such disapproval, so long as he retained the favour of the Sultan and the Grand Vizier (the gambler and *roué* of the Rue Royale and Rue Scribe having now developed into a hard-working Under-Secretary of State for Foreign Affairs). He quite determined to live his private life as he pleased, since he devoted his public life to the service of his country, and when the day's work was over and he embarked on his steam-launch on his return journey to his palace, to leave behind him the Turkish statesman and become again purely and simply the cosmopolitan man of pleasure.

Of other permanent guests beside himself at the palace, Hippy found but three—his old friend, a well-known gambler and breaker and taker of banks, Lord Melrose; an amusing French newspaper man, Emile Bertonneux by name, of the Paris *Œil de Bœuf*, and last, but not least, the universally popular Tony Jeratczesco, whom Hippy had last seen in the Birdcage at Newmarket some months before, and whose sudden and mysterious disappearance from St. James's Street, which loved him so well, in order to (as rumour asserted) go and take possession of a property just left him in some outlandish country by a recently deceased relation, was still the talk of London. Not that London had any reason to be astonished at anything, whether good or evil, that might befall the popular sportsman; for Tony Jeratczesco was altogether a mystery, and nobody knew anything whatever about the man familiarly nicknamed "Cheery and Cheeky," whether he was rich or poor, married or single, patrician by birth or plebeian, nor indeed of what nationality he might boast himself to be, whether Austrian, Hungarian, Bohemian, Pole, Moldavian, Russian, Wallachian, Servian, Bulgarian, or Montenegrin, Jew, Christian, Mohammedan, Buddhist, or what not. He was good-looking, amiable, refined, and well-dressed, and moreover, was endowed to a very marked degree with the rare and precious gift of being able to both win and lose money admirably well; in no wise allowing either the smiles or frowns of fortune to disturb the serene reign of the perfect good taste which presided over all his affairs; and when this had been said, and the facts chronicled, that he was fond of cards and racing, and always seemed to have plenty of money to justify his interest in both these expensive forms of speculation, and that he enjoyed a close personal friendship with some of the most exalted personages of the realm—the authentic data wherewith to compose a biographical sketch of Count Jeratczesco would be perhaps exhausted, although of course scandal, both benevolent and malignant, was constantly taking up the wondrous tale of the great success of this mysterious stranger and adventurer in the best of our rude island society, and enriching it with rare and marvellous broideries of fancy.

For once, however, rumour, in dealing with the private affairs of "Cheery and Cheeky," would appear to have been correct. A relative had died—an uncle—and left Tony a mysterious castle and many acres in Moldavia, not far from the little town of Sereth, and the count had come on to stay with Djavil solely because he knew Hippy Rowan, Lord Melrose, and others *ejusdem farinæ*, would be gathered together under the Pacha's hospitable roof-tree, and he was desirous of making up a house-warming party of friends to accompany him to his new possessions, and enjoy some of the shooting for which the place was famous. This plan met with general approval, and Jeratczesco found no difficulty in forming a pleasant party to return with him to Moldavia from among the Pacha's numerous guests. For although, as we have said, Dick Rowan, Lord Melrose, the Count, and the French *chroniqueuer*, were the only permanent residents beneath the Pacha's roof during this fortnight, the four remaining guest-chambers in the palace were never empty; for Djavil's house was literally Liberty Hall, and there was a constant ebb and flow of all kinds of persons there, more or less invited by the Pacha: people from our Embassy, and people from every other Embassy, people of every rank and position: from a very Broad-Church English divine, who was sent on out of sheer mischief by our ambassador, Lord Malling, and who came, accompanied by his florid, comely, and substantial spouse, both inclined to be slightly querulous about the Holy Places, until they had tasted the water, drinking Djavil's incomparable *Yquem*; to a very beautiful and wayward Italian diva, who came accompanied by two of her adorers, likewise blest with the gift of song, and who made everyone weep (including the chef from Bignon's, who listened outside) when she and her friends after dinner (and all three slightly intoxicated) interpreted, as only angels fired with a few goblets of St. Marceaux can, Verdi's divine Requiem; persons of both sexes, and of every nationality and religion, who would arrive in time for dinner one evening, stay the night, and perhaps the following day and night, and then disappear without thinking of subjecting their host to a formal leave-taking, being well aware that his excellency's time was very precious, since he was up and about by six o'clock every morning, and very often steaming down in the direction of Stamboul to look after the foreign affairs of the empire before many of his guests had awakened from their slumbers. So pleasantly did the time pass that it was with regret Colonel Rowan saw the termination of his visit drawing nigh, and heard one morning Jeratczesco, impatient to assume his unwonted role of host, solemnly announce that in four days' time he should depart to his home in Karpaks, taking with him the followers he had selected. Then, to celebrate the approaching departure of the popular Hippy Rowan, Djavil gave a sylvan picnic, which for many months after was the subject of much gossip on both sides of the Bosphorus, and from the Black Sea to the Sea of Marmora—an entertainment destined, alas, to be fraught with fatal consequences to the gentleman in whose honour it was given. The rendezvous was for ten o'clock in the morning, at the sweet waters of Asia—where an insignificant little streamlet loses itself in the Bosphorus—and the guests, about twenty in number, arrived at the place of meeting with surprising punctuality—some coming with Djavil in his steam-launch, and some from Constantinople.

But for our limited space we would introduce each one of these somewhat notable individualities singly to our readers:—Leopold Maryx, the dissipated and irregular and eccentric savant, the renowned specialist for nervous diseases, who had been summoned from Vienna on purpose to see the Sultan; Lord Malling, our delightful but impossible ambassador; Lord, and especially Lady, Brentford, the champion political bore in petticoats, the victim to high principles, who had bullied her half-witted husband into believing he had a conscience on the occasion of the Reform Bill of 1867, and expressing his delighted surprise at the discovery of his novel possession in a fashion so offensive to his party as to have merited and brought about his final extinction at the hands of "the impetuous earl, the Rupert of debate," and who, since then, had been dedicating her life to impotent though vigorous denunciations of what she termed the "treachery" of the Tory county members, and the "infamy" of the county caucus; Mr. Leonard P. Beacon, the New York millionaire and sportsman, a rough, boasting, but withal good-hearted giant, who, although vulgar beyond even the power of dynamite to purify, was vastly amusing, owing to the fact of his having only begun his boisterous youth at the age of forty-five (he had been a collier till then), and who thus at fifty experienced the delightful surprises of a lad of eighteen, and confided them to you with a frankness which would even have brought blushes to the cheeks of Jean Jacques; Frank Silveyra, the famous Hebrew financier and prince of good fellows, from Vienna, and his friend, the no-less-delightful young Jewish millionaire and artist, Raphael Sciama; the smart and enterprising little Alec Torquati, who had won our Derby at far-distant Epsom the previous year with "Kyber"; and, finally, three very beautiful and witty, and altogether attractive, ladies of high degree from Paris, who, accompanied by their husbands, had come all the way from the Seine to the Bosphorus on purpose to be admired, and three very magnificent young Cavaliers of the Guard who had come all the way from the Neva to the Bosphorus on purpose to admire them and manifest their admiration.

Ten carriages awaited Djavil's guests on the Asian coast, and into nine of these they clambered; the tenth and last being reserved for a *valet-de-chambre* provided with all that could be required for the dispensing of light refreshments en route. And thus, with servants of the Pacha mounted on faultless little Arab horses racing up and down on either side of the carriages, bringing every now and then from the hindmost vehicle fruit and sandwiches, and bottles of champagne and Bordeaux wherewith the weary travellers might be refreshed, this gay and brilliant party dashed into the interior of Asia at full gallop. It had been arranged that the *déjeuner champêtre* should take place in the forest of Alem-Dagh; and when, after a drive at steeplechase speed for about three hours' duration, this spot was reached, it was indeed made manifest that Djavil had neglected nothing to make this fantastic breakfast a success. Here, to this wild, deserted, picturesque spot in the heart of a forest in Asia, a romantic nook apparently miles away from any trace of European civilisation, this very *grand seigneur* had sent the evening before—accompanied by an army of marmitons—his cordon bleu, whose education had been perfected in the famous kitchen on the corner of the Chaussée d'Antin and the Boulevard des Italians; and with this great artist and his assistants had come vast and numerous vans drawn by bull-ocks, and containing all the requisites for cooking, and the food, and wine, and silver, and decorations, and furniture—in fact, all that could be imagined by a wealthy and experienced voluptuary and man of the world to be necessary to make this *déjeuner sur l'herbe* for twenty persons an entertainment worthy of both host and guests. The viands provided by Djavil (who, being a Turk, possessed that stubborn and rough Oriental palate which apparently can never be trained to a proper appreciation of the most precious and delicate secrets and traditions of *la grande cuisine*) were of a very substantial character; but the long journey had aroused appetites wholly beyond the power of sandwiches and goblets of St. Marceaux to satisfy, and the Pacha's guests eagerly sought consolation in the introductory *œufs à la Béchamel* as a hidden orchestra of the best musicians to be found in Constantinople ravished the Asian air with heaven-inspired passages telling of the jealousy of Amneris and of the ill-fated love of Radamès and Aïda.

"This is the most perfect still champagne I ever drank! Where did you get it, Djavil?" And so speaking, Mr. Leonard P. Beacon put down his glass and felt in his pocket for the notebook wherein he was accustomed to inscribe such precious addresses. Life at best is short, but he, Mr. Leonard P. Beacon, had, to speak Hibernicé, only begun when already half through it; and as he always wanted the best of everything and had no time to lose in personal quests after supreme excellence, he was always glad to take advantage of short cuts through

the experience of friends. But the good-natured and adipose Pacha
shook his head and smiled.

"No, no, *mon cher*. 'Tis a secret. Were I to tell you, you'd buy it all
up and take it back with you to America. But, if you like it, I daresay
I can spare you a few dozen. Ask Hassan yourself."

Here a very high-pitched "Oh! how terrible!" from Lady Brentford disturbed the wit-winged chatter of the three lovely Seine-side
dames with their three adoring flowers of Slav chivalry; disturbed the
husbands of these dames, who were engaged in an animated discus-
sion among themselves as to the merits of cooking in oil; disturbed
the Dowager Duchess, who, while listening to Raphael Sciama's
enthusiastic account of the priceless Giulio Clovio he had unearthed
a fortnight before in Venice, had been endeavouring, and not without
success, to rekindle by means of a visual current of sympathy with the
youthful Alec Torquati, the flame of passion in those orbs which had
first flashed with that all-devouring fire early in the fifties; disturbed
Tony Jeratczesco, who was explaining some Newmarket matters to
Baron Silveyra, while Lord Brentford and our ambassador listened;
and disturbed, in fact, the original cause of this disturbing cry, the
loud-voiced Leopold Maryx, whose remarks to Hippy Rowan had
elicited this startling exclamation from Lady Brentford, who sat next
to him and had overheard them.

"Dr. Maryx is saying such awful things," said her ladyship, shaking
her head. "He says he believes in people being possessed of devils."
Then, even as she spoke, her mind reverted to the terrible events of
1867, those famous "Resolutions" and the way the borough members had been treated, and she felt that the great professor might not
perhaps after all be mistaken.

"Ah, no! you misunderstood me. Lady Brentford!" exclaimed
Maryx, laughing. "What I said was, I saw no reason why, if people
were ever possessed of evil spirits, as we are told they used to be, we
should believe such things to be impossible now. Is the world any
better now than it was on the day when the swine ran down that
steep place and were choked in the lake? I didn't say that I believe in
such things, for I don't; but, certainly, if I believed they ever existed, I
should think they were as likely to exist now as ever."

"Maryx was telling me about the Children of Judas," remarked
Hippy Rowan, by way of explanation.

"The Children of Judas!" echoed Emile Bertonneux, the Parisian
newspaper man, scenting a possible *article àsensation*—for it is, we

suppose, hardly necessary to remind our readers that in so cosmopolitan a gathering the conversation was carried on in French—"Who are they? I had no idea that Judas was a *père de famille*."

"It's a Moldavian legend," replied the great specialist. "They say that Children of Judas, lineal descendants of the arch traitor, are prowling about the world seeking to do harm, and that they kill you with a kiss."

"Oh, how delightful!" murmured the Dowager Duchess, glancing at Alec Torquati, as if inviting, and indeed expecting, just such homicidal osculatory cruelty at the lips of the young Derby winner.

"But how do they get at you to kiss you?" gasped Mr. Leonard P. Beacon, his thirst for information leading him to ignore the fact that his mouth was full of *loup sauce homard*.

"The legend is," said Maryx, "that in the first instance they are here in every kind of shape—men and women, young and old, but generally of extraordinary and surpassing ugliness, but *are* here merely to fill their heart with envy, venom, and hatred, and to mark their prey. In order to really do harm, they have to sacrifice themselves to their hatred, go back to the infernal regions whence they came—but go back by the gate of suicide—report to the Chief of the Three Princes of Evil, get their diabolical commission from him, and then return to this world and do the deed. They can come back in any form they think the best adapted to attain their object, or rather satisfy their hate: sometimes they come as a mad dog, who bites you and gives you hydrophobia—that's one form of the kiss of Judas; sometimes as the breath of pestilence, cholera, or what not—that's another form of the kiss of Judas; sometimes in an attractive shape, and then the kiss is really as one of affection, though as fatal in its effect as the mad dog's bite or the pestilence. When it takes the form of a kiss of affection, however, there is always a mark on the poisoned body of the victim—the wound of the kiss. Last summer, when I was at Sinaia in attendance on the Queen, I saw the body of a peasant girl whose lover had given her the kiss of Judas, and there certainly was on her neck a mark like this:"—and Maryx took up a fork and scratched on the tablecloth three X's, thus, XXX. "Can you guess what that's supposed to signify?" inquired the great physician.

"It looks like a hurdle," remarked Torquati.

"Thirty," exclaimed Lady Brentford.

"Of course," replied Maryx, "thirty—the thirty pieces of silver, of course—the mark of the price of blood."

"*Vous êtes impayahle, mon cher!*" exclaimed Djavil, grinning. "Whenever you find it no longer pays you to kill your patients you can always make money at the *foires*. Set Hippy Rowan to beat the drum at the door and you sit inside the van telling your wonderful *blagues*, and you'll make a fortune in no time."

"I hope you don't tell those horrible tales to the Sultan, Leopold," said Lord Malling, laughing. "You cure nervous diseases by frightening people to death, I think."

But the great professor paid no attention to these flippant remarks; he was, indeed, notwithstanding his marvellous intelligence and extraordinary science and experience and skill, at very heart a charlatan and mountebank in his love of a gaping crowd; and the interest he saw depicted on the faces of his listeners delighted him.

"Did you say that in the first instance these Children of Judas are supposed to be very ugly?" inquired Colonel Rowan, his thoughts reverting to the awful face of that man, Isaac Lebedenko, who had assaulted him on the boat.

The incident had almost wholly passed away from his memory until then, though he had noted it down in his carefully kept diary; and he had, by the way, long ago told himself that he must have been mistaken in what he thought that horrible muffler had disclosed to him; that such things could not be, and that he must have been deceived either by some trick of shadow, or by some prank played on him by gout astride of his imagination.

"Yes," replied Maryx; "so runs the legend. This physical ugliness betokens, of course, the malignant spirit within. At that stage they may be recognised and avoided or, better still, slain; for they only really become dangerous when their hatred has reached such a pitch that they are prompted to seek a voluntary death and reincarnation in order completely to satisfy their malignancy; for it is by the gate of suicide alone that they can approach the Arch-Fiend to be fully commissioned and equipped to return to earth on their errand of destruction. So if they are killed in their first stage of development, and not allowed to commit suicide, they are extinguished. When they return fully armed with power from hell, it is too late; they cannot be recognised, and are fatal—for they have at their command all the weapons and artillery of Satan, from the smile of a pretty woman to the breath of pestilence. This voluntary self-sacrifice of hate in order to more fully satisfy itself by a regeneration, this suicide on the *reculer pour mieux sauter principle*, is of course nothing but a parody of the divine sacrifice of Love on which the Christian religion is based."

"I'm both sorry and astonished, my dear Leopold," said Baron Silveyra, smiling, "to see that your knowledge of diabolical matters is so faulty. How can you speak of three princes of evil? You must know there are seventy-two!"

"Ah! you believe in the old system," rejoined Maryx, laughing, and pouring himself out a tumblerful of Mouton Rothschild: "six multiplied by twelve, and then the seven million four hundred and five thousand nine hundred and twenty-six demons of inferior rank. But, *mon cher*, that's altogether out of fashion now; that brings you to six multiplied by one million two hundred and thirty-four thousand three hundred and twenty-one, or the old mysterious 'tetrade' of Pythagoras and Plato counting both ways.[2] We've altogether changed that down in Hades now."

And then the great savant, who delighted above all things in gravely clothing nonsense in a garb of erudition, launched forth into a fantastic and witty description of the internal economy of the kingdom of Satan, a satire in which he not only displayed an extraordinary amount of mystical knowledge, but which he enlivened by sly and apposite allusions to the Governments represented by Djavil and Lord Malling respectively; and these gentlemen replying to this banter in the same spirit, and appealing to the other guests, the conversation soon became general.

When the repast was at length over, every one began strolling about the woods, and Hippy Rowan, lighting a cigar, started for a ramble with his old friend Lord Malling. But they had not gone far when their host sent a servant after them to request his lordship to return and speak with him; and so, the ambassador turning back, Hippy continued his saunter by himself, penetrating by degrees into a somewhat remote and secluded part of the forest, the voices and

---

[1] Perhaps the meaning of the professor will be more apparent if we put the numbers in figures. He speaks of 72 princes of darkness (6 multiplied by 12) and 7,405,926 demons of an inferior rank. This last number, so strange apparently, is still the product of 6 multiplied by 1,234,321; and, as our readers can see, 1,234,321 presents to us both from right to left and from left to right the four numbers constituting the mysterious "tetrade" of Pythagoras and of Plato.

laughter of the other guests becoming gradually fainter and fainter as he strolled on. Suddenly, from behind a tree, a man sprang out upon him, and a knife gleamed in the sunlight, swiftly descending upon his heart. Hippy, quick as lightning leapt to one side, striking up as he did so with his heavy walking-stick at the would-be assassin's arm, and with such force that he sent the knife flying out of the man's hand into the air; and then turning, he dealt the villain a blow on the side of the head which brought him to the ground as one dead. It was the Moldavian, Isaac Lebedenko. Hippy had recognised the eyes gleaming over the dirty-white muffler the moment the man sprang out upon him; and now, as he lay on the ground insensible, there could of course be no shadow of doubt about the man's identity, although he had so fallen on one side that the wrapper had not been disarranged from his face. We have said that, although enjoying the well-merited reputation of being the best-natured man in London, Dick Rowan had laid himself open to the reproach of having been most unduly harsh and severe in the numerous wars in which he had been engaged; and this hardness, not to say cruelty, presumably ever latent in his nature, but which seemed only to be called to the surface under certain special conditions closely connected with peril and the excitement engendered thereby, now made itself apparent. The Moldavian had fallen on his side, and the shock of his fall had been so violent that, while one hand lay palm upwards and half open on the trunk of a large fallen tree, the other hand, palm downwards, had been thrown upon its fellow. It was rather a peculiar position for the shock resulting from a fall to have thrown the hands into, and of course indicated that the blow had been so severe that the man had not been able to make any attempt to break his fall, but had sunk to the ground like a doll. Such, at least, was the way Rowan explained the matter as he stood over his prostrate enemy, wondering in his mind how he could possibly contrive to secure the violent would-be assassin until such time as he should be able to obtain assistance and have him handed over to the authorities for punishment; and just as he noticed the position of his hands his eyes caught the gleaming of the knife, which had fallen a little farther on in the grass. Hippy went to where it lay and picked it up. It was a murderous looking weapon indeed: broad, double-edged, and very sharp, though rather thick and not long, and fitted with a big round handle of lead, destined, of course, to lend terrible momentum to any blow struck by it. Rowan looked at the knife, and then at the hands of the Moldavian, lying in so diabolically tempting a position; and just then a quivering of the man's legs plainly indicated that he was recovering his senses. If it was to be done at all there was evidently no time to be lost, so Rowan, taking the sharp instrument, and poising it point downwards over the man's hands, which were already beginning to twitch with returning consciousness, and using his huge walking-stick as a hammer, with one powerful blow on the broad heavy handle of the knife, drove it through both the hands of the Moldavian and into the trunk of the tree up to the very hilt. A slight and almost inaudible groan came from behind the white wrapper—that was all; but Rowan could see that under the sting of the sudden pain the man had completely recovered consciousness, for the awful eyes, just visible above the muffler, were now open and fixed upon him.

"You miserable scoundrel!" exclaimed Rowan in German, his voice hoarse with anger. "You may think yourself lucky I didn't kill you like a dog when you lay there at my mercy. But I'll have you punished—never fear. Lie quiet there until I have you sent for to be put in prison."

The man said nothing; his awful eyes simply looked at Rowan.

"I have been forced, as you see," continued the colonel, leisurely taking out a cigar and lighting it, "to nail you to the tree to prevent your escaping. Vermin is often treated so, you know. But I shan't inconvenience you for long. In a very few minutes I shall be sending people to unpin you and bind you properly, and have you taken off to prison. We have not seen the last of each other yet, my good friend—believe me, we have not."

Then the man spoke—it was almost in a whisper, but the words came with the horrible liquid lisp Rowan remembered with so much distrust. "No," he murmured, "we have not seen the last of each other yet—we have not."

"There's but little fear, I fancy, of your not being here when I send for you," resumed Rowan, after a moment's pause, during which he and the Moldavian had been steadfastly gazing at each other. "So we needn't waste more time now, and especially as you must be rather uncomfortable. So à bientôt." Then, just as he was turning away, he stopped. "In case," said he very quietly, "you should succeed in wriggling away before I send for you, and prefer mutilating your hands to suffering the very many lashes I shall certainly have administered to you, it's as well you should know, perhaps, that when travelling I invariably carry a revolver. I'm without it to-day—very luckily for you—by the merest accident. But I'm not likely to forget it again. So take care." And then Rowan turned and began strolling very leisurely back to where he had left his friends. His last words had not been idly spoken, but were intended to first of all suggest to the miserable wretch whom he had left nailed to the fallen tree, that escape was not altogether impossible, provided he were ready to pay the terrible price of self-mutilation required; and, secondly, to indicate the humiliating nature and severity of the punishment in store for him, that he might decide whether escape at any cost were not preferable to such torture and degradation. For, as a matter of fact, Hippy Rowan, directly the first moment of anger and the accompanying spasm of malignant cruelty had passed away, had decided in his mind to proceed no further in the matter, and by no means to take upon himself the ennui and trouble of having the paltry villain more seriously punished than he had already been. Had he had his revolver with him, he would of course have killed the man; but as it was, he had nailed him as vermin to a tree in a lonely forest in Asia, and there he would leave him to his fate. He might starve to death there, or escape by a terrible mutilation, or possibly with his teeth remove the knife; or somebody might happen to pass by and relieve him, though this last was hardly likely: but at all events he, Hippy Rowan, having warned the villain what to expect in the event of his again molesting him, would have nothing more to do with the matter, and, indeed, not even mention the disagreeable episode to his friends—at least, not at present.

When Rowan got back to the scene of the picnic, he found the preparations for departure just being completed; and in a few minutes all Djavil's guests were once more comfortably ensconced in the carriages and on their way back to the Bosphorus, but this time by another road, which their host had reserved as an agreeable surprise, and which led through scenery of great beauty—first, after fairy vistas of sylvan solitudes and entanglements, through a squalid though picturesque little village, the inhabitants of which, men and women and children, came running out after the carriages in great excitement, calling out and holding up their hands for alms; then past an encampment of tziganes, who were singing and playing and dancing; then across a lonely plain, over which here and there in the far distance, and standing out in bold relief against the horizon, now all ablaze with the glory of the setting sun, passed bullock carts full of peasants, grouped together with Oriental and artistic grace, going home after the day's toil; and then at last, as the sun disappeared to

their left behind the islands of the Sea of Marmora, to where the
splendid panorama of the Bosphorus bathed in twilight lay at their
feet. There, by the waterside, the party broke up—all but those persons staying with Djavil going back to Constantinople in a steamboat
provided for their convenience by their host, and the others, including of course Hippy Rowan, returning to the Pacha's palace in his
excellency's steam-launch.

The scene returning home was beautiful indeed, but so familiar
to Colonel Rowan that the loveliness of what he saw could hardly
have been the sole and only cause of the deep feeling of melancholy
which stole over him as he walked the deck and heard the music of
the orchestra, which the others were taking back with them to Constantinople, growing fainter and fainter in the distance. It was quite
night, and the sea was very quiet, for after sundown no boat leaves
the Bosphorus, neither is any vessel allowed to enter therein before
the dawn; so that the only sound which broke the stillness, when
the music had died away in the distance, was the noise of the screw,
which, working in the phosphorescent waters, rolled out showers
and sheets of gold as the little steam-launch plodded, plodded, plodded on its course, cleaving and leaving on either side and behind
a way of liquid fire. Above were the heavens sparkling with stars,
below and around the sea of molten gold, while on either side on
the silent banks of the Bosphorus gleamed and streamed innumerable lights from the different harem windows, at some one of which
every now and then an inquisitive head would appear, peeping out
at the passing vessel. All Djavil's guests were tired; so after dinner, and
a little music and chatting, and some very harmless gambling, they
retired to rest much earlier than usual. Rowan being indeed glad
when the time came that, unobserved and alone, he could deliver
himself up wholly to his reflections, which, as we have said, happened
that night to be of a strangely melancholy complexion. His rooms
were on the ground floor, the windows indeed opening out on to
the garden which sloped down to the marble terrace bordering the
Bosphorus; and since it was to meditate rather than to sleep that
Rowan sought retirement, and as it was early and the night divine,
the colonel, when he had sent the faithful Adams to bed, lit a cigar
and went out, descending to the waterside to enjoy the view. Hardly
had he reached the terrace, however, when from the farther end of
it, which lay in shadow, emerged, crawling in the moonlight along
the white marble pavement, an awful figure, which he knew but too

well—that of Isaac Lebedenko the Moldavian, the man whom he had left but a few hours before nailed to a tree in the forest in Asia. As Rowan saw the man, the man saw him; and as Hippy stepped back and hurriedly felt in his pocket for his revolver, remembering, even as he did so, that he had left that useful weapon on his dressing-table, the Moldavian drew himself up and sprang towards his enemy, pulling, as he advanced, with one hand the muffler from his face, and disclosing with hideous distinctness in the moonlight the indescribable horror of that countenance of a monster not born of woman, while with the other he fumbled in his pocket.

"The only way!" he gasped, in lisping German—"the only way! But I am ready—glad; for I shall come to you now and you cannot escape me! See!" And so saying, and before Rowan could realise what was taking place, the man stabbed himself to the heart, and with a loud groan fell backwards into the waters of the Bosphorus, which closed over him.

Chapter III

"And you say you were not frightened?" exclaimed Bertonneux of the Œil de Bœuf.

Hippy Rowan shook his head and smiled. "No, of course not," he said. Then he added, lowering his voice lest the others should hear him, "Do you know, it's a strange thing *mon cher*, that never in my life have I known what fear is. It's no boast, of course, but a fact; and you can ask anyone who's been with me in danger. There are plenty of them about, for I began with Inkermann and only ended with Candahar, not to speak of innumerable little private adventures more or less unpleasant between times, like the one I've just been telling you about, in fact. You know me well enough to know that I'm neither a fool nor a coxcomb, and as a matter of fact this is not exactly courage, I fancy, but rather an absolute inability to entertain such a sentiment as fear. Just as some people are born blind and deaf and dumb."

The scene was an immense and lofty chamber, luxuriously furnished, half drawing-room and half smoking-room, in Tony Jeratczesco's house in Moldavia, in the Krapak Mountains, and the time about a month after the events had taken place recorded in the last chapter. It had been raining all day, as it only can rain in the Danubian principalities, and so the sportsmen had been unable to get

out: a particularly deplorable *contretemps*, seeing that, with the exception of the small contingent which had come on from the Bosphorus,
and which included Rowan, the French journalist, Lord Melrose, the
three very magnificent Cavaliers of the Guard from the shores of the
Neva, and Mr. Leonard P. Beacon, the guests of "Cheery and Cheeky,"
were wild, rough, and boisterous neighbouring magnates, many of
whom had never travelled beyond Bucharest, and none of whom
possessed any of those very rare and precious qualities of heart and
head, a combination of which in a fellow-captive can alone reconcile
us to the common chain. These boyars were indeed so inconceivably
rough and uncouth that Tony Jeratczesco greatly regretted having,
on the occasion of his taking possession of his property, conformed
to the almost feudally hospitable custom of the country, and invited
these loud-voiced Nimrods and their retainers to take up their residence under his roof-tree for such time as the sport in the neighbourhood might meet with their approval. As it was, however, the
mistake had been made: these strange beings had been asked and had
come, and the evil was past recall; and although at certain times, and
especially after dinner, and when the alcohol began to lift its voice,
the society of the wealthy barbarians became almost unendurable, it
had, of course, to be put up with and made the best of; all that Tony's
more civilised friends could do being, almost in self-defence, as it
were, to keep to themselves as much as was possible without risking
giving offence to their unpleasant fellow-guests by this reserve. The
house-party was composed entirely of men, which of course did not
add to the refinement of the gathering; and when, as at the beginning of this chapter, the tedium of a long and rainy day, thoroughly
saturated with alcohol and tobacco, had reached the hour preceding
midnight, the atmosphere of Jeratczesco's salon, either from an ethical
or from a purely social point of view, would assuredly have compared
unfavourably with that of most drawing-rooms in Mayfair.

To the French journalist Rowan had already told the story of his
horrible adventure with Isaac Lebedenko and of the man's suicide—
all of which events, together with minutes of what Maryx had said
about the Children of Judas, were found carefully noted down in the
colonel's diary after his death, from which source of information and
the testimony of Adams, the present authentic account of the strange
facts is taken;—but Mr. Leonard P. Beacon not having heard the
story before, Hippy had been prevailed upon to repeat it to him, the

question and answer with which this chapter opens being the immediate consequences of the telling of this tale.

Hippy had spoken in a low tone, to avoid attracting attention;
but he had not taken into consideration the boisterous nature of
his American auditor, who now exclaimed at the top of his voice—
"What! do you mean seriously to tell me, Rowan, that you have
never known what fear is? That you simply can't be frightened by
anything?"

Annoying as it was, under the circumstances, to have such a question put in so trumpet-tongued a fashion, Hippy plainly saw that the
American would insist upon a reply to his thundered query, and that
it would in nowise better matters to delay giving it.

"I do," said he simply; and then added, in a half-whisper, "I wish
you wouldn't yell so, Beacon."

But it was too late; the half-tipsy boyars, bored to death and eager
to seize upon any topic of conversation likely to furnish a pretext
for much violence of language, had heard the question and the
answer, and an uproar ensued which Jeratczesco was powerless to
quell, and in the course of which the amiability and good breeding
of Dick Rowan were both put to a severe test by the clumsy banter and coarsely expressed incredulity of these uncouth noblemen.
One gentleman especially, a certain Prince Valerian Eldourdza, who,
owing to the fact of his having been educated at a Lycée in Paris, was
looked upon as the Admirable Crichton of that part of Moldavia,
pressed Hippy very hard, plying him with most personal and impertinent questions as to his belief in a future life, future punishment,
the devil, and so forth, and at last, indeed, going so far as to solemnly
declare that not only did he not believe in Colonel Rowan's inability to experience terror, but that he would himself undertake, under
a penalty of £4,000, to frighten him. This somewhat offensive boast
had, in the first instance, fallen from Eldourdza's lips in the heat of
excitement, and probably without the speaker himself attaching any
very great meaning or importance to his words; but the statement
having been received with vociferous approval by the other boyars,
his highness had been constrained to repeat the bet, and the second
time give it a more specific form. "One hundred thousand francs,"
he repeated, bringing his very small and very unclean fist down on
the table with much violence, "that I frighten you, colonel, before
you leave here—that is, of course, always provided you're not leaving
at once."

"My friend is staying with me another month," interposed Jeratczesco rather angrily. "But I can't allow such bets to be made in my house, Eldourdza. I hate practical jokes—we have quite enough of that kind of folly in England."

"They're afraid already!" sneered a very unpleasant-looking old Moldavian statesman, all lip and nose, chewing at his cigar in the corner of his mouth after the fashion of a dog with a bone.

"You leave this to me, Tony," said Rowan to his host, speaking quickly, and in English; then, turning to Eldourdza—"Let's understand each other plainly, prince. What do you mean by fright? Of course you can startle me by jumping out from a dark corner, or any trick of that kind. I make no bet about that kind of thing, of course; but I'll bet you an even hundred thousand francs, if you like, or a hundred and fifty thousand francs, that you don't make me experience what is generally and by everyone understood by the word fright—a sentiment of fear, or of anything even remotely resembling fear. How shall we define it, for we must be clear on this point?"

"Hair standing on end and teeth chattering," suggested Mr. Leonard P. Beacon, who was greatly delighted at the turn affairs had taken, foreseeing an adventure and new experience of some kind.

"Exactly," replied Eldourdza, who had been consulting in a whisper with his friends, and absorbing yet another gobletful of champagne strongly laced with brandy. "Let those very words be used if you like—I'll bet you an even hundred and fifty thousand francs—two hundred thousand if you like" (Hippy nodded), "that before you leave this place, four weeks from today, you will be so frightened that your hair will stand on end, your teeth will chatter, and what's more, you'll call for help."

"Very well," assented Rowan, laughing, "C'est entendu; but I shan't make you go so far as that, my dear prince. I shall be quite ready to pay up if you do more than merely startle me in the way I spoke of just now—by some sudden noise, or jumping out at me, or some such silly prank. Anything even approaching fear, much less terror, of course, and I pay up at once. And," he added good-naturedly—for he was fond of winning money, and the certainty of this £8,000 was very pleasant to him—"luckily for you, Eldourdza, I happen to have the money to pay with if I lose. I was on every winner the last day at Baden—couldn't do wrong—and sent it all on to Gunzburg at once, where it is intact, for I didn't want to be tempted to gamble till I got to the Yacht Club."

And so this strange bet was made, and duly noted down with the approval of all, even Jeratczesco withdrawing his objection when he saw the very evident satisfaction with which the colonel regarded what he felt sure to be the only possible result of this absurd wager. But if HippyRowan had foreseen the wholly-unexpected way in which this waiting day by day, night after night, and hour by hour, for the surprise—of course of an apparently unpleasant nature—which Eldourdza and his friends must be preparing for him, had he, we say, foreseen the peculiar and unprecedented way in which this really absurd suspense was destined to gradually, and by almost imperceptible degrees, affect his nerves in the course of the next month, he would most assuredly have let the prince's silly wager pass unnoticed. And what made this never-absent feeling of care, of perpetual caution, of unceasing vigilance, the more acutely irksome to Hippy was, that these quite novel sensations could be ascribed but to one altogether disagreeable and detestable cause—namely, the advance of old age. His experience of life had told him that the constitution of a man who had lived as he had lived was apt to break down suddenly, no matter how robust it might be apparently; the supports, the foundation, which kept the structure in its place and seemingly firm and upright, having been little by little, and very gradually but very surely, removed in the course of years, the nights of which had been worn to very morning in the fatigue of pleasure, and the days of which had been scornful of repose. He had seen innumerable friends of his, apparently as strong and vigorous as himself, suddenly give way in this fashion—fall down like a house of cards, as it were, and be swept away into the outer darkness. Could it be owing to the approach of some such sudden and disastrous conclusion to his mundane affairs, that he found day by day, as the next four weeks wore on, his nerves, hitherto apparently of steel, becoming more and more unstrung by this suspense, the cause of which was in reality so utterly puerile and contemptible? This was very certainly not his first experience of suspense: he had been in danger of his life very often, and on a few occasions this danger had been imminent for a considerable period of time, and yet never could he recall having felt before this uneasiness of mind, this perpetual questioning of his heart, which now, while merely waiting for these boorish savages to play some more or less gruesome, and even perhaps dangerous, practical joke on him, he experienced. So it must be old age; it could be nothing else—old age, and the beginning, perhaps, of a general breaking-up of the system;

the first intimation, as it were, of the second and final payment being about to be required of him for those extravagances by Seine side already alluded to, those myrtles sacred to the sparrow-drawn goddess, those prolonged and oft -repeated saunters from midnight to dawn arm-in-arm with Bacchus and baccarat; such outriders of death's chariot. Rowan told himself, it must be that induced him, greatly to his own surprise, to waste so much of his time twisting and turning over in his mind all kinds of possible and impossible speculations as to how these wretched Moldavians were going to try and frighten him, led him to carefully examine his apartments every night before retiring to rest, see that his revolver had not been tampered with and was safely under his pillow, and finally, indeed, and just before the end, brought about so chronic a condition of nervous restlessness as to render his seeking that pillow for purposes of prolonged repose, a mockery.

Of course this very abnormal condition of mind, which in no-wise even remotely resembled fear and was one merely of perpetual watchfulness, was of very gradual growth, and Hippy Rowan was throughout the whole course of its development, until just before the end, quite sufficiently master of himself to conceal his feelings, not only from his friends, but even from his valet, the omniscient Adams; and the very visible change in the colonel's appearance and manner, which by and by came to be remarked, was ascribed by all—and in a great measure justly ascribed—to a very severe chill which he caught shortly after the night of the wager, and which confined him to the house, and indeed to his room, for many days. Neither Prince Eldourdza nor anyone else had made any even covert allusion, in Rowan's hearing, to the wager since the night on which it had been made and formally noted down; and this fact in itself, this studied silence, became in the course of time, and as Rowan's nervous irritability increased, a source of annoyance to him, and induced him at length suddenly one morning, when they were all at breakfast together, to himself boldly allude to the matter, which was becoming more and more constantly uppermost in his mind.

"Pardon me, prince," said he, smiling, and with well-assumed care-lessness, "if I allude to the matter of our wager, which you seem to have forgotten, for you have only ten days left now, and"—

"Plenty of time!" interrupted Eldourdza roughly. "Forgotten it? Not I—have I?" he continued, turning to his friends. "You know whether I have forgotten it or not!" Significant and sinister grins

and much shaking of heads in negation responded to this appeal—
a pantomime which excited the colonel's curiosity not a little.

"Well," said he, "I'm glad to hear it, for I shouldn't like to take your
money without your having had some semblance of a run for it. All I
want to tell you was this, and I feel sure you'll agree with what I now
say. Of course I've no idea what kind of prank you're going to play on
me to endeavour to frighten me, but no doubt it will be as horrible
and awful a thing as you can concoct, for I suppose you've no intention of making me a present of two hundred thousand francs."

"Certainly not!" laughed Prince Valerian; "if you get it at all you'll
have to pay dear for it, believe me."

"Very well," replied Hippy, "anything you like; but that's just what I
wanted to speak about. Of course I'm at your disposal to do anything
you like with, and to try and frighten in any way and every way
you can contrive; but you can easily understand that there must be
a limit to my endurance, otherwise you'd make me look like a fool.
What I mean is, that you're at perfect liberty, say, to send any ghost,
or vampire, or wild beast, or devil, or anything else you can think
of, to my room to try and frighten me, and for that purpose I am
glad to lend you all the aid in my power. As it is, I leave my door
unlocked every night now, as perhaps you know. But there must be
some limit to this—I mean that your endeavour to frighten me must
have some limit in time, and can't go on for ever. Suppose we put it
at one hour—for one hour let your ghost or devil do its worst; then
at the end of that time, if it has failed to frighten me, your goblin
will become merely a nuisance, and I think I shall be justified in
extinguishing it, don't you?"

"Most assuredly," replied Eldourdza. "In less than an hour: we don't
ask for an hour—half an hour will do; after half an hour you are
perfectly at liberty to do as you like—provided always," he added
grimly, "that by that time you are not half dead with fright."

"Very well, then," rejoined Hippy; "so that's understood. After half
an hour from the time your test, whatever it may be, begins, I shall be
free to use any means I care to adopt to put a stop to this test, provided by that time, of course, I have not felt anything even remotely
resembling alarm. As, in the event of your test being something really
offensive and disagreeable to me, I should probably use my revolver,
I thought it only fair to have this plainly understood, so that what is
really only a silly practical joke may not, by a misunderstanding, end
in a tragedy."

The prince nodded in acquiescence. "You are quite right," he said, "After half an hour do as you please. But you're mistaken in looking upon this as a practical joke, Colonel Rowan; it will be no joke, and may indeed, even against your will, end in a tragedy."

As may be readily imagined, these few mysterious words of menace from the man pledged to, in some way or other, cause him within ten days' time to experience the novel, but doubtless unpleasant, sensation of terror, did not tend to bring the colonel to a more restful state of mind; and his never-ending speculations as to what scheme these savages might perchance be planning wherewith to frighten him, began again after this conversation to torment his brain with renewed persistency. Of course, Eldourdza would do all he could to win his bet—not for the sake of the money, perhaps, for that could be nothing to him, but for the pleasure and delight of triumph; and, equally of course, at least so Hippy told himself, this desired fright the prince and his friends would only endeavour to bring about by some pseudo-supernatural agency, for they could hardly imagine that any of the vulgar dangers of life—say an attack of many adversaries, whether men or brutes, peril from water, fire, or what not, in fact, any of the thousand-and-one not uncommon evils which threaten human existence—could possibly affright so hardened and experienced a soldier and traveller as he was, a man whose record of perilous adventures was so well known. The supernatural, therefore, the terrors which owe their horror to the fact of their being inexplicable, the power of them unfathomable; the awful enemies which may be lurking crouched behind the last breath of life ready to spring upon us as the heart stops beating; such, or rather the semblance of such, would doubtless be alone the influences which these wild barbarians would seek to bring to bear upon his nerves to try them. And when this probability had been suggested to his imagination, Colonel Rowan began recalling to mind all the gruesome stories he had ever heard of about ghosts, hobgoblins and the like, his restlessness and nervous watchfulness (to which he only gave way when in the privacy of his own chamber of course) so increasing as the last ten days sped by, that at length Adams, who slept in the next room, remarking his master's condition, arranged, without of course the knowledge of anyone, to keep watch and ward over the colonel during these last few nights by means of an aperture high up in the wall, through which he could obtain a perfect view of his master's sleeping apartment, and see all that took place therein.

And thus it came to pass that, on the last night but two, Hippy never retired to rest until the dawn, having decided, after mature reflection, that no matter what absurd practical joke his friends might be going to play on him, he would cut a less ludicrous figure in his dressing-gown than in bed, and that it might indeed be advisable to be thus prepared to follow the tormenting masqueraders from his chamber to punish them elsewhere, and before the whole household, in the event of their conduct proving too outrageous. And so, after having as usual carefully examined every hole and cranny of his sleeping apartment (as the unobserved Adams from his peephole above very plainly saw him do), and lighted many tapers about the old-fashioned and vast chamber, and put many cheering logs upon the fire, the colonel lit a cigar and began pacing up and down the room, turning over of course in his mind the perpetual question, "What are these uncouth madmen going to do?" and the query for ever followed by the usual reflection, "They can do as they please, provided they don't, by their folly, make me look a fool." There would probably be the rattling of chains and bones, and some very cleverly-contrived apparition; and even, in fact, some real danger, perhaps, for these men were really perfect savages, who would stop at nothing to attain their end; and Hippy would certainly not have been surprised to have found a box of dynamite concealed beneath his bed. "Luckily, this is the last night but two," he said to himself; "and after all, this bet has taught me one thing I never so plainly realised before, and in a certain sense I have really lost the wager, for there is one thing I am afraid of, and very much afraid of, more and more afraid of every minute, and that is being made a fool of." Then he stopped in his perambulation and stared at himself in the looking-glass. Yes; he was certainly growing old: the grey hairs he cared nothing about—they were entirely insignificant, and the crows' feet and wrinkles were of no importance—they did not in the least annoy him; but the eyes, ah! the eyes were losing their light—that light that had disported itself over so many beautiful things, and for so many years, was now being withdrawn—going perhaps to join the fair and dear and dead, or indeed worse than dead, women who had inspired its most brilliant and most ardent scintillations. But then even a youthful face would look sad in so mystic a mirror—for it was very old and evidently Venetian, and had doubtless been in that room, in that castle, in that remote corner of Moldavia, for years, and seen perchance strange things, and was destined, (who could tell?) before three nights were over, to reflect images of even more fantastic terror than had ever darkened it before.

What a pity that this old looking-glass could not recall some of the most pleasant images that had been reflected in it in the long-ago to keep him company that night! If he stared at it long enough, would he not, perhaps, at length perceive far, far away, there in the most remote and distant and least-lighted corner of the room, the fair sad reflected face dimly advance of some Moldavian dame who had wept and kissed and loved and lost in the old days of the Hospodars?

> *"Les miroirs par les jours abrégés de Décembre*
> *Songent—telles les eaux captives—dans les chambres,*
> *Et leur mélancolie a pour causes lointaines*
> *Tant de visages doux fanés dans ces fontaines*
> *Qui s'y voyaient naguere embellis de sourires."*

Then, drawing up a comfortable arm-chair before the blazing logs, he seated himself, and taking up *Le Rouge et le Noir*, which he happened to find lying on the table by his side, ere long had read himself to sleep over the marvellous narrative of the vicissitudes of Julien Sorel, only awaking, indeed, when the

> "fair-faced sun,
> Killing the stars and dews and dreams and desolations of the night,"

was plainly visible through the curtains, and the noises of the awakening household warned him that another day had begun. Then he arose and went to bed, fondly believing that by this little comedy he was deceiving the omniscient Adams, who, as a matter of fact, perched on a step-ladder in the adjoining apartment, had kept an unceasing watch over his master's slumbers.

That day, Rowan's last day on earth, passed without any incident worthy of notice. Jeratczesco announced at breakfast that he had engaged a band of *laoutari*—gipsy minstrels—to enliven his friends, but that, as he only expected them to arrive late that night, his guests would not have the opportunity of enjoying their wild and delightful music until the morrow.

"I shall lodge them in your wing of the house, where they'll be quiet," explained Tony to Colonel Rowan, later on in the day, when they happened to be alone, "You know how beautiful some of these tzigane women are, and how jealously guarded by their men. I don't want a row here, and there's no knowing what mad folly Eldourdza and his friends might be up to when drunk."

And that the prudent Tony was quite justified in taking all precautionary measures to ensure peace and tranquillity during the sojourn of the gypsies beneath his roof, was amply proved that very night when they arrived late, for the Moldavian magnates, who, with Eldourdza at their head, would seem to have intentionally got drunk rather earlier than usual that evening, were only with the greatest difficulty restrained by their host from rushing out into the moonlit courtyard and embracing the women of the minstrel band, as they were seen and heard passing and chattering and singing on their way to their quarters. The arrival of these gypsies, and the prospect of the break which their performances would make in the monotony of the daily life at the chateau (which, by the way, all save the most enthusiastic sportsmen would have found intolerably tedious), greatly enlivened Hippy Rowan's spirits; and when he retired for the night—the last night but one of this absurd waiting for surprises, as he reminded himself with a smile—he opened his window and looked out across the quadrangle to the lights in the rooms occupied by the wandering musicians, wondering whether indeed this band contained any of those really beautiful women such as he remembered having remarked among the Strelna gypsy musicians of Moscow—women unlike any other to be found in any class or country in the world, and whose peculiar charm is as indescribable as it is indisputable, possessing as it does a power partaking of the supernatural, springing as it were from a fountain of fascination infernal. What a splendid night! And nearly Christmas too, the very season for ghostly masquerading, and—But hark! a woman's voice singing.

Hippy leaned out and listened. The voice was low and very sweet, though the woman singing was evidently engaged in some other occupation which absorbed her attention, for there would be careless pauses in her song, the words of which, in a Roumanian dialect, ran somewhat as follows:

> "Love shot his arrow o'er the sea,
> And all the waters leaped with joy,
> Lifting their foam-wreathed arms in glee,
> To bid the sunlight hold the boy;
> But the sun said
> 'My beams are shed
> To cheer with flowers the lonely dead.'"

Here the singing ceased for a moment, but presently a man's voice took up the song, singing in the same careless fashion, stopping every now and then—

"Death spread his pinions o'er the sea,
And all the waves with stormed-thrilled breath
In sobs besought the moon that she
Might break the tear-plumed wings of death.
But the moon cried
'My silver tide
Will only— '"

But here a merry burst of laughter interrupted the singer, and though for some time after Rowan could hear the voices of the gypsies laughing and talking, he could not distinguish what was being said, and there was no more singing.

"What a strange people!" murmured Rowan to himself, as he closed the window, "and what suitable neighbours to have on such a night as this, when at any moment now I may expect to see a cavalcade of ghosts come galloping into the room!"

Then the watchful Adams saw his master make his usual careful inspection of the room, seat himself by the fire, take up Stendhal again, and read himself to sleep, as on the previous night. Suddenly Rowan awoke, roused by a sound that stole into his ears very gradually and very gently, but which, when his drowsy faculties had understood its meaning, stirred them to instant activity—the sound of weeping. He sprang to his feet and looked around the room. He was alone; the apartment was brilliantly illuminated, thanks to two large lamps and several tapers in girandoles, and he could plainly see into the farthest corner: nobody—no animated creature was visible. He listened: not a sound broke the stillness of the night. He must have been dreaming. But no—hark! there it was again, the sound of weeping, of someone in great and bitter distress; it came from the corridor, and not far from his chamber door. Should he go and see what it was? Could this be any part of the Moldavians' masquerading? Surely not! Hardly would they begin their attempt to frighten a man by such heart-rending expressions of anguish, which could evoke but pity and compassion.

Again! Oh, what a wealth of woe! And a woman too; the long-drawn, gasping, tear-clogged suspiration was pitched in a key of peculiar pathos, which that treasury of divine tenderness, a woman's heart, alone can find to woo compassion. Again—yes, certainly a woman: could it perchance be one of the *laoutari*? The corridor led to the part of the house where they were sleeping, and so far as he knew they were the only women in the house except the servants. Surely Eldourdza had nothing to do with this, and even if he had, what then? Had not this drunken Moldavian boor already occupied his mind quite long enough with speculations as to what he might, and what he might not, be about to do? Let him do as he pleased, and what he liked, and go to the devil! There was a woman in terrible distress just outside his door, and he, Hippy Rowan, must go to her without delay—that was very clear.

So, taking his revolver in his hand in case of need, Rowan advanced to his door, opened it wide, and looked out into the sombre corridor; Adams, greatly frightened, watching his master the while and, having heard nothing, being at a loss to understand the colonel's conduct. Even as he opened the door Rowan saw that he had guessed aright, and that it was a woman who was giving utterance to these most pitiful and heart-rending expressions of anguish. There she lay, not very near his door after all, weeping bitterly, her face buried in her hands—lay prone as if she had been praying on her knees for mercy, and in a very agony of supplication had fallen forward. Rowan saw at once that those white and shapely hands must belong to a young woman, and so his voice assumed a tone of very special tenderness and compassion, as he said in the Roumanian dialect in which he had heard the gypsies singing—

"What is it, lady? Can I help you?"

The mourner, who apparently had not remarked the opening of the door, at the sound of Hippy's voice ceased her lamenting, and after a moment's pause slowly raised her head, withdrawing her hands from her face as she did so, and revealing to Rowan's astonished eyes the most faultlessly lovely countenance he had ever gazed upon in living woman. It was a youthful copy of the most perfect type of the Mater Dolorosa, and never, Rowan told himself, had he known, until he saw those tearful and uplifted eyes, the sweet and wondrous power that violets could lend to grief to stir compassion with; nor, till he noted the delicate oval of that face, all the poetic value and pathetic eloquence of form; nor, till he marked the quivering of those parted, perfect lips, with what resistless tenderness sorrow could light upon the very throne of kisses. That the woman was not a gypsy was very evident, for her skin was of the most fine and delicate fairness, and her hair, which fell in caressing curls over her forehead, of a soft and tender brown, and, moreover, her dress was entirely unlike that of a tzigane, both in colour and in form, being all black, and fashioned, so far as Rowan could see, as that of a member of some religious order, the beautiful face being, as it were, framed round about in a covering not unlike a cowl. Rowan had heard, he thought, of some sisterhood in the neighbourhood: perhaps this fair mourner belonged to such a community—at all events she was assuredly a very lovely woman, and it behoved him, both as a man of heart and as a man of taste, to console her in her sorrow. But to attain this desired end, of course the first and most necessary step would be to make himself understood, and that, apparently, he had not so far succeeded in doing.

The lustrous violet eyes looked at him, indeed, with startled surprise and fawn-like timidity, though there was assuredly nothing redoubtable in the kind aspect of Hippy's handsome face, and he had instinctively hidden the revolver in his pocket the moment he had seen the pathetic prostrate figure in the corridor; but beyond this half-frightened expression there was nothing to be recognised but sorrow in that lovely countenance, not the slightest indication that his words had conveyed to the mourner's mind any idea of sympathy and compassion. Again he addressed her, this time in no dialect, but in the purest Roumanian, and in a still more tender and sympathising tone than before, but the look of timid wonder in the sweet Madonna face remained unchanged. Then, feeling that the situation was becoming rather ludicrous, he said, this time speaking in German and beckoning towards the open door of his apartment—

"Lady, let me beg of you to tell me what troubles you! Come into my room and rest and warm yourself. Believe me, there is nothing I would not gladly do to be of service to you. You have only to command me; I am an Englishman, a gentleman, and a soldier—so you may trust me. Let me help you, lady; come, I beg of you."

Then, after a pause, and as the mourner neither spoke nor moved, Hippy bowed and, motioning her to follow him, walked slowly into his room, turning every now and then and repeating his gesture of invitation, she the while remaining upon her knees looking after him, indeed, but making no attempt to rise and follow.

Although Adams had at no time lost sight of his master, whose back, as he seemed to be engaged in conversation with some invisible person far down the corridor, had always been within the range of the faithful servant's vision, still it was with a feeling of great relief that he now saw the colonel come back into the room unharmed, although the expression of tenderness and pity in his master's face rather puzzled the man, as did also the colonel's conduct in turning when he had reached the fireplace and looking anxiously back towards the door, which he had left open behind him as if expecting and indeed longing for the arrival of some visitor. And at length, after the lapse of a few minutes—a delay which, though brief, the servant could plainly see his master bore impatiently—the longed-for visitor came; and slowly emerging from the darkness of the corridor with faltering steps, until at length she came to stand framed in the doorway, against one side of which, as if to support herself, she lightly placed a small white hand, Adams saw the slender black-robed figure of the sweet girl-mourner appear, and for the first time in his life was astonished, nay, astounded rather, for the marvellous resemblance in depth of tenderness, in purity of sorrow-hallowed loveliness, between this nocturnal lady visitor to his master, and the most inspired efforts of genius to depict the countenance of the Virgin Mother of God, so struck and so amazed the travelled and cultured valet, that he could hardly perhaps have been more filled with wonder had he actually seen a Madonna from a canvas, say, of Raphael, step down and stand before him clothed in flesh.

Perhaps some such fantastic idea of an incarnation of one of Raphael's Holy Virgins occurred to Rowan as he bowed low and advanced to welcome his fair visitor, for this time he addressed her in Italian, thanking her for the great honour she was doing him, making all kinds of graceful and very Italian protestations of sympathy and respect, and concluding a very pretty speech by begging her not to stay there on the threshold, but to come in and seat herself by the fire, adding that if his presence were in any way distasteful to her, he would at once withdraw and leave her in undisturbed possession of the room. But this attempt, clothed in the choicest Tuscan, to inspire confidence met with no greater measure of success than had attended its Roumanian and German predecessors. The sweetly-sorrowful lady stood on the threshold in the same timid attitude, staring at the colonel with no abatement in the tender melancholy of her face, but apparently in nowise understanding his words, and even indeed ignoring his gesture inviting her to enter and be seated.

What was to be done? He could hardly, of course, take this lovely girl-Madonna in his arms and drag her into his room by force, and yet it seemed intolerably absurd, and indeed impossible, to leave her

standing there in the doorway. Why had she come even to the threshold of his door, if she had not intended coming farther in the event
of her seeing nothing to alarm her? Of course, and beyond all doubt,
if he could only make her understand his sympathy and respect, and
that she need have no fear of him, she would come in and perhaps
tell him the cause of her distress and let him help her; and on the
other hand, knowing so many languages and even dialects and patois
as he did, it seemed almost impossible that he should not be able at
length to hit upon some form of speech by which he could convey
to this most perfect incarnate type of spiritual purity and loveliness
the expression of his devoted homage. So he started off on a wild
polyglottic steeplechase, making protestations of respect and sympathy and offers of aid and friendship in every language and dialect
he could remember, from his native English to the patois spoken by
the Jews in White Russia. But all to no purpose; and at length he was
constrained to pause and acknowledge that he was utterly defeated
and quite at the end of his tether, for although in the course of his
chatter his hands even had not been idle (for the horrible possibility
of this beautiful woman being a deaf mute had occurred to him),
nothing that his tongue or fingers could find to tell had been able to
bring the faintest gleam of recognition or even of curiosity to that
perfect face.

"You're very beautiful," said he at last, with a sigh, speaking in his
native English, the inability of his fair auditor to understand him possessing at least the meagre and thankless advantage of allowing him to
express his admiration in words no matter how impassioned, provided,
of course, he took care his face should not betray the significance
and ardour of his speech—"the most beautiful woman I think I ever
saw, but you're a beautiful riddle, and I don't know how to read you.
What language can you speak, I wonder? Only the language of love,
perhaps! Were I to kneel down there before you, or take you in my
arms and kiss you, in what language would you repulse me, or—?"

Here he paused, greatly surprised—were his eyes deceiving him,
or was at length a change stealing over the Madonna face, and the
timidity and sadness in it slowly giving place to an expression of some
brighter sentiment? That she could not understand the language he
was speaking he felt sure, for he had already addressed her in it and
his words had evidently failed utterly to convey any meaning to her
mind. But surely there was a difference now, and something he had
said, or some gesture he had made, or some expression in his face, had

been pleading to her, for the great shadow of melancholy was slowly passing from her face. But between the language, the English he had used before and that which he had just spoken, what difference was there? None, of course, save in the sense; then the words had been of respect and sympathy, now of love and tenderness. Could it be that by some marvellous intuition her woman's instinct had at once divined the more tender words? Or indeed was it not possible, nay, likely, that in speaking them he had involuntarily let their meaning be reflected in his eyes, and that she had read it there? But then such tenderness and affection were not displeasing to her, and this mask of the Madonna, this ideal type of womanly purity, could be lighted by the joy of love?

The thought set Rowan's blood coursing through his veins like fire, and made his heart beat as if he had been but twenty. He must see, and at once: he would speak to her again in words of affection, and let his eyes partly and by degrees interpret what he said, but carefully of course, and always guided by what he should see her eyes reply to his, lest he should offend her. And so he began telling this lovely woman in very low, quiet, and grave tones, but in words of great tenderness, how fair he found her, and as he spoke his eyes expressed the meaning of his words more and more clearly and ardently as he recognised with ever-growing delight that the Madonna face was being gradually illuminated and transfigured by joy, as word after word of ever-increasing passion, echoed in tender glances from his eyes, fell from his lips. And as he spoke he did not advance towards her, but only clasped his hands and stood still: far from her, looking at her in the doorway, while she, more and more visibly affected by his ever-growing emotion, first withdrew her hand from the side of the door where she had leant it, and pushed back the cowl from her face a little, still further disclosing, by so doing, the wavy wealth of soft brown curls, and then, as the violet eyes became by degrees lighted with great joy and the sweet lips melted to a smile of ineffable rapture, clasped both hands together just beneath her cheek in an attitude of girlish and innocent delight.

So she stood until the fervour of Rowan's words and voice and eyes rose to an ecstasy of passion, and then leaning forward her head, not indeed to hide the sweet blushes which were rising to her cheeks, but as a child eager to rush to a beloved embrace, and her eyes answering the ardour she read in those she gazed into, she half stretched forth her arms as if her longing to twine them in a caress were but restrained by maiden bashfulness. Rowan saw the gesture, stepped forward, opened wide his arms, and the girl–Madonna rushed to his embrace, nestling her blushing face upon his neck, as in a rapture of fondness he clasped her to his bosom.

At the same moment a terrible cry rang through the room and through the house, waking the tziganes, who sprang from their beds in mad terror, and startling the stupid Moldavians, who, despairing of really frightening Rowan, had decided on merely making him look a fool, and were at that very moment creeping up the staircase, dressed in absurd costumes and armed with monster squirts and all kinds of grotesque instruments—the cry of a strong man in an agony of terror; and the horrified Adams saw his master hurl the woman from him with great violence, snatch his revolver from his pocket, discharge three chambers of it at her in quick succession, and then reel and fall forward on his face, the woman rising from the floor apparently unhurt, and gliding from the apartment by the still open door.

When Adams reached his master's side he found him quite dead, and the body presenting two most remarkable peculiarities: first, a very strong odour of musk, and, secondly, on the neck three small wounds shaped like three X's joined together.

The medical man, a German, who was immediately called in, ascribed the death of Colonel Rowan to aneurism of the heart, and declined to attach the least importance to the three small wounds or bites on the neck, the post-mortem examination proving that, so far as the cause of death was concerned, the physician was right in his conjecture.

As for the strange lady with the Madonna face, Adam was far too shrewd a man of the world to make known the extraordinary circumstance to everyone. He told Tony Jeratczcsco, and inquiries were made, but no such person had been seen or heard of, and so the matter dropped, and it is only within the last few months that Mr. Adams, now retired from his delicate and difficult profession of valet, and living in the neighbourhood of Newmarket, could be prevailed upon to give a detailed account of all the strange facts connected with the death of his master, show Hippy Rowan's diary, and complete his story by producing a photograph, which he himself had taken of the dead man's neck, on which is plainly visible the imprint of the Kiss of Judas.

The Crimson Weaver

R. Murray Gilchrist

Robert Murray Gilchrist (1867–1917) was a poet, novelist, and playwright of Scottish descent, though he lived most of his life in his beloved Derbyshire. That is the setting for much of his later work, and though full of atmosphere, little of it involves the supernatural. But early in his career, as he was establishing himself, he immersed himself in the decadent literary movement that so epitomized the 1890s, and produced a singular volume of strange tales, The Stone Dragon and Other Tragic Romances, *published in 1894. Critic and literary historian Everett Bleiler has described the stories as "probably as close to Beardsley in prose as one can get." The following story was written later and appeared in that flagship magazine of the movement,* The Yellow Book, *for July 1895, but remained uncollected for over a hundred years. This was where the vampire entered the phantasmagoric.*

The Crimson Weaver

R. Murray Gilchrist

My Master and I had wandered from our track and lost ourselves on the side of a great "edge." It was a two-days' journey from the Valley of the Willow Brakes, and we had roamed aimlessly; eating at hollow-echoing inns where grey-haired mistresses ministered, and sleeping side by side through the dewless midsummer nights on beds of fresh-gathered heather.

Beyond a single-arched wall-less bridge that crossed a brown stream whose waters leaped straight from the upland, we reached the Domain of the Crimson Weaver. No sooner had we reached the key-stone when a beldam, wrinkled as a walnut and bald as an egg, crept from a cabin of turf and osier and held out her hands as a warning.

"Enter not the Domain of the Crimson Weaver!" she shrieked. "One I loved entered.—I am here to warn men. Behold, I was beautiful once!"

She tore her ragged smock apart and discovered the foulness of her bosom, where the heart pulsed behind a curtain of livid skin. My Master drew money from his wallet and scattered it on the ground.

"She is mad," he said. "The evil she hints cannot exist. There is no fiend."

So we passed on, but the bridge-keeper took no heed of the coins. For awhile we heard her bellowed sighs issuing from the openings of her den.

Strangely enough, the tenour of our talk changed from the moment that we left the bridge. He had been telling me of the Platonists, but when our feet pressed the sun-dried grass I was impelled to question him of love. It was the first time I had thought of the matter.

"How does passion first touch a man's life?" I asked, laying my hand on his arm.

His ruddy colour faded, he smiled wryly.

"You divine what passes in my brain," he replied. "I also had begun to meditate. . . . But I may not tell you. . . . In my boyhood—I was scarce older than you at the time—I loved the true paragon. 'Twere sacrilege to speak of the birth of passion. Let it suffice that ere I tasted of wedlock the woman died, and her death sealed for ever the door of that chamber of my heart. . . . Yet, if one might see therein, there is an altar crowned with ever-burning tapers and with wreaths of unwithering asphodels."

By this time we had reached the skirt of a yew-forest, traversed in every direction by narrow paths. The air was moist and heavy, but ever and anon a light wind touched the tree-tops and bowed them, so that the pollen sank in golden veils to the ground.

Everywhere we saw half-ruined fountains, satyrs vomiting senilely, nymphs emptying wine upon the lambent flames of dying phoenixes, creatures that were neither satyrs nor nymphs, nor gryphins, but grotesque adminglings of all, slain by one another, with water gushing from wounds in belly and thigh.

At length the path we had chosen terminated beside an oval mere that was surrounded by a colonnade of moss-grown arches. Huge pike quivered on the muddy bed, crayfish moved sluggishly amongst the weeds.

There was an island in the middle, where a leaden Diana, more compassionate than a crocodile, caressed Actæon's horns ere delivering him to his hounds. The huntress' head and shoulders were white with the excrement of a crowd of culvers that moved as if entangled in a snare.

Northward an avenue rose for the space of a mile, to fall abruptly before an azure sky. For many years the yew-mast on the pathway had been undisturbed by human foot; it was covered with a crust of greenish lichen.

My Master pressed my fingers. "There is some evil in the air of this place," he said. "I am strong, but you—you may not endure. We will return."

"'Tis an enchanted country," I made answer, feverishly. "At the end of yonder avenue stands the palace of the sleeping maiden who awaits the kiss. Nay, since we have pierced the country thus far, let us not draw back. You are strong, Master—no evil can touch us."

So we fared to the place where the avenue sank, and then our eyes fell on the wondrous sight of a palace, lying in a concave pleasaunce, all treeless, but so bestarred with fainting flowers, that neither blade of grass nor grain of earth was visible.

Then came a rustling of wings above our heads, and looking sky-wards I saw flying towards the house a flock of culvers like unto those that had drawn themselves over Diana's head. The hindmost bird dropped its neck, and behold it gazed upon us with the face of a mannikin!

"They are charmed birds, made thus by the whim of the Princess," I said.

As the birds passed through the portals of a columbary that crowned a western tower, their white wings beat against a silver bell that glistened there, and the whole valley was filled with music.

My Master trembled and crossed himself. "In the name of our Mother," he exclaimed, "let us return. I dare not trust your life here."

But a great door in front of the palace swung open, and a woman with a swaying walk came out to the terrace. She wore a robe of crimson worn into tatters at skirt-hem and shoulders. She had been forewarned of our presence, for her face turned instantly in our direction. She smiled subtly, and her smile died away into a most tempting sadness.

She caught up such remnants of her skirt as trailed behind, and strutted about with the gait of a peacock. As the sun touched the glossy fabric I saw eyes inwrought in deeper hue.

My Master still trembled, but he did not move, for the gaze of the woman was fixed upon him. His brows twisted and his white hair rose and stood erect, as if he viewed some unspeakable horror.

Stooping, with sidelong motions of the head, she approached; bringing with her the smell of such an incense as when amidst East-ern herbs burns the corse. . . . She was perfect of feature as the Diana, but her skin was deathly white and her lips fretted with pain.

She took no heed of me, but knelt at my Master's feet—a Magdalene before an impregnable priest.

"Prince and Lord, Tower of Chastity, hear!" she murmured. "For lack of love I perish. See my robe in tatters!"

He strove to avert his face, but his eyes still dwelt upon her. She half rose and shook nut-brown tresses over his knees.

Youth came back in a flood to my Master. His shrivelled skin filled out; the dying sunlight turned to gold the whiteness of his hair. He would have raised her had I not caught his hands. The anguish of foreboding made me cry:

"One forces roughly the door of your heart's chamber. The wreaths whither, the tapers bend and fall."

He grew old again. The Crimson Weaver turned to me.

"O marplot!" she said laughingly, "think not to vanquish me with folly. I am too powerful. Once that a man enter my domain he is mine."

But I drew my Master away.

"'Tis I who am strong," I whispered. "We will go hence at once. Surely we may find our way back to the bridge. The journey is easy."

The woman, seeing that the remembrance of an old love was strong within him, sighed heavily, and returned to the palace. As she reached the doorway the valves opened, and I saw in a distant chamber beyond the hall an ivory loom with a golden stool.

My Master and I walked again on the track we had made in the yew-mast. But twilight was falling, and ere we could reach the pool of Diana all was in utter darkness; so at the foot of a tree, where no anthill rose, we lay down and slept.

Dreams came to me—gorgeous visions from the romances of old. Everywhere I sought vainly for a beloved. There was the Castle of the Ebony Dwarf, where a young queen reposed in the innermost casket of the seventh crystal cabinet; there was the Chamber of Gloom, where Lenore danced, and where I groped for ages around columns of living flesh; there was the White Minaret, where twenty-one princesses poised themselves on balls of burnished bronze; there was Melisandra's arbour, where the sacred toads crawled over the enchanted cloak.

Unrest fretted me; I woke in spiritual pain. Dawn was breaking—a bright yellow dawn, and the glades were full of vapours.

I turned to the place where my Master had lain. He was not there. I felt with my hands over his bed: it was key-cold. Terror of my loneliness overcame me, and I sat with covered face.

On the ground near my feet lay a broken riband, whereon was strung a heart of chrysolite. It enclosed a knot of ash-coloured hair—hair of the girl my Master had loved.

The mists gathered together and passed sunwards in one long many-cornered veil. When the last shred had been drawn into the great light, I gazed along the avenue, and saw the topmost bartizan of the Crimson Weaver's palace.

It was midday ere I dared start on my search. The culvers beat about my head. I walked in pain, as though giant spiders had woven about my body.

On the terrace strange beasts—dogs and pigs with human limbs,—tore ravenously at something that lay beside the balustrade. At sight of me they paused and lifted their snouts and bayed. Awhile afterwards the culvers rang the silver bell, and the monsters dispersed hurriedly amongst the drooping blossoms of the pleasaunce, and where they swarmed I saw naught but a steaming sanguine pool.

I approached the house and the door fell open, admitting me to a chamber adorned with embellishments beyond the witchery of art. There I lifted my voice and cried eagerly: "My Master, my Master, where is my Master?" The alcoves sent out a babble of echoes, blended together like a harp-cord on a dulcimer: "My Master, my Master, where is my Master? For the love of Christ, where is my Master?" The echo replied only, "Where is my Master?"

Above, swung a globe of topaz, where a hundred suns gambolled. From its center, a convoluted horn, held by a crimson cord, sank lower and lower. It stayed before my lips and I blew therein, and heard the sweet voices of youth chant with one accord.

"Fall open, oh doors: fall open and show the way to the princess!"

Ere the last of the echoes had died a vista opened, and at the end of an alabaster gallery I saw the Crimson Weaver at her loom. She had doffed her tattered robe for one new and lustrous as freshly drawn blood. And marvellous as her beauty had seemed before, its wonder was now increased a hundredfold.

She came towards me with the same stately walk, but there was now a lightness in her demeanour that suggested the growth of wings.

Within arm's length she curtseyed, and curtseying showed me the firmness of her shoulders, the fulness of her breast. The sight brought no pleasure: my cracking tongue appealed in agony.

"My Master, where is my Master?"

She smiled happily. "Nay do not trouble. He is not here. His soul talks with the culvers in the cote. He has forgotten you. In the night we supped, and I gave him of Nepenthe."

"Where is my Master? Yesterday he told me of the shrine in his heart—of ever-fresh flowers—of a love dead yet living."

Her eyebrows curved mirthfully.

"'Tis foolish boys' talk," she said. "If you sought till the end of time you would never find him—unless I chose. Yet—if you buy of me—myself to name the price."

I looked around hopelessly at the unimaginable riches of her home. All that I have is this Manor of the Willow Brakes—a moorish park, an ancient house where the thatch gapes and the casements swing loose.

"My possessions are pitiable," I said, "but they are all yours. I give all to save him."

"Fool! fool!" she cried. "I have no need of gear. If I but raise my hand, all the riches of the world fall to me. 'Tis not what I wish for."

Into her eyes came such a glitter as the moon makes on the moist skin of a sleeping snake. The firmness of her lips relaxed; they grew child-like in their softness. The atmosphere became almost tangible: I could scarce breathe.

"What is it? All that I can do, if it be no sin."

"Come with me to my loom," she said, "and if you do the thing I desire you shall see him. There is no evil in't—in past times kings have sighed for the same."

So I followed slowly to the loom, before which she had seated herself, and watched her deftly passing crimson thread over crimson thread.

She was silent for a space, and in that space, her beauty fascinated me, so that I was no longer master of myself.

"What you wish for I will give, even if it be life."

The loom ceased. "A kiss of the mouth, and you shall see him who passed in the night."

She clasped her arms around my neck and pressed my lips. For one moment heaven and earth ceased to be; but there was one paradise, where we were sole governours. . . . .

Then she moved back and drew aside the web and showed me the head of my Master, and the bleeding heart whence a crimson cord unravelled into many threads.

"I wear men's lives," the woman said. "Life is necessary to me, or even I—who have existed from the beginning—must die. But yesterday I feared the end, and he came. His soul is not dead—'tis truth that it plays with my culvers."

I fell back.

"Another kiss," she said. "Unless I wish, there is no escape for you. Yet you may return to your home, though my power over you shall never wane. Once more—lip to lip."

I touched against the wall like a terrified dog. She grew angry; her eyes darted fire.

"A kiss," she cried, "for the penalty!"

My poor Master's head, ugly and cadaverous, glared from the loom. I could not move.

The Crimson Weaver lifted her skirt, uncovering feet shapen as those of a vulture. I fell prostrate. With her claws she fumbled about the flesh of my breast. Moving away she bade me pass from her sight. . . .

So, half-dead, I lie here at the Manor of the Willow Brakes, watching hour by hour the bloody clew ever unwinding from my heart and passing over the western hills to the Palace of the Siren.

The Woman With the "Oily Eyes"

Dick Donovan

*Dick Donovan, or to give him his real name, James Muddock (1843–1934)—
though he later called himself Joyce Emerson Preston Muddock—was a
journeyman writer. He produced scores of books—93 by Richard Dalby's
count—some of which were bestsellers. These were almost all the ones under
the Donovan alias and were almost all stories of crime and detection. Indeed
Donovan—which was the name of Muddock's detective as well as the alias—
rose to fame at the same time as Conan Doyle's Sherlock Holmes, starting
with the collection* The Man-Hunter *in 1888, and for a while Donovan's
popularity was close to that of Holmes. The* Strand *even ran a series of
Donovan's "Romances from a Detective's Case-Book" alongside the Holmes
stories in 1892. Now and then Muddock would turn to a story of the supernatural, frequently over melodramatic and suitably bloodthirsty, but at times
he would temper this and produce more thoughtful, even insightful stories.
One such is the following, included in his now very rare 1899 collection,*
Tales of Terror, *which was reissued as* The Corpse Light and Other
Tales of Terror *a hundred years later.*

The Woman With the "Oily Eyes"

The Story as told by Dr. Peter Haslar, F.R.C.S. LOND.

Dick Donovan

ALTHOUGH OFTEN urged to put into print the remarkable story which follows I have always strenuously refused to do so, partly on account of personal reasons and partly out of respect for the feelings of the relatives of those concerned. But after much consideration I have come to the conclusion that my original objections can no longer be urged. The principal actors are dead. I myself am well stricken in years, and before very long must pay the debt of nature which is exacted from everything that lives.

Although so long a time has elapsed since the grim tragedy I am about to record, I cannot think of it even now without a shudder. The story of the life of every man and woman is probably more or less a tragedy, but nothing I have ever heard of can compare in ghastly, weird horror with all the peculiar circumstances of the case in point. Most certainly I would never have put pen to paper to record it had it not been from a sense of duty. Long ago certain garbled versions crept into the public journals, and though at the time I did not consider it desirable to contradict them, I do think now that the moment has come when I, the only living being fully acquainted with the facts, should make them known, otherwise lies will become history, and posterity will accept it as truth. But there is still another reason I may venture to advance for breaking the silence of years. I think in the interest of science the case should be recorded. I have not always held this view, but when a man bends under the weight of years, and he sniffs the mould of his grave, his ideas undergo a complete change, and the opinions of his youth are not the opinions of his old age. There may be exceptions to this, but I fancy they must be very few. With these preliminary remarks I will plunge at once into my story.

It was the end of August 1857 that I acted as best man at the wedding of my friend Jack Redcar, C.E. It was a memorable year, for our hold on our magnificent Indian Empire had nearly been shaken loose by a mutiny which had threatened to spread throughout the whole of India. At the beginning of 1856 I had returned home from India after a three years' spell. I had gone out as a young medico in the service of the H.E.I.C., but my health broke down and I was compelled to resign my appointment. A year later my friend Redcar, who had also been in the Company's service as a civil engineer, came back to England, as his father had recently died and left him a modest fortune. Jack was not only my senior in years, but I had always considered him my superior in every respect. We were at a public school together, and both went up to Oxford, though not together, for he was finishing his final year when I was a freshman.

Although erratic and a bit wild he was a brilliant fellow and while I was considered dull and plodding, and found some difficulty in mastering my subjects, there was nothing he tackled that he failed to succeed in, and come out with flying colours. In the early stage of our acquaintance he made me his fag, and patronised me, but that did not last long. A friendship sprang up. He took a great liking to me, why I know not; but it was reciprocated, and when he got his Indian appointment I resolved to follow, and by dint of hard work, and having a friend at court, I succeeded in obtaining my commission in John Company's service. Jack married Maude Vane Tremlett, as sweet a woman as ever drew God's breath of life. If I attempted to describe her in detail I am afraid it might be considered that I was exaggerating, but briefly I may say she was the perfection of physical beauty. Jack himself was an exceptionally fine fellow. A brawny giant with a singularly handsome face. At the time of his wedding he was thirty or thereabouts, while Maude was in her twenty-fifth year. There was a universal opinion that a better matched couple had never been brought together. He had a masterful nature; and nevertheless was kind, gentle, and manly to a degree.

It may be thought that I speak with some bias and prejudice in Jack's favour, but I can honestly say that at the time I refer to he was as fine a fellow as ever figured as hero in song or story. He was the pink of honour, and few who really knew him but would have trusted him with their honour, their fortunes, their lives. This may be strong, but I declare it's true, and I am the more anxious to emphasise it because his after life was in such marked contrast, and he presents a study in psychology that is not only deeply interesting, but extraordinary.

The wedding was a really brilliant affair, for Jack had troops of friends, who vied with each other in marking the event in a becoming manner, while his bride was idolised by a doting household. Father and mother, sisters and brothers, worshipped her. She was exceedingly well connected. Her father held an important Government appointment, and her mother came from the somewhat celebrated Yorkshire family of the Kingscotes. Students of history will remember that a Colonel Kingscote figured prominently and honourably as a royalist during the reign of the unfortunate Charles I.

No one who was present on that brilliant August morning of 1857, when Jack Redcar was united in the bonds of wedlock to beautiful Maude Tremlett, would have believed it possible that such grim and tragic events would so speedily follow. The newly-married pair left in the course of the day for the Continent, and during their honeymoon I received several charming letters from Jack, who was not only a diligent correspondent, but also possessed a power of description and a literary style that made his letters delightful reading. Another thing that marked this particular correspondence was the unstilted—I may almost say florid—praise he bestowed upon his wife. To demonstrate what I mean, here is a passage from one of his letters:—

"I wish I had command of language sufficiently eloquent to speak of my darling Maude as she should be spoken of. She has a perfectly angelic nature; and though it may be true that never a human being was yet born without faults, for the life of me I can find none in my sweet wife. Of course you will say, old chap, that this is honeymoon gush, but, upon my soul, it isn't. I am only doing scant justice to the dear woman who has linked her fate with mine. I have sometimes wondered what I have done that the gods should have blest me in such a manner. For my own part, I don't think I was deserving of so much happiness, and I assure you I am happy—perfectly, deliciously happy. Will it last? Yes, I am sure it will. Maude will always be to me what she is now, a flawless woman; a woman with all the virtues that turn women into angels, and without one of the weaknesses or one of the vices which too often mar an otherwise perfect feminine character. I hope, old boy, that if ever you marry, the woman you choose will be only half as good as mine."

Had such language been used by anyone else I might have been disposed to add a good deal more than the proverbial pinch of salt before swallowing it. But, as a matter of fact, Jack was not a mere gusher. He had a thoroughly practical, as distinguished from a sentimental, mind, and he was endowed with exceptionally keen powers of observation. And so, making all the allowances for the honeymoon romance I was prepared to accept my friend's statement as to the merits of his wife without a quibble. Indeed, I knew her to be a most charming lady, endowed with many of the qualities which give the feminine nature its charm. But I would even go a step farther than that, and declare that Mrs. Redcar was a woman in ten thousand. At that time I hadn't a doubt that the young couple were splendidly matched, and it seemed to me probable that the future that stretched before them was not likely to be disturbed by any of the common-place incidents which seem inseparable from most lives, I regarded Jack as a man of such high moral worth that his wife's happiness was safe in his keeping. I pictured them leading an ideal, poetical life—a life freed from all the vulgar details which blight the careers of so many people—a life which would prove a blessing to themselves as well as a joy to all with whom they had to deal.

When they started on their tour Mr. and Mrs. Redcar anticipated being absent from England for five or six weeks only, but for several reasons they were induced to prolong their travels, and thus it chanced I was away when they returned shortly before Christmas of the year of their marriage. My own private affairs took me to America. As a matter of fact a relative had died leaving me a small property in that country, which required my personal attention; the consequence was I remained out of England for nearly three years.

For the first year or so Jack Redcar wrote to me with commend-able regularity. I was duly apprised of the birth of a son and heir. This event seemed to put the crown upon their happiness; but three months later came the first note of sorrow. The baby died, and the doting parents were distracted. Jack wrote:—

My poor little woman is absolutely prostrated, but I tell her we were getting too happy, and this blow has been dealt to remind us that human existence must be checked in order that we may appreciate more fully the supreme joy of that after-life which we are told we may gain for the striving. This, of course, is a pretty sentiment, but the loss of the baby mite has hit me hard. Still, Maude is left to me, and she is such a splendid woman, that I ought to feel I am more than blest.

This was the last letter I ever received from Jack, but his wife wrote at odd times. Hers were merely gossipy little chronicles of pass-ing events, and singularly enough she never alluded to her husband, although she wrote in a light, happy vein. This set me wondering, and when I answered her I never failed to inquire about her husband. I continued to receive letters from her, though at long intervals, down to the month of my departure from America, two years later.

I arrived in London in the winter, and an awful winter it was. London was indeed a city of dreadful night. Gloom and fog were everywhere. Everybody one met looked miserable and despondent. Into the public houses and gin palaces such of the poor as could scratch a few pence together crowded for the sake of the warmth and light. But in the streets sights were to be seen which made one doubt if civilisation is the blessing we are asked to believe it. Starving men, women and children, soaked and sodden with the soot-laden fog, prowled about in the vain hope of finding food and shelter. But the well to-do passed them with indifference, too intent on their own affairs, and too wrapped in self-interests to bestow thought upon the great city's pariahs.

Immediately after my arrival I penned a brief note to Jack Redcar, giving him my address, and saying I would take an early opportunity of calling, as I was longing to feel once more the hearty, honest grip of his handshake. A week later a note was put into my hand as I was in the very act of going out to keep an appointment in the city. Recognising Mrs. Redcar's handwriting I tore open the envelope, and read, with what feelings may be best imagined, the following lines:—

For God's sake come and see me at once. I am heart-broken and am going mad. You are the only friend in the world to whom I feel I can appeal. Come to me, in the name of pity.
"Maude Redcar."

I absolutely staggered as I read these brief lines, which were so pregnant with mystery, sorrow, and hopelessness. What did it all mean? To me it was like a burst of thunder from a cloudless summer sky. Something was wrong, that was certain; what that something was I could only vaguely guess at. But I resolved not to remain long in suspense. I put off my engagement, important as it was, and hailing a hansom directed the driver to go to Hampstead, where the Redcars had their residence.

The house was detached and stood in about two acres of ground, and I could imagine it being a little Paradise in brilliant summer weather; but it seemed now in the winter murk, as if a heavy pall of sorrow and anguish enveloped it.

I was shown into an exquisitely furnished drawing-room by an old and favoured woman, who answered my knock at the door. She gave me the impression that she was a sullen, deceptive creature, and I was at a loss to understand how such a woman could have found service with my friends—the bright and happy friends of three years ago. When I handed her my card to convey to Mrs. Redcar she impertinently turned it over, and scrutinised it, and fixed her cold bleared grey eyes on me, so that I was induced to say peremptorily, "Will you be good enough to go to your mistress at once and announce my arrival?"

"I ain't got no mistress," she growled. "I've got a master"; and with this cryptic utterance she left the room.

I waited a quarter of an hour, then the door was abruptly opened, and there stood before me Mrs. Redcar, but not the bright, sweet, radiant little woman of old. A look of premature age was in her face. Her eyes were red with weeping, and had a frightened, hunted expression. I was so astounded that I stood for a moment like one dumbfounded; but as Mrs. Redcar seized my hand and shook it, she gasped in a nervous spasmodic way:

"Thank God, you have come! My last hope is in you."

Then, completely overcome by emotion, she burst into hysterical sobbing, and covered her face with her handkerchief.

My astonishment was still so great, the unexpected had so completely paralysed me for the moment, that I seemed incapable of action. But of course this spell quickly passed, and I regained my self-possession.

"How is it I find this change?" I asked. It was a natural question, and the first my brain shaped.

"It's the work of a malignant fiend," she sobbed.

This answer only deepened the mystery, and I began to think that perhaps she was literally mad. Then suddenly, as if she divined my thoughts, she drew her handkerchief from her face, motioned me to be seated, and literally flung herself on to a couch.

"It's an awful story," she said, in a hoarse, hollow voice, "and I look to you, and appeal to you, and pray to you to help me."

"You can rely upon my doing anything that lies in my power." I answered. "But tell me your trouble. How is Jack? Where is he?"

"In her arms, probably," she exclaimed between her teeth; and she twisted her handkerchief up rope-wise and dragged it backward and forward through her hand with an excess of desperate, nervous energy. Her answer gave me a keynote. She had become a jealous and embittered woman. Jack had swerved from the path of honour, and allowed himself to be charmed by other eyes to the neglect of this woman whom he had described to me as being angelic. Although her beauty was now a little marred by tears and sorrow, she was still very beautiful and attractive, and had she been so disposed she might have taken an army of men captive. She saw by the expression on my face that her remark was not an enigma to me, and she added quickly: "Oh, yes, it's true, and I look to you, doctor, to help me. It is an awful, dreadful story, but, mind you, I don't blame Jack so much; he is not master of himself. This diabolical creature has enslaved him. She is like the creatures of old that one reads about. She is in possession of some devilish power which enables her to destroy men body and soul."

"Good God! this is awful," I involuntarily ejaculated; for I was aghast and horror-stricken at the revelation. Could it be possible that my brilliant friend, who had won golden opinions from all sorts and conditions of men, had fallen from his pedestal to wallow in the mire of sinfulness and deception.

"It is awful," answered Mrs. Redcar, "I tell you, doctor, there is something uncanny about the whole business. The woman is an unnatural woman. She is a she-devil. And from my heart I pity and sorrow for my poor boy."

"Where is he now?" I asked.

"In Paris with her."

"How long has this been going on?"

"Since a few weeks after our marriage."

"Good heavens, you don't say so?"

"You may well look surprised, but it's true. Three weeks after our marriage Jack and I were at Wiesbaden. As we were going downstairs to dinner one evening, we met this woman coming up. A shudder of horror came over me as I looked at her, for she had the most extraordinary eyes I have ever seen. I clung to my husband in sheer fright, and I noted that he turned and looked at her, and she also turned and looked at him.

" 'What a remarkable woman,' he muttered strangely, so strangely that it was as if some other voice was using his lips. Then he broke into a laugh, and, passing his arm round my waist, said: 'Why, my dear little woman, I believe you are frightened.'

" 'I am,' I said; 'that dreadful creature has startled me more than an Indian cobra would have done.'

"'Well, upon my word,' said Jack, 'I must confess she is a strange-looking being. Did ever you see such eyes? Why, they make one think of the fairy-books and the mythical beings who flit through their pages.'

"During the whole of the dinner-time that woman's face haunted me. It was a strong, hard-featured, almost masculine face, every line of which indicated a nature that was base, cruel, and treacherous. The thin lips, the drawn nostrils, the retreating chin, could never be associated with anything that was soft, gentle, or womanly. But it was the eyes that were the wonderful feature—they absolutely seemed to exercise some magic influence; they were oily eyes that gleamed and glistened, and they seemed to have in them that sinister light which is peculiar to the cobra, and other poisonous snakes. You may imagine the spell and influence they exerted over me when, on the following day, I urged my husband to leave Wiesbaden at once, notwithstanding that the place was glorious in its early autumn dress, and was filled with a fashionable and light-hearted crowd. But my lightest wish then was law to Jack, so that very afternoon we were on our way to Homberg, and it was only when Wiesbaden was miles behind me that I began to breathe freely again.

"We had been in Homberg a fortnight, and the incident of Wiesbaden had passed from my mind, when one morning, as Jack and I were on our way from the Springs, we came face to face with the woman with the oily eyes. I nearly fainted, but she smiled a hideous, cunning, cruel smile, inclined her head slightly in token of recognition, and passed on. I looked at my husband. It seemed to me that he was unusually pale, and I was surprised to see him turn and gaze after her, and she had also turned and was gazing at us. Not a word was uttered by either of us, but I pressed my husband's arm and we walked rapidly away to our apartments.

"'It's strange,' I remarked to Jack as we sat at breakfast, 'that we should meet that awful woman again.'

"'Oh, not at all,' he laughed. 'You know at this time of the year people move about from place to place, and it's wonderful how you keep rubbing shoulders with the same set.'

"It was quite true what Jack said, nevertheless, I could not help the feeling that the woman with the oily eyes had followed us to Homburg. If I had mentioned this then it would have been considered ridiculous, for we had only met her once, and had never spoken a word to her. What earthly interest, therefore, could she possibly take in us who were utter strangers to her? But, looked at by the light of after events, my surmise was true. The creature had marked Jack for her victim from the moment we unhappily met on the stairs at Wiesbaden. I tell you, doctor, that that woman is a human ghoul, a vampire, who lives not only by sucking the blood of men, but by destroying their souls."

Mrs. Redcar broke down again at this stage of her narrative, and I endeavoured to comfort her; but she quickly mastered her feelings sufficiently to continue her remarkable story.

"Some days later my husband and I moved along with the throng that drifted up and down the promenade listening to the band, when we met a lady whom I had known as a neighbour when I was at home with my parents. We stopped and chatted with her for some time, until Jack asked us to excuse him while he went to purchase some matches at a kiosk; he said he would be by the fountain in ten minutes, and I was to wait for him.

"My lady friend and I moved along and chatted as women will, and then she bade me goodnight as she had to rejoin her friends. I at once hurried to the rendezvous at the fountain, but Jack wasn't there. I waited some time but still he came not. I walked about impatiently and half frightened, and when nearly three-quarters of an hour had passed I felt sure Jack had gone home, so with all haste went to our apartments close by, but he was not in, and had not been in. Half distracted, I flew back to the promenade. It was nearly deserted, for the band had gone. As I hurried along, not knowing where to go to, and scarcely knowing what I was doing, I was attracted by a laugh—a laugh I knew. It was Jack's, and proceeding a few yards further I found him sitting on a seat under a linden tree with the woman with the oily eyes.

"'Why, my dear Maude,' he exclaimed, 'wherever have you been to? I've hunted everywhere for you.'

"A great lump came in my throat, for I felt that Jack was lying to me. I really don't know what I said or what I did but I am conscious in a vague way that he introduced me to the woman, but the only name caught was that of Annette. It burnt itself into my brain; it has haunted me ever since.

"Annette put out her white hand veiled by a silk net glove through which diamond rings sparkled. I believe I did touch the proffered fingers, and I shuddered, and I heard her say in a silvery voice that was quite out of keeping with her appearance.

"'If I were your husband I should take you to task. Beauty like yours, you know, ought not to go unattended in a place like this.'

"Perhaps she thought this was funny, for she laughed, and then patted me on the shoulder with her fan. But I hated her from that moment—hated her with a hatred I did not deem myself capable of.

"We continued to sit there, how long I don't know. It seemed to me a very long time, but perhaps it wasn't long. When we rose to go the promenade was nearly deserted, only two or three couples remained. The moon was shining brilliantly; the night wind sighed pleasantly in the trees; but the beauty of the night was lost upon me. I felt ill at ease, and, for the first time in my life, unhappy. Annette walked with us nearly to our door. When the moment for parting came she again offered me the tips of her fingers, but I merely bowed frigidly, and shrank from her as I saw her oily eyes fixed upon me.

"'Ta, ta!' she said in her fatal silvery voice; 'keep a watchful guard over your husband, my dear; and you, sir, don't let your beautiful little lady stray from you again, or there will be grief between you.'

"Those wicked words, every one of which was meant to have its effect, was like the poison of asps to me; you may imagine how they stung me when I tell you I was seized with an almost irresistible desire to hurl the full weight of my body at her, and, having, thrown her down, trample upon her. She had aroused in me such a feeling of horror that very little more would have begotten in me the desperation of madness, and I might have committed some act which I should have regretted all my life. But bestowing another glance of her basilisk eyes upon me she moved off, and I felt relieved; though, when I reached my room, I burst into hysterical weeping. Jack took me in his arms, and kissed and comforted me, and all my love for him was strong again; as I lay, with my head pillowed on his breast, I felt once more supremely happy.

"The next day, on thinking the matter over, I came to the conclusion that my suspicions were unjust, my fears groundless, my jealousy stupid, and that my conduct had been rude in the extreme. I resolved, therefore, to be more amiable and polite to Annette when I again met her. But, strangely enough, though we remained in Homberg a fortnight longer we did not meet; but I know now my husband saw her several times.

"Of course, if it had not been for subsequent events, it would have been said that I was a victim of strong hysteria on that memorable night. Men are so ready to accuse women of hysteria because they are more sensitive, and see deeper than men do themselves. But my aversion to Annette from the instant I set eyes upon her, and the inferences I drew, were not due to hysteria, but to that eighth sense possessed by women, which has no name, and of which men know nothing. At least, I mean to say that they cannot understand it."

Again Mrs. Redcar broke off in her narrative, for emotion had got the better of her. I deemed it advisable to wait. Her remarkable story had aroused all my interest, and I was anxious not to lose any connecting link of it, for from the psychological point of view it was a study.

"Of course, as I have begun the story I must finish it to its bitter end," she went on. "As I have told you, I did not see Annette again in Homberg, and when we left all my confidence in Jack was restored, and my love for him was stronger than ever if that were possible. Happiness came back to me. Oh! I was so happy, and thinking I had done a cruel, bitter wrong to Jack in every supposing for a moment that he would be unfaithful to me, I tried by every little artifice a woman is capable of to prove my devotion to him.

"Well, to make a long story short, we continued to travel about for some time and finally returned home, and my baby was born. It seemed to me then as if God was really too good to me. I had everything in the world that a human being can reasonably want. An angel baby, a brave, handsome husband, ample means, hosts of friends. I was supremely happy. I thanked my Maker for it all every hour of my life. But suddenly amongst the roses the hiss of the serpent sounded. One day a carriage drove up to our door. It brought a lady visitor. She was shown into our drawing-room, and when asked for her name made some excuse to the servant. Of course, I hurried down to see who my caller was, and imagine my horror when on entering the room I beheld Annette.

"'My dear Mrs. Redcar,' she gushingly exclaimed, emphasizing every word, 'I am so delighted to see you again. Being in London, I could not resist the temptation to call and renew acquaintances.'

"The voice was a silvery as ever, and her awful eyes seemed more oily. In my confusion and astonishment I did not inquire how she had got our address; but I know that I refused her proffered hand, and by my manner gave her unmistakably to understand that I did not regard her as a welcome visitor. But she seemed perfectly indifferent. She talked gaily, flippantly. She threw her fatal spell about me. She fascinated me, so that when she asked to see my baby I mechanically rang the bell, and as mechanically told the servant to send the nurse and baby in. When she came, the damnable woman took the child from the nurse and danced him, but he suddenly broke into a scream of terror, so that I rushed forward; but the silvery voice said:

"'Oh, you silly little mother. The baby is all right. Look how quiet he is now.'

"She was holding him at arm's length, and gazing at him with her basilisk eyes, and he was silent. Then she hugged him, and fondled him, and kissed him, and all the while I felt as if my brain was on fire, but I could neither speak nor move a hand to save my precious little baby.

"At last she returned him to his nurse, who at once left the room by my orders, and then Annette kept up a cackle of conversation. Although it did not strike me then as peculiar, for I was too confused to have any clear thought about anything—it did afterwards—she never once inquired about Jack. It happened that he was out. He had gone away early that morning to the city on some important business in which he was engaged.

"At last Annette took herself off, to my intense relief. She said nothing about calling again; she gave no address, and made no request for me to call on her. Even had she done so I should not have called. I was only too thankful she had gone, and I fervently hoped I should never see her again.

"As soon as she had departed I rushed upstairs, for baby was screaming violently. I found him in the nurse's arms, and she was doing her utmost to comfort him. But he refused to be comforted, and I took him and put him to my breast, but he still fought, and struggled, and screamed, and his baby eyes seemed to me to be bulging with horror. From that moment the darling little creature began to sicken. He gradually pined and wasted, and in a few weeks was lying like a beautiful waxen doll in a bed of flowers. He was stiff, and cold, and dead.

"When Jack came home in the evening of the day of Annette's call, and I told him she had been, he did not seem in the least surprised, but merely remarked:

"'I hope you were hospitable to her.'

"I did not answer him, for I had been anything but hospitable. I had not even invited her to partake of the conventional cup of tea.

"As our baby boy faded day by day, Jack seemed to change, and the child's death overwhelmed him. He was never absolutely unkind to me at that period, but he seemed to have entirely altered. He became sullen, silently even morose, and he spent the whole of his days away from me. When I gently chided him, he replied that his work absorbed all his attention. And so things went on until another thunderbolt fell at my feet.

"One afternoon Jack returned home and brought Annette. He told me that he had invited her to spend a few days with us. When I urged an objection he was angry with me for the first time in our married life. I was at once silenced, for his influence over me was still great, and I thought I would try and overcome my prejudice for Annette. At any rate, as Jack's wife I resolved to be hospitable, and play the hostess with grace. But I soon found that I was regarded as of very little consequence. Annette ruled Jack, she ruled me; she ruled the household.

"You will perhaps ask why I did not rise up in wrath, and, asserting my position and dignity, drive the wicked creature out of my home. But I tell you, doctor, I was utterly powerless. She worked some demon's spell upon me, and I was entirely under the influence of her will.

"Her visit stretched into weeks. Our well tried and faithful servants left. Others came, but their stay was brief; and at last the old woman who opened the door to you was installed. She is a creature of Annette's and is a spy upon my movements.

"All this time Jack was under the spell of the charmer, as I was. Over and over again I resolved to go to my friends, appeal to them, tell them everything, and ask them to protect me; but my will failed and I bore and suffered in silence. And my husband neglected me; he seemed to find pleasure only in Annette's company. Oh, how I fretted and gnawed my heart, and yet I could not break away from the awful life. I tell you, doctor, that that woman possessed some strange, devilish, supernatural power over me and Jack. When she looked at me I shrivelled up. When she spoke, that silvery voice seemed to sting every nerve and fibre in my body, and he was like wax in her hands. To me he became positively brutal, and he told me over and over again that I was spoiling his life. But, though she was a repulsive, mysterious, crafty, cruel woman, he seemed to find his happiness in her company.

"One morning, after a restless, horrible, feverish night, I arose, feeling strangely ill, and as if I were going mad. I worked myself up almost to a pitch of frenzy, and, spurred by desperation, I rushed into the drawing-room, where my husband and Annette were together, and exclaimed to her:

"'Woman, do you not see that you are killing me? Why have you come here? Why do you persecute me with your devilish wiles? You must know you are not welcome. You must feel you are an intruder.'

"Overcome by the effort this had cost me, I sank down on the floor on my knees, and wept passionately. Then I heard the silvery voice say, in tones of surprise and injured innocence:

"'Well, upon my word, Mrs. Redcar, this is an extraordinary way to treat your husband's guest. I really thought I was a welcome visitor instead of an intruder but, since I am mistaken, I will go at once.'

"I looked at her through a blinding mist of tears. I met the gaze of her oily eyes, but only for a moment, as I cowered before her, shrank within myself, and felt powerless again. I glanced at my husband. He was standing with his head bowed, and, as it seemed to me, in a pose of shame and nomination. But suddenly he darted at me, and I heard him say: 'What do you mean by creating such a scene as this? You must understand I am master here.' Then he struck me a violent blow on the head, and there was a long blank.

"When I came to my senses I was in bed, and the hideous old hag who opened the door to you was bending over me. It was some little time before I could realise what had occurred. When I did, I asked the woman where Mr. Redcar was, and she answered sullenly:

"'Gone.'

"'And the—Annette; where is she?' I asked.

"'Gone, too,' was the answer.

"Another blank ensued. I fell very ill, and when my brain was capable of coherent thought again I learnt that I had passed through a crisis, and my life had been in jeopardy. A doctor had been attending me, and there was a professional nurse in the house; but she was a hard, dry, unsympathetic woman, and I came to the conclusion—wrongly so, probably—she, too, was one of Annette's creatures.

"I was naturally puzzled to understand why none of my relatives and friends had been to see me, but I was to learn later that many had called, but had been informed I was abroad with my husband, who had been summoned away suddenly in connection with some professional matters. And I also know now that all letters coming for me were at once forwarded to him, and that any requiring answers he answered.

"As I grew stronger I made up my mind to keep my own counsel, and not let any of my friends know of what I had gone through and suffered; for I still loved my husband, and looked upon him as a victim to be pitied and rescued from the infernal wiles of the she-demon. When I heard of your arrival in England, I felt you were the one person in the wide world I could appeal to with safety, for you can understand how anxious I am to avoid a scandal. Will you help me? Will you save your old friend Jack? Restore him to sanity, doctor, and bring him back to my arms again, which will be wide open to receive him."

I listened to poor Mrs. Redcar's story patiently, and at first was disposed to look upon it as a too common tale of human weakness. Jack Redcar had fallen into the power of an adventuress, and had been unable to resist her influence. Such things had happened before, such things will happen again, I argued with myself. There are certain women who seem capable of making men mad for a brief space; but under proper treatment they come to their senses quickly, and blush with shame as they think of their foolishness. At any rate, for the sake of my old friend, and for the sake of his poor suffering little wife, I was prepared to do anything in reason to bring back the erring husband to his right senses.

I told Mrs. Redcar this. I told her I would redress her wrongs if I could, and fight her battle to the death. She almost threw herself at my feet in her gratitude. But when I suggested that I should acquaint her family with the facts, she begged of me passionately not to do so. Her one great anxiety was to screen her husband. One thing, however, I insisted upon. That was, the old woman should be sent away, the house shut up, and that Mrs. Redcar should take apartments in an hotel, so that I might be in touch with her. She demurred to this at first, but ultimately yielded to my persuasion.

Next I went to the old woman. She was a German Suisse—her name was Grebert, I told her to pack up her things and clear out at once. She laughed in my face, and impertinently told me to mind my own business. I took out my watch and said, "I give you half an hour. If you are not off the premises then I will call in the police and have you turned out. Any claim you have on Mrs. Redcar, who is the mistress here—shall be settled at once."

She replied that she did not recognise my authority, that she had been placed there by Mr. Redcar, who was her master, and unless he told her to go she should remain. I made it plain to her that I was determined and would stand no nonsense. Mr. Redcar had taken himself off, I said; Mrs. Redcar was his lawful wife, and I was acting for her and on her behalf.

My arguments prevailed, and after some wrangling the hag came to the conclusion that discretion was the better part of valour, and consented to go providing we paid her twenty pounds. This we decided to do rather than have a scene, but three hours passed before we saw the last of the creature. Mrs. Redcar had already packed up such things as she required, and when I had seen the house securely fastened up I procured a cab, and conveyed the poor little lady to a quiet West-end hotel, close to my own residence, so that I could keep a watchful eye upon her.

Of course, this was only the beginning of the task I had set myself, which was to woo back the erring husband, if possible, to his wife's side, and to restore him to the position of happiness, honour, and dignity from which he had fallen. I thought this might be comparatively easy, and little dreamed of the grim events that were to follow my interference.

Three weeks later I was in Paris, and proceeded to the Hotel de l'Univers, where Mrs. Redcar had ascertained through his bankers her husband was staying. But to my chagrin, I found he had departed with his companion, and the address he had given for his letters at the post-office was Potes, in Spain. As I had taken up the running I had no alternative but to face the long, dreary journey in pursuit of the fugitives, or confess defeat at the start.

It is not necessary for me to dwell upon that awful journey in the wintertime. Suffice to say I reached my destination in due course.

Potes, it is necessary to explain, is a small town magnificently situated in the Liebana Valley, in the Asturian Pyrenees, under the shadow of Pico de Europa. Now, what struck me as peculiar was the fugitives coming to such a place at that time of the year. Snow lay heavily everywhere. The cold was intense. For what reason had such a spot been chosen? It was a mystery I could not hope to solve just then. There was only one small hotel in the village, and there Annette and Redcar were staying. My first impulse was not to let them know of my presence, but to keep them under observation for a time. I dismissed that thought as soon as formed, for I was not a detective, and did not like the idea of playing the spy. But even had I been so disposed, there would have been a difficulty about finding accommodation. Moreover, it was a small place, and the presence of a foreigner at that time of year must necessarily have caused a good deal of gossip. The result was I went boldly to the hotel, engaged a room, and then inquired for Redcar. I was directed to a private room, where I found him alone. My unexpected appearance startled him, and when he realised who I was, he swore at me, and demanded to know my business.

He had altered so much that in a crowd I really might have had some difficulty in recognising him. His face wore a drawn, anxious, nervous look, and his eyes had acquired a restless, shifty motion, while his hair was already streaked with grey.

I began to reason with him. I reminded him of our old friendship, and I drew a harrowing picture of the sufferings of his dear, devoted, beautiful little wife.

At first he seemed callous; but presently he grew interested, and when I referred to his wife he burst into tears. Then suddenly he grasped my wrist with a powerful grip, and said:

"Hush! Annette mustn't know this—mustn't hear. I tell you, Peter, she is a ghoul. She sucks my blood. She has woven a mighty spell about me, and I am powerless. Take me away; take me to dear little Maude."

I looked at him for some moments with a keen professional scrutiny, for his manner and strange words were not those of sanity. I determined to take him at his word, and, if possible, remove him from the influence of the wicked siren who had so fatally lured him.

"Yes," I said, "we will go without a moment's unnecessary delay. I will see if a carriage and post-horses are to be had, so that we can drive to the nearest railway station."

He assented languidly to this, and I rose with the intention of making inquiries of the hotel people; but simultaneously with my action the door opened and Annette appeared. Up to that moment I thought that Mrs. Redcar had exaggerated in describing her, therefore I was hardly prepared to find that so far from the description being an exaggeration, it had fallen short of the fact.

Annette was slightly above the medium height, with a well-developed figure, but a face that to me was absolutely repellent. There was not a single line of beauty nor a trace of womanliness in it. It was hard, coarse, cruel, with thin lips drawn tightly over even white teeth. And the eyes were the most wonderful eyes I have ever seen in a human being. Maude was right when she spoke of them as "oily eyes." They literally shone with a strange, greasy lustre, and were capable of such a marvellous expression that I felt myself falling under their peculiar fascination. I am honest and frank enough to say that, had it been her pleasure, I believe she could have lured me to destruction as she had lured my poor friend. But I was forearmed, because forewarned. Moreover, I fancy I had a much stronger will than Redcar. Any way, I braced myself up to conquer and crush this human serpent, for such I felt her to be.

Before I could speak, her melodious voice rang out with the query, addressed to Jack:

"Who is this gentleman? Is he a friend of yours?"

"Yes, yes," gasped Jack, like one who spoke under the influence of a nightmare.

She bowed and smiled, revealing all her white teeth, and she held forth her hand to me, a delicately shaped hand, with clear, transparent skin, and her long lithe fingers were bejewelled with diamonds.

I drew myself up, as one does when a desperate effort is needed, and, refusing the proffered hand, I said:

"Madame, hypocrisy and deceit are useless. I am a medical man, my name is Peter Haslar, and Mr. Redcar and I have been friends from youth. I've come here to separate him from your baneful influence and carry him back to his broken-hearted wife. That is my mission. I hope I have made it clear to you?"

She showed not the slightest sign of being disturbed, but smiled on me again, and bowed gracefully and with the most perfect self-possession. And speaking in a soft gentle manner, which was in such startling contrast to the woman's appearance, she said:

"Oh, yes; thank you. But, like the majority of your countrymen, you display a tendency to arrogate too much to yourself. I am a Spaniard myself, by birth, but cosmopolitan by inclination, and, believe me, I do not speak with any prejudice against your nationality, but I have yet to learn, sir, that you have any right to constitute yourself Mr. Redcar's keeper."

Her English was perfect, though she pronounced it with just a slight foreign accent. There was no anger in her tones, no defiance. She spoke softly, silvery, persuasively.

"I do not pretend to be his keeper, Madame; I am his sincere friend," I answered. "And surely I need not remind you that he owes a duty to his lawful wife."

During this short conversation Jack had sat motionless on the edge of a couch, his chin resting on his hands, and apparently absorbed with some conflicting thoughts. But Annette turned to him, and, still smiling, said:

"I think Mr. Redcar is quite capable of answering for himself. Stand up, Jack, and speak your thoughts like a man."

Although she spoke in her oily, insidious way, her request was a peremptory command. I realised that at once, and I saw as Jack rose he gazed at her, and her lustrous eyes fixed him. Then he turned upon me with a furious gesture and exclaimed, with a violence of expression that startled me:

"Yes, Annette is right. I am my own master. What the devil do you mean by following me, like the sneak and cur that you are? Go back to Maude, and tell her that I loathe her. Go; relieve me of your presence, or I may forget myself and injure you."

Annette, still smiling and still perfectly self-possessed, said:

"You hear what your friend says, doctor. Need I say that if you are a gentleman you will respect his wishes?"

I could no longer control myself. Her calm, defiant, icy manner maddened me, and her silvery voice seemed to cut down on to my most sensitive nerves, for it was so suggestive of the devilish nature of the creature. It was so incongruous when contrasted with her harsh, horribly cruel face. I placed myself between Jack and her, and meeting her weird gaze, I said, hotly:

"Leave this room. You are an outrage on your sex: a shame and a disgrace to the very name of woman. Go, and leave me with my friend, whose reason you have stolen away."

She still smiled and was still unmoved, and suddenly I felt myself gripped in a grip of iron, and with terrific force I was huried into a corner of the room, where, huddled up in a heap. I lay stunned for some moments. But as my senses returned I saw the awful woman smiling still, and she was waving her long white bejewelled hand before the infuriated Jack, as if she were mesmerising him; and I saw him sink on to the sofa subdued and calmed. Then addressing me she said:

"That is a curious way for your friend to display his friendship, I may be wrong, but perhaps as a medical man you will recognise that your presence has an irritating effect on Mr. Redcar, and if I may suggest it, I think it desirable that you should depart at once and see him no more."

"Devil!" I shouted at her. "You have bewitched him, and made him forgetful of his honour and of what he does to those who are dear to him. But I will defeat you yet."

She merely bowed and smiled, but deigned no reply and holding her arm to Jack, he took it, and they passed out of the room. She was elegantly attired. Her raven hair was fascinatingly dressed in wavy bands. There was something regal in her carriage, and gracefulness in her every movement; and yet she filled me with a sense of indefinable horror; a dread to which I should have been ashamed to own to a little while ago.

I tried to spring up and go after them, but my body seemed a mass of pain, and my left arm hung limp and powerless. It was fractured below the elbow. There was no bell in the room, and I limped out in search of assistance. I made my way painfully along a gloomy corridor, and hearing a male voice speaking Spanish, I knocked at door, which was opened by the landlord. I addressed him but he shook his head and gave me to understand that he spoke no English. Unhappily I spoke no Spanish. Then he smiled as some idea flitted through his mind, and bowing into the room he motioned me to be seated, and hurried away. He returned in about five minutes accompanied by Annette, whom he had brought to act as interpreter. I was almost tempted to fly at her and strangle her where she stood. She was undisturbed, calm, and still smiled. She spoke to the man in Spanish, then she explained to me that she had told him I had slipped on the polished floor, and falling over a chair had injured myself, and she had requested him to summon the village surgeon if need be.

Without waiting for me to reply she swept gracefully out of the room. Indeed, I could not reply, for I felt as if I were choking with suppressed rage. The landlord rendered me physical assistance, and took me to my bedroom, where I lay down on the bed, feeling mortified, ill, and crushed. Half an hour later a queer-looking old man, with long hair twisted into ringlets, was ushered into my room, and I soon gathered that he was the village surgeon. He spoke no English, but I explained my injury by signs, and he went away, returning in a little while with the necessary bandages and splints, and he proceeded rather clumsily to bandage my broken arm. I passed a cruel and wretched night. My physical pain was great, but my mental pain was greater. The thought forced itself upon me that I had been defeated, and that the fiendish, sinister woman was too much for me. I felt no resentment against Jack. His act of violence was the act of a madman, and I pitied him. For hours I lay revolving all sorts of schemes to try and get him away from the diabolical influence of Annette. But though I could hit upon nothing, I firmly resolved that while my life lasted I would make every effort to save my old friend, and if possible restore him to the bosom of his distracted wife.

The case altogether was a very remarkable one, and the question naturally arose, why did a man so highly gifted and so intelligent as Jack Redcar desert his charming, devoted, and beautiful wife, to follow an adventuress who entirely lacked physical beauty. Theories without number might have been suggested to account for the phenomenon, but not one would have been correct. The true answer is, Annette was not a natural being. In the ordinary way she might be described as a woman of perverted moral character, or as a physiological freak, but that would have been rather a misleading way of putting it. She was, in short, a human monstrosity. By that I do not mean to say her body was contorted, twisted, or deformed. But into her human composition had entered a strain of the fiend; and I might go even further than this and say she was more animal than human. Though in whatever way she may be described, it is certain she was an anomaly—a human riddle.

The morning following the outrage upon me found me prostrated and ill. A night of racking pain and mental distress had told even upon my good constitution. The situation in which I found myself was a singularly unfortunate one. I was a foreigner in an out-of-the-way place, and my want of knowledge of Spanish, of course, placed me at a tremendous disadvantage.

The landlord came to me and brought his wife, and between them they attended to my wants, and did what they could for my comfort. But they were ignorant, uncultivated people, only one removed from the peasant class, and I realised that they could be of little use to me. How the nearest important town to this mountain village was Santander, but that was nearly a hundred miles away. As everyone knows who has been in Spain, a hundred miles, even on a railway, is a considerable journey; but there was no railway between Santander and Potes. An old ramshackle vehicle, called a diligence, ran between the two places every day in the summer and twice a week in the winter, and it took fourteen hours to do the journey. Even a well-appointed carriage and pair could not cover the distance under eight hours, as the road was infamous, and in parts was little better than a mule track. I knew that there was a British consul in Santander, and I was hopeful that if I could communicate with him he might be able to render me some assistance. In the meantime I had to devise some scheme for holding Annette in check and saving my friend. But in my crippled and prostate condition I could not do much. While lying in my bed, and thus revolving all these things in my mind, the door gently opened and Annette glided in—"glided" best expresses her movement, for she seemed to put forth no effort. She sat down beside the bed and laid her hand on mine.

"You are ill this morning," she said softly. "This is regrettable, but you have only yourself to blame. It is dangerous to interfere in matters in which you have no concern. My business is mine, Mr. Redcar's is his, and yours is your own, but the three won't amalgamate. Jack and I came here for the sake of the peace and quietness of these solitudes; unhappily you intrude yourself and disaster follows."

Her voice was as silvery as ever. The same calm self-possessed air characterised her; but in her oily eyes was a peculiar light, and I had to turn away, for they exerted a sort of mesmerising influence over me, and I am convinced that had I not exerted all my will power I should have thrown myself into the creature's arms. This is a fact which I have no hesitation in stating, as it serves better than any other frustration to show what a wonderful power of fascination the remarkable woman possessed. Naturally I felt disgusted and enraged, but I fully recognised that I could not fight the woman openly; I must to some extent meet her with her own weapons. She was cunning, artful, insidious, pitiless, and the basilisk-like power she possessed not only gave her a great advantage but made her a very dangerous opponent. At any rate, having regard to all the circumstances and my crippled condition, I saw that my only chance was in temporising with her. So I tried to reason with her, and I pointed out that Redcar had been guilty of baseness in leaving his wife, who was devoted to him.

At this point of my argument Annette interrupted me, and for the first time she displayed some emotion, like passion, and her voice became hard and raucous.

"His wife," she said with a sneer of supreme contempt. "A poor fool, a fleshly doll. At the precise instant I set my eyes upon her for the first time I felt that I should like to destroy her, because she is a type of woman who make the world commonplace and reduce all men to a common level. She hated me from the first and I hated her. She would have crushed me if she could, but she was too insignificant a worm to do that, and I crushed her."

This cold, brutal callousness enraged me; I turned fiercely upon her and exclaimed:

"Leave me, you are a more infamous and heartless wretch than I believed you to be. You are absolutely unworthy of the name of woman, and if you irritate me much more I may even forget that you have a woman's shape."

She spoke again. All trace of passion had disappeared. She smiled the wicked insidious smile which made her so dangerous, and her voice assumed its liquid, silvery tones:

"You are very violent," she said gently, "and it will do you harm in your condition. But you see violence can be met with violence. The gentleman you are pleased to call your friend afforded you painful evidence last night that he knows how to resent unjustifiable interference, and to take care of himself. I am under his protection, and there is no doubt he will protect me."

"For God's sake, leave me!" I cried, tortured beyond endurance by her hypocrisy and wickedness.

"Oh, certainly, if you desire it," she answered, as she rose from her seat. "But I thought I might be of use. It is useless your trying to influence Mr. Redcar—absolutely useless. His destiny is linked with mine, and the human being doesn't exist who can sunder us. With this knowledge, you will do well to retrace your steps; and, if you like I will arrange to have you comfortably conveyed to Santander, where you can get a vessel. Anyway, you will waste your time and retard your recovery by remaining here."

"I intend to remain here, nevertheless," I said, with set teeth. "And, what is more, Madame, when I go my friend Redcar will accompany me."

She laughed. She patted my head as a mother might pat the head of her child. She spoke in her most insidious, silvery tones. "We shall see, *mon chier*—we shall see. You will be better tomorrow. *Adieu!*"

That was all she said, and she was gone. She glided out of the room as she had glided in.

I felt irritated almost into madness for some little time but as I reflected, it was forced upon me that I had to deal with a monster of iniquity, who had so subdued the will of her victim, Redcar, that he was a mere wooden puppet in her hand. Force in such a case was worse than useless. What I had to do was to try and circumvent her, and I tried to think out some plan of action.

All that day I was compelled to keep my bed, and, owing to the clumsy way in which my arm had been bandaged, I suffered intolerable pain, and had to send for the old surgeon again to come and help me to reset the fracture. I got some ease after that, and a dose of chloral sent me to sleep, which continued for many hours. When I awoke I managed to summon the landlord, and he brought me food, and a lantern containing a candle so that I might have light. And, in compliance with my request, he made me a large jug of lemonade, in order that I could have a drink in the night, for I was feverish, and my throat was parched. He had no sooner left the room than Annette entered to inquire if she could do anything for me. I told her that I had made the landlord understand all that I desired, and he would look after me, so she wished me goodnight and left. Knowing as I did that sleep was very essential in my case, I swallowed another, though smaller, dose of chloral, and then there was a blank.

How long I slept I really don't know; but suddenly, in a dazed sort of way, I saw a strange slight. The room I occupied was a long, somewhat meagerly furnished, one. The entrance door was at the extreme end, opposite the bed. Over the doorway hung a faded curtain of green velvet. By the feeble light of the candle lantern I saw this curtain slowly pulled on one side by a white hand; then a face peered in; next Annette entered. Her long hair was hanging down her back, and she wore a nightdress of soft, clinging substance, which outlined her figure. With never a sound she moved lightly towards the bed, and waved her hand two or three times over my face. I tried to move, to utter a sound, but couldn't; and yet what I am describing was no dream, but a reality. Slightly bending over me, she poured from a tiny phial she carried in the palm of her hand a few drops of a slightly acrid, burning liquid right into my mouth, and at that instant, as I believe, it seemed to me as if a thick, heavy pall fell over my eyes, for all was darkness.

I awoke hours later. The winter sun was shining brightly into my room. I felt strangely languid, and had a hot, stinging sensation in my throat. I felt my pulse, and found it was only beating at the rate of fifty-eight beats in the minute. Then I recalled the extraordinary incident of the previous night, which, had it not been for my sensations. I might have regarded as a bad dream, the outcome of a disturbed state of the brain. But as it was, I hadn't a doubt that Annette had administered some subtle and slow poison to me. My medical knowledge enabled me to diagnose my own case so far, that I was convinced I was suffering from the effects of a potent poisonous drug, the action of which was to lower the action of the vital forces and weaken the heart. Being probably cumulative, a few doses more or less, according to the strength of the subject, and the action of the heart, would be so impeded that the organ would cease to beat. Although all this passed through my brain, I felt so weak and languid that I had neither energy nor strength to arouse myself, and when the landlord brought me in some food I took no notice of him. I knew that this symptom of languor and indifference was very characteristic of certain vegetable poisons, though what it was Annette had administered to me I could not determine.

Throughout that day I lay in a drowsy, dreamy state. At times my brain was clear enough, and I was able to think and reason; but there were blanks, marked, no doubt, by periods of sleep.

When night came I felt a little better, and I found that the heart's action had improved. It was steadier, firmer, and the pulse indicated sixty-two beats. Now I had no doubt that if it was Annette's intention to bring about my death slowly she would come again that night, and arousing myself as well as I could, and summoning all my will power, I resolved to be on the watch. During the afternoon I had drunk milk freely, regarding it as an antidote, and when the landlord visited me for the last time that evening I made him understand that I wanted a large jug of milk fresh from the cow, if he could get it. He kept cows of his own; they were confined in a chalet on the mountain side, not far from his house, so that he was able to comply with my request. I took a long draught of this hot milk, which revived my energies wonderfully, and then I waited for developments. I had allowed by watch to run down, consequently I had no means of knowing the time. It was a weary vigil, lying there lonely and ill, and struggling against the desire for sleep.

By-and-by I saw the white hand lift the curtain again, and Annette entered, clad as she was on the previous night. When she came within reach of me I sprang up in the bed and seized her wrist.

"What do you want here?" I demanded angrily. "Do you mean to murder me?"

Her imperturbability was exasperating. She neither winced nor cried out, nor displayed the slightest sign of surprise. She nicely remarked in her soft cooing voice, her white teeth showing as her thin lips parted in a smile:

"You are evidently restless and excited tonight, and it is hardly generous of you to treat my kindly interest in such a way."

"Kindly interest!" I echoed with a sneer, as, releasing her wrist, I fell back on the bed.

"Yes; you haven't treated me well, and you are an intruder here. Nevertheless, as you are a stranger amongst strangers, and cannot speak the language of the country, I would be of service to you if I could. I have come to see if you have everything you require for the night."

"And you did the same last night," I cried in hot anger, for, knowing her infamy and wickedness, I could not keep my temper.

"Certainly," she answered coolly; "and I found you calmly dozing, so left you."

"Yes—after you had poured poison down my throat," I replied.

She broke into a laugh—a rippling laugh, with the tinkle of silver in it—and she seemed hugely amused.

"Well, well," she said; "It is obvious, sir, you are not in a fit state to be left alone. Your nerves are evidently unstrung, and you are either the victim of a bad dream or some strange delusion. But there, there; I will pardon you. You are not responsible just at present for your language."

As she spoke she passed her soft white hand over my forehead. There was magic in her touch, and it seemed as if all my will had left me, and there stole over me a delightful sense of dreamy languor. I looked at her, and I saw her strange eyes changed colour. They became illumined, as it were, by a violet light that fascinated me so that I could not turn from her. Indeed, I was absolutely subdued to her will now. Everything in the room faded, and I saw nothing but those marvellous eyes glowing with violet light which seemed to fill me with a feeling of ecstasy. I have a vague idea that she kept passing her hand over my face and forehead; that she breathed upon my face; then that she pressed her face to mine, and I felt her hot breath in my neck.

Perhaps it will be said that I dreamed all this. I don't believe it was a dream. I firmly and honestly believe that every word I have written is true.

Hours afterwards my dulled brain began to awake to things mundane. The morning sun was flooding the room, and I was conscious that somebody stood over me, and soon I recognised the old surgeon, who had come to see that the splints and bandages had not shifted. I felt extraordinarily weak, and I found that my pulse was beating very slowly and feebly. Again I had the burning feeling in the throat and a strange and absolutely indescribable sensation at the side of the neck. The old doctor must have recognised that I was unusually feeble, for he went to the landlord, and returned presently with some cognac, which he made me swallow, and it picked me up considerably.

After his departure I lay for sometime, and tried to give definite shape to the vague and dreadful nightmares that haunted me, and filled me with a shrinking horror. That Annette was a monster in human form I hadn't a doubt, and I felt equally certain that she had designs upon my life. That she had now administered poison to me on two occasions seemed to me beyond question, but I hesitated to believe that she was guilty of the unspeakable crime which my sensations suggested.

At last, unable to longer to endure the tumult in my brain, I sprang out of bed, rushed to the looking-glass and examined my neck. I literally staggered back, and fell prostrate on the bed, overcome by the hideous discovery I had made. It had the effect, however, of calling me back to life and energy, and I made a mental resolution that I would, at all hazards, save my friend, though I clearly realised how powerless I was to cope with the awful creature single-handed.

I managed to dress myself, not without some difficulty then I summoned the landlord, and made him understand that I must go immediately to Santander at any cost. My intention was to invoke the aid of the consul there. But the more I insisted, the more the old landlord shook his head. At length, in desperation, I rushed from the house, hoping, to find somebody who understood French or English. As I almost ran up the village street I came face to face with a priest. I asked him in English if he spoke my language, but he shook his head. Then I tried him with French, and to my joy he answered me that he understood a little French. I told him of my desire to start for Santander that very day, but he said that it was impossible, as, owing to the unusual hot sun in the daytime there had been a great melting of snow, with the result that a flooded river had destroyed a portion of the road; and though a gang of men had been set to repair it, it would be two or three days before it was passable.

"But is there no other way of going?" I asked.

"Only by a very hazardous route over the mountains," he answered and he added that the risk was so great it was doubtful if anyone could be found who would act as guide. "Besides," he went on, "you seem very ill and weak. Even a strong man might fail, but you would be certain to perish from exhaustion and exposure."

I was bound to recognise the force of his argument. It was a maddening disappointment, but there was no help for it. Then it occurred
to me to take the old priest into my confidence and invoke his aid.
Though, on second thoughts, I hesitated, for was it not possible—
nay, highly probable—that if I told the horrible story he and others
would think I was mad. Annette was a Spanish woman, and it was
feasible to suppose she would secure the ear of those ignorant vil-
lagers sooner than I should. No, I would keep the ghastly business
to myself for the present at any rate, and wait with such patience
as I could command until I could make the journey to Santander.
The priest promised me that on the morrow he would let me know
if the road was passable, and, if so, he would procure me a carriage
and make all the preparations for the journey. So, thanking him for
his kindly services, I turned towards the hotel again. As I neared the
house I observed two persons on the mountain path that went up
among the pine trees. The sun was shining brilliantly; the sky was
cloudless, the air crisp and keen. The two persons were Annette and
Redcar. I watched them for some minutes until they were lost to
sight amongst the trees.

Suddenly an irresistible impulse to follow them seized me. Why I
know not. Indeed, had I paused to reason with myself it would have
seemed to me then a mad act, and that I was risking my life to no
purpose. But I did not reason. I yielded to the impulse, though first
of all I went to my room, put on a thicker pair of boots, and armed
myself with a revolver which I had brought with me. During my
extensive travelling about America a revolver was a necessity, and by
force of habit I put it up with my clothes when packing my things in
London for my Continental journey.

Holding the weapon between my knees, I put a cartridge in each
barrel, and, providing myself with a stick in addition, I went forth
again and began to climb the mountain path. I was by no means a
sanguinary man; even my pugnacity could only be aroused after much
irritation. Nevertheless, I knew how to defend myself, and in this
instance, knowing that I had to deal with a woman who was capable
of any crime, and who, I felt sure, would not hesitate to take my life
if she got the chance, I deemed it advisable to be on my guard against
any emergency that might arise. As regards Redcar, he had already
given me forcible and painful evidence that he could be dangerous;
but I did not hold him responsible for his actions. I regarded him as
being temporarily insane owing to the infernal influence the awful

woman exercised over him. Therefore it would only have been in the very last extremity that I should have resorted to lethal weapons as a defence against him. My one sole aim, hope, desire, prayer, was to rescue him from the spell that held him in thrall and restore him to his wife, his honour, his sanity. With respect to Annette, it was different. She was a blot on nature, a disgrace to humankind, and, rather than let her gain complete ascendancy over me and my friend, I would have shot her if I had reason to believe she contemplated taking my life. It might have involved me in serious trouble with the authorities at first for in Spain the foreigner can hope but for little justice. I was convinced, however, that ultimately I should be exonerated.

Such were the thoughts that filled my mind as I painfully made my way up the steep mountainside. My fractured arm was exceedingly painful. Every limb in my body ached, and I was so languid, so weak that it was with difficulty I dragged myself along. But worse than this was an all but irresistible desire to sleep, the result, I was certain, of the poison that had been administered to me. But it would have been fatal to have slept. I knew that, and so I fought against the inclination with all my might and main, and allowed my thoughts to dwell on poor little Maude Redcar, waiting desolate and heartbroken in London for news. This supplied me with the necessary spur and kept me going.

The trees were nearly all entirely bare of snow. It had, I was informed, been an unusually mild season, and at that time the sun's rays were very powerful. The path I was pursuing was nothing more than a rough track worn by the peasants passing between the valley and their hay chalets dotted about the mountains. Snow lay on the path where it was screened from the sun by the trees, I heard no sound, saw no sign of those I was seeking save here and there footprints in the snow. I frequently paused and listened, but the stillness was unbroken save for the subdued murmur of falling water afar off.

In my weakened condition the exertion I had endured had greatly distressed me; my heart beat tumultuously, my pulses throbbed violently, and my breathing was stertorous. I was compelled at last to sit down and rest. I was far above the valley now, and the pine trees were straggling and sparse. The track had become very indistinct, but I still detected the footsteps of the people I was following. Above the trees I could discern the snow-capped Pico de Europa glittering in the brilliant sun. It was a perfect Alpine scene, which, under other circumstances. I might have revelled in. But I felt strangely ill, weak, and miserable, and drowsiness began to steal upon me, so that I made a sudden effort of will and sprang up again, and resumed the ascent.

In a little time the forest ended, and before me stretched a sloping plateau which, owing to its being exposed to the full glare of the sun, as well as to all the winds that blew, was bare of snow. The plateau sloped down for probably four hundred feet, then ended abruptly at the edge of a precipice. How far the precipice descended I could not tell from where I was, but far far below I could see a stream meandering through a thickly wooded gorge. I took the details of the scene in with a sudden glance of the eye, for another sight attracted and riveted my attention, and froze me with horror to the spot. Beneath a huge boulder which had fallen from the mountain above, and lodged on the slope, were Annette and Redcar. He was lying on his back, she was stretched out beside him, and her face was buried in his neck. Even from where I stood I could see that he was ghastly pale, his features drawn and pinched, his eyes closed. Incredible as it may seem, horrible as it sounds, it is nevertheless true that that hellish woman was sucking away his life blood. She was a human vampire, and my worst fears were confirmed.

I am aware that an astounding statement of this kind should not be made lightly by a man in my position. But I take all the responsibility of it, and I declare solemnly that it is true. Moreover, the sequel which I am able to give to this story more than corroborates me, and proves Annette to have been one of those human problems which, happily for the world, are very rare, but of which there are several well authenticated cases.

As soon as I fully realised what was happening I drew my revolver from the side pocket of my jacket and fired, not at Annette, but in the air; my object being to startle her so that she would release her victim. It had the desired effect. She sprang up, livid with rage. Blood—his blood—was oozing from the sides of her mouth. Her extraordinary eyes had assumed that strange violet appearance which I had seen once before. Her whole aspect was repulsive, revolting, horrible beyond words. Rooted to the spot I stood and gazed at her, fascinated by the weird, ghastly sight. In my hand I still held the smoking revolver, levelled at her now, and resolved if she rushed towards me to shoot her, for I felt that the world would be well rid of such a hideous monster. But suddenly she stooped, seized her unfortunate victim in her arms, and tore down the slope, and when the edge of the precipice was reached they both disappeared into space.

The whole of this remarkable scene was enacted in the course of a few seconds. It was to me a maddening nightmare. I fell where I stood, and remembered no more until, hours afterwards, I found myself lying in bed at the hotel, and the old surgeon and the priest sitting beside me. Gradually I learnt that the sound of the shot from the revolver, echoing and re-echoing in that Alpine region, had been heard in the village, and some peasants had set off for the mountain to ascertain the cause of the firing. They found me lying on the ground still grasping the weapon, and thinking I had shot myself they carried me down to the hotel.

Naturally I was asked for explanations when I was able to talk, and I recounted the whole of the ghastly story. At first my listeners, the priest and the doctor, seemed to think I was raving in delirium, as well they might, but I persisted in my statements, and I urged the sending out of a party to search for the bodies. If they were found my story would be corroborated.

In a short time a party of peasants started for the gorge, which was a wild, almost inaccessible, ravine through which flowed a mountain torrent amongst the debris and boulders that from time to time had fallen from the rocky heights. After some hours of searching the party discovered the crushed remains of Jack Redcar. His head had been battered to pieces against the rocks as he fell, and every bone in his body was broken. The precipice over which he had fallen was a jagged, scarred, and irregular wall of rock at least four thousand feet in height. The search for Annette's body was continued until darkness compelled the searchers to return to the village, which they did bringing with them my poor friend's remains. Next day the search was resumed, and the day after, and for many days, but with no result. The woman's corpse was never found. The theory was that somewhere on that frightful rock face she had been caught by a projecting pinnacle, or had got-jammed in a crevice, where her unhallowed remains would molder into dust. It was a fitting end for so frightful a life.

Of course an official inquiry was held—and officialism in Spain is appalling. It was weeks and weeks before the inevitable conclusion of the tribunal was arrived at, and I was exonerated from all blame. In the meantime Redcar's remains were committed to their eternal rest in the picturesque little Alpine village churchyard, and for all time Potes will be associated with that grim and awful tragedy. Why Annette took her victim to that out of the way spot can only be guessed at. She knew that the death of her victim was only a question of weeks, and in that primitive and secluded hamlet it would arouse no suspicion, she being a native of Spain. It would be easy for her to say that she had taken her invalid husband there for the benefit of his health, but unhappily the splendid and bracing air had failed to save his life. In this instance, as in many others, her fiendish cunning would have enabled her to score another triumph had not destiny made me its instrument to encompass her destruction.

For long after my return to England I was very ill. The fearful ordeal I had gone through, coupled with the poison which Annette had administered to me, shattered my health; but the unremitting care and attention bestowed upon me by my old friend's widow pulled me through. And when at last I was restored to strength and vigour, beautiful Maude Redcar became my wife.

Note by the Author

The foregoing story was suggested by a tradition current in the Pyrenees, where a belief in ghouls and vampires is still common. The same belief is no less common throughout Styria, in some parts of Turkey, in Russia, and in India. Sir Richard Burton deals with the subject in his "*Vikram and the Vampire*." Years ago, when the author was in India, a poor woman was beaten to death one night in the village by a number of young men armed with cudgels. Their excuse for the crime was that the woman was a vampire, and had sucked the blood of many of their companions, whom she had first lured to her by depriving them of their will power by mesmeric influence.

Emptiness

Brian Stableford

Brian Stableford (b. 1948) is a prolific writer of science fiction and fantasy who has a particular interest in fiction of the decadent 1890s, and has created his own treatment of an alternate history of the world where vampires become all-powerful. This began with his story "The Man Who Loved the Vampire Lady" (1988), which formed the basis of the novel The Empire of Fear *(1988). Later novels include* Young Blood *(1992) and the wonderful steampunk extravaganza, "The Hunger and Ecstacy of Vampires" (1995). Behind all of these stories is a science-fiction premise that considers vampires as genuine products of evolution. There is a scientific basis to the following story as well, but the result is something altogether different and more poignant.*

Emptiness

Brian Stableford

IT WAS five o'clock on Tuesday morning, with an hour still to go before dawn, when Ruth found the abandoned baby. The plaintively mewling infant—who was less than a week old, if appearances could be trusted—had been laid in a cardboard box in a skip outside a former newsagent's in St. Stephen's Road. The skip was there because the shop was in the process of being refitted as an Indian takeaway. Ruth was coming home from the offices of an insurance company in Queen Street, where she'd been sent to work the graveyard shift by the contract cleaning firm that employed her. She was all washed out, drained of all reserves of strength and momentum.

Ruth knew that she ought to call the police so that they could deliver the baby to social services, and that was what she vaguely intended to do when she plucked the child's makeshift crib out of the skip. The first thing she did thereafter, obviously, was to stick an experimental finger into the baby's open mouth. When she felt the nip of the newborn's tiny teeth the vague intention ought to have hardened into perfect certainty, but it didn't. She was adrift on the tide of her own indolence, rudderless on the sea of circumstance.

The baby sucked furiously at the futile finger, desperate to assuage a building hunger. In order to get it out of the infant's mouth Ruth had to tear the finger free, but the ripped flesh on either side of the nail didn't bleed. The pain quickly faded to a numbness that was not unwelcome.

The baby had thrashed around vigorously enough to work free of the shit-stained sheet in which it had been wrapped, and Ruth took note of the fact that he was a boy before wrapping him up as best she could in the cleaner part of the sheet. Her own kids were both girls. Frank had done a bunk while they were supposedly still trying for a boy; if they had succeeded in time, she would have stood exactly the same chance as everybody else of giving birth to a vampire—the publicly-quoted odds had been as short as one in fifty even then, fourteen years ago.

The nearest payphone was a quarter-mile up the road, practically on the doorstep of the estate. By the time Ruth drew level with the booth she had not brought her resolve to do the sensible thing into clearer focus. The baby had stopped crying long enough to look into her eyes while she rearranged the sheet by the glare of a sodium street-light, but it had only been a glimpse. Temptation had not closed any kind of grip upon her—but fear, duty and common sense were equally impotent. When she reached the phone booth she paused to rest and consider her options.

★

If she did as she was supposed to do the baby would be fitted with a temporary mask and whisked away to one of the special orphanages that were springing up all over. Once there he would be fitted with a permanent eyeshield, stuck in a dormitory with a dozen others and fed on animal blood laced with synthetic supplements. He would go straight into a study-programme and would remain in it for life.

The primary objective of the study programmes was to find a cure for the mutant condition, enabling its victims to survive on other nourishment than blood. Their secondary objective was to find a way of helping the afflicted to survive longer than was currently normal. Nobody thought the scientists were knocking themselves out to obtain the latter achievement while the former remained tantalisingly out of reach. There was a certain social convenience in the fact that real vampires, unlike the legendary undead, rarely survived to adulthood. The average life-expectancy of an orphanage baby was no more than thirteen years; the figure was probably three or four years higher for babies raised at home, but they were in a minority even in the better parts of town. The best reason why so many vampire babies were abandoned was that they were direly unsafe companions for young siblings; the more common one was that the neighbours would not tolerate those who harboured them.

In theory, Ruth's younger daughter was still living with her in the flat, but in practice fifteen-year-old Cassie spent at least five nights a week with her boyfriend in a ground-floor squat. Even if she were unwise or unlucky enough to become fixated on the child, sharing donations with her mother wouldn't do her any harm. In any case, Cassie's blood was probably too polluted by various illegal substances to offer good nourishment to a fortnight-old vampire. All in all, Ruth thought, there was no very powerful reason why she shouldn't look after the baby herself for a little while, if she wanted to.

Carefully, she counted reasons why she might want to hesitate over the matter of handing the baby over to the proper authorities.

Firstly, the flat had been feeling empty ever since Judy had moved to Cornwall with the travellers, even before Cassie took up with Robert. No matter how much she hated the work itself, Ruth simply didn't know what to do with herself any more when she wasn't working.

Secondly, she'd put on a lot of weight lately, and everyone knew that nursing a vampire baby, if only for a couple of weeks, was one hell of a slimming aid.

There wasn't a thirdly; Ruth wasn't the kind of person to take any notice of those middle class apologists for the "new humankind" who were fond of arguing that vampire children were the most loving, devoted and grateful children that anyone could wish for and ought not to be discriminated against on account of unfortunate tendencies they couldn't help. She didn't have any expectations of that kind— her own children hadn't given her any reason to.

In the end, Ruth decided that there was no hurry to make the call. Surely nobody would care if she waited for a little while, provided that she didn't hang on too long. If it were only for three or four days, she could probably keep the baby's presence secret from the Defenders of Humanity, and if she couldn't she could hand the baby over as soon as she had to. It was no big deal. It was just something to do that might even do her a tiny bit of good. Just because she was pushing forty, there was no reason to let go of the hope that she might still be worth something to *someone*.

★

Unfortunately, Cassie made one of her increasingly rare raids on her wardrobe later that morning, before Ruth had had time to get her head down for a couple of hours. The baby was asleep but Ruth hadn't taken him into her bedroom. The dirty sheet had been swapped for a clean one but he was still in the old cardboard box—which was anything but unobtrusive, sat as it was on the living-room table.

"Why aren't you in school?" Ruth demanded, hoping to distract her daughter's attention and ensure that she didn't linger.

"Free period," Cassie replied, ritualistically. "What's *that?*"

"None of your business," said Ruth, defiantly.

"Whose is it? Is baby-minding a step up from office cleaning or a step down? Can't its mum find anything better to keep it in than a cardboard box?"

Cassie peered into the makeshift cot as she spoke, but the baby's eyes and lips were closed, and there was nothing to betray its true nature.

"Shh!" said Ruth, fiercely. "You'll wake him up." There was, of course, little chance of that, given that the sun was shining so brightly, but Ruth figured that there was no need to let Cassie in on her secret yet if she could possibly avoid it. Her tacit arrangement with the baby was, after all, strictly temporary.

Fortunately, Cassie showed no inclination to inspect the visitor more carefully. Sexual activity hadn't made her broody. In fact, when Ruth had first tackled her on the subject of contraception, Cassie had sworn that if ever she fell pregnant and couldn't face an abortion she'd jump off a top-floor balcony. Most people who said things like that didn't mean them, but Cassie was short for Cassandra, and ever since Robert had told her what the name signified in mythology Cassie had taken the view that whenever it was time for one of her gloomy prophecies to come true she'd have to make bloody sure that it did.

When Cassie had gone Ruth unearthed an old cot from the junk-cupboard under the stairs. Two baby-blankets and a couple of baby-gros were still folded neatly within it, although she had to run the vacuum over them to get rid of the dust. She left the baby asleep with the bedroom curtains drawn while she hiked over to Tescos in search of Pampers, red meat, Lucozade, iron tablets and various other items which now had to be reckoned essentials. Luckily, she'd been off-shift on Friday and Saturday and hadn't been able to collect her pay until Monday, so she was as flush as she ever was.

By the time she got back the sun was at its zenith and she was twice as exhausted as before, but the baby was awake and whimpering and she knew that she'd have to feed him again before getting some sleep on her own account.

The thought of putting the vampire to her breast again made her hesitate over the wisdom of her decision not to call Social Services, but as soon as she looked down into the child's tear-filled eyes her squeamishness vanished, as it had the first time when the child had been terrified and starving. His gaze had filled up once again with

tangible need. He was thin and pale and empty, and the pressure of his eyes renewed Ruth's awareness of her own contrasting *fullness:* her too-substantial flesh; her still-extending life; her superabundant blood.

It did hurt when the teeth clamped down for the second time on the tenderised rim of the nipple, but once they were lodged the anaesthetic effect of the baby's saliva soothed the ache away.

Ruth couldn't feel or see the flow of blood as the child took his nourishment. Vampires only used their teeth for holding on—they took the blood by some kind of suction process that drew it through the skin without breaking it. When he released her again, already falling back to sleep, there was no leakage from the residual wounds. The control which vampires exercised over the flesh of their donors was ingenious enough to forbid any waste.

When she had put a clean disposable on the baby and put him down again Ruth fought off her tiredness for the fourth time and made herself a meal. She knew that she had to eat regularly and well if she were to be adequate to the baby's needs, even for a fortnight. She had a second cup of tea in order to maintain her fluid balance but she left the Lucozade for later. Before she finally went to bed she phoned the agency to say that she had flu and that she would have to come off the roster for at least a week, until further notice. Her supervisor didn't protest; Ruth's attendance record was better than average and there was no shortage of night-cleaners in the area.

She slept very soundly, as was only to be expected. She didn't dream—not, at any rate, that she could remember.

★

Cassie didn't figure out what kind the baby was until Thursday evening, at which time she threw an entirely predictable tantrum.

"Are you completely crazy?" she demanded of her mother. "It's kidnapping, for God's sake—and the thing will bleed you to death if you let it. It's a monster!"

"He's a human being," Ruth assured her. "His mother obviously couldn't cope—but she didn't turn him over to the authorities either. She'd be grateful to me if she knew. It's only temporary, anyhow. It's kindness, not kidnapping."

"It's suicide!"

"No it's not. They're not dangerous to adults, even in the long run. A couple of weeks will only make me leaner and fitter. I need to be

fitter to do that bloody job five and six nights a week. It'd be different
if there was a child in the house, but there isn't, is there?"

"They're cuckoos," Cassie blustered. "They're *aliens*, programmed
to eliminate all rivals for their victims' affections. Why do you think
they keep them masked in the homes? That's where he belongs, and
you know it—in a home."

"He is in a home," Ruth pointed out. "A real home, not a lab
where they'll weigh and measure and monitor him like some kind
of white rat. He's entitled to that, for a little while at least. There's no
need to tell anyone—it's my business, not yours or anyone else's."

"It is *so* my business," Cassie retorted, hotly. "I live here too—I'm
the rival that the cuckoo is programmed to squeeze out while he
squeezes you dry and leaves you a shrivelled wreck."

"I thought you had decided that this place is just a hotel," Ruth
came back, valiantly. "A place to keep your stuff, where you can get
the occasional meal and take a very occasional bath whenever you
happen to feel like it."

"Don't be ridiculous, Mum. I want that thing out of here—now,
not next week or next month."

"Well, it's not what I want," Ruth informed her, firmly. "It's just
for a few more days. Stay away if you want to. You usually do. Don't
interfere."

Cassie told her boyfriend straight away, of course, but it turned out
that she didn't get the response she expected. If he'd been the kind of
Robert who condescended to be called Rob or Bob he'd have run
true to form, but even on the estate there were kids with intellectual
pretensions. Robert hadn't left school until he was eighteen and he
would tell anyone who cared to listen that he could have gone to
university if it hadn't been for the fact that the teachers all hated him
and consistently marked down the continuously assessed work he had
to do for his A levels.

★

Robert came up to inspect the infant at eleven o'clock on Friday morning. Ruth had had a busy night but her nipples had now
adapted themselves to the baby's needs and the flow of her blood
had become wonderfully smooth and efficient. The numbness left
behind when the child withdrew wasn't in the least like sexual
excitement but it was delicious nonetheless. She was tired, certainly,
but she wasn't dish-rag limp, the way she had been after finishing a

long night-session in some glass-sided tower. Although she was keen to get to bed she knew that she could stay awake if she had to, and she knew that she had to persuade Robert not to do anything reckless. It was a pleasant surprise to find that he was a potential ally.

"Do you know whose he is?" Robert wanted to know, as he stared down into the cot with rapt fascination. The baby's eyes were closed, so the fascination was spontaneous.

"No," said Ruth. "I've kept my ears open, but I didn't want to ask around. The neighbours haven't cottoned on yet—Mrs. Hagerty next door's as deaf as a post and if the Gledhills on the other side have heard him whimpering they haven't put two and two together. He doesn't scream like ordinary babies, no matter how distressed he gets—not that he gets distressed, now that he's safe. He's a very sensible baby."

"I could probably find out who dumped him," Robert bragged. "It must be one of the slags on the estate—it's easy enough to do a disappearing bump census when you've got connections."

Robert didn't have connections, in any meaningful sense of the word. He was a small-time user, not a dealer. He didn't even have any friends, except Cassie—who would presumably dump him as soon as she found someone willing to take her on who was slightly less of an outcast.

"It doesn't matter where he came from," Ruth said. "The important thing is to make sure that he doesn't come to any harm. You have to stop Cassie shooting her mouth off to the Defenders."

"She wouldn't do that," Robert assured her, with valiant optimism. "She's with me—she knows that all the scare stories are rubbish. We don't believe in demons or alien abductions or divine punishment. We know that it's natural, just a kind of mutation—probably caused by the hormones they feed to beef cattle or pesticide seepage into the aquifers."

Ruth knew that Robert probably hadn't a clue what an aquifer was, but she didn't either and she wasn't about to give him the opportunity to run a bluff.

"He needs me, for now," she said. "That's all that matters. It's only temporary. When he's strong enough, I'll hand him over."

"Does it hurt?" he wanted to know. Ruth didn't have to ask him what he meant by *it*.

"No," she said. "And it isn't like a drug either. Not pot, not ecstasy. He isn't even particularly lovable. Little, helpless, grateful . . . . but no cuter than any ordinary baby, no more beautiful. Alive, hungry, maybe even greedy . . . . but it's my choice and it's my business. I don't need saving from him—and I certainly don't need saving from myself."

"They must always have existed, mustn't they?" Robert said, following his own train of thought rather than trying to keep up with hers. "Much rarer than nowadays, of course—maybe one in a million. Intolerable, in a pre-scientific age. Automatic demonization. The idea that the dead come back as adult vampires must be an odd sort of displacement. Guilt, I guess. Never seen one close up before. Quite safe, I suppose, while the sun's up. Safe anyway, of course, if you're sensible. Adaptation makes sure that they don't kill off their primary hosts. What's good for the host is good for the parasite."

"He still needs to feed during the day," Ruth pointed out. "He wakes up from time to time. But it's perfectly safe. He doesn't intend to hurt anyone. He doesn't hurt anyone."

She smiled faintly as Robert took a reflexive step backwards, mildly alarmed by the thought that the child might open its eyes and captivate him on the instant—but Robert regained his equilibrium as she finished the last sentence.

"What do you call him?" Robert asked. He was being pedantic. He hadn't asked what the baby's name was because he knew that Ruth couldn't know what name the child's real mother had given him, and wouldn't feel entitled to give him a name herself when she knew that she would have to hand him over in a matter of days.

"I don't call him anything," Ruth lied, before adding, slightly more truthfully: "Just the usual things. What you'd call *terms of endearment.*"

Cassie's boyfriend nodded, as if he knew all about terms of endearment because of all the things he said to Cassie while subjecting her exceedingly willing flesh to statutory rape.

The boy was long gone by the time the baby bared his teeth again and searched for his anxious provider with his pleading and commanding eyes. Ruth was certain that Robert had had nothing to worry about; the infant knew by now who his *primary host* was, and he only had eyes for her.

★

It was Ruth's rapid weight-loss that finally tipped off Mrs. Hagerty, and it was Mrs. Hagerty—despite the fact that her own kids were in their thirties and long gone—who passed the word along to the

Gledhills so that the Gledhills could make sure it got back to the local chapter of the Defenders of Humanity.

Fortunately, the conclusion to which the stupid old bat had jumped was only half-correct, and the rumour that actually took wing was that the child was Cassie's and that Ruth had decided to take him on in her daughter's stead. This error qualified as fortunate, in Ruth's reckoning, because it persuaded the Defenders of Humanity that shopping her as a kidnapper would be a waste of time. If the baby had been Cassie's, the whole thing would have been a family matter, much more complicated than it really was.

When she knew that the secret was out Ruth expected shit and worse through the letter-box and a flood of anonymous letters in green crayon, but the Defenders of Humanity were canny enough to try other gambits for starters. The first warning shot fired across her bows was a visit from the vicar of St. Stephen's. She could hardly refuse entry to her flat to an unarmed and unaccompanied wimp in a dog-collar, although she wasn't about to make him a cup of tea.

"You must put your mind at rest, my dear," said the vicar, hazarding an altogether unwarranted and faintly absurd familiarity. "It is not because it was conceived in sin that the child is abnormal."

"No," said Ruth, as non-committally as she could.

"There is no need for shame," the vicar ploughed on. "It is not your duty to accept this burden. There is no reason at all why you should not deliver the infant into the hands of the proper authorities, and every reason why you should."

"That's what God wants, is it?" Ruth asked.

"It is the reasonable and responsible thing to do," the vicar assured her. "Your first duty in this matter is to your daughter, your second is to your neighbours and your third is to yourself. For everyone's sake, it is better to have the child removed to a place of safety. While it remains on the estate it is bound to be seen as an increasing danger, not merely to your own family but the families of others. I do not ask you to concede that the child is an imp of Satan, but I do ask you to consider, as carefully as you can, that even if it is not actively evil it is an unnatural thing whose depredations pollute the temple of your body. It is a bloodsucker, my dear, which only mimics the forms of humanity and innocence in order to have its wicked way with you— and I use that phrase advisedly, for what it does is a kind of violation equally comparable to vile seduction and violent rape."

"Suffer the little children to come unto me," Ruth quoted, endeavouring to quench the fire of zealotry with a dash of holy water—but to no avail.

"It is not a child, my dear," the vicar insisted, all the while keeping his eyes averted from the cot. "It is a leech, an unclean instrument of temptation and torment. If you would be truly merciful, you must give it up to those who would keep it safely captive."

"Well," said Ruth, "I'm grateful for the lesson in Christian charity, but I think he's about to wake up. I'm sure that modesty forbids . . . ."

Modesty did forbid—and the first note didn't arrive until the following day, when the vicar had washed his hands of the matter.

GET RID OF IT, the note said. IF YOU DON'T WE WILL. Apart from the lack of punctuation it was error-free, but given that the longest word it contained was only four letters long it was hardly a victory for modern educational standards.

The notes which followed were mostly more ambitious, and the fact that the longer words tended to be misspelled didn't detract from the force of their suggestion that if Ruth wanted to spill her blood for vampires there were plenty of people living nearby who would be glad to lend her a helping blade.

★

Cassie was incandescent with rage when she heard what was being said about her.

"*How dare you?*" she yelled at her hapless mother. "How dare you let them believe that it's mine?"

"I never said so," Ruth pointed out.

"But you didn't bloody deny it, did you? You let that shit the vicar blether on without ever once telling him that you found the little bastard in a rubbish skip. Mud sticks, you know. Some round here will remember this for ever, and God help me if I ever have a kid of my own. Well, I'm done protecting you. Robert wouldn't let me phone 999 myself, but I've put the word out that you have no claim at all on the cuckoo, and that the fastest way to get it off the block is in a police van. Expect it tonight."

That was on the second Saturday, by which time Ruth had had the child in her care for twelve days. She had not really intended to keep him so long, and his tender care had already turned nine-tenths of her spare fat into good healthy muscle, so one of her reasons for keeping him had melted away. As for the other, she was almost out of cash and she really needed to get back to work. The fact that she would have nothing to do when she wasn't working was no longer a significant issue, given that if she couldn't feed herself properly she'd soon be no use at all to the baby.

For once, reason stood fair square with bigotry. Both asserted that she must not keep the baby any longer—but their treaty had been made too late. Ruth's devotion to blood-donation had passed beyond the bounds of reason, and whatever failed intellectuals like Robert might think about the cleverness of the adaptive strategies of vampires, baby bloodsuckers had no means of dispossessing themselves of primary hosts that were no longer adequate to their needs. The baby was just a bundle of appetites, a personification of need. He had learned to lust after Ruth's breast, and he could not help the instinct that guided his tiny teeth. He could not let her go—and his incapacity echoed in her own empty heart.

Despite what Cassie had said, the police did not put in an appearance on Saturday night; they had their own cautious rules about picking up vampire babies after sunset. Ruth contemplated doing a runner, but she hadn't got anywhere to run to so she decided to front it out. When the WPC turned up on her doorstep on Sunday morning Ruth wouldn't take the chain off to let her in.

"There's no baby here, and if there was he wouldn't be a vampire, and if he was he'd be mine and I wouldn't be interested in giving him up," Ruth said, breathlessly. "Don't come back without a warrant, and even then I won't believe that it gives you any right."

"It's not my problem if you don't care to co-operate, love," said the WPC, shaking her head censoriously. "Just don't come crying to me when your hall carpet goes up in flames."

*

Ruth had taken the child to the supermarket a couple of times before the word got out, but she didn't dare do it once the local Defenders knew the score and she certainly didn't dare to go out and leave the poor little mite alone while she spent the last vestiges of her meagre capital. She wasn't surprised when Cassie refused point blank to fetch groceries for her—but she was pleasantly astonished when Robert not only said that he would but that he would chip in what he could spare to help her out.

"We shouldn't give in to ignorance," he declared. "We have to stand up for our right to take our own decisions for our own reasons in our own time according to our own perceptions of nature and need." The false-ringing speech didn't mean much, so far as Ruth could see, and even if it had it wouldn't have been applicable to her situation, but she figured that Robert's muddy principles would buy her a few extra days before she finally had to let go. Even though she'd always intended to let go in the end, she thought that she was damned if she'd give the so-called Defenders of so-called Humanity the satisfaction of seeing her do it one bloody minute before she had to.

There were no more notes, and nothing repulsive came through the letter-box in their stead. The Defenders of Humanity knew that the message had been delivered, and they also knew that they only had to wait before it took effect. They knew that as long as they were vigilant—and they were—there was no danger to any human life they counted precious. Besides which, they simply weren't angry enough to march up the concrete stairs like peasants storming Castle Frankenstein, demanding that the child be handed over to them for immediate ritual dismemberment. Things like that had happened twenty years before, but even the most murderous of mobs had lost the capacity to take the invasion personally once the numbers of vampire babies ran into the thousands. Even the most extreme religious maniacs lacked the kind of drive that was necessary to sustain a diet of stakes through the heart, lopped-off heads and bonfires night after night after night without any end in sight. By now, even the dickheads on the estate couldn't summon up energy enough to do much more than write a few notes and wait for inevitability and the law to take their natural course.

In a way, Ruth regretted the lack of strident enmity. There was something strangely horrible in the isolation that was visited upon her as she eked out her last supplies and went by slow degrees from slim but robust to thin and tired. It was, she thought, as much the loneliness of her predicament as the baby's ceaseless demands that made her so utterly and absolutely tired. She had not realised before how much it meant to her to be able to shout good morning at Mrs. Hagerty or glean the available gossip from Mrs. Gledhill's semi-articulate ramblings.

The baby was a continuous source of comfort, of course, and that would have been enough in slightly kinder circumstances, but his powers of communication were limited to moaning and staring, and they just weren't enough to sustain a person of Ruth's intellectual capacity. He loved her with the kind of unconditional ardour that only the helpless could contrive, and she was glad of it, but it simply wasn't the answer to all her needs.

She knew that the end of the adventure was coming, so she made every attempt to milk it for all it was worth. She became vampiric herself in her desire to extract every last drop of comfort from her hostage. She had never been subject to a desire so strong and yet so meek, a hunger so avid and yet so polite. She had never been looked at with such manifest affection, such obvious recognition or such accurate appraisal.

She flattered herself by wondering whether even a vampire would ever be able to look at any other host with as true a regard as her temporary son now looked at her. She took what perverse comfort she could from the fact that nothing the orphanage would or could provide for him would ever displace her as an authentic mother. For as long as the baby lived, it would know that she was the only human being who had ever really loved it, the only one who had ever tended unconditionally to its real needs.

But it wasn't enough, and not just because there wasn't enough time.

★

By the time she had had the baby for nineteen days Ruth was at the end of her tether. Cassie had not come near her for a week, and had somehow contrived sufficient emotional blackmail to keep Robert away too. The wallpaper had begun to crawl along the walls. She was out of Pampers, out of Lucozade and out of tinned soup.

She decided, in the end, that she would rather die than hand the baby over, although she knew as she decided it that she was being absurd as well as insincere. She tried with all her might to persuade him to feed more and more often, but he would not take from her more than he needed or more than she could give, and she had always known that this was the way that things would finally work out. She grew weaker and weaker while she could not bring herself to bite the bullet, but she was never drained to the dregs.

In the end, she didn't need to contrive any kind of melodramatic gesture. She only had to make her way next door and ask the Gledhills to call an ambulance, not for her but for the child. It would not take him to a hospital, but that wasn't the point. It was far, far better—or so it seemed—to surrender him into the arms of a qualified paramedic than to let him be snatched away by a blinkered police-woman or a so-called social worker.

She cried as she handed him over. Her tears dried up for a while but when night fell and the time of his usual awakening arrived she began to cry again. Her breasts ached with frustration, and the waiting blood turned the areoles crimson. She knew that the hurt would fade, but she also knew that the nipples would be permanently sensitised. She would never recover the lovely numbness that she had learned so rapidly to treasure. She would never see eyes like his again. No one would ever understand her as he had. No one would ever think her the most delicious thing in the world.

She wondered whether they used contract cleaners at the orphan-ages. She wondered whether it would be possible, in spite of her lack of formal qualifications, to retrain as a nurse or a laboratory assistant, or any other kind of worker that might be considered essential by the scientists for whom vampires were merely an interesting problem. She made resolutions and sketchy plans, but in the end she went to sleep and did not dream—at least so far as she could remember.

She went back to work the next night. It was hell, but she survived.

The labour left her desperately devitalised for the first couple of weeks, but she soon began to put on weight again and her deso-lation turned first to commonplace debilitation and eventually to everyday enervation. Mrs. Hagerty began to respond to her shouted good mornings and Mrs. Gledhill began filling her in on the gossip. Cassie resumed regular expeditions to her wardrobe, and slightly-less-frequent ones to the bathroom. Robert dropped in more often than before, stayed longer, and talked nonsense to her for hours on end.

It wasn't great, but it was normal. Ruth had learned the value of normality—but that wasn't why she remembered the baby so fondly, and sometimes cried at night.

★

Things had been back to normal for nearly three months when Cassie, still three weeks short of her sixteenth birthday, found out that she was pregnant, panicked and jumped off a top-floor balcony.

The autopsy showed that the child would have been a vampire, but Ruth knew that that didn't even begin to justify Cassie's panic, or even to reinforce the ironic significance of her name. She would have been able to get an abortion. She would have been able to hand the baby over to Social Services. She would have been all right. She would have been able to resume normal life. There was no reason to kill herself but stupidity and sheer blind panic. It wasn't Ruth's fault. It wasn't anybody's fault. It was just one of those things. It would have happened anyway—and it wouldn't have happened at all if Cassie had only had the sense to talk to somebody, and let them soothe her terror away.

Robert was heartbroken. He moved out of the squat into Cassie's old room, but the consolation with which he and Ruth provided one another was asexual as well as short-lived. Within a month he was gone again, just like Frank, along with the intensity of his grief and the pressure of his need.

Once Robert had gone, Ruth never did figure out what to do with herself during the day, or during the long and lonely nights when she wasn't on shift cleaning up the debris of other people's work and other people's lives—but every time she went past a rubbish-skip while walking the empty streets in the early hours of the morning she kept her eyes firmly fixed on her fast-striding feet, exactly as any sensible person would have done.

With the Vampires

Sidney Bertram

I have been unable to find any information about Sidney Bertram, not even if that was his full name. It's possible he may have been Australian, as were several of the little-known contributors to Phil May's Annual *in which the following story appeared in 1899. If so, he may have been something of a traveler, especially if he is the same Sidney Bertram who wrote* The Free-booters; or, the Adventures of Jack Richards in South Africa, *published in 1930. Whoever he was he creates a powerful atmosphere in this story, which has never been reprinted until now.*

With the Vampires

Sidney Bertram

"Is'POSE we'd better get on the road again to-morrow," said Courtney, as he carefully filled his meerschaum and prepared for a comfortable half-hour after supper; "it's no use wasting our time on these frauds of caves any longer."

"Hear, hear!" exclaimed Sammy, as he scratched a match on his trousers.

Charlie Grant looked at his two companions in a somewhat disdainful manner.

"You fellows," he said in a half-injured tone, "take no real interest in exploring,—at any rate, from a scientific point of view. You, Sammy, look upon it only as a means of supplying 'copy,' whilst Courtney is wofully disappointed if he does not find a gold-mine or a diamond-studded hill about. Why, having got so far, it is absurd to turn back without thoroughly exploring these caves! They might have been the dwellings of a race of creatures never so much as dreamt of!"

"Rats!" rudely exclaimed Courtney, puffing at his pipe.

Sammy declared he was going for a shoot in the morning, and the caves could "go hang."

"Then Charlie must have the glory of discovering traces of the race of mammoths all to himself, as I'm with you for a little sport," said Courtney.

"Well, you two can do as you please. I intend to explore that big cave we saw high up in the cliff, whatever happens," was all that Charlie deigned to reply.

These three men—William Courtney, civil engineer; "Sammy" Woods, journalist; and Charles Grant, a world-wide explorer—had set out up the Amazon with a number of native bearers. Their starting-point was Guatevera, a small inland town six hundred miles from the sea-coast, and they had taken a week to reach their present location. Their journey had been through dense forests and over broad waterways, until they had come upon this stretch of rugged country in the hills, which Charlie Grant, the real explorer of the trio, prophesied to be of pre-historic interest. The limestone cliff was simply honeycombed with caves, and he meant to examine them minutely, the large one in particular. All three were enthusiastic at first, and on the day after fixing their camp had wandered in and out of these gaping crevices, finding them, however, of but little interest. Hence the conversation recorded above. But Charlie's curiosity, or rather thirst for knowledge, for he was a born explorer, made him anxious and determined to investigate the largest of them all.

Consequently, next morning the two sportsmen left the camp in search of game, and Charlie prepared for his climb up the cliff. He selected half a dozen iron tent-pegs for use in scaling the heights, some candles, a lantern, and a small coil of rope.

At the base of the cliff the ascent was very steep; an incline of débris, which years of storm and rain had caused to fall from the face of the overhanging limestone, gave him a little trouble; but though he was handicapped by his tools, he succeeded in reaching the actual cliff within ten feet of the cave. By the aid of the pegs, which he drove into the cracks of the limestone, he quickly reached the yawning mouth of the recess.

As he climbed on to the ledge, disappointment awaited him. What had appeared from below a huge cave now turned out to be only a blind cavity in the rock, and he cursed his luck bitterly that he had not gone shooting with his companions.

The entrance was capacious, probably thirty feet high and twenty wide; but what had seemed to be the dark interior now proved to be a black back-wall not five yards in.

Turning away in disgust, he was about to descend when his eye caught a glimpse of a fissure in the far corner of the cave. Advancing towards it, to his joy he beheld a narrow passage, but so narrow that at first he thought it impossible to enter.

The crack was perpendicular. On a level with his face it was about a foot wide, but widened out at the bottom. He stooped and peered in, but could see very little. So lighting his lantern, and pushing it in front of him, he crawled in after it.

Yes, there was a passage, and a fairly good one, widening out considerably inside the opening. Returning to daylight, he blew out his lantern, lit a candle, got down on his stomach, and again crawled in.

Charlie was a man of iron nerve, but he had never entered a cave quite in this way before, and it gave him a feeling of compression which for the first few seconds produced an unpleasant, suffocating sensation. It soon wore off, however, for as he got farther in the passage became considerably higher, and very soon enabled him to walk in an upright position. The first thing that struck him was the peculiar smell emanating from the interior, a smell he had not noticed in any of the other caves. The floor was very wet and slippery, and inclined downwards to an alarming extent.

He had hardly proceeded more than twenty yards when he heard a peculiar sound that made him halt and listen. He strained his ears to distinguish what it was. At first it sounded like running water, but he noticed that it pervaded the whole place, now here, now there, sometimes overhead, and again in the distance, so that he was soon convinced of his mistake.

It was some few moments before he could determine to his own satisfaction what the noise was; however, he was not left long in doubt, for as he stood there something flew past him with a rush, brushing his face with its wings, extinguishing his candle, and leaving him in darkness.

"Bats," he murmured, re-lighting his lantern.

Having satisfied himself on this point, he stuffed the extinguished candle in his pocket, and slipping and sliding on the reeking floor he plodded on.

Charlie's enthusiasm increased the farther he penetrated, notwithstanding the difficulty he had in keeping his feet. At every step he took the hollow echoes of his footfall seemed to recede more and more into the dim recesses of the immense cave; and as the light of his lantern fell upon them, great stalactites sparkled and glistened all around him.

The air reeked with foulness, and became more oppressive. His lantern showed, however, no signs of failing, so he continued onward.

A lonely feeling took possession of him as he almost felt his way along in these vast depths, and he could not help wishing his two friends were with him.

Suddenly something came whirring round his head. He put up his hand to ward it off, and it sailed away. Back it came again, this time brushing his face with its wings with such force he jumped back to avoid the contact; his foot slipped on the slimy floor, and he fell headlong to the ground.

He sprang to his feet, and relit his lantern, determined not to let a poor innocent bat alarm him again. Such is the curious constitution of the human nervous system, that the simplest, unusual thing, if not visible to the eye, frequently produces a strained tension of the nerves, upsetting the strongest philosophical ideas and common sense. Charlie was no exception to this rule, and he felt a sensation down his back, while his scalp tingled at the thought of another such encounter.

He had to use the utmost care now, for the incline had become so precipitous that the least step might, for all he knew, prematurely consign him to eternity.

The most unpleasant part of this cave to him was the noise made by the wings of its inhabitants. The steady drone got on his nerves, it irritated him, it became in effect like the steady drip, drip of water on the brain of a man put to torture.

With dogged persistency he took a few more steps forward, his heart as keenly in his work as ever. Without the least warning there was again a sudden rush and a whir—r—r of wings. Before he could duck, something soft, warm, and black struck him in the face. With a cry he fell backward, his feet shooting from under him as though he were on ice. Instantly he was impelled forward with terrible velocity. His lantern went out, and he clutched wildly at the slimy wet ground to stay his slide and to give him time to get a foothold, but it was useless. He was precipitated over the edge of a chasm, and fell with force on the hard rock.

His senses had not left him in his fall, and as he lay helpless he felt an acute pain the left leg. For some time he lay there in a half-dazed condition, hardly realising the terrible predicament he had been placed in, but keenly alive to the dreadful pain of his leg. His mind began to clear, and at the same time thoughts of self-preservation asserted themselves. He felt about for his lantern, having a dim consciousness that he had heard it fall with him. Failing to discover its whereabouts, he endeavoured to move his body and so reach farther into the darkness; but the first attempt made him cry out in agony, and he threw himself back, gasping in exhaustion of pain.

He felt so helpless, so solitary, and the pain of his leg was becoming so excruciating, that he began to wonder how it would all end. Would his friends come and find him? and if so, would they be able to get him out? Surely he could not have fallen far! He gazed into the blackness above him, and endeavoured to calculate the distance of his fall. No, it could not have been more than ten feet at the outside: and yet—he reached his hand behind his head, touching, as he did so, a slimy wall.

Once more he became conscious of the droning of wings that had so irritated him before. They came nearer and nearer, and several times he put up his hands to ward off the loathsome creatures as they flew close down over his face. Three or four times this occurred. What could he do? At last, almost in desperation, he suddenly thought of the candle in his pocket. With, the greatest care he raised himself, and after considerable trouble and pain he succeeded in drawing it out. Another misfortune awaited him: his matches had become damp, and he used nearly half the box before he at last succeeded in striking a light.

As the faint glimmer cast its rays around he almost wished he had been left in darkness. The horror of his position was now staring him in the face, and he shrank back. The pain of his leg appeared to increase tenfold as he drew himself away from what his horror-stricken gaze revealed to him.

He had fallen on what he fondly imagined to be the bottom of an inner cave, but it proved to be a small projection measuring about six feet square in the side of a black yawning chasm. Around and below him was black space. One false move and he would probably be dashed to pieces hundreds of feet below.

The situation was awful to contemplate, and he shuddered as he realised what might have been his fate had he fallen two or three feet on either side of his present position. The instinct of self-preservation would not allow him to die there like a captive in some mediaeval dungeon. He would act, and that promptly. He turned on his side to rise, but quickly fell back again. It was useless. He could not move—his leg, the torture of it nearly drove him mad. He lay back, almost fainting.

Presently the pain subsided a little, and holding up his candle with one hand he supported himself with the other, while he stared intently above, contemplating the only way he could see out of his difficulty.

Suddenly came a rush of something huge and black swooping down over him, flapping its wings in his face as it went. Out went his candle, and he was once more plunged in a darkness that could almost be felt.

His nerves were becoming unstrung, and he trembled in every limb. The noise of wings became louder and closer to him, while the awesome feeling of something weird and uncanny surrounding him, almost palsied him.

He struggled to relight his candle. The intolerable darkness, and the awful droning that came from the depths of the cavern, were terrifying. After two or three failures he succeeded in getting a match to ignite, and with returned light his nerves steadied themselves, although the expectancy of those great black creatures plunging him in darkness again made him gaze around in superstitious fear. He groaned aloud with pain, and the cave echoed back his moans, until the place sounded like a pit of the wailing damned.

He reached down and, pulling up his trouser leg with great care, allowed the burning flesh to rest on the cool wet stone. He shouted for help, with little hope,—but anything to relieve his strain of mind, anything to give vent to his overburdened feelings. Only the echoes came in answer, and, as they died away, the monotonous droning of the wings.

He lay with eyes closed. A slight noise at his feet attracted his attention. "What's—that?" He rubbed his eyes and looked again, "My God!—What is it?" he half exclaimed. He seemed to see some gruesome object. Was it a phantasy of his distorted imagination, a creation of his fevered brain? Again he glared.

"Yes;—no, no;—yes." He saw it move, and with a fearful cry he rose to a sitting posture.

"What?—Who?" He tried to articulate, but ere he could frame the question his tongue clove to the roof of his mouth, and the words died on his lips. His hair fairly bristled on his head, his eyes seemed to start from their sockets, and he trembled like an aspen. Close at his feet sat, or rather wallowed, three huge black creatures. He reached his candle forward to make sure it was no delusion, and then with a shrieking cry he fell back, the cave echoing and re-echoing "Vampires!"

There was no mistaking them as they sat there. No detail of their loathsome bodies could he now fail to distinguish. The candle only intensified the horror of the two sharp incisor teeth in front, and the lancet-shaped fangs at the sides of their mouths; but worst of all, the split leaf-like appendage with which they suck the blood of their victims.

Bitterly he regretted his folly in having ventured into the cave alone. What the end would be he dared not think, now that he was confronted by this fresh terror. Crippled and helpless, he must lie there and await his doom, those terrible creatures sitting by, and only waiting for him to become unconscious before making their attack.

He determined to keep his senses, and leant back, keeping his eyes fixed on the vampires; they should not suck his life's blood from him.

As he arrived at this determination there was another terrific rush of wings, and his candle was knocked from his hand. With a frantic lunge he tried to recover it, but failed. He groped about in the dark with feverish haste, the thought of those three swaying figures at his feet spurring him on to find it.

His whole body was aching and throbbing with the gnawing pain of his leg. Each effort warned him that if he taxed his powers of endurance too far the pain would overcome him, and he would quickly become a prey to the voracious vermin at his feet.

With a sinking heart he at last had to give up the search, and to lie back exhausted and faint, fancying one of the creatures was crawling towards him.

It was merely a trick of his imagination, and he knew it; but the horror made him groan aloud. "My God!"—would it never end, this ceaseless terror, this horrid nightmare! His thoughts ran wild. His whole life seemed to pass panorama-like before his mind's eye.

The droning above and around him still continued, and his endurance began to give way. He thought he could hear one of the creatures move. He clenched his hands to steady himself, and glared out into the darkness. Was it fancy or fact? In that pitch blackness he could distinctly see one of the vampires creeping towards his leg. A minute passed. His head was swimming, he was conscious of nothing but the vampire. Heavens! he felt a cool air on his leg! He reached down, but the pain became so acute that he lay back once more breathing hard.

Spasmodically, he kicked out, nearly fainting with the pain. He struck something soft, which squeaked at his blow. My God!—the first attack warded off!

A fresh horror now came upon him. One of the vampires swept over his face. Again it came, again and yet again, as though looking for a place on which to alight.

He put up his hands, and hit out right and left to ward the creature off. Still it circled ominously around, every now and then its wings brushing some part of him.

He threw his arms wildly about, suffering agonies the while. Again came the cool sensation over his leg. He kicked out as well as hit; he was losing his reason; he kicked with the broken limb; he made furious efforts, his brain reeled, and with a despairing groan his limbs fell and all became a blank.

Then an awesome silence reigned, broken only by the noise of the circling bats above. Emboldened by the stillness of their victim they had so patiently awaited, the three gruesome figures edged nearer the bare white leg. Still no movement to stay their sanguinary quest. Flop, flop—they came nearer and nearer. One reached the glistening white leg, and as it did so its wings slowly oscillated. A few moments passed, as if the creature were waiting to make sure the unconscious figure roused not.

Slowly its head sank on to the flesh, and the regular pulsations of its body told their tale. The blood-thirst was being assuaged. Encouraged by the success of their leader, the others ranged themselves beside the limb: and the slow beating of the three pairs of wings steadily kept time.

Hopelessly inanimate lay poor Grant, as the terrible work of the sanguinary creatures continued. The vampires shifted sluggishly as their bodies became distended; but ever the insatiable creatures bent forward for more.

The flesh of the victim began to shrink on the bones it covered, as the blood was drawn out; and vitality ebbed through the punctures made by the sharp teeth of the assailants. Half an hour passed, and one of the creatures fell off, wallowing on the slimy ground. A few moments after it returned again to its loathsome work. In turn each of the vampires left the body, but only to return.

Suddenly one of the legs of the victim moved convulsively. The three creatures tried to fly, but their loathsome bodies refused to move. They were too full of the blood of their victim, and the wings were not powerful enough to lift them.

Then a light appeared above, followed by a sound of voices. A vicious squeak came from the creatures, angry at being disturbed. Failing to rise, they rolled their heavy bodies over the ledge, and spreading their wings, sailed round the chasm, floating heavily down-wards into the depths of darkness.

Fortunately, Courtney and Woods met with little success in their search for sport, and, returning to camp, followed on Grant's trail only just in time to save him from a miserable death. The perilous work of rescuing their injured and unconscious comrade, and bringing him through the cave crevice to the camp, was the heartrending labour of hours. But, nevertheless, loyalty and grit accomplished it; and when, many months later, Grant rose from a bed of dangerous illness, with his cruel experience carved in furrows on his face and splashed in grey on his hair, they were repaid a thousandfold with the delight of his recovery.

To-day Grant appears to have almost forgotten the horrors of the cave, but his shooting at feathered game becomes shockingly bad when the birds rise close enough for the whirr of their wings to be audible.

Appendix

A Fragment
Lord Byron

We end where we began, with the tragic figure of George Gordon Byron (1788–1824), later 6th Baron Byron and the leading poet of the English Romantic movement. He found fame with the publication of Childe Harold's Pilgrimage *in 1812, and at the same time found notoriety because of his very public affair with the married Lady Caroline Lamb. In 1815 he married Caroline's cousin Anne Millbanke, but the marriage lasted barely a year and when they separated in 1816 Byron left England forever. That was how he came to be at the Villa Diodati in Switzerland in the summer of 1816 with Claire Clairmont, (who subsequently bore him a daughter), Claire's half-sister Mary Godwin, and Mary's future husband, Percy Shelley. It was at that gathering that Byron challenged them all to write a horror story out of which came the following fragment that Byron never completed but which his physician, John Polidori, reworked into "The Vampyre" and began literature's obsession with the creatures.*

Polidori modeled his vampire, Lord Ruthven, on Byron, and that image of the tragic, haunted and doomed aristocrat has become iconic in vampire literature ever since. But Byron was also heroic and died the hero's death, helping the Greeks fight in their war of independence against the Ottoman Empire. Lady Caroline Lamb once famously said of him that he was "mad, bad and dangerous to know," which would be a fitting epithet for any vampire.

A Fragment

Lord Byron

"IN THE year 17—, having for some time determined on a journey through countries not hitherto much frequented by travellers, I set out, accompanied by a friend, whom I shall designate by the name of Augustus Darvell. He was a few years my elder, and a man of considerable fortune and ancient family, advantages which an extensive capacity prevented him alike from undervaluing and overrating. Some peculiar circumstances in his private history had rendered him to me an object of attention, of interest, and even of regard, which neither the reserve of his manners, nor occasional indication of an inquietude at times approaching to alienation of mind, could extinguish.

"I was yet young in life, which I had begun early; but my intimacy with him was of a recent date: we had been educated at the same schools and university; but his progress through these had preceded mine, and he had been deeply initiated into what is called the world, while I was yet in my novitiate. While thus engaged, I heard much both of his past and present life; and, although in these accounts there were many and irreconcilable contradictions, I could still gather from the whole that he was a being of no common order, and one who, whatever pains he might take to avoid remark, would still be remarkable. I had cultivated his acquaintance subsequently, and endeavoured to obtain his friendship, but this last appeared to be unattainable: whatever affections he might have possessed seemed now, some to have been extinguished, and others to be concentred: that his feelings were acute, I had sufficient opportunities of observing; for, although he could control, he could not altogether disguise them; still he had a power of giving to one passion the appearance of another, in such a manner that it was difficult to define the nature of what was working within him; and the expressions of his features would vary so rapidly, though slightly, that it was useless to trace them to their sources. It was evident that he was a prey to some cureless disquiet; but whether it arose from ambition, love, remorse, grief, from one or all of these, or merely from a morbid temperament akin to disease, I could not discover: there were circumstances alleged which might have justified the application to each of these causes; but, as I have before said, these were so contradictory and contradicted, that none could be fixed upon with accuracy. Where there is mystery, it is generally supposed that there must also be evil: I know not how this may be, but in him there certainly was the one, though I could not ascertain the extent of the other—and felt loth, as far as regarded himself, to believe in its existence. My advances were received with sufficient coldness: but I was young, and not easily discouraged, and at length succeeded in obtaining, to a certain degree, that common-place intercourse and moderate confidence of common and every-day concerns, created and cemented by similarity of pursuit and frequency of meeting, which is called intimacy, or friendship, according to the ideas of him who uses those words to express them.

"Darvell had already travelled extensively; and to him I had applied for information with regard to the conduct of my intended journey. It was my secret wish that he might be prevailed on to accompany me; it was also a probable hope, founded upon the shadowy restlessness which I observed in him, and to which the animation which he appeared to feel on such subjects, and his apparent indifference to all by which he was more immediately surrounded, gave fresh strength. This wish I first hinted, and then expressed: his answer, though I had partly expected it, gave me all the pleasure of surprise—he consented; and, after the requisite arrangement, we commenced our voyages. After journeying through various countries of the south of Europe, our attention was turned towards the East, according to our original destination; and it was in my progress through these regions that the incident occurred upon which will turn what I may have to relate.

"The constitution of Darvell, which must from his appearance have been in early life more than usually robust, had been for some time gradually giving away, without the intervention of any apparent disease: he had neither cough nor hectic, yet he became daily more enfeebled; his habits were temperate, and he neither declined nor complained of fatigue; yet he was evidently wasting away: he became more and more silent and sleepless, and at length so seriously altered, that my alarm grew proportionate to what I conceived to be his danger.

"We had determined, on our arrival at Smyrna, on an excursion to the ruins of Ephesus and Sardis, from which I endeavoured to dissuade him in his present state of indisposition—but in vain: there appeared to be an oppression on his mind, and a solemnity in his manner, which ill corresponded with his eagerness to proceed on what I regarded as a mere party of pleasure little suited to a valetudinarian; but I opposed him no longer—and in a few days we set off together, accompanied only by a *serrugee* and a single janizary.

"We had passed halfway towards the remains of Ephesus, leaving behind us the more fertile environs of Smyrna, and were entering upon that wild and tenantless tract through the marshes and defiles which lead to the few huts yet lingering over the broken columns of Diana—the roofless walls of expelled Christianity, and the still more recent but complete desolation of abandoned mosques—when the sudden and rapid illness of my companion obliged us to halt at a Turkish cemetery, the turbaned tombstones of which were the sole indication that human life had ever been a sojourner in this wilderness. The only caravanserai we had seen was left some hours behind us, not a vestige of a town or even cottage was within sight or hope, and this 'city of the dead' appeared to be the sole refuge of my unfortunate friend, who seemed on the verge of becoming the last of its inhabitants.

"In this situation, I looked round for a place where he might most conveniently repose: contrary to the usual aspect of Mahometan burial-grounds, the cypresses were in this few in number, and these thinly scattered over its extent; the tombstones were mostly fallen, and worn with age: upon one of the most considerable of these, and beneath one of the most spreading trees, Darvell supported himself, in a half-reclining posture, with great difficulty. He asked for water. I had some doubts of our being able to find any, and prepared to go in search of it with hesitating despondency: but he desired me to remain; and turning to Suleiman, our janizary, who stood by us smoking with great tranquility, he said, 'Suleiman, *verbana su*,' (*i.e.* 'bring some water,') and went on describing the spot where it was to be found with great minuteness, at a small well for camels, a few hundred yards to the right: the janizary obeyed. I said to Darvell, 'How did you know this?' He replied, 'From our situation; you must perceive that this place was once inhabited, and could not have been so without springs: I have also been here before.'

"'You have been here before! How came you never to mention this to me? and what could you be doing in a place where no one would remain a moment longer than they could help it?'

"To this question I received no answer. In the mean time Suleiman returned with the water, leaving the *serrugee* and the horses
at the fountain. The quenching of his thirst had the appearance of
reviving him for a moment; and I conceived hopes of his being able
to proceed, or at least to return, and I urged the attempt. He was
silent—and appeared to be collecting his spirits for an effort to speak.
He began—

"'This is the end of my journey, and of my life; I came here to die;
but I have a request to make, a command—for such my last words
must be.—You will observe it?'

"'Most certainly; but I have better hopes.'

"'I have no hopes, nor wishes, but this—conceal my death from
every human being.'

"'I hope there will be no occasion; that you will recover, and—'

"'Peace! it must be so: promise this.'

"'I do.'

"'Swear it, by all that—' He here dictated an oath of great
solemnity.

"'There is no occasion for this. I will observe your request; and to
doubt me is—'

"'It cannot be helped, you must swear.'

"I took the oath, it appeared to relieve him. He removed a seal ring
from his finger, on which were some Arabic characters, and presented
it to me. He proceeded—

"'On the ninth day of the month, at noon precisely (what month
you please, but this must be the day), you must fling this ring into
the salt springs which run into the Bay of Eleusis; the day after, at the
same hour, you must repair to the ruins of the temple of Ceres, and
wait one hour.'

"'Why?'

"'You will see.'

"'The ninth day of the month, you say?'

"'The ninth.'

"As I observed that the present was the ninth day of the month,
his countenance changed, and he paused. As he sat, evidently becoming more feeble, a stork, with a snake in her beak, perched upon a
tombstone near us; and, without devouring her prey, appeared to be
steadfastly regarding us. I know not what impelled me to drive it
away, but the attempt was useless; she made a few circles in the air,
and returned exactly to the same spot. Darvell pointed to it, and

smiled—he spoke—I know not whether to himself or to me—but the words were only, 'Tis well!'

" 'What is well? What do you mean?'

" 'No matter; you must bury me here this evening, and exactly where that bird is now perched. You know the rest of my injunctions.'

"He then proceeded to give me several directions as to the manner in which his death might be best concealed. After these were finished, he exclaimed, 'You perceive that bird?'

" 'Certainly.'

" 'And the serpent writhing in her beak?'

" 'Doubtless: there is nothing uncommon in it; it is her natural prey. But it is odd that she does not devour it.'

"He smiled in a ghastly manner, and said faintly, 'It is not yet time!' As he spoke, the stork flew away. My eyes followed it for a moment—it could hardly be longer than ten might be counted. I felt Darvell's weight, as it were, increase upon my shoulder, and, turning to look upon his face, perceived that he was dead!

"I was shocked with the sudden certainty which could not be mistaken—his countenance in a few minutes became nearly black. I should have attributed so rapid a change to poison, had I not been aware that he had no opportunity of receiving it unperceived. The day was declining, the body was rapidly altering, and nothing remained but to fulfil his request. With the aid of Suleiman's *ataghan* and my own sabre, we scooped a shallow grave upon the spot which Darvell had indicated: the earth easily gave way, having already received some Mahometan tenant. We dug as deeply as the time permitted us, and throwing the dry earth upon all that remained of the singular being so lately departed, we cut a few sods of greener turf from the less withered soil around us, and laid them upon his sepulchre.

"Between astonishment and grief, I was tearless."